SEVEN DAYS OF FRIDAY

A Women of Greece Novel

ALEX A. KING

ALSO BY ALEX A. KING

For B & C, the two great loves of my life

PROLOGUE

Wᴇɴ ᴛʜᴇ ɢᴀʀʙᴀɢᴇ ᴅɪsᴘᴏsᴀʟ choked, eleven-year-old Vivi Pappas began planning her imminent funeral. A big Greek affair, with all the requisite wailing and coffin-hugging.

"Elias, fix the garbage disposal!" her mother yelled into the basement.

"I don't have the tools for that."

"You have tools for everything, but you do not have tools for that?"

Back and forth, back and forth, went her parents.

Closed casket, Vivi thought. Definitely a closed casket. She'd be in chunks by the time Mom was done with her.

———

The plumber showed up the next afternoon. Late. Dusty footprints across her mother's glowing linoleum. Vivi sat at the kitchen table waiting to die, and her mother hovered at the plumber's side, waiting for him to screw up.

He didn't screw up. Unlike Vivi's father, he had the right tools for the job. And it wasn't a big job. Within minutes (long, long hours to

Vivi, who was mentally crafting her obituary) he had made a countertop collage of the asphyxiated disposal and its stalwart pieces. He looked down at the mess, scratched his shoulder.

"I ain't ever seen nobody put underwear in the garbage disposal before." Then: "Heh. I guess someone around here really hates Fridays."

Eleni Pappas turned. She looked at Vivi – looked at Vivi *hard*.

"You better run," she said. "Because I am going to kill you."

———

There was a reason for the Friday underwear. Not a good reason (in Vivi's estimation), but still a reason.

Vivi is short for Paraskevi.

Paraskevi is Greek for Friday.

The name was a hand-me-down from her father's mother, because that's how Greeks name their kids. Paternal grandparents first, then Mom's parents get a shot. No new name unless they run out of grandparents before they run out of kids.

So Eleni Pappas (a.k.a. Vivi's mother and part-time sadist) bought her daughter underwear with her name stamped on the front. Seven days of Friday. Easier to see which underwear was whose, she claimed. Clever, no?

No.

Not clever, at all.

Riding a wave of fury and humiliation, Vivi fed all seven Fridays into the garbage disposal, banishing each one from her underwear drawer forever. The disposal didn't mind – at first. They're not known for being discerning, and usually only stop for silverware. But it gagged while gulping down last pair, and the water began to rise.

Vivi scooped out the water with a tablespoon.

Why not put the Fridays in the garbage, like anyone else who wants to throw perfectly good stuff away?

Good question.

For that there is a good answer.

Eleni Pappas goes through their trash – all their trash – looking for secrets.

She misses nothing, that woman.

Almost.

I

VIVI

THE RAKE IS IN Vivi's hand. She wants to slam it into John's face.

"Vivi," John repeats. "I'm leaving you."

"Excuse me?" A small headshake. "Sorry, I was just fantasizing about your death."

"My death?"

"Yes, your death."

"You're a strange woman, Vivi," he says. "I said I'm leaving you."

"I heard you the first time. Leaving me what?"

"Leaving you. Leaving the house. I'm moving out. Vivi, are you listening?"

"Oh. I thought that's what you meant, but I wanted to be sure." Vivi tilts her head. Her dark ponytail lurches right. "Forever?"

"Yes, forever," John says.

"Okay. Don't forget to pack clean underwear."

"I'm not going to change my mind. This is what I need to do."

"If you say so."

"I'm going tonight – now. I'll be back during the week to pick up my things."

"Okay. Do you think you could drop dead before then?"

He shakes his head as though she's the asshole standing on their manicured lawn. "Vivi, come on."

His delivery sucks. He needs to work on that.

"Jesus, Vivi. Say something."

"I don't know what you want me to say, John. Some warning might have been nice."

The rake falls. Vivi crouches, scoops a crunchy handful of desiccated leaves into a gaping black bag, before asking the only thing that really matters when a relationship ends:

"Is there someone else?"

The sound John makes reminds her of their neighbor's old hairball-afflicted Tomcat.

"No. Shit. No, there's no one else."

Shifty eyes. Pretty, sky blue – but shifty.

Shitty poker player, John. No bluffing gene. Anytime she asks what he wants for his birthday, Christmas, anniversary, and he says, "Nothing, Honey," his eyes go epileptic. Now he gives her that look: the disapproving, nostril flaring look of a man who thinks he's standing a rung higher on the social ladder.

He's on a ladder, all right, except they're called shoe lifts. In bare feet he's five-ten, but he likes the boost.

Vivi says, "Your face . . ."

"What about it?"

"It's not doing that thing."

"What thing?"

She waves a hand over her own face. "Moving, like you're a normal human being."

It's true, John's face doesn't move much. Thank you, Botox.

Business expense, he had insisted. It wouldn't do for the fastest-selling real estate agent in town to slap an airbrushed glamour shot on his business card. "They want the real deal, an honest face," he said in his own defense, seconds before the doctor stabbed his forehead.

Speaking of honest:

Capped teeth. John has them in Arctic white. Sometimes, at night, Vivi thinks about tapping them with her fingernails, see if she can play

Chopsticks in his mouth. She can't play the piano, but what else is she going to do when she can't sleep?

Anyway, Vivi knows there's someone else.

She knew something was up when John went in for his cosmetic overhaul, but she didn't think, at the time, that it was his dick.

That was the first (conveniently ignored) clue.

Clue number two (also conveniently ignored): What looked (and, okay, smelled) like spots of semen on the tie their daughter bought him for Father's Day, year before last. Since their sex life had devolved into a biannual affair, Vivi assumed John (like her) had been doing a hasty DIY in a private place.

Hopefully not in a park near an elementary school.

And now look at him, guilt splashed all over his sculpted, artificially preserved face.

"Let's be reasonable about this for Melissa's sake," John says, in a tense voice, like he's trying not to shit his pants.

"Let's be reasonable," she mimics, in a way she knows will drive him the bad kind of crazy. "You don't want to be in this marriage, fine. You might have said something years ago. That would have been much more helpful."

"I didn't know then, did I, that it wasn't going to work."

Okay, that's fair, but Vivi doesn't want to hear about fair right now. With the last of summer's little jagged corpses in the bag, she knots the flaps and stalks to the curb. John follows.

She says, "Okay. You can fuck off and die now."

Harsh words, but her tone is pure sugar.

Blatantly ignoring her serving suggestion: "What about Melissa?"

Her fingers fumble with the thick gardening gloves. "What about Melissa?"

Melissa, their fifteen-year-old, spends most of her time with her nose in a book. Probably she won't even notice her father is gone. She carries her books to every family meal, hiding herself between the covers, while she ignores them both.

On nights he's home, John drones on and on about sales figures and escrow over pot roast, or chicken, or some French thing he read about that Vivi has to cook. His eyes glaze over whenever she interrupts and offers some small detail about her day. As the years slip by, Vivi has been doing it less and less. Why bore someone to death when silence is easier on the fraying ego?

"We can talk about it later, I guess," he says.

Silence.

"I have to go now."

More silence.

"I'm sorry, Vivi. I really am. Say something?"

She ignores him until he wafts away.

It's cold, Vivi knows, plotting her husband's sudden (yet simultaneously slow, painful, disfiguring) death, but it's been sixteen years in the making. Tonight's revelation is nothing more than canned icing on box cake.

Her morbid fantasy plays out like a grisly scene from one of those old B movies they show near Halloween. Picture Vivi Tyler holding the rake, while John Tyler (handsome in that all-American golden boy way) bleeds. Mouth slack with astonishment. Arms waving. Eyes –

Yeah, the steel tines prevent his eyes from doing much at all.

And near his end, she lifts her foot, puts it right in his middle and pushes.

"Get off my damn rake," fantasy Vivi says.

The (Bloody) End.

On the outside, Vivi is drama-lite. Which is why there's simmering rage instead of homicide. Which is also why she doesn't flip him off as he glides away in his status-mobile.

She and her rake go back into the garage. John doesn't do yard work. No time, no inclination. Vivi picked up his slack years ago. She's the reason he doesn't need a scythe to get to his car.

All done in the same hour, her marriage and the yard work. Only one of those feels good and satisfying.

Now she stomps back inside, where all her loneliness resides.

Beautiful house, the Tyler house. Gleaming planks, fashionable furniture, no soul.

John's choice. Cold and expensive. Vivi has never loved it the way John does. Her hands shake as she curls her fingers around the kitchen counter's granite rim. White-knuckled, she wills her knees to stay steady, to never fold. A tsunami of grief slams against her heart, leaving her gasping.

John is gone.

Nothing can bring him back; it was in his eyes.

Fucking asshole.

———

Not even five minutes later:

The phone nags. It only nags when her mother calls. Anyone else and it just plain rings.

Snot travels down her nose into a tissue. A second tissue catches tears. She needs a quick fix-it before she snatches up the phone.

"I can't talk right now, Mom." Sounds like her face met Mike Tyson.

"What, you do not say hello to your mother?" Screech, screech, squawk – in thickly accented English. "That is no way to answer a phone. You have a cold? Your nose sounds stuffy."

For the record, Vivi didn't major in disappointing her mother (not a single college in this country offers those classes), but it always feels that way. She rubs her forehead, waits for the genie to pop out and offer wishes.

"Now's not a good time," she says.

"Always too busy to spend five minutes talking. Maybe I have something important to say, but you would never know it because you do not have time to listen."

Eyes closed, Vivi conks her head on the polished counter. "So then talk already!"

"No, no, you are in a bad mood. I should call back when you are not menstruating . . ."

This – this is what she has to live with.

" . . . But then why spend good money on phone calls when I already have you here? Dinner. Saturday. You are coming." Not a request. "And put some rubbing alcohol on your chest. It will fix your cold."

"I –"

Click.

An Eleni Pappas click is louder than any other. That woman ends a call like she means it.

Vivi should have told her mom about John, but she figures it's much more fun to play the emotional masochist, torture herself by dragging it out until she's in a deranged neurotic frenzy.

Shouldn't take long.

———

Food processor. Now that would be a cool story to tell at John's funeral.

Poor John, he slipped in the kitchen and fell into the fancy processor he just had to have. All his limbs gone. The mortician tried, but . . . Closed casket, no choice. Poor, poor, tragic John.

Vivi's all foggy on the inside.

She pulls out a chair and embraces the cold. Over the cherry dining room table, with its mirror shine, she weeps. Then she wipes the tears away with a sleeve, because John would have a fit if he saw his precious table all damp.

Look at this house, filled with things John loves. But she isn't one of them.

These shaking hands, they're all about John, but not the crying. It's been years since she shed a tear over him. A broken marriage is awful, so is the idea of Melissa being shuffled between two homes. And she's an idiot, because who doesn't move when they see a derailing train smashing its way closer?

(Vivi Tyler, that's who.)

So her stupidity is a semi-decent excuse for this river she's sourcing.

But the banks are flooding, going pre-1970s Nile, because of her mother.

Her inevitable gloating is going to drive Vivi insane. Eleni will throw an *I Told You So* party, with a special *You Should Have Listened to Me and Married a Good Greek Boy cake.*

And Vivi loves cake.

🦂 2 🦂

MELISSA

MELISSA TYLER DOESN'T CARE if he is the most popular guy in school; Josh Cartwright is the biggest jerk-off in the universe, which is really saying something, because the universe is (allegedly) infinite.

"Your dad's a cocksucker, Tyler. I bet you take after him. Come on, show us."

Josh Cartwright and his posse of dickless friends didn't care that they were in the gym and everyone was listening. That was kind of the point. Everything those guys do is for show; you can't be important and popular if no one is watching.

"How come you never told us your old man's a faggot? I'm pretty sure he was checking my ass out when he sold my folks our house."

"Bite me," she had said, volleyball in hand, the rest of her team waiting on her to serve. It was so like Josh to make up bullshit to get a reaction.

"It's true," he called out across the gym. "I saw your dad blowing some homeless guy in Midland Park last night."

Everybody turned around and stared, like Josh was talking about her.

"You're full of crap," she said.

"No way. I couldn't make that shit up if I wanted to." He appealed to his grinning buddies. "Hey, the homeless need blow-jobs too. Your dad's not a just fag, he's a fucking humanitarian."

"Josh, language," Mr. Hector called out.

Josh flipped him a peace sign. "Think about it, Tyler. Was your dad home last night around nine?" He held a fist up in the air, jerked it. "Guess you're living proof homos can have kids."

"And you're living proof that a person can talk through their asshole."

Melissa flipped him off just as Mr. Hector looked over.

"Tyler, detention!"

And that's the main reason Melissa hates Josh's guts. The others rate way lower than that.

"Josh is cute, but he's got rocks in his head," Tonya said when Melissa caught up with her in the library. "He's projecting his latent homosexual tendencies onto other people."

Tonya is Melissa's best friend, so she's supposed to say stuff like that. But Melissa could see she had doubts, like she was trying to convince Melissa Josh was lying, without really believing it herself.

Which is why Melissa is typing "gay parents" into Google. That and she's quietly freaking out. Josh was right about one thing: Dad was out late last night. And Mom and Dad aren't exactly the smoochy types. Some kids are always half bragging, half repulsed because they caught their folks pretending to "wrestle" on a Saturday morning.

Not Melissa. She's never seen her parents do more than peck.

Weird, right?

Tonya's parents are always chasing each other around the house; Melissa has even seen Tonya's dad slip her mom the tongue. It was weird but also kind of cool, in an "Ewww, look at the sweet old people!" kind of way.

Thousands of results pop up in the browser, but Mom's done with the yard work, which means she might be coming this way. Dad is gone, too – but not really. From her window she can see he's parked a few feet back from the STOP sign at the end of their street, talking into his phone.

The front door slams. Melissa's search history goes bye-bye while she thinks about what to do next. They were arguing on the lawn, and when Mom and Dad argue, Dad always leaves. Paperwork is always his lame excuse, but now she's thinking about Josh effing Cartwright.

She has to work fast.

Melissa's bedroom has two windows, one at the front of the house and the other overlooking the side. It's totally Hollywood, but there really is an old oak tree in the yard, with fat branches that brush against the siding. Her mother is always nagging Dad to trim them, but he never does. They creep along the walls, scratching with their nails, when it's windy; make Halloween noises when it's dark. The tree's sounds used to scare her when she was little, but now she hardly ever hides under the bed on a windy night.

After shimmying down the tree, it's a breeze to get her bike from the shed and ride down to the huge bush on the street corner. Five minutes later, Dad inches past in his silver Lexus, barely pausing at the STOP sign.

Good thing it's November and the sun goes to bed early. A month earlier, no way she could hide.

Melissa peddles hard, churning fast enough to make her lungs sting. Sidewalks fly by. She keeps her eyes on the silver sedan.

Then the car signals right. Dad turns down a side street. The Lexus drops to cruising speed. Sweet (lung) relief.

Dad maneuvers the car up a short sloping driveway that leads to a neat beige house, a whole lot like chez Tyler. She hunkers down behind some bushes across the street. Dad must be selling this house.

Josh is wrong. Her parents love each other. So what if Dad works late a lot? Loads of parents do.

Right?

Dad gets out of the car, ear to his iPhone. Face all lit up like a Christmas tree, his walk ten years younger. She's watching a stranger, some thief who pick-pocketed Dad's face. He hardly ever smiles now.

Does he hate them so much that he can't smile?

The front door yawns. It's a deep, shiny black. Her saliva dries up, her stomach goes sour. A man steps out, younger than her dad, but dressed in a similar suit. Another real estate agent? As the men approach each other, she's dead certain they're going to shake hands, all businesslike. But she's totally wrong.

Hug. No handshake.

Her skin is flashing hot and cold, pulse banging pots and pans in her ears. Their lips are moving, but she can't hear them over the sound of her horror.

The younger guy pulls out of the hug. Now — now they'll break away. They're just friends.

But, no. He plants a kiss on Dad-who-isn't-Dad's lips. Dad-who-isn't-Dad kisses back, like it feels good, like they're on a date. Then, arm in arm, they walk into the house, an old married couple.

She shoves her coat sleeve down her throat, all the way to the dangly thing at the back, and murders her own scream.

3

MAX

Twenty times.

Twenty-one. Not even noon and his phone is blinking an urgent red. He tilts the face until the numbers swim into focus.

Mama.

Again.

Twenty-two.

Max's parents gave him a boxful of fate while he was in the cradle, some thirty-four years ago. The cradle, passed down through the Andreou family line, had been his father's before his. Christ on His cross looked down from the carved headboard, keeping watch over Max's mortal soul. He watched patiently and tirelessly while Max overcame colic and infancy.

The way Mama tells it, Max's lungs were so strong, his screaming so loud, his father worried endlessly that his first son would become a pop singer.

Unacceptable.

Each week his father would light a candle, praying to Christ and the Virgin Mary that it would not be so; his oldest son would go to an English university, before returning home to become a doctor and raise a family of his own.

Expectation is a heavy load to dump on a kid. Better men than Max have fought expectation and lost. Greek culture was built on the backs of children following their parents' word. The world has changed, but older generations are still stuck in ancient mud.

Change, in Greece, takes time.

Max is the good son. Mama loves to tell him this. He took his place at Oxford and began a love affair with medicine, according to the plan. His younger brother Kostas was more daring. He defied the plan, and chose the love of God over law.

Then Kostas ripped out their hearts and shit on them when he entered the priesthood before he chose a wife, destroying any hope of grandchildren. Now the burden to continue the Andreou name is on Max's shoulders. His younger brother's strength is both an inspiration and a steel cage.

But . . .

Life is good.

Work is satisfying.

Max has money.

He dates lots of pretty women – some of them more than once. Sometimes they break his heart a little. Sometimes he breaks theirs.

Last night, the Fates snapped the leash. The three sisters, who measure the lives of all men and women at birth, shoved him to his knees with one voicemail.

"Maximos, I have found you a wife," Mama crowed.

Delete.

He doesn't want or need a wife, and he doesn't want or need Mama to find one for him.

And now she's calling him at work.

She knows the rule: Never call while he's on duty, unless it's a life or death emergency.

Q: But does she care?

A: No.

He ducks into his Spartan office, hits 2 on speed dial, waits for a connection he doesn't want.

"Maximos," his mother says, before the phone completes its first ring. "There is a girl I want you to meet."

A girl. Why not a woman? He outgrew girls a long time ago.

"Forget it, Mama." He peers around the door. Time for morning rounds and the other doctors are gathering outside the pediatrics ward. Last night he admitted a three-year-old with gastroenteritis, and he's eager to check on her progress. "You can't call me at work like this."

Mama is a bulldozer. "I called last night and you didn't call back. And I thought, 'Max is lying dead in a gutter somewhere.' You have no idea how much a mother worries. When you have your own children you will understand. My heart, it can't handle all this worry."

She pauses for him to agree.

"Mama, I'm too busy to meet anybody."

"No! You must. Her mother is my very good friend. I promised her you would marry her daughter."

"Call her and tell her no."

"Oh, Maximos. After all we do for you? Your father and I sacrificed everything our whole lives for our sons. We survived earthquakes and the rule of that madman Papadopoulos so we could give you a good future, and how do you boys repay us? Kostas goes to the church to become lovers with Christ. He broke my heart. He broke your father's heart, and look how it killed him! It will be my fate to die alone with no grandchildren, and the family name will be no more. Every day I tell the Virgin Mary she should have given me daughters. They are much more obedient. Daughters would have given me many grand-babies!"

She comes on like the hundred-handed *Briareos* commanding an ocean storm. Max is tired. His defenses are low. So, he folds.

He owes her.

He owes his father.

Perhaps the time has come to settle down. Besides, what harm could it do to meet this girl? Worst case, they'll hate each other on sight and there will be no wedding. Who knows, maybe he'll find her attractive, and they can have some fun before going their separate ways. It's been three weeks and counting since he got laid.

"Okay, I'll meet her. But I'm not making any promises."

"You will like her. She is very beautiful and clever – a paralegal. She will be a good wife for you and you will make beautiful babies together."

Translation: she has two legs, all her own teeth, and can read without moving her lips.

"I'll try. But if the hospital – "

"Always with the emergencies! What happens if I die before I see my grandchildren? That is an emergency. It is bad enough that your father left us before he could see you married. Come, make an old, sick woman happy."

The woman isn't sick or old. She's as cunning as a fox and twice as manipulative as any politician.

This is nothing new.

"If you don't come home for the holidays, I'll die," she told Max when he left for Oxford. Mama's toolbox is filled with what-ifs and veiled threats.

Time to compartmentalize.

He shuts the office door, and with it, their conversation. His boots squeak on the freshly waxed linoleum. Most days he doesn't hear it, but the ward is quiet after a busy winter of pneumonia and bronchitis.

A passing nurse smiles up at him. She's cute. It makes him happy when women find him attractive, even when they aren't attractive to him. There's no sign of gray in his hair, and his skin, once pale from British gloom, is now a healthy light gold. He's tall and he stays fit – a habit he acquired during his two years of compulsory national service. Finding a pretty woman for relief and fun has never been a problem.

But Max rarely shits where he eats, so he keeps the smile professional and grabs his patient's chart. Test results: E-Coli negative, which means it's probably garden-variety stomach flu. He crosses himself, hopes she has improved overnight.

"How is Toula today?"

Better. He can see for himself, but he wants to hear it from her mother.

The tired young mother smiles. "She's stopped vomiting."

He mirrors her smile, warms the stethoscope with his hands. The toddler's heart beats steady. Her lungs are clear. She giggles when he tickles her under the chin with one finger. A healthy flush has replaced last night's pallor.

"That's a lot of progress. It means the medicine is working. And the diarrhea?"

"Not since dawn."

"Good." He makes his notes while he's waiting for the nurse to take Toula's temperature. Almost normal. "Keep up the ice chips, and when lunch comes give her a few bites and we'll see how she does. I'll be back this afternoon."

Next, it's one of his regulars, a teenager with beta thalassemia. Kids like Vassili don't make enough hemoglobin. Hemoglobin hitches a ride on red blood cells to make its regular oxygen deliveries. Symbiosis: hemoglobin needs red blood cells, which need hemoglobin. Less hemoglobin means fewer red blood cells, which means anemia, an enlarged spleen, increased chance of infection, and heart problems – if you've got it bad. Neither of Vassili's parents has the disease, and none of his five siblings show any symptoms. He's one of the luckier ones: no heart problems and no bone deformities. Regular blood transfusions are keeping his motor running.

Max sees them all the time, these losers of the genetic lottery. They're scattered all over the Mediterranean.

The teenager waves when he sees Max. "Hey, Doc, think the girls will like my new gear?" He thumbs at the I.V. as the technician adjusts a bag of deep red blood.

Once again, Max warms the stethoscope between his hands.

"The scars will impress them more. Girls like men with mysterious scars."

Heartbeat steady but rapid. All that damaged blood is a strain on his heart, and it's gridlock in his spleen. "How do you feel?"

"Tired. But not too tired to check out a hot girl." He grins. Good looking kid; Max hopes he won't let the disease hold him back.

"That's normal before the transfusion, but you know that by now." Max straddles a chair. When was the last time he had just sat? Anytime his backside is in a chair, he has papers to read and files to update.

"Doesn't mean I have to like it," Vassili says. "I really want to finish the whole football season."

"You planning on playing for the Superleague?"

"Hell yeah! If my body will cooperate."

Fingers drumming the chair, considering the options. "We could move your treatment up to three week intervals, see how you do."

"What about the iron?"

Most kids don't read the literature the hospital gives them, and parents don't always force the issue. The dark is a nice stress-free zone for their kids. What he sees is the opposite: children who understand what they're facing fight harder. Vassili's parents gave him the straight facts, and it helps that his Google-Fu is mighty. If anyone finds a cure, Max bets Vassili will know it before he does.

Anyway, the iron problem. More transfusions mean more iron. But these days there's a pill for everything. Chelation is just a *pop-pop-pop* away. Those extra iron molecules get a one-way ticket to the kidneys before the bladder spits them out. Downside is, iron levels drop and white blood cells right along with them, if you're not lucky.

Sometimes medicine is the art of picking the poison that does the least harm for the most comparative good.

"We'll need to monitor your white blood cell count. That means more needles. Still want to change your schedule?"

Vassili thinks about it for a moment. "I'm tired of being too tired for football. Let's do it."

"I'll clear it with your parents. Hang in there. I expect to see you playing for a Superleague team." Max claps him on the shoulder before moving on.

Rare day. Not only is there time to eat, but there's time to leave.

He chows down a slice of *kaseri* cheese and bread without interruption, but his hands are shaking. Good thing he's not a surgeon.

Quick jog down the stairs to the parking garage. The Jeep his mother hates is waiting there. The engine comes alive, jolts out into the city street.

The mountain is waiting.

———

Lots of tiny villages dot the sides of Mt Pelion – all of them SUPER ADORABLE (always in capitals) if you're a *tourista*. But there's only one Church of the Holy Mother. The whole place is underground, hiding in the rock's cool gut. Outside, there's a door, a crucifix, and that's it.

Blink and you'll miss it.

The Holy Mother isn't an elaborate church by Greek Orthodox standards. Not nearly gold enough. Greeks love to cake their churches in the shiny stuff. No such thing as too much. So the Holy Mother is an anomaly. Simple village above, simple church below. Perfect symmetry. Inside it's close to silent. Nothing except the faintest plinks of an underground spring. Anemic lighting, almost all of it coming from a few thin candles pressed into sand. This house of God is the most peaceful place on Earth.

It's hypnotic.

Max steps inside and lets the sudden coolness take him.

He's not devout, but he's Christian enough to keep his soul out of boiling water. Dark head bowed, he pays homage to the portrait of the Virgin Mary and her infant Christ, in the Orthodox way: with a kiss.

A male voice slices through the dim light.

"You carry many worries, my son."

"Is it that obvious?"

"Man cannot hide his troubles from God."

"Apparently, this man can't even hide his troubles from his own brother."

Big, bold laugh for a holy man. "I grew up looking at that ugly face of yours." He emerges from the dark, clad in the traditional black garments of the Greek Orthodox priest. Good thing the Andreou boys look great in black.

Brothers, no doubt about it. Same dark hair, same dark eyes – although the priest's eyes hold a touch of humor missing from the doctor's. A lighter (holier) heart. Same strong jaw and their mother's cheekbones.

Used to be they had the same nose, but now Kostas's leans left. Hell raiser, that one, until God hired him.

Max grins. "Looking well, Kostas. For a monster." The church suits his brother. He's settled, peaceful, the way he never was before.

Kostas knows Max isn't here to pray; Max does his praying in the hospital. He guides Max through the church, up six steps to a humble living space overlooking the ocean.

Humble, yeah. With a million dollar view from the small balcony. A round table and four chairs help his brother enjoy his lookout over paradise.

"Mama wouldn't say so," the priest says. "I can see her clutching her chest, wailing about how I'm wasting my life and killing her by not providing her with dozens of grandchildren, no?"

Out on the ocean, a cement ship is heading out to sea, cutting a foamy path between the ant-sized fishing vessels. The world is different up here. Miniature. Benevolent. He could be Zeus from up here.

"She says the same shit to me." His head is pounding, hands still shaking. "She's driving me crazy. Sometimes I wish she'd just go to the devil. You're the only person who knows what she is like. She's like a wild dog with a bloody bone."

"What?" Kostas says, feigning horror. "You didn't come here just to visit and pray?"

"God and I keep a comfortable distance from each other, you know that. I do my job, he does his. When we talk, it's business."

"Ah, you doctors who love to play God."

Max laughs. "No, if I wanted to play God I'd be surgeon."

"I'll fix you something that will throw you into a sugar coma – at least temporarily. And then we'll talk."

The younger brother pulls a jar from the kitchen cupboard, eases off its lid. Two tall glasses go on the counter, side by side. A spoon scoops a sticky white substance from the jar. He drops it in the glass, spoon and all. Twice he does this, before filing both glasses with cold water from the refrigerator. One each.

"You know," he says, "one of the best things about not being a kid is that we can have this anytime we want."

This is vanilla *hyporvrychio*, a thick glob of confectionary that sticks to the spoon. The white sweet, with its strong vanilla flavor, is a Greek childhood favorite. A few years of that and your tiny white teeth will turn black. When Mama was out, they used to take turns sneaking spoons into the pantry. Minor miracle they made it to adulthood with any teeth.

Instead of sucking and licking the spoon, Max bites into the white and waits for the sugar grenade to go off in his mouth before swallowing. He could eat the whole jar in one sitting. No shame.

"Do you suppose Zeus himself created this up on Mt Olympus?"

"I think God gave him the recipe."

"Blasphemer," Max says, laughing. Feels good to be with his brother again. Things come easy.

Kostas sucks the spoon before speaking. "So how is Mama punishing you this time? Greek guilt? 'We did everything for you, blah, blah,' or '*Panayia mou*, I'm dying without grandchildren'?"

"This time? Both. She's pushing me to marry."

"Have you met someone?"

"No, but Mama has. She wants to introduce us."

Kostas shakes his head, spoon bobbling in his mouth like he's a kid again. When he pulls it from his mouth, it makes a small pop. "You're a stronger man than me. I would have tossed her into the sea by now."

"And they say you're the holy one."

"God turned the wrong woman to salt." Another suck of the spoon. "So who's your bride to be?"

Max shrugs. "Mama said she's the daughter of a friend."

"Which could mean anything."

"Exactly."

"So what will you do? Marry her?"

"No." The cement ship drifts out of sight. "Maybe. I wish I knew. Mama gave me the family honor speech. She already promised this woman I would marry her daughter."

"Tricky situation. Tell her no."

"I can't."

"Of course you can. What is she going to do, take your stethoscope away?"

Max gulps down what's left of the vanilla water. If only life could be as simple and sweet as this dessert. But no, life is more like a soufflé: destined to crumble and fall under the slightest change in pressure.

"Aren't you going to give me some priestly advice about honoring our mother and father?"

"Is that what you want to hear?" Kostas waits for a nod, receives a shrug. "Would you like to hear my opinion as a brother or a priest?"

Max says, "Both."

"Then as a priest and a brother I will tell you the same thing: This is a new century and parents no longer choose for their children. Do what you think is best."

"It's not that easy."

"Yeah," the priest says, "it is."

Max groans. "I should have entered the priesthood."

Not the worst idea ever, but close.

"Come, let's go light a candle for you. Perhaps God will help you to see the way. Or maybe, if we are very lucky, He will cut out our mother's tongue."

The idea of their mother deprived of her favorite weapon makes them laugh. They don't stop until the incense-laden serenity of the church below envelops them. On the hottest July days, the underground church stays October cool.

Max lights a candle, sends a silent prayer to God for direction. Better to double up, he thinks. Ask the old gods of Olympus to take mercy on his soul, just in case God's busy today.

Kostas taps the collection box. Max feeds it a ten Euro note.

"The church thanks you, Brother. Now go and be the man you want to be. Don't be Mama's bitch."

Light twinkles down the far end of a dark, hopeless tunnel.

Five minutes later, he's navigating the twisty mountain. Everything will be fine. He'll tell Mama "No," and she will have to understand.

That's how it's going to happen. Easy.

The phone starts howling in his pocket, but he's too busy dodging an overflowing bus to get it. Not until he reaches the bottom does he get a chance to check his voicemail.

One message. Mama, of course.

"Max, you are coming for dinner Saturday night at seven. Wear something nice and don't be late. If you have an emergency I will know you don't love your Mama or your poor dead *Baba*. Grandchildren, Max. I'll die of a broken heart if you don't give them to me soon."

He gives the gas pedal hell.

𝕾 4 𝕾
VIVI

DAY ONE: VIVI MAKES believe John is out showing houses.
    That goes okay until dinnertime. With no one to babble endlessly about square footage, Vivi gets even more bored than usual. She rolls a pea at Melissa, hoping to start a food fight, but Melissa keeps on reading.

———

Day two: She crafts a crude voodoo doll out of a sock and hair John dumped in the bathroom trashcan. Permanent marker face. No needle, so she uses a knife to give it a few whacks.
    Now he's headless. Headless John.

———

Day three is the day of promises she has no intention of keeping.
    If John comes back, I promise not to stare at his shiny forehead or comment on his expression of perpetual surprise. If John comes back, I promise to not kick him in the nuts for leaving. If John comes back, I promise not to spit in his lunch and put Nair in his shampoo.

———

Days four through six: dedicated to the art of crying.

———

On the seventh day, Vivi caves. She squeezes *Nair* into John's shampoo.

———

She thinks of it as the week of accomplishment, because it's been seven days of avoiding her mother. But (tick tock, tick tock) time is running out. Dinner at her parents' place is tomorrow night.

Melissa creeps in and out of the house like a pretty blonde ghost. Once in a while, she offers to make coffee or toast, but mostly she locks herself away in her room with a stack of books for company. She took the news wordlessly for the most part, asked where she was going to live.

With me, of course, Vivi told her. And Melissa's tense face relaxed back into its new, bland mask

Vivi really doesn't want to call her mother.

The phones are mocking her, the way she knew they would. They're too sleek and modern, slick like car salesmen. Not the kind of thing you use to settle into a nice long conversation with coffee in one hand and a good friend in the other.

Pick up. Put down.

Pick up. Put down.

Twenty times.

A short prayer: Oh God, let it be fast and easy.

Throw Mother Nature and Eleni Pappas in a boxing ring and Eleni will be the last woman standing – guaranteed. It's happened before.

Take Vivi's period. Hers arrived in time to make the beginning of sixth grade a year to really remember.

"Impossible," Eleni Pappas had said. "You are too young."

All (bloody) evidence to the contrary.

But what happened? No more bleeding for a whole year.

After that, Vivi was scared. Her mother was magic, she was sure. If she could delay a period, surely she could do bigger damage, to something like her height or cup size.

And now look at her, stuck at five-two.

Exhibit Two: Junior year, Vivi's first date. Eleni wailed and stamped her foot when she discovered the object of Vivi's affection, Mike Clemens, wasn't Greek. She stood in the doorway staring him down, barring him from entering, Vivi from exiting. Eleni went all out with the war paint, a thick layer of frosted green shadow and engine sludge gluing her lashes together.

"Just because my daughter is Greek," Eleni Pappas announced, "doesn't mean you get to go Greek with her."

Vivi sank into the purple-pink rug.

The date didn't happen. Mike decided he had somewhere else to be, like, with a normal girl whose mother didn't openly discuss anal sex.

School ended and Vivi applied to colleges two hundred or more miles away from home. Last thing she needed was Eleni deciding she'd pop in for a visit without prior warning, her double-edged tongue slicing, both faces with their eagle eyes nitpicking every detail of her new life.

She froze Vivi out for a month when her daughter picked UCLA.

The freeze lasted until Vivi's first night in California, when she began a torrential downpour of phone calls. Twenty times a day she'd be on the phone, giving Vivi her own special brand of Eleni advice.

"Vivi, do not forget to change your underwear every day."

Or, "Vivi, sit at the front of class. You learn more if you are not looking at the back of the people's heads."

And Vivi's personal favorite: "Vivi, keep your legs shut. I do not want your friends to think I raised a whore."

She sent Vivi a quarter, told her to hold it between her knees.

Vivi got knocked up, anyway, which was the Worst Thing Ever, until John married her. All Eleni said after that was, "Two years, mark my words. You will wish you had listened to your mother and married a good Greek boy."

Vivi makes the call she doesn't want to make.

Eleni pounces on the other end. "Whatever you are selling, I do not want it. We are poor."

These are people who have caller I.D., so her mother knows damn well who's calling.

Vivi throttles back the scream. "Jesus, it's just me. I need to tell you – "

"Vivi, my doll, you do not have to call me Jesus. You are coming for dinner Saturday, yes? I'm making your favorite *galaktobouriko*."

Vivi shuts her eyes, fantasizes about a swift death (her own) before then. "No, Mom. I mean yes, Melissa and I will be there."

"Good, good." She can almost hear the tap tapping of Eleni's ubiquitous low heels. "And Yanni?"

It's waaay too early in the conversation to lose control. "It's John. He's not Greek, we are, remember? We're separated, Mom. A week ago. So to answer your question: No, John will not be coming."

Vivi doesn't have to be there to know her mother is waving her hands at the heavens. "*Ay-yi-yi*! What did you do now? Why did he leave you?"

"Who said he left me? Maybe I told him to go."

"No, he left you," she says smugly. "A mother knows these things. Did you burn his dinner? I told you not to use that microwave. It is unnatural to cook that way. Or did you forget to iron his underwear?"

"You don't iron Dad's underwear."

"Maybe you neglected him in the bedroom, eh? Some men have strange needs. Your father he likes to – "

Jesus, God, anyone with a spare lightning bolt, strike her down

"Mom, no. Look, it's done, okay? No more John."

Silence.

"Mom?"

"Okay," Eleni says, all sunshine and puppies. "So you will be here Saturday?"

The plot is gurgling in its cauldron. Witchy-Poo is saving the interrogation for Saturday. That way she's got plenty of time to sharpen her tools.

It's going to be a hostage situation.

"Yeah," Vivi says, inching toward the slaughter. "Mel and I will see you tomorrow."

There is triumph in Eleni's voice as she says, "You would not have this problem if you married a good Greek boy."

———

A door slams.

Vivi's asleep again, until that happens. On the sofa (of course) where she's been anesthetizing her brain with a concoction of soaps and talk shows. She can't be bothered showering, dressing; her bones are limp and untrustworthy.

She's a cliché. A stereotype. Smells like it, too. There's an environmental disaster happening on her skin and in her hair. The EPA is coming any day now to begin cleanup.

"Is that you, Mel?"

Melissa casts a slight shadow. She's a scrap with a nimbus of gold light illuminating her blonde hair. The open kitchen blinds have allowed the sun to sneak in where it's not welcome. She's in school clothes, a backpack over one shoulder.

Is it a school day? It must be.

What kind of mother is she?

A shitty one, apparently. Must run in the family.

Vivi counts off the days on trembling fingers and comes up with Friday. Still exactly one week since John left, same as it was before the nap. The days are glissading into one another.

"Have you been there all day?" The 'again' is silent.

"I made coffee. I went to the bathroom. Does that count?"

The halo moves. "I've got homework."

Before Vivi has a chance to offer help, Melissa's bolting up the stairs.

Now Vivi is wondering, if she's such a cliché, how do other women cope? Is it a gradual process? Will she wake up one morning and discover she's still alive?

She's thinking about following Melissa upstairs when the phone kills her plan.

It's John. Her pulse quickens.

"I'm coming over to pick up a few of my things. Is that convenient?" He sounds like funeral director: polite, apologetic, detached. *So sorry about your dead marriage.*

His things . . .

Melissa and Vivi used to be his things.

"That's fine. There are boxes in the garage." Why is she making this easy for him? "Come to think of it, why don't you take all your stuff? I can have it all boxed and waiting in the driveway."

"I was hoping I could see Mel, too. Is she home?"

Asshole. He waited a whole week to ask.

A bright thread of hysteria winds itself around her words. "Of course she's here. Where else would she be? She's up in her room with her nose in a book where she always is."

"Don't make this harder, Vivi . . ."

The invisible rubber band that has been slowly winding tighter since he left suddenly snaps.

"Hey, don't you dare put this on me. You threw me away. Come and see our daughter. Come and get your things if you have to, but don't put the blame on me. We'll be here, but make it snappy or your things are going out with the trash!"

She throws the phone, but it doesn't know how to fly. Immediate regret; now that's John's gone, how long is it going to be before the money runs out? She needs to be practical. They have to talk money and soon. She and Melissa can't stay in this house with its mortgage and crippling property taxes.

Keeping house doesn't pay the bills, and she can't – won't – rely on alimony for long. Besides, the idea of doing something for herself looks new and shiny.

She has a B.A. in nothing much, and an M.B.A. she completed part time after Melissa started school. Her plan involved working, but John wanted a wife at home – one who could impress on demand.

Yeah, she sure impressed him.

If she had any balls, she would pack everything up and move. But their lives are here, aren't they? And no way will the courts let her move Melissa too far from John.

Nice fantasy, though. She feels better – feels better all the way upstairs and into the bathroom.

Goodbye, grime and sweat.

When she's done showering, she raps on Melissa's door and waits her customary four beats before going in.

Melissa's busy with a book. She doesn't look up.

"Hey, Kiddo, I thought you were doing homework."

She lifts the book so Vivi can see the title. "I am."

Times have changed. No way would her school have put Bram Stoker's Dracula on the reading list. Her school was old school.

"Nice," she says. "Your dad is on his way over."

Nothing but silence.

"Kiddo, your father loves you. Just because we're separated – "

"I don't care," Melissa murmurs.

"Of course you do. This is just going to take some getting used to."

"I don't care." She slams the book shut. Contempt turns her eyes a hard, glossy brown. "And you shouldn't either. God, look at you, you got all dressed up for him. You're pathetic."

Wow, Vivi thinks, because Melissa just punched every other word out of her head. Just . . . Wow.

Is that how her daughter really feels? That Vivi's a pathetic creature to be pitied?

Yeah, no. Not even close.

Okay, maybe a bit.

"Well, I might be pathetic, but I'm still your mother and while you're living under my roof, I'd like some respect. After that, we can renegotiate."

Vivi sulks in her room for thirty seconds. Knees tight against her chin, shins mashed against her thighs. She's a hedgehog, stripped of its needles.

She's still got a spine though, hasn't she?

John walked out and the world is still spinning. Melissa is safe, healthy, and in the next room. John's leaving hasn't killed Vivi – he doesn't have the power.

Her head falls back, bangs the wall.

"I can hear you, Mom," Melissa calls out. "Quit spying on me."

Yeah, that's enough brooding for today.

The boxes are in the garage, like she remembered, flat and stripped of old packing tape. Like a machine, she goes at them, pushing cardboard chunks back into shape, sealing their bottoms with tape.

A whole second is how long she gives herself to admire her handiwork, when she's done. She grabs four, then it's upstairs for cleanup duty.

The closet steps up to the plate first.

Once upon a time, she loved this closet. Now, looking at John's suits, sorted by color and season, she hates its guts.

These stupid suits have got to go. She rips them from their hangers, dumps them in the boxes. Shirts, underwear, socks stuffed in the box. Shoes on top of those, leather-soled fabric weights. Watches? Dumped in the box. Cufflinks? Dumped in the box. Everything John's? Dumped in the box.

The lavender drawer liners can stay.

Box four goes in the bathroom. She shoves it up to the counter – the His side.

Dozens of bottles crowding the counter, crowding the cupboard. John does love his potions. Promise John youth and he's there, swiping his credit card.

In one smooth move, she sweeps every last bottle and jar over the edge. Some don't make it, and that's okay. She cleans the mess with toilet paper, and does what?

Dumps it in the box.

Let him clean up his own mess.

Now the boxes are overflowing with John's junk, so she climbs in one box at a time, stamps, stomps, makes wine.

It takes a lot of tape to keep all that together. Good thing she has an abundance of tape.

Hair pops loose from her ponytail. While she shoves it back in she's humming. There's nothing like a good spring (or, um, fall) cleaning to blast away the cobwebs.

Now all she needs is a good way to get John's shit downstairs.

———

John's timing is . . .

33

5

VIVI

"IMPECCABLE," VIVI HOLLERS OUT the bedroom window.

One box to go. Her hip persuades it to jump.

She's not gloating – she's not. But her lips are curving up, enjoying the sight of the box crashing on the concrete driveway. Like its three predecessors, it bounces slightly before the cardboard splits and it's disemboweled.

He's gaping in his car, the man who would be a fish.

Vivi gives her husband a one-fingered wave. "Pick up your things, would you? Curb appeal, John. Curb appeal."

John's all action now, falling out of his shiny, shiny car in a tangle of limbs and seatbelt. He scuttles here and there, snatching up his belongings, stuffing them into the car.

The cold wind doesn't bite the smile off Vivi's face.

"You're a crazy bitch," he shouts.

Tense jaw, eyes sunken slits, rigid plastic forehead. He's a stranger.

"I love you, too, John!"

The neighbors are getting a great show for free. They're slow-walking their dogs, mowing the same patch of grass, staaaaaring out their windows. Good times at the Tyler house. Don't miss the performance; after tonight, it's going dark.

34

Vivi drops the window, goes looking for Melissa, who hasn't moved.

"Dad's here," she says.

Melissa lowers the book. "What's that noise?"

Vivi leans in the doorway, describes the scene in Technicolor.

"No kidding?"

"Would I lie about something like that?" A tiny smile from Melissa. Better than nothing. "So are you coming down to see him?"

"Nope."

What's a mother to do? The girl is old enough to make up her own mind.

Still, it doesn't take a genius to see Melissa is taking this harder than Vivi anticipated. Her attitude toward her father is downright hostile. What is going on her lovely head? Vivi wonders if she should arrange for her daughter to see the school counselor. Maybe she'll talk to an impartial third party the way she won't talk to Mom.

Which sucks.

It seems like yesterday Melissa used to share every tiny detail about her day. Now they're adversaries, glaring across the battlefield.

Vivi doesn't like it. She wants her girl back – the one with sweet breath and a fuzzy head; the gap-toothed girl with pigtails, the girl who fizzed.

She loves Melissa so much it hurts.

What's she going to do to bring the happy girl back?

———

John's in the kitchen brewing espresso in the fancy machine he gave her for Christmas a couple of years ago.

She leans against the door jamb, watches him go through the familiar routine. Looks like he's got homicide on his mind.

"We need to talk," she says.

"Where's Mel?"

"Doing homework."

"Go and get her. I'm taking her out."

"I told her. She said nope."

His face goes mental. "You're poisoning her against me. Just wait until the courts – "

"What did you do, John? I only gave her the bare facts about you leaving – which is about all you gave me. You might be a cheating scumbag, but you're the only father she's got. So you must have fucked up somehow."

"There's no one else."

"Bullshit. I deserve better than that. If you push me to it, I can probably even prove it."

"Are you going somewhere with this shit?"

"We need to talk about money."

"My lawyer will be in touch."

"Play fair, John. We've been together a long time."

He slumps against the counter. "What do you want? Everything I suppose."

She crosses the room, pats his shoulder, gives him the comfort she's always given.

"I'm not greedy, I just want what's fair. And I want you to buy out my half of this house, sell it if you have to. I never liked it much, anyway. You picked it out so you can have it. Mel and I will do just fine in something much smaller."

"Why didn't you say something – about the house?"

"I did, but you were too excited to listen."

"Vivi – "

"It doesn't matter. Not now."

They go quiet – for a spell.

"What else?"

"Full custody and child support."

John digests her words while he finishes making coffee. "I can live with that," he says flatly. "Visitation?"

"As much as you and Melissa want."

"I'll talk to my lawyer." In his condescending movie-star voice.

"You do that," she says. "And soon."

———

Did she ever love John? Now . . . It's hard to say. And if she did – when did it start, the withering?

She picks at her memories, pulls strings, searches for that most recent glittering moment of love, that time when his touch burned and turned her thermostat to fever.

But . . .

It's never been that way.

They were never a romcom or a paperback novel. The tale of Vivi and John started as a Dear Abby letter, and it's ending in the same, sad column.

❧ 6 ❧

VIVI

VIVI GOT KNOCKED UP same way most girls her age do.
Vivi loved John. John loved talking about how much he loved Vivi. Not the same thing, but who knows that when they're nineteen?

Okay, maybe some people, but not Vivi. She was too busy being blinded by his glow.

John Tyler was sweet. Old fashioned. He liked holding hands and cuddling. He wanted to wait and she wanted to not wait.

Exhibit A (also known as Melissa Jane Tyler) proves that John eventually caved, and caved, and caved.

And caved.

John liked caving when there was a gallon of beer involved.

So, John was drunk and she was sober enough to realize somewhere along the way his dick shed the condom.

The doctor said, "No," to emergency contraception. Didn't consider college girls having accidents a bona fide emergency. Said, "Come back if you miss your period."

Four weeks later, the same doctor said, "You've got three choices . . ."

Not one of them involved the doctor paying for the cost of raising a child, or stepping into a time machine so he could scribble UNDO on that prescription pad.

———

Eleni said: "I will kill you."

No one abuses the power of an empty threat like Eleni Pappas.

7

MELISSA

OKAY, SO MELISSA'S NOT totally naïve. She's seen gay porn on the Internet and she knows what men do together. She can totally deal with it. That kiss is the problem. Even if she keeps her eyes open, that kiss is seared onto her corneas.

And . . .

Josh Cartwright was right.

Which totally sucks.

Dad's really gay, and everyone at school knows it. Yesterday, Josh brushed past her and whispered, "Your dad sucks balls," with a big smirk on his stupid face. Tonya told him to screw himself, but guys do that all the time anyway, so it was a wasted opportunity to really zing Josh.

Afterward, she hid in the library. It's not that Melissa doesn't appreciate Tonya standing up for her, but it would be so much better if no one knew; she could pretend things were totally normal.

"You okay there, Honey?"

Is Mom high? No, she's not okay. She's not even in the same dictionary as okay.

They're on their way to Grams' and Grampy's house for dinner. Mom is smiling, but it makes her look crazy, not happy. Grams is going to know Mom has lost it. Grams can sniff out insanity from a mile away. Uncle Chris says crazy people know their own kind.

Fine," she says.

Melissa sounds empty, like a missing person. Looks crazy (lots of that going around) sitting there wrapped around her backpack, staring at the great suburban nothing on the other side of the glass. Her fingernails are biting into her palms. Yeah, it hurts, but in a good way. Her hand is the only part of her that feels alive.

"Don't worry about the dragon. Let me handle her."

Mom thinks she's worried about Grams? Not even. She shrugs. Says, "Fine, whatever," and Mom goes back to smiling at the road.

Grams and Grampy live in the same house they've always lived in, from before Mom and Uncle Chris were even born. Years ago, Dad tried to sell them another one, and Grams told him the bones of her enemies were buried under this house. Dad was like, "Oooookay . . ." He quit asking in case it was true.

Too cold now, but in spring and summer her grandparents sit outside on the covered porch, drinking doll-sized cups of muddy coffee, while they watch the neighbors and mind everyone else's business. Melissa has seen the world from their porch, and mostly it consists of old people hunched over walkers, or kids her age practically making out in the street. Grams always yells, "Just you wait, I'm going to tell your mother she raised a whore!" And Grampy always says, "Eleni, let them be young, eh? Remember when we used to be young?" And then Grams says, "I am still young, but in an old woman's body."

The front door flies open before the car stops. Grams is there with a smile for Melissa and a mouthful of "I told you so" for Mom.

"Don't even say it," Mom says.

Grams gives her a dark look. "Too late, I already said it. And I will say it again, soon." She turns her attention back to Melissa. "My angel, you look more Greek every day!"

Then Grampy's there, dishing out hugs.

"I have to use the bathroom," Melissa says.

Mom steers them both into the house. "You just went before we left the house."

"Maybe she has a urinary infection," Grams says. "Look at her. You let her wear such skimpy clothes. Probably her bladder got a chill. Even the prostitutes put on warm clothes in winter."

Whaaaat? No way. Her jeans are barely low and she's wearing a long sweater with a cropped jacket. Not exactly the latest in hooker fashions.

"I have to go again. It's probably that shitty generic cola we buy now."

"Language," Vivi says. "And we only bought it once."

Grams crosses herself. "*Ay-yi-yi*! You let her drink that poison?"

"We have to conserve money. It doesn't exactly grow on trees," Mom says.

"Actually, it kind of does," Melissa says. "It's mostly cotton, which grows on shrubs."

Vivi says, "Mom, she's my daughter – "

"And she is my granddaughter. All that sugar!"

"It's diet," Melissa mutters, but no one is listening to her now – Melissa the ghost.

The ghost of Melissa Tyler slips past the arguing women. Eyes shut, she makes her way to upstairs, fingers brushing the wall. She knows this house by heart.

The arguing dims. By the time she closes the guest bathroom's door, it's just her and her footsteps.

Melissa Tyler, last person on earth. Sounds okay.

Out the tiny window, she watches the neighbor's dog stop its squirrel chase to crap.

Melissa wants a dog. Melissa has always wanted a dog.

But no – of course. Dad is allergic to cats, dogs, and any pet Melissa has ever wanted.

Probably a lie, like everything else.

She leans on the counter, takes a good look in the mirror. Leans, leans, until the knobby elbow joints ache.

Relax, Mel. Enjoy it.

She relaxes. The pain fades to pastels. Then she pushes down, until her bones sing.

End result: Purple, pink, no bruise.

Too bad.

What does this mirror have to say?

Nothing she doesn't already know. Lots of ugly black dots on her nose. She put those nose strips on Mom's shopping list, but if she bought them, they never made it home. She'll be sorry when clogged pores conquer Melissa's whole face.

And another thing: Grams is full of crap. Melissa doesn't look anything like Greek. She looks like Dad; everyone says so, except Grams.

Her whole family is so full of crap that they're drowning in crap soup. Except Grampy, but he's always so busy at the lab, or with his woodwork, that he doesn't bother anybody.

She sits on the fuzzy pink toilet cover that goes with the rest of the room. Used to be she loved this bathroom and its bright pink everything. Now it looks like Pepto-Bismol puke.

Way too bright. Way too loud.

Melissa closes her eyes just to make the room shut up. Her hand dives into the backpack's front pocket. Fingers dance around the tight corners.

There it is – her just-in-case. A tiny, silver safety pin Mom put there along with a few quarters.

Just in case, she said.

She thumbs the sharpened tip. Four scabs on her wrist. About to be five.

The mirror watches her stick her tongue out the way it did when she was a kid, poring over a coloring book, focused on staying inside the lines.

She goes slow. Draaaaags the point along a parallel path.

Melissa is flint. Together she and the pin create sparks of bright, shiny pain. The walls are nothing compared to the stars they make.

The pink cotton room cradles her, while she rides the wave.

Nothing else matters except here, except now.

She is alive. She is dead.

She is numb.

❧ 8 ❧
VIVI

HOSTAGE SITUATION – VIVI KNEW it.
All she can do is sit and fake invisibility until the inevitable regimen of torture commences. Dad folds his newspaper, winks, vanishes to his hideaway beneath the house.

Neat trick. Now it's just her in the audience.

Eleni pulls an extended-family-sized tray of *pastitsio*, with its bubbling béchamel sauce, from the oven, eases the whole pasta and meat dish onto a large wooden chopping board. Then it's goodbye, oven mitts.

She won't sit yet. No tactical advantage.

"I made *galaktobouriko*, too. Plenty for you to take home."

Figures. "You just reprimanded me for giving Melissa sugary drinks, but desserts are okay?"

Eleni waves her magic hand and Vivi's objections disappear. "It is the chemicals. My *galaktobouriko* is natural – no preservatives or colors made in a laboratory."

Her *galaktobouriko*, Vivi's ass.

Eleni can't make sweets to save her own life. A thousand times, Vivi and Chris sat in this kitchen, ate her mistakes like they were good, ate like they had a choice.

Too sweet.

Too salty.

Too Hindenburg.

Ten bucks says Eleni rushed down to the local Greek restaurant this afternoon, demanded a whole tray of the custard and pastry dish. If Vivi checked the trash she'd find the foil stashed at the bottom, under the bags – guaranteed.

"What is that look for, eh?"

Vivi says, "What look?"

"That look."

"There's no look."

"Trust me, there is a look. Your brother loves my desserts. I always fix them for him. He comes every weekend."

Yeah, that's a lie. Vivi spoke to Chris a week ago, before her world exploded. Six weeks Eleni-free, he bragged. Laughed about how he deserved a chip.

"How's Trish?"

Trish is a sweetheart, but not a good enough wife for Chris, in Eleni's book. Not rich enough, not fertile enough, not Greek enough.

She doesn't say it now, though. She's too busy poking through the liquor cabinet, searching for something that doesn't seem to be there. "He called last night to talk to his mama. He is such a good boy."

Typical Mom, sidestepping the question. "Trish is good for him. She keeps him grounded."

Mom straightens up. "No more brandy."

"I don't mind."

"But your father will. We must get some. Where is Melissa?"

Melissa materializes in the doorway. "Here."

Eleni tugs off her apron, scoops the handles of her purse over one forearm. "Your mother is driving us to the store."

Melissa flops into a chair. "I'm not going."

"Of course you are going," Eleni says. "What else is there to do?"

Shrug. "Read, or I'll go to the garage with Grampy."

"She can stay here if she wants to. She'll be fine with Dad." Vivi says.

Eleni licks her finger, rubs at invisible smut on Vivi's cheek. "I don't think so," she says in distant voice.

Five minutes later Melissa leaves the house with them. The Eleni Pappas steamroller crushed the protest right out of her, too.

———

The Liquor Shack isn't far. A couple of blocks. Mom barks directions; plays drill sergeant while Melissa slouches in the backseat.

What's she going to do with that girl?

Parking lot full, liquor store empty. The red-roofed Pizza Hut is where the party is happening. The Liquor Shack's Indian clerk looks up when they walk in. Short guy in a white turban.

He nods at Melissa. "Is she twenty-one?"

"Twenty-two," Eleni says.

"She does not look twenty-two."

"Okay." Eleni turns on one heel. "Come, Vivi, Melissa. We go somewhere else where they do not hate Greek customers and call us liars."

"He didn't call me a liar," Vivi says. "He called you a liar."

The clerk doesn't look like a happy man. "I do not hate Greek customers, just underage customers, because the authorities will take away my liquor license."

"I already told you she is twenty-three," Eleni says.

"You said twenty-two."

Eleni shrugs. "Today is her birthday."

Yeah, he's still not happy. But he's not in any hurry to chase Melissa out. It's been a slow day, and the middle woman looks thirsty.

Eleni shuts up until they're a row away from the liqueurs. Then she says, "Why did John leave you?"

Panic, panic.

Vivi throws a glance over one shoulder, but the clerk's not interested in them – just their money. He won't come alive again until they wave some green under his nose. "Jeez, Mom, not here, okay?" Vivi tries to roll the polyester boulder, but her mother won't budge.

It's a trap.

Vivi walked (and drove) right into it.

Eleni brought Vivi here so she can do her grilling in public, where Vivi won't make a scene. The verdict is still out on whether the brandy is a lie or not.

Well, Vivi isn't playing this game.

"Forget it. Not here, not now. The end."

Eleni puts on her bulldog face.

Vivi says, "I said no."

Meanwhile, Melissa has caught up with them, bored with staring at booze she can't buy for a few more years, unless a forger hooks her up with a fake ID.

"I figured you knew, Grams." One finger traces an invisible line across the rum bottles. "Dear old Dad is gay."

Vivi's head snaps around. "Melissa, that's not true."

Melissa shrugs, in that teenage way. No one can give a shit less than a teenager. "If you say so."

"Jesus, Melissa. Why would you make up something like that?" Vivi grabs her by the shoulders. Checks her eyes for a lie. "What happened? Did Dad do something to you?"

"She has to blame someone," Eleni says.

Vivi glares.

"When two men kiss on the mouth, it means they're gay," Melissa says. "And I saw Dad kiss a man on the mouth."

In a flash, the semen-splattered tie pops into Vivi's mind: John's or not? All the times they didn't screw in the past fifteen years. All the kissing they never did. Intimacy that never came.

She goes cold, stiff. Total paralysis, except her right hand slicing through the air. That hand strikes Melissa's face, cuts her down.

"You little brat!"

Vivi hurls the words, but they don't stick. Melissa's wearing body armor made of smug fascination. No reaction trumps reaction.

Vivi cues a second slap.

Eleni grabs her arm. "Vivi, enough!"

This is Melissa's *carpe diem* moment. Her hand blurs, finds her mother's face.

Vivi freezes. Can't move. Can't speak. Can't *believe*.

"People in school are talking about Dad." Melissa spits the words out. "Josh Cartwright saw him cruising the park for gay sex. How do you think that makes me feel? All you care about is yourself!"

Hands on hips, eyes and mouth accusing Vivi of being a bad mother. And she's right: poor kid has two shitty parents.

The clerk peers out from behind the cash register.

"Don't say anything," Eleni snaps.

"I say nothing, crazy lady."

"John can't be gay," Vivi says.

Melissa opens her mouth to speak, but her grandmother clamps her palm across that open mouth.

"He can't be gay. He married me. He chose me. We have a child!"

"I knew there was something I never liked about him," Eleni says. "At first I thought it was just his eyes were too close together. Then I thought, 'Eleni, do not be prejudiced because he has squinty eyes and big nostrils,' because your father, Vivi, his family have the big nostrils. But see, I was right! Now that I think about it, one time I saw John watching your father's buttocks."

Vivi wants to go ogre, sweep these bottles off the shelves, aim a few at her mother.

"Mom! Jesus! Enough! My husband is gay and he never thought to drop that little tidbit into the conversation, oh, say before we got married? He should never have married me. Maybe I'd be married to someone straight and I wouldn't be standing here in a grungy liquor store with my lunatic mother and a daughter who loathes my guts! Marrying John is the worst thing that ever happened in my whole stupid life!"

It's one of life's slow motion moments: Melissa walks backwards, hands in the air. She's done. She's *so* out of here.

Hate is about the only thing tougher and shinier than diamonds. And Melissa, she's shimmering with the stuff.

The warning bells are much too late. Vivi's mouthing, *I'm sorry, I didn't mean that, Baby*, but the damage is done and her girl is gone.

Too late. Too, too late.

"Mel – " she starts.

"She is a better daughter than you deserve right now," Eleni says.

Vivi turns on her. "You just had to meddle, didn't you? You had to bring us here and poke with that sticky beak, instead of just asking. You have no empathy, Mom. I really hope you're happy."

Off in the (increasingly less distant) distance, sirens wail. Probably a fire. House fires are popular in winter, all those fireplaces puffing smoke and creosote into the air, all those people too cold to go outside for a smoke.

Except there's no fire this time.

The dime drops when a couple of police officers push into the store, slap bracelets on Vivi's wrists.

"You have the right to – "

"Remain silent, I know," she says.

Eleni says, "My daughter doesn't know how to be silent."

Pot. Kettle. Black.

Melissa's outside, watching, crying. And the cashier is suddenly interested in everything.

"Thanks a lot, asshole," Vivi says, because who else could have made the call?

"Child abusers get what they deserve," he says.

"I'm not a child abuser," Vivi says – to him, to her mother, to her daughter, to the cops herding her out the door.

Palm raised: "Talk to the hand, crazy lady."

Humiliating, being dragged away from a liquor store in handcuffs, flanked by cops twice her size. Lots of people outside, more than one holding up a phone, ready to make Vivi a YouTube "star."

The worst part? Melissa was right. The second she said it a bell tolled in Vivi's soul. John is different, their marriage a sham; deep down, below the itchy, uncomfortable surface, she has known it all along.

She's not unlovable, undesirable, after all.

It was always him.

A firm hand shoves her head.

"That's my daughter!" Eleni shouts. She appeals to the swelling crowd. "Look at the police, they are brutalizing her because they are prejudiced against the Greek people! What, you don't like *baklava* and *gyro*? You people owe everything to Greece. It is the birthplace of civilization!"

Vivi climbs into the police cruiser. It's an Eleni-free zone.

"That your mother?" one of the cops wants to know.

"Yeah."

"Apple doesn't fall far from that tree."

Ha-ha.

9

MAX

"GOODNIGHT, MAX. MISS ME while you're gone," the nurse says. She's giving him that look, the one telling him she wouldn't mind a rerun of their brief affair.

Ha. Some affair.

He fucked her one night in his Jeep, after a staff party. First and only time he touched a hospital employee.

Bad idea.

She got weird and clingy after that, started telling everyone they were dating. Left cute cards in his office. Invited him to meet her parents.

He was kind, but honest about no possibility of a future.

Now he gives her a polite, dismissive, "Have a good night," and he's out of there.

———

It's a shitty night. The Pagasetic Gulf is its usual calm self – it's Max who is the storm.

All week, he's been hoping for a disaster. A pandemic or a huge earthquake. Maybe a good war. Anything to stop this night from happening.

One night, one dinner, he tells himself. He'll do this once, but that's it. And he'll make Mama understand.

Yeah right. Good luck with that. Mama doesn't understand anything she doesn't like.

He finds a parking space in a side street near the Volos promenade.

Warmish out, not cold. But the cold is coming. Summer's had enough of Greece for this year, and soon it will swap places with winter. It'll change its mind, be back again, when it gets bored with the southern hemisphere.

He walks like a kid on his way to detention. Hands shoved deep in his pockets. Eyes on the ground. He means to walk slowly, but old habits have a tendency to fight for their lives.

A smart man would have parked one street over, so he could see them before they see him.

Too late. Mama's there, waving her black handkerchief his way.

He picks up the already fast pace.

The good son.

No longer officially summer, but the promenade is still closed to traffic. A string of *tavernas* line the street, their chairs and tables set out along the water. On the ribbon of road between, couples stroll. Arms linked, talking, flirting, seeing and being seen. Colored lights wink at the sky.

A good place to bring a beautiful woman or hang with friends.

He's not surprised Mama chose this place. It was his parents' favorite, for times they wanted to impress. The food is good and inexpensive. A meal can speed up or slow down and the wait staff doesn't mind.

He should have invited his brother, but Kostas isn't stupid; smart men don't accept uninviting invites. So, Max is going into the viper pit alone.

"Here he is!" A cool leathery cheek to his. Mama reeks of Estée Lauder. "Maximos, you are late."

It takes some doing, extricating himself from her iron embrace. "I'm right on time, Mama. The exact time you gave me."

"Ah, Max, you are so unkind to me." She gives him a warning glance only he can see, before turning back to her guests. "Don't mind our little joke. My son is very respectful."

Mama looks . . .

Old.

Older than she should. Now that his father is dead, she's committed to wearing black for the rest of her life. Not everyone is made for black; it's stealing the color from her face, even with all that makeup. A web of silver winds its insidious way though her tight bun.

When did this happen?

When did she get *old?*

Her tongue hasn't dulled, though. It's still razor sharp on both edges and can fillet a human being, with a few well-places slashes.

Tired through to the bone, he checks out the others. He recognizes his mother's friend Tasoula, though he hasn't seen her since he graduated from high school. Which would make her daughter . . .

Wow!

Gorgeous. Hot, hot, hot.

A woman like that, a man throws himself happily on those rocks.

The vision unfolds her long legs, stands. A delicate hand reaches for his.

"Hello, Max, I'm Anastasia." Her voice is honey – of course. "Do you remember me? I used to follow you around, begging you to play with me."

Barely. Ten years difference when you're a kid is a lot.

Now, it's different. Now he wants to play.

Oh yeah, he wants to play. And play hard.

"Did I play with you?" he asks.

"No." She laughs. "You had more important things to do."

His mother's arm is a vine, winding possessively around his. "My Maximos is a doctor," she says proudly.

"And your other son? Am I remembering correctly that you have another son?" Tasoula asks. Mama's sour expression doesn't deter her. "Younger, I think."

"Yes," Mama says. "Kostas. He was to become a lawyer. I grieve every day."

Tasoula makes the sign of the cross: forehead to chest, shoulder to shoulder. "I'm sorry. We have been in Thessaloniki too many years, I did not hear he had passed."

Mama has gone too far. Max says, "Kostas isn't dead, he's a priest."

"A noble calling." Tasoula looks confused.

"Before he married," Max explains.

"Max!" Mama pinches his arm, the way she did when he was a boy.

Tasoula nods. "Ah . . ."

Mama raises her palms, like she's calling on Jesus for backup. "What's a mother to do?"

Max has to give her credit; she's holding herself together, dialing down the crazy. Good thing, too. What would her guests think if she erupted in her usual way? They might think her insanity is genetic, and then Anastasia would be jerked out of (his) reach.

Reality check: Anastasia is stunning, but can he seriously consider marriage with a woman he doesn't know?

He drinks her in, her long, lean body, that soft skin. She's all legs and beauty. What does she smell like, he wonders, when she's up close, caramel hair pulled away from her neck? How does she look on her knees?

Mama's watching him expectantly, waiting on him to push in her chair. When she's settled, she sighs. "My only hope for grandchildren now is my Maximos. But he spends all his time with other people's children when he should be busy making his own."

Same old song, same old dance.

"I'm a pediatrician," he explains. "It's my job to make sick children well. You wanted me to become a doctor and I'm a doctor."

But she's never satisfied. "You should have been a real doctor, then you might have done your father some good."

Tasoula smiles politely. "There is a great deal of money in medicine. Plenty of money for a wife and many children. And your brother's work is impressive, also. It is important work bringing God's word to the people."

Mama crosses herself. "Kostas is cursed. He did not get our blessing. My husband died from the grief."

"*Baba*," Max says, using the affectionate word for father, "had cancer."

"And would he have got the cancer if your brother had not ignored our wishes and become a priest? No!" She clutches her chest and the jet crucifix resting there. "Your brother murdered his father."

He wants to shake her, change her channel. Instead he puts on his own show and smiles. "Forgive her, she's old and feeble. She could drop dead at any minute."

"How am I cursed with such a son?" She pats his hand, but the look in her eyes tells him this isn't over. To stay in her good graces now, it's dance, dance, dance on the end of her strings.

He glances at Anastasia's legs, wishes his father was still alive – for a million reasons. He kept Mama in check, gave her a constant project.

"Anastasia," he says. "What are you going to have?"

She's smiling. "Not hungry. I think I'd prefer to walk first."

He grins. Both mothers are watching.

"Let's do it," he says.

———

Anastasia bides her time.

It's not until they've melded with the crowd that her fingers reach for his.

Electricity shoots straight up his arm and down into his cock.

"Are you a good fuck, Max?"

Yeah, he keeps his cool, outside where it counts. He's had plenty of practice. Forward women aren't rare; he's had his share of the forward and the backward kind. But this is different.

"You move fast."

She bites her lip. He knows it's calculated, but tonight he doesn't care.

"So old fashioned. I didn't expect that from the boy who used to piss on his mother's gardenias." Her laugh is thin, girlish. "Come on."

He goes.

———

There's a park nearby. Max knows it well. He dumped his virginity there during his fourteenth summer. An amicable breakup.

Anita was her name. Pretty, German, Eighteen. Easy in the best possible way. God bless horny girls.

"They won't be expecting us back for a while. They'll just be glad we're bonding," Anastasia says. She smiles her angel's smile, her making-a-secret smile.

"Hey, gardenias like acid," he says, belatedly.

"I don't care. Do you?"

The heavily wooded park behind St Constantine's Church is the color of carbon at night. No lights, except on the edge closest to the church. It's a good place for lovers and the merely lustful.

He goes, he goes, following her steps.

Like wearing a blindfold.

Max is a man who likes playing with blindfolds.

He groans when her soft hands pull his face to hers, lips parted, tongue waiting to be captured. Fuck, she makes him want to lose control, like some overeager teenager. It takes everything he's got to grind her into the tree's bark, good and slow.

"Fuck me, Max," she whispers.

"No."

She stops. "No?"

"No."

One hand goes up her skirt, makes her naked from the waist down. He lets her really feel his fingers.

"Why not?"

"It's not a debate," he says. Maybe he'll be getting married soon, maybe not. But until then, there's fun. "I haven't decided if you're going to be mine."

"A game. I like games," she breathes.

He doesn't like games, but Max sure loves to play.

10

VIVI

R OCK BOTTOM WAS LAST week. And now look, a new rock
bottom.

Rock bottom's bottom?

Life, you are one funny bitch, Vivi thinks.

Nice holding cell. A cozy six-by-eight. Shiny, shiny toilet and the
worst bed taxpayers' money can buy. Is it too soon to make a shiv, or
should she wait?

She flops on the bed. The pillow doesn't pretend to care – it keeps
on being a rock.

John is gay. John is gay. Hip-hip-hooray.

In the old days, gay meant happy. She doesn't feel happy. But then
she's not the gay one, is she?

Is John happy?

Someone has to be happy.

Round and round in circles, until someone comes for her.

She shuffles, on her way to death row – stupid woman walking. Into
a grim room with sad walls and an equally sad table and chairs. Her
escort points her to the bad-guy side of the table. Then another police
officer comes in and sits on the good-guy side.

Oh God, she'd rather eat shit than call John to make bail.

"Sounds like you're a woman on the edge," the officer says. She's one of those big, no bullshit types. Ten bucks says she'd never be dumb enough to hook up with a gay man. Or any man.

"You have no idea."

"Guess we should be grateful we don't have to charge you with homicide. Killing someone means more paperwork. I really don't like paperwork."

"I would never kill my daughter," Vivi says. "It was just a slap. And I regret it, I swear."

The officer holds up her hand. Vivi shuts up.

"I'm talking about that husband of yours. Your mother gave us the lowdown on his dooooown low. That woman sure can talk. She kept calling him a *pousti*. At first I thought she was talking about some kind of Italian sandal, until your kid translated."

"Are you charging me with anything?"

"No, you can go home – this time. You family is waiting on you out front." She holds the door open. "If I were you, I would have ripped off little Willie and the twins and fed them to the dog."

"We don't have a dog."

"So get a dog."

Eleni and Melissa are sitting on a battered wood bench in the lobby. Melissa won't look at her, and her mother won't talk to her.

Which is fine. She just wants to go home and scrub the humiliation off her soul.

Then she's going to deal with the two of them.

———

Vivi searches "how to get a life."

But the Internet being the Internet, it only wants to sell her stuff.

So she tackles the problem old school: with a notepad and a thinking cap.

She's there on the couch, wide-awake, when the night peels back from the sky and flaunts its golden petticoat.

It's an omen. Spring is coming, and in spring anything is possible – not just allergies.

Vivi wants a brand spanking new life. The old one is a tatty pair of sweats, all baggy around the knees. It makes her look and feel like shit.

The big question: Is selling the house and finding a new neighborhood a big enough change?

Life won't be the same, no matter where they go. Staying nearby, she runs the risk of bumping in John and his Mr. Perfect. Who needs that?

Last night Melissa came clean, told her all about what the kids at school have been saying. Vivi didn't say it, but she wanted to kill John for his indiscretions. It's one thing to betray her, but Melissa? Not cool. She wonders how many nights he spent cruising the park, looking for some action, while she and Melissa ate alone.

Is he even practicing safe sex?

Never mind. Of course he is. The man is the epitome of paranoid and O.C.D. when it comes to cleanliness. Every time they had sex, he couldn't get to the shower fast enough.

Doesn't matter, she's still making an appointment to get things checked out under her hood. Can't start a new life with someone's secondhand, thirdhand, diseases.

A new life. She can do it. They can do it.

But where?

Someplace unfamiliar. None of the same restaurants, none of the same people. But not too far from family.

Back to the computer.

Google Maps is useless, for once. It shows her pictures of a better life, better places, but it's skimpy on the finger snapping make-it-happen part.

She snaps her fingers. Clicks her heels.

Nothing happens.

11

VIVI

S AME OLD NUMBER, BUT the phone doesn't nag.

Vivi says, "Dad?"

"How did you know it was me and not your mother?"

"You wouldn't believe me if I told you."

"Eh, probably not. I accepted a long time ago that the women in my life are all strange."

Vivi can hear the smile. "Are you okay? Is Mom okay?"

"Of course we are okay. But I need to ask you to do a thing for me. It is a secret, and I know you can keep a secret, especially from your mother."

"Are you in trouble?"

"No. It's nothing. Someone is sending me a package, and I do not want your mother to know. If they send it to your house, will you keep it there for me?"

"Sure," Vivi says. "Of course."

"Thank you. You are a good girl. I know you have problems right now, but I can't ask your brother. One twist and he would tell your mother everything. Chris could not keep a secret even from a stranger."

Vivi laughs because, hey, it's true. "It's no problem, Dad. I'll let you know when it gets here."

"Thank you," he says. "Thank you."

He ends the call on a distracted note.

———

The package shows up a couple of days later. Vivi scribbles her signature on the pink form, and then it's just her and the box.

It's . . .

A box.

Unremarkable.

The boxiest box ever.

Only thing interesting is the return address. It flew express, rocketing across the top half of the globe from Greece. The customs form is next to useless. There's a big, fat smudge across its details.

Huh, she thinks.

Then it's off to Google for more intel. But Google's got nothing to say, except what looks like an address is the Greek equivalent of a P.O. Box.

So, basically Vivi's at a dead end.

But not quite.

Two days late, that finger snapping and heel clicking pays off. Not instant teleportation (which is okay, because on one hand there's Star Trek, but on the other? The Fly), but an idea busts into her head, waving a bright white on blue banner.

Greece.

Yeah, she could handle that. It meets her criteria: unfamiliar, different restaurants, close to family. Throw in the beaches, the history, the culture, and all the Greek food they can eat.

Her language skills are covered in a sprinkling of rust, but they'll polish up just fine.

Greece?

Why not?

———

Her father shows up for the package during his lunch break. He never looks like Dad in a suit.

"Where's the lab coat?" she asks.

"Big meeting this afternoon," he says. "The company is launching a new drug, soon. They asked me to be impressive, so I wear something impressive, that way the FDA lackeys concentrate on my suit and not on my big, confusing words. How are you doing, my love?"

"Amazing. No, better than amazing. What's better than amazing?"

"Wonderful?"

"Then that's what I am. Do you want coffee?"

"Not today," he says. "What if I spill it on my suit?"

She laughs and gives him the box. "What is it? A surprise for Mom?"

"Yes, it is a surprise for your mother."

"I won't say a word."

But he has already checked out, fingers skating over the label. "Eh?"

"I won't tell her. About the box."

"Good," he says. "You are a good girl, Vivi."

12

VIVI

MELISSA SAYS, "BUT WHHHHHHHY?"

(So much angst packed into one syllable.)

"Because it's the best idea ever."

"No way." She's shaking that blonde head so hard, Vivi thinks there's a good chance it's going disconnect itself from the rest of her and slam a cranium-shaped hole in the living room wall. Not good. No way is Vivi redecorating before they move to Greeker pastures.

"Too bad," she says. "You're outnumbered. You get one vote, I get two."

"Not fair. I'll stay with Dad."

"And his boyfriend?"

"Okay, I'll stay with Uncle Chris and Aunt Trish."

"You're not staying with Chris and Trish."

"Grams and Grampy? They love me."

"I love you."

"Could we have a dog?"

"Maybe."

"What about my friends?"

"They're an email away. And you'll make new ones."

"I don't want new ones. I like the old ones."

"And you'll learn to like the new ones. Isn't this exciting?"

"Yeah right," Melissa says.

13

VIVI

A COUPLE OF MONTHS mosey on by while she's plotting her way out of the United States. Christmas comes . . . and goes. The New Year kicks the old one out of its seat.

Vivi pinky swears Melissa to silence. Easy, because the girl's vocabulary has shrunk to a handful of monosyllabic words. Doesn't seem likely that she's going to go on a sudden chatting spree, least of all to her grandmother.

Passports, Visas, tickets. And on top of everything, a whole house to pack. John's selling the house, moving on and away – from her, from their marriage. Everything she and John collected during their tenure will be divided; her half will go into storage until she decides whether staying in Greece is viable option. John gets first shot at buying out her life if she starts calling Greece "home."

It gives her a kind of fever.

John doesn't say much when Vivi fills him in. She's being nice about it, not bitchy. Flexible, too. But not flexible enough to leave Melissa behind.

He's okay with that – he's okay. They'll work something out. They really will. There's the Internet and Skype and airplanes to slash the miles.

Meanwhile, she's making a mushroom out of her mother, shoving her in a dark place and feeding her bullshit. One poorly timed word, and Mom will spin out of control. When Eleni gets going, she's like a flaming star, thrown off its axis, burning everything in its path.

The house sells fast. One day it's still theirs, the next it's not. The buyers have a family and they want the perfect family home.

Well, they can have it.

They sit there in the title office, John and Vivi, and sign away the largest purchase of their marriage for two small pieces of paper. Vivi weighs her piece in one hand. Funny how so much money can feel light and insignificant. Checks and credit cards have a way about them, of transforming something into nothing at all.

She's pretty sure banks count on that. It's easier to spend dollars you can't see.

"Are you sure you want to do this?" John touches her hand. He feels rubbery, unnatural.

"I'm not sure of anything."

"So, why go then? Get a new place and find a job here. That way Melissa won't have to go to a new school in a strange country. Surely that would be better for you."

"Better for you, you mean."

"That's not what I mean." He escorts her to her car. "Reconsider. Please, Vivi."

She can hardly stand to look at him, but she makes herself do it, look at the stranger.

Who is he?

Who is she?

"Were you thinking about men all those times we were screwing? Was fantasizing about them the only way you could get off with me?"

"God, Vivi. No. How could you think that?" A guilty man looks her in the eye. "How did you find out?"

The knife slides in easy. His back is butter.

"I didn't know, until Melissa told me. She saw you. Followed you to your boyfriend's house."

He goes pale – face and shirt merge where they meet. Despite the Botox, the facials, the dermabrasion, he leaps forward a decade.

66

"When?"

"The night you left. After some kid at her school saw you at the park, she followed you. This kid and his buddies have been giving her hell about it."

He slumps against the cold car. "God, Vivi, how did we screw up this bad?"

"You shouldn't have lied to yourself. That never works out."

"But I loved you."

"Not in the way you should have loved me. Not in the way I wanted to be loved. It's better this way, don't you think?"

She drives away feeling every synonym for sad. When a marriage dies, there's no corpse to grieve over, no place to put flowers.

✿ 14 ✿

VIVI

LIFE IS TOUGH IN the gulag.

It's only temporary, Vivi tells herself. She's balancing a magazine and a roll of flower-printed toilet paper on her knees in the pink bathroom. Living with her mother is enough to literally give her the shits.

One week until they escape.

Her mother insists on a family dinner, though she still has no idea Vivi and Melissa are about to fly her coop. That means Chris will be here with his wife. Trish is one of those good through to her gooey center types, an optimist who sees the sunny side of everything, even taxes. Have to pay for schools somehow, she says. Aside from Melissa and John, she's the only one who knows about Vivi's plan. She helped Vivi with the details, never once begging her to stay.

She gets it, Trish does.

Eleni pulls on her pissy pants before Chris and Trish walk in the door. She's tweaking the sheers as the Suburban butts up to the garage. "Why do they need that thing? So big. It is not like they have a family."

Aaaand . . . that right there is the crux of it. Vivi's sister-in-law doesn't want kids, though she and Chris dote on Melissa. Like all

Greek mothers, Eleni expects Vivi and Chris to provide her with at least ten bouncing babies. Clearly, she was temporarily deaf all those times Chris pointedly mentioned they're happy living in a childfree zone.

Vivi says, "Lots of people drive big cars. So what?"

"So much gasoline. So expensive." She scurries to the kitchen, where she gets busy pretending she's overworked and underpaid; she wants homage before hugs. "Tell him I'm in the kitchen."

"Them."

"That is what I say."

It all goes as Eleni planned. Vivi opens the door, hugs them both, then she says, "Mom's in the kitchen." Chris goes on ahead, leaving the women to link arms and take their time.

The sound of Eleni smothering her son with kisses wafts down the hall. Then she starts berating him for hair she considers too long. Jesus had long hair, Chris tells her.

"So how's it going?" Trish asks.

"Do you know how to make a noose?"

"For you or Eleni?"

"Does it matter?"

Trish laughs. "I can't believe you're leaving me alone with her."

Vivi laughs, too. But it annoys her that five years into their marriage, Eleni still acts like Trish is Chris's imaginary friend.

"Mostly, I'm trying to stop Melissa from going completely mute."

Into the kitchen, where the wild thing is.

"Speaking of Mel, where is my favorite girl?" Chris grabs a handful of sunflower seeds from the bowl on the table. He nibbles out the center before spitting the shell on a napkin Trish slides in front of him.

"In the garage with Dad," Vivi says. "Probably got her nose stuck in one of his woodworking books."

"She sure likes to read," Trish says.

Eleni snorts. "Reading is very good for you. My Melissa is a smart girl."

"Trish knows that. She's a teacher, remember?" Chris lifts his wife's hand, drops a kiss on her pinkie.

Vivi wants to cry, but she won't do it here.

Fuck you, John. Nothing but a thief, who stole her shot at romance and happiness. And she let him. She's the one who sat back and said, "Yes please," to the few crumbs he tossed her way.

No way will that happen again. She wants cake, not crumbs.

Footsteps in the hall, then her dad appears. He winks at Vivi, smiles his wide, friendly smile.

"Would you look at this, all of my favorite people in the same room. Except my girl." He drops a kiss on Trish's cheek. "Melissa will be up in a minute. She is reading about some *malakas* named Humbert Humbert."

(*Malakas*: A man who masturbates so frequently, so furiously, that his brain turns to mush.)

Eleni glares at Vivi across the room. "Why do you let her read these things? It is not appropriate."

"Lolita is a classic," Trish says. "And if Vivi's okay with it, I don't see the problem."

"It is smut," Eleni says.

"Oh, have you read it?"

"I don't need to read it to know it is smut."

Chris winks at Vivi; Trish can hold her own with Eleni Pappas and he loves it. Vivi wishes she had that gift, but it's easier when you didn't pop out of Eleni's womb while she was walking to work in the snow – barefoot and uphill both ways, of course.

Worrying about Melissa is Vivi's new hobby. She's always quiet, always sullen – times ten if she's been out with John.

Because Melissa H-A-T-E-S Ian. And Ian's always around.

Vivi talked to John about it, told him it wasn't cool to flaunt his fling in front of their daughter, but John told her this is how it is, and if Vivi doesn't like it, they can let the lawyers scrap over the details.

Anyway, the worrying, it's reaching critical mass. So, when Melissa is happy, Vivi's happy. And reading makes Melissa happy, which means . . .

There's zero chance Vivi's going to mess with that.

"It's on the school reading list," she says. "It's not like she's leafing through Playboy."

Mom makes a huffing sound over the boiling potatoes. "It is pornography."

A loud thwack of newspaper on wood makes her stop. Her husband glares at her over the top of his wire-rimmed glasses. "Eleni, always with the nagging. You never stop. Leave the poor girl alone."

"How can I leave her alone when she is in the garage reading dirty books? She is not here to leave alone."

"Mom – " Chris starts.

Mom slams the lid on the potatoes, hurls the spoon across the room. The wooden spoon strikes the hutch, bounces off the fruit bowl, hits Vivi on the head with a skull-echoing thud.

"Now look what you have done," Elias Pappas says. Trish hurries to Vivi's side, but she's fine. No dents, no cuts, no life-threatening outpouring of blood.

It's all good. Except for the screaming in her head that won't shut up.

Eleni waves her hands at the ceiling. "I am the one who is hurting and you take her side? My daughter is getting divorced, has no job, has no husband, and now no home. What am I supposed to tell people?"

Vivi looks at the lunatic. "I don't care what you tell them. I'm too busy trying to make a new life with my daughter."

"What are you trying to do? You sit here in my kitchen and eat *baklava* while my granddaughter reads filth."

"Well, this time next week we'll be gone."

"You found a place?" Chris asks.

Vivi glances at Trish, who shakes her head. She hasn't said a thing because, as previously mentioned, Chris can't keep secrets.

"Sort of," she says. "Melissa and I are going away. To Greece." She doesn't look at her mother, but thanks to the power of peripheral vision, she catches the instant weather change.

"Good for you!" Chris says. "Is this like a holiday?"

"More like a maybe-permanent thing. Or maybe not. We're testing the warmer waters."

He whistles. "Damn, Vivi. Good for you." He looks at his wife. "Babe, did you know about this?"

Trish nods. "It wasn't an easy secret to keep, but Vivi needed a sounding board and some advice about education."

Eleni is a statue. The tantrum is coming, the drama ratcheting. The air pressure shifts, the way it does when a storm is bundling up its energy for the big strike.

Vivi says, "What do you think, Dad?"

He shrugs. "Eh. If you think it is best."

"No," Eleni whispers. "I forbid it."

All eyes on the two of them. Vivi and Eleni in the ring alone, only one will be left standing.

"Too late. The tickets are in my handbag."

Eleni runs out of the kitchen.

"That went well," Chris says.

Trish slaps his arm. "Vivi, are you okay?"

Is she okay?

Is a train wreck okay?

Is a meteor headed straight for Earth okay?

Oh yeah, she's okay. And now her mother is pouting in the bedroom where she'll stay until they all take turns comforting her and Vivi begs for forgiveness.

That's the Eleni protocol.

Right now, in this moment, Vivi feels every day of a million years old.

"Yeah, I'm okay," she says.

"Are you sure about this?" her father asks. His forehead is wearing more creases than usual, probably from the constant pressure of Mom's thumb.

"It's already done. All Mel and I have to do is get on the plane."

There's a scuffle in the hallway. Eleni runs back into the kitchen, Vivi's handbag in her fists.

"You want to go to Greece, eh? I do not think so!"

She upends the lot on the kitchen floor. Lipstick bouncing, tampons rolling, receipts fluttering to the floor. She moves fast, pouncing on the floppy plastic ticket holder, yanks them from their protective coating.

"You want to go to Greece? How will you do that without tickets?"

She makes confetti. Sprinkles some, crams the rest into her mouth.

"I can print new ones," Vivi says. "It's all electronic, anyway."

Eleni raises both hands (chewing, chewing), makes them shiver in the air, as though she's at one of those Holy Roller services.

"The spirits . . . they are saying you should not go! Bad things will happen if you do!"

"She always says that when it's convenient," Chris says, in a stage whisper.

"Trust my words," Eleni says. "If you go to Greece you will regret it. There is nothing for you there except unhappiness."

So, just like here, then?

———

Things have changed. In the old days Eleni said no to night-lights. "Why we want to pay for light we don't see, eh?" Now there's a tiny LED nightlight in every room that isn't a bedroom. The hallway reminds her of an airport's landing strip, with its white-blue glow.

It's Eleni's way of acknowledging the passing of the years. Vivi's parents are not as young as they used to be, nor are they as old as they will be soon.

Vivi goes to the kitchen, raids the *galaktobouriko* Eleni didn't bake.

"Cut me a piece, too, eh?" Elias says, from the doorway.

"Can't sleep, Dad?"

"The older your mother gets, the more she talks in her sleep. Tonight she is having a conversation with a shoe."

"What kind of shoe?"

"An old shoe."

Two plates, two forks, two desserts. Two silent eaters.

When his plate is clean, her father says, "Your mother is upset with you, but she will get over it. Like she did with the Friday underwear – remember?"

Like Vivi could forget. Eleni swore she would kill Vivi, but that didn't work out. Vivi wound up with a mouthful of pepper, and seven years of dishwashing. One year for each pair.

Elias leans back in his chair, pats his belly. "When you go to

Greece, maybe people will tell you some stories, eh? About me, about your mother."

"What kind of stories?"

"It has been so long . . . Who knows what the stories will be now. Time changes the shape of a story. Enough time passes and only the original idea is the same as it was. Everything else becomes different. The truth is no longer true, the names change. You will see. Fifty years from now, you will look at this time and you will not recognize the character of Vivi as yourself."

Okay . . .

"Don't believe everything you hear, eh? When somebody gossips, they are not doing you a favor by giving you information. They are trying to elevate their position, to seem more important than they are. And they are trying to extract information from you, also. Remember that."

"Does this have anything to do with that box, Dad?"

"What box?" he says. "There was no box."

———

Yeah, right. No box.

But that's okay. It's not her business.

Elias and Eleni Pappas are not John and Vivi Tyler. Their marriage is a rock.

✣ 15 ✣

MELISSA

ELISSA IS MAKING PROGRESS of the backwards kind.
Regress?

If anyone pointed that out to her, she'd say, "Whatever," and keep on cutting.

Nobody her age wears a watch anymore. They've all got phones to give them life's Cliff's Notes. Time, date, number of "friends" at any given moment. Bored? Your cell phone's got that covered, too.

But Melissa dug out her watch from three years ago, strapped the silver-on-white face to her wrist, risked being uncool. And – voila! – it's the perfect hiding place. So what if leather on shredded skin stings? That's kind of the point. It's a modern day take on the hair shirt. Things start rolling down that slope, her head gets muddled, all she has to do is rub, press, and everything floats away, courtesy of fresh pain.

Three days to go.

She saw Dad last night and she's seeing him again tonight. He promised Ian wouldn't be there, but he promised that last night, too.

Ian can't help himself. He's desperate to be friends.

Well. Was.

Last night he was playing at being her BFF, asking too many questions about stuff Melissa doesn't want to talk about. Boys, friends, blah, blah, blah. And all the pressing and rubbing on her wrist wasn't making him go away. So, she stalked off to the bathroom and made an old cut new.

She came back ready to deal. Said, "Did Dad tell you how a guy from my school saw him sucking dicks in the park?"

Melissa expected:

An explosion.

A fight.

Screaming, tears, and one last look at Ian's back as he stormed out of the house.

Yeah, none of those things happened.

Ian gave her a steel smile and said, "John and I love each other very much, but we don't chain each other to the bed. Much."

Dad said, "Ian!"

Ian said, "What? Your kid was asking for it."

While they were bickering, Melissa puked two slices of pepperoni and twelve ounces of Fanta onto Ian's plate.

Now Melissa can't wait to fly away to the Ian-free zone. Her safety pin is all packed.

16

VIVI

VIVI IS THE TITANIC and Eleni is the iceberg. But the way Eleni's behaving, anyone would think she's the doomed ship. This time, the ship's not going down; if it does, Vivi has lifeboats. Chris and Trish are at the airport with them. They're all hovering in a small, noisy cluster near the security checkpoint.

Time marches to the right. Nobody says goodbye.

"Is Dad coming?" Melissa wants to know.

"He said he'd be here, Honey."

Eleni makes a face. "Some nerve he has, showing his face to this family."

"Chill out, Mom," Vivi says. "He's Mel's dad."

"And that's as it should be," Trish says, hugging her around the neck. "I know you need to go, but I don't want you to."

"She does not have to go." Eleni cups Melissa's cheeks in her hands and kisses her forehead over and over, until it's Revlon orange. "She is deserting me, depriving me of my beautiful granddaughter."

Vivi wants to scream, but the TSA guys already look jumpy.

"Eleni, they need to go," her father says.

The line is growing exponentially. Harried travelers, annoyed and tired before they even take off their shoes and dump their belongings into those plastic tubs, are being sucked into the security vortex.

"Dad's here!"

Vivi looks up, and sure enough, John is striding their way in his dark blue pinstripe. She must have taken that thing to the dry cleaners' a hundred times. But as he gets closer, she sees the slightly different cut of the lapels, the shinier buttons. It's new – a post-Vivi suit.

"I got caught up with a client." He drops an awkward kiss on Vivi's cheek before scooping Melissa into a bear hug.

Next, John shakes hands. Trish gets her usual peck, and then he closes in on Eleni.

Eleni is glowering, a dangerous shine to her eyes. They're all skating along a paper-thin line. One wrong word and she'll explode.

Vivi holds her breath.

He leans closer.

Eleni's hand shoots up, steel trap gripping his mouth. He looks like a shocked goldfish. Fresh Botox amplifies his distress.

"Wha – ?" he starts, but her other hand clobbers him around the ear.

"Do not touch me with that mouth," she says. "Your breath smells like a man's penis."

"As opposed to a woman's penis," Chris says for everyone's benefit. Melissa's eyes bug. Trish elbows him.

"Go and wash the penis off your mouth, then you can come back and kiss me. Go!" Her fingers unclamp, she shoves him in the direction of the men's room. John walks away, dazed.

"Mom," Vivi says, into her hands.

"Eleni, enough," her father says.

"What? He smelled like a penis. I do not want that on my face. Who knows where he has been?"

Vivi covers Melissa's ears. "Mom, enough. Don't make this unpleasant."

Hands in the air. "Unpleasant? This is already unpleasant. You think I want to be here sending my child alone into the snake pit? Greece will eat you alive. You will come crawling back bleeding, crying,

'You were right, Mama,' and, 'Why didn't I listen to you when I had the chance, Mama?' Trust me, you will be back."

"Hey, Mel," Trish says cheerfully. "Let's go get some magazines for the trip."

Mel's face says that's a great idea.

Vivi wags her finger under her mother's nose. "Don't make this harder for my daughter. Do you think this is easy? I packed up our whole lives because I want to make something better. I don't want Mel to grow up with one of those weepy divorcees for a mother, who just lies around the house watching soaps and reading magazines, wishing she had a life. Don't you want more for me than that? Aren't you supposed to want me to make my life better?"

Olympic-level eye rolling.

Her dad reels her in for a hug. She holds him tight. "Thanks, Dad."

"If you need anything, you call us, okay?" he says into her hair.

Chris says, "Ditto, Sis."

John is on his way back from the bathroom. The minty fresh mouthwash reaches them before he does.

"Good boy," Eleni says. "Much better. Did you wash your hands, too?"

"What did I say, Mom?"

She ignores Vivi, offers her cheek to John.

Trish and Melissa return with an armload of magazines. Her sister-in-law slides a couple into Vivi's carry-on bag. "It's a long flight. Celebrity gossip will either keep you amused or put you to sleep. You can't lose."

Hugs. Tears. I love yous.

"I'd give you a tissue, but I'm not sure which compartment they're in," Vivi says. Their half-hearted laughter is damp. The security line is waiting. "We have to go now."

John hugs her again. "Don't be a stranger," he says.

Like you? But she's beyond that now; time for a clean slate, and that means letting go. "We'll call you when we get there."

Chris goes next. "Don't do anything I wouldn't do."

Trish scoffs. "That's like giving her an open checkbook. If you decide to stay for good, we're coming for Christmas."

Eleni is horrified. "And who will I have Christmas with? Everyone is leaving me."

"What, I am chopped gyro meat now?" her husband asks. He hugs them again. "Remember what I said. You need anything, you call."

"I will."

And finally, it's mother and daughter, staring each other down.

"You will regret this," Eleni says.

"I'll regret it more if I don't go."

"Do as you please."

"Mom . . ."

"Fine, go. Your aunt Dora will pick you up in Volos. She is less of a snake than the others, but she is still a small snake. Never forget."

Snakes. Got it.

Then she and Melissa are wending their way through the paranoia zone.

"Mom?" Melissa inches closer. Vivi wraps an arm around her shoulders. Melissa doesn't flinch, thank God.

"What, Honey?"

"What's that?" She points to a TSA guy brandishing a handheld metal detector.

"Don't worry, it's not for a cavity search."

"A what?"

"Never mind," Vivi says. "When we get to Greece, you call Dad, ask him to explain it."

Okay, so it's going be a while before the bygones are, well, bygone.

17

MAX

EVERYTHING ABOUT ANASTASIA IS a mystery, except what's between her legs. She sizzles one moment, freezes him the next.

Sometimes she makes him beg to come. Next day, she claws his clothes off, like fucking him is going to keep her alive.

It's a new game – her game.

She's playing, playing, and he's eating her up like a starving beast. He doesn't care, he just wants more.

Tonight:

She peels her skin off his, skin damp and glowing with light sweat. "Was that good?"

His heartbeat takes its time finding normal. "Always."

"Do you mean that?" She drags a fingernail across his chest, carves her name there.

"Mmm hmm."

Max," she says, in a petulant girlish voice. "Are you going to marry me?"

Okay, should have seen that one coming. Now what?

He kicks the covers aside, ditches the condom. "If I ask you, you'll know."

Kaboom!

Anastasia takes the top sheet with her. Wrapped from head to toe in cotton, she gathers her clothes, stalks into the bathroom.

The door slams and clicks.

This is his cue: Anastasia wants to be pursued, cajoled. Won.

And Max doesn't like games.

He takes his time. Pulls his boxer briefs on. Sits on the edge of the bed and scratches his head, while he thinks about his current crop of patients, thinks about scheduling the Jeep for maintenance.

Eventually he gets up, knocks on the bathroom door.

"You don't love me. What else could we possibly have to talk about?" The door muffles her voice.

"You're putting word in my mouth. I never said that."

"If you're just using me for sex, be a man and tell me."

They've had this argument before – at least twice. "Anastasia, just come out and talk like an adult. You're making something out of nothing."

"No! You don't tell me what to do!"

The familiar hiss of the shower tells him the conversation is over. He stands there until it stops.

"Do you want me to tell you if I'm going to propose? Wouldn't you prefer a romantic surprise? Isn't that what women expect?"

Anastasia is driving him crazy. At this rate he's going to end up marrying her just to stop the insanity.

"Maybe," she says, after a short pause. "Leave me alone now."

Back to the bedroom. After five minutes of pacing, he flops on the bed and groans. He really needs to piss. His apartment has only one bathroom.

Decision time about his future with Anastasia has come sooner than he anticipated. He was hoping for some prolonged fun and games while he sorts out his feelings – if he even has any for her.

Shit, he has no idea what he wants.

Anastasia's controlling him with that pout and that hard-soft body.

Is that enough?

She has a point: They have nothing to talk about. That's not what she meant, but doesn't make it less true. She has no interest in his work, resents his patients, hates the Jeep, and never opens her own purse to pay for anything.

Not that he minds spending money on a woman – he's spent all kinds of money on girls and women over the years. But an offer would be cool.

Then there's that body, that face, that heat.

Anastasia is electric.

But there have been plenty of other women, many of them electric.

Question is: Is she special?

The bathroom door creaks. Anastasia comes out, skin damp, firm breasts bouncing, smile on her face as if their argument never happened.

Her towel hits the floor.

She pins him to the bed, and Max, he just lies there, faking help-lessness, waiting to see what she'll come up with next.

Anastasia doesn't say a word. She wiggles her way backward and downward, until he's buried in her throat.

He moans – he can't help it. She's good. She elevates sex to art.

Max, you're a fucking idiot. Walk away, man. Walk away.

Run.

❧ 18 ❧

VIVI

THE LONG ARM OF the Mediterranean curls northwards, past the east coast of Greece, to form the flat palm of the Aegean Sea. Its fingers twist and turn around the islands between the mainland and Turkey, and the crook of one digit holds the calm seas of the Pagasetic Gulf.

Vivi knows this because Google Maps said so.

Now she's getting a load of the real deal in tiny oval-shaped chunks. A hundred swirling shades of blue. Cerulean bleeding into aquamarine bleeding into cyan bleeding into ultramarine.

Melissa is missing it all. Eyes shut, ears clogged with white buds, she's busy being fifteen. When Vivi leans over her to get a better look, Melissa frowns, buries herself deeper in the seat.

The plane dips closer to land. Grey and brown buildings with their red roofs materialize out of the blips and dots. The Acropolis rises, a goddess above her subjects, Parthenon forming the crown upon her head. The crumbling ruins look whole. Easy to imagine how it looked on opening day.

Vivi tugs one of Melissa's buds out. "You're missing the best view ever."

It's a big burden – huge, but Melissa indulges her mother. Her nose wrinkles. "It looks like a big dirty city."

Yeah, it's a big dirty city. It's obvious the shades of brown and gray are buildup from smog and dust, and the streets are jammed with thousands of bug-sized vehicles. But Vivi isn't about to let a little dirt overshadow the adventure.

"Look. There's the Parthenon. Remember during the Athens Olympics when we saw it all lit up? You said you wanted to see it in person more than anything in the whole world. Everything back home is so new and shiny compared to this. This is living history. This is where you came from."

"You're worse than Grams. Greece this, Greece that. I'm going to the restroom."

"Forget it, Kiddo." Vivi nods to the lighted Fasten Seatbelt sign. "We're stuck here until we land."

"Figures," she says, jamming the bud in her ear. But she doesn't quit looking out the window.

The airport shows up with its miniature runways and toy blocks. Time to get the plane into position.

The ground charges.

They don't crash.

An electrical current zips through the crowd. Phones out, texts sent. Mostly tourists onboard, weighted down with the requisite morbidly obese travel bags. The plane jerks to a stop at the terminal and passengers rise from their seats like the walking dead. An army, lurching towards the doors, wielding their belongings.

Vivi waits until they're no longer in the decapitation zone, then they work their way out.

Hot on the jet bridge. Breathing is like kissing a handful of molten sand. Eyes everywhere; a security guard carrying a machine gun looks through them, constantly on the lookout for the next potential terrorist.

Vivi grabs her daughter's hand. "These guys mean business. Stay close to me, okay? I don't want to lose you in this place."

Signs in Greek and English all over the place, arrows pointing in a million different directions. "Let's get our bearings and figure out where we're going."

Melissa shrugs. "Shouldn't we just follow the rest of the people from the plane?"

Great plan. They do that.

Until Melissa has to pee.

In the restroom, Vivi stifles a scream. She has carry-on luggage under her eyes, and she's wearing a Shar Pei.

There's a whoosh and Melissa appears in the mirror. In flats she's almost Vivi's height. "Carnival mirror?"

The hag in the mirror says, "Nope. That's how we really look."

"Wow. Not cool."

Immigration is a breeze. The immigration officer is one of those new-fangled robot people who work in airports now. He asks wooden questions and scans their faces for lies. With a stamp to their passports, he waves them on; time to process the next body in line.

Their luggage isn't lost, and they have nothing to declare. And they must look okay, because customs waves them through.

They are almost charmed.

19

VIVI

THEY'RE GOING TO DIE, and it will be the cab driver's fault.

He picked them up at the airport's exit, a round guy in a Greek fisherman's hat.

His mustache asked, "Where you go?"

"The Liosion bus station," Vivi said.

"No train?"

"Does it go to Volos?"

"Eh," he said, raising both hands. "I don't know, I just drive taxi."

"In that case take us to the bus station."

"Okay."

Now he's zipping in and out of traffic like he took driving lessons from NASCAR. Melissa is a pale sheet hanging from the handgrip, and Vivi knows she's just as limp.

"You want to see Olympic stadium? Maybe National Garden?"

"Just the bus station."

"You are sure?" The mustache rises and falls in the rearview mirror.

His tip is shrinking by the second.

"I'm Greek, so stop trying to con me."

He laughs big. "You are not Greek, you are *tourista*."

"My parents were born here, which makes me Greek. So just take us to the station."

Grudging respect on Melissa's face. Finally Vivi is doing something right.

"You are American, yes? I have cousin in America. Maybe you know her?"

Surely he isn't serious. "I doubt it."

"She lives in New York. Do you know it?"

"Sure, I've been there a few times."

"Where you live?"

"Oregon."

"That is close to New York, yes?"

"Nope."

"How far can it be? America is not so big."

"Two days drive – if you don't stop."

He twists in the seat, until he's looking her in the eye. The cab is still moving. "I don't believe it."

"Look at a map."

He goes back to the road. A honk from behind and he smashes his foot on the gas pedal. Another honk, from up ahead, and he slams the brakes, blasts his horn. Tires screech.

"You know Robert DeNiro? Maybe he is your friend, eh?"

"No." She swaps her terrified face for a bored one, but he rolls right over her.

"Are you sure? He's very famous. Best actor in the world."

"I know his movies, but I don't know him personally."

"You are certain?"

The traffic starts to move again.

"Positive."

Vivi reads his mind: *Stupid American.*

"People say I look like him." He points to a mole on his face. "Say hello to my little friend," he says. "That sounds like him, yes?"

Melissa bites her lip, goes far, far away.

"Scarface. That was Pacino."

"No! It was DeNiro."

"Pacino."

He swivels in the beaded seat, face like a rock. "Prove it!"

"I'm in a cab – your cab – how am I supposed to prove anything?"

He turns back around, smashes his palm on the horn. "Go to the devil!" he hollers out the window. "It is DeNiro."

"Fine, it's DeNiro. You win."

He grunts again, zooms another few feet before crunching down on the brake. Oh look, they can fly.

"Get out," he barks. "This is bus station."

He tosses their bags on the grimy sidewalk, waves his hand for the fare. Ten percent tip. A fair price for a near-death experience.

Melissa covers her nose. "It smells weird."

Swanky place. Doesn't reek too much of stale urine and old tobacco.

"Try not to breathe," Vivi says.

She steers them past a group of old men sitting in a smoke cloud, all the way to an empty bench. The old men fiddle and flip their worry beads, gold teeth shining at the pretty women. She dumps their bags, says, "Sit. Stay. If anything weird happens, scream."

"I'm not a dog. Woof."

So her kid's a smart ass. Vivi's glad to see the return of her spark. "I mean it. I'm going to get bus tickets."

A woman with a bad perm and a pretty smile sells her two tickets to Volos, departing in about an hour. Vivi drops coins in the pay phone and leaves a message for her aunt.

Ten minutes out of Athens and Vivi's asleep. Two hours after that she wakes with a head full of cotton and salt in her eyes. Melissa gives her what's left of a warm Coke.

Caffeine and sugar don't take long to strike. She comes alive, more or less.

They're on a bus with a mixture of tourists and natives. It's language soup in here. A bit of everything from all over Europe. Lots of pale-skinned people in eye-gouging colors, wearing sandals for the first time in what looks like forever. But they're happy-happy. And who wouldn't be? It's paradise on the other side of the window. Even the dry patches are new and different. Vivi likes the way nature struggles in places, the way the olive trees punch their fists out of the dirt and claw up toward the sun.

"What's that smell?" Melissa says.

———

Most people who follow showbiz news know the story of how a bunch of actors trained for months so they could be in a movie cobbled together with special effects. Their Thermopylae pass was a green screen, their King Leonidas some Scottish guy. Three hundred Spartans play-fought and play-lost to a CGI Persian army, while a giant Xerxes (clearly an escapee from a BDSM porno) flipped between stomping his foot and gloating.

What most people don't know is that the real world Thermopylae stinks.

Hot springs.

Greece sits on a nest of fault lines.

———

Vivi says, "Sulfur."

"It smells like really bad farts."

"So hold your nose."

"I am holding my nose. See?"

A group of Germans sees Melissa holding her nose and they start to laugh and hold theirs. Then Melissa is laughing at their laughing.

"*Po-po,*" the old Greek woman across from them says, waving a hand in front of her face.

Vivi can't help herself – laughter spreads faster than Ebola.

———

The bus is in decent shape, but it's the wrong shape for prolonged sitting. Vivi is a volatile mixture of uncomfortable and anxious.

Hurry up, hurry up.

Slow down, slow down.

All the way into Volos.

Now that she's basically a captive in a tin can, she has time to think about what she's done. There's something unsettling about the idea of staying with family she's never met. Eleni grudgingly arranged for Vivi's aunt Dora – Eleni's older sister – to meet them at the bus station. From there they will travel the few minutes or so to Agria, a fishing village that used to be its own entity, but has now (on paper) been assimilated into the city. Resistance was futile.

Vivi doesn't know a thing about her aunt, except that she's apparently a small snake. She's seen pictures, black and white and wrinkle-free, but that's it. Nothing about character and temperament.

Stress, stress, stress.

Now they're here, and she's steering Melissa ahead of her, off the bus and into the vindictive light. She barely has time to step away from the door, when she's accosted by a pillow with arms.

"Vivi, you are here! Come, let me look at you!"

Her aunt has an addiction to exclamation points, while her younger sister lives an *italicized, underscored* life.

She's a big woman, but soft in body and face. Greying hair, but so what? She wears it like she's happy for it to be there.

"*Thea* Dora?" Vivi asks. *Thea* being the Greek word for aunt.

"Yes, I am *Thea* Dora." She reaches for Melissa. "And this is little Melissa. What a beauty!" The large woman leans back and spits without letting saliva fly.

Melissa looks horrified.

"It's okay," Vivi says in English. "It's to ward off the evil eye."

Turns out her aunt speaks English.

"Yes, the evil eye. You do this when someone pays you a compliment. Evil likes to attach itself to beauty, so you spit to cancel the compliment. It is one of the old, Greek ways, from the time when we had our own gods."

Melissa's eyes grow even wider. "Do you believe in God, too?"

"Of course! It is his work we do when we remove the evil eye. Just do not mention it in church, that is all, or they will chase us away with their brooms." Mischief dances naked in her hazel eyes. "And now come, we will go home. You both look like you could use a good meal."

She shakes her head. "So skinny, you American girls. My daughter – your cousin Effie – she is fat. She eats too much, does nothing for exercise except nag her husband and children."

She talks and talks and talks her way to a tiny BMW, circa nineteen-eighty-something, with rust bubbling all over its yellow paint. Sea air loves to eat. The car has two speeds: fast and faster.

Thea Dora's mouth runs on the same engine. Questions, historical factoids, gossip – she never stops.

"Your mother and I, we used to dive off that pier every day during summer," and, "Look, they make the best *frappe* in town right there." And, when a man walking two donkeys with packs comes into view: "Look, a Greek car!"

Vivi laughs.

"What's *frappe*?" Melissa asks. "Is that like a Frappuccino?"

"Iced coffee. You will try some when we get to the house."

"Mom doesn't let me drink coffee."

"You don't let the girl drink coffee?"

"Maybe this once," Vivi says.

Melissa shoots her a look.

"How is my sister?" *Thea* Dora wants to know.

"The same. She never changes."

Not a grain of sand on the beach. The shore is made up of rocks and pebbles, but swimmers and sunbathers don't seem to care. The water is slightly more perfect than the weather – that's what matters.

Thea Dora laughs at the sky. "That is Eleni. Our parents were stricter with her. It was a big scandal when she married your father."

Vivi perks up. "Scandal?"

But her aunt is three conversations down the road already. "See, there is our Church, *Agios Yioryios* – St George."

An elderly woman in black is lugging a huge red bottle up the road. She's leaning way left, hem bobbing several inches above a black knee-high stocking.

Melissa says, "What's she carrying?"

"Water. It comes down from the mountains. The water here is not so good, so we go to faucets around town and fill bottles with good spring water."

"Why don't you buy it at the store, like Fiji water?"

Hands off the wheel, *Thea* Dora roars with laughter. "Why we want to give money for it when this way is free? Soon we go up to Makrinitsa. In the mountains you will drink the best water in the world. Like a spoonful of cold, wet sugar!"

"Sounds like heaven," Vivi says.

"That's why God put it so close to the sky, so He can smile down upon it when He is having a bad day."

———

Kids and young lovers everywhere. Holding hands, sharing ice cream, pausing to kiss.

It hurts Vivi hard. She doesn't miss John, but she misses all the frills she's never had, the things lovers do because they have love.

The wheel turns and they bounce around a corner. Now the BMW is crawling up a narrow street with concrete straight out of a war zone.

This is not a postcard, but it has its own brand of . . . can she really call it charm?

Stucco houses, pastel paint, flattop roofs. Red flower pots everywhere. Bright, dipped-in-paint red. Gardenias in some, geraniums in others. That's just the plants she knows.

The car stops at the top of the street, outside a white house with peeling iron teeth. The fence used to be blue, before it took a few thousand glances at the sun and gave up.

There's a view of the gulf, of the heart of an emerald.

"It's so quiet," Vivi says in wonder.

Her aunt slams the car door, shatters the silence.

"It is siesta time. Everyone is sleeping. Wait until tonight, you will not find it so peaceful when the children come out to play."

Vivi looks over Melissa's shoulder. She's fiddling with her iPod.

"So what do you think, Kiddo?"

Shrug. "I don't know. *Thea*, do you have cable?"

The older woman raises her hands to the sky. "My doll, you are in the land of the gods. You won't have time to watch TV."

20

MELISSA

S HE'S DYING TO PEE.

Being here is like . . . being here but also not being here.

But if she's not here, where is she?

Nowhere.

"Can't we stay in a hotel?" she whispers to Mom. Thea Dora is busy making coffee and something she called *finikia*.

"Shh," she says with a weird look on her face. "Let's give it a chance."

A couple of minutes later, her aunt (great-aunt, if you want to get all picky about it) bustles back in carrying a big black tray. On top are three tiny coffee cups and three small plates.

She kind of wants to throw up, because there's a damp turd on each plate.

Except it's not a turd, it's a kind of cookie, and the wet stuff is honey syrup.

It's pretty much the best thing she's ever eaten. Way better than Grams's desserts, for sure. Not that she would ever say that aloud, because Grams can turn people to stone.

She nibbles the cookie while Mom and her aunt talk. She can't hear a word they're saying, so they look funny with their mouths moving out of rhythm with the music. She makes up a little play in her head, where *Thea* Dora is berating Mom for being the shittiest mom ever.

What about Dad? Does he even miss her?

Does she miss him?

It's complicated. She doesn't miss him so much as she misses old Dad. Seeing your father French another guy changes things. He dumped them for Ian. He dumped her.

Thea is staring at Melissa, lips moving. She wonders if *Thea* knows she's got hair on her chinny, chin, chin.

Mom tugs on the ear buds, and sound pours out. After the smoothness of music, speech sounds harsh and jangled.

"So, Melissa." *Thea* Dora says it like she hitched her name to the back of a car and dragged it a few miles. *Meeleessaa*. It sounds weird but she kind of likes it. "Are you good in school?"

She looks down at the plate. Empty. If they were home she'd go get another one.

"I guess. I don't love it or anything, but I do okay."

"You have lots of friends?"

Shrug. "Just the one. But since we're here now, I guess I'm down to none." Mom's mouth droops, but Melissa doesn't care. "*Thea*, where's the bathroom? I really need to go."

"Down the hall and second left," *Thea* Dora says.

She leaves and they keep talking. Probably talking about Melissa and what a screw up she is. Hey, it wasn't exactly her idea to move here, to this . . . this . . . thriving metropolis. Heavy on the sarcasm.

Metropolis. Cool word.

That's what she wants, to live in a metropolis filled with people. Blend in. Become invisible.

Vanish.

Second door to the left.

She steps insides, closes the door and lets the darkness hide her from her own critical eyes. A temporary vanishing.

How long can she stay?

Not long. Too long and they'll think she's doing number two, and that's embarrassing. So, she can't stay forever.

Say goodbye to the dark, Mel. On with the light.

She blinks.

Something is really, really fuc –

✿ 21 ✿

VIVI

Vivi says, "What?"

Her aunt is on the phone, chatting to someone in Greek. Something about Effie and soap.

Melissa huffs.

"I can't hear you," Vivi says. "You'll have to speak up."

Melissa gives her the "But moooom" look, with fifteen years of exasperation dumped in those extra vowels. She tries again.

"The toilet is broken. Remember that time you and Dad replaced the toilet in my bathroom and there was just that big round pipe underneath?"

Vivi nods.

Oh yeah, she remembers. She scraped away the gooey wax herself, and dragged the old toilet to the curb on her own, because John couldn't, wouldn't, shouldn't risk messing up his manicure.

"Well it looks like that. You know, a big hole in the ground."

"What – no toilet?"

"Nope. Just a round hole."

This she has to see.

In she goes. Light on.

No toilet. Dead ahead is the hole Melissa described.

Good news? It's not broken.

Bad news? It's not broken.

Vivi knows a hole when she sees one, and this once is surrounded by white porcelain. Two wavy foot-sized patches straddle the opening.

She contemplates the physics.

That's not all. It gets worse.

A small wicker trashcan sits within grabbing distance. No lid. Inside, small pieces of soiled toilet paper.

Perfect, she thinks. Perrrrfect.

Outside the bathroom, her smile goes back on. What the hell is she thinking, uprooting their lives, racing across the world to see what shade of green the grass is here?

(For the record, the grass she's seen so far is sparse and leans toward the brown spectrum.)

Her marbles are gone.

She looks at Melissa.

"How hard can you cross your legs?"

22

MAX

G OOD FOOD.
      Uninterrupted sleep.
Satisfying sex.

Most men need all three to thrive.

Max has all three, but he's not thriving.

He watches Anastasia dress. First time she's been over in three days and he just feels tired.

Her lens is focusing, zooming. "Why don't you redecorate this place? It's so . . ."

"Masculine?"

"Boring. You don't even have pictures."

She leans forward, drops her breasts into the lace cups. He feels nothing. The urgency he felt earlier has evaporated, same as their sweat.

"What for?" He rolls over, grabs his own clothes. "I sleep here, that's all."

"You should think about buying a house."

He thinks about the money rolling, rolling, rolling in his bank account for exactly that.

"Maybe one day."

"How old are you, Max?"

"You know how old I am."

Her cleavage disappears behind the shirt's buttons. Only a promise remains.

"What will you do when you get married?"

When we get married, she means. He can't miss the thin, whining undercurrent of Anastasia winding up for another fight. What he thinks is that she likes the arguing more than she likes the sex.

"Then I guess my wife and I will buy a house to raise our children in."

"Your wife? Are you planning on making someone else your wife?" Pencil skirt next, thin belt through the loops. "Max, are you seeing another woman?"

"I'm too tired to see anyone else."

True.

Long days at the hospital. Long nights with Anastasia.

She's sucking the life out of him through his balls.

And then there are the phone calls from Mama.

Have you proposed yet?

No.

Have you bought a ring?

No.

Why not?

Yeah, Max. Why not?

Because he doesn't love her, he just loves fucking her.

Anastasia zeros in on her handbag. She pulls out a severe black tube, wields the lipstick, the make-believe dagger.

"That's not an answer, Max. That's avoidance. Do you know what I will do if I find out you are cheating on me?" Lipstick slashes through air.

I don't care, he thinks. Just hurry up and do it and go away.

"Max?"

He grabs her wrist, holds it still. "There's no one else. I promise."

She smiles, that bitch. "I know. I just wanted you to know how I feel." Now she's someone else, a smiling angel. "Let's go and get coffee."

He's tying his boots when the phone beeps.

"Sorry," he tells Anastasia. "No coffee this morning."

Her cold gaze stalks him. "Always the hospital."

"Baby, it's my job. When we get married it will buy you lots of nice things." When, not if. Is he trying to placate her or sabotage his life?

"Promise?"

"Of course." And they're out the door.

Alone in his Jeep at last. He looks in the rearview mirror and sees a stranger sitting where he's sitting. The other guy is holding up a noose.

Don't make me use this, he says.

Then Max laughs, because what is he so afraid of? A life with a beautiful woman?

Fool.

———

A child dies on his watch. Not because of negligence or lack of skill. It happens because sometimes it happens – and fuck you, God.

He tells the parents, but they don't want to know.

He understands; he doesn't want to know, either.

———

The ghost of Max gets away early, but not much. He and Anastasia have plans for dinner at a café near St Nicholas Square.

St Nicholas, patron saint of sailors and children.

Maximos Andreou, patron saint of nothing, wanders like a man lost. He looks at jeans. Skims titles in a bookstore. He stops at a jewelry store's window, temporarily blinded by the glare.

No price tags. What a racket.

So, he goes in.

Why? Because there's no good reason not to. The store wants money and he has money to spend.

Anastasia is winding his hormones around her pinky, but after today . . .

Max doesn't care.

He wants a wife and family to come home to. He needs to see something warm after a day like today, his own child to distract him with play, a woman to curl up on the inside of his spoon.

What would Kostas say?

Not much. He gave his blessing as long as the choice was Max's – Didn't he?

He could – should – cut Anastasia loose, let her find some other head to fuck with, but he doesn't want to deal with the shit storm. He doesn't have time to fight a battle on two fronts. The constant text messages from Anastasia and Mama, the non-stop phone calls – threats one minute, contrition the next.

Breakups get bad enough when you're dealing with one person who won't disappear.

He thinks about how their children might look – her golden eyes, his dark hair. Maybe after they marry the fights will slow to an occasional downpour.

Maybe the sex will crumble, too.

Doesn't matter. He's going to buy a ring, and when the right moment comes he'll propose.

Even tired and beat up from the day, Max looks like money. The saleswoman is tripping on her own feet to get to him, euro signs dancing in her eyes.

Max doesn't like to let a woman down, so he lays his plastic on the counter, points to the window

"The one in the middle."

"A beautiful choice, sir."

Choice.

Max chooses peace.

❀ 23 ❀
VIVI

VIVI IS ON A desert island, knocking back pina coladas, when Melissa pokes her.

She opens her eyes. Reality is made of pink walls and blue shutters. Bold choices.

The sun is glaring through the thin gap where the shutters don't quite meet. Every house has them here – practical, not ornamental. Shutters stay closed during the heat of day, and then they're thrown wide at night so cool air can offer respite. Between shutters and marble floors, houses stay a bearable shade of sauna during daylight hours.

Melissa is balanced on the bed's edge, ear buds curled around one hand, watermelon wedge in the other. For once she's not plugged in and there's no book in sight. She looks worried.

"Are you okay?" Vivi asks.

"I'm okay. Are you okay?"

"Sure, why?

"Well, you've only been asleep for nearly two days."

Vivi hasn't slept more than seven consecutive hours since high school. "Wow. What day is it?"

Melissa shrugs – her new signature move. "Saturday. *Thea* took me to the store. And I met some of the neighbors. There's this really weird old lady across the street. She has these funny chickens and she let me pat them. Plus she kept babbling at me and I couldn't understand anything she said. Well, hardly anything. Just the bit about Grams."

"What about Grams?"

Melissa shrugs (again). "Don't know. Just something about her and Grampy."

Very mysterious. First the accidental mention of a scandal, and now this. Everyone seems to be in the loop but her and Melissa. Might have been nice if her mother had declared her baggage before Vivi rolled it across the world.

Then there's Dad's box, the one that never existed . . .

Outside a horn honks. Right on its heels, a megaphone crackles to life.

"Watermelon." The voice is chipped, broken. "Watermelon with the knife!"

"Gypsies," Melissa says. "You should see them. They wear all these really colorful clothes that totally clash, and their kids don't go to school. How cool is that? *Thea* says if you're not careful they'll put a gypsy curse on you. They're selling watermelon. You should try it, it's really good."

Gypsies. Watermelon. Curses. Oh my.

"Romani," Vivi says. "They're Romani." Sleep. She needs more sleep.

"And," Melissa continues, "you know how we buy those tiny bottles of olive oil back home and you're always complaining about how expensive it is? *Thea* has a huge metal container of it on the counter. Do you suppose she drinks it? Because that's just weird."

"I don't think so," Vivi mumbles. "Maybe it's cheaper to buy bulk."

"Mom?" Melissa hasn't used this many words in months. "Can we go to the beach?"

Best idea ever – and when she says so, Melissa beams.

"And can we go to McDonalds?"

Thousands of miles from the USA, some of the best cuisine in the world, and her kid wants McDonald's?

"If there's a McDonald's, we'll find it."

Melissa crams the buds back into her ears. Says, "Cool. Whatever," before slinking out of the room.

Now Vivi is alone in the false night.

Once upon a time, she was a teenager. Doesn't mean she's qualified to raise one of her own.

———

Up close, the ocean is the color of a cool forest. Seaweed swishes its fingers through the warm, gentle water. Colorful wooden fishing boats bob to the same languid rhythm, while teenagers swarm the decks, laughing and diving from the highest points.

Is anything better than sixteen?

Is anything worse?

"Can I – " Melissa starts.

Vivi is wearing her psychic mommy hat. "Forget it. I don't want you diving off those boats."

"Mom . . ."

"Those boats belong to someone. Would you want a bunch of kids using your things?"

"But everyone else is doing it." She flops back on the towel, her life obviously O-V-E-R. "Don't say it."

"If everyone else was jumping off a cliff, would you do it, too?"

"If it was fun, yeah. Maybe."

Jumping off a cliff *is* fun. Vivi knows – she did it, back in the pre-John, pre-Melissa, post-Eleni days.

"Nice try, but do I look like Little Bo Peep?"

Bodies back and forth, sunburned and suntanned and sunstroked. Every shape and age. The less-than-perfects own every inch of themselves. Good for them. Paranoia and hiding beneath XXL T-shirts is the American way.

There's a kiosk butted up to the beach, selling more drinks and cigarettes than anything else. They have ice cream, too.

Vivi pulls out money, waves it in front of Melissa's nose. Foreign currency, but her kid can smell cash a mile away. Must be something in the ink.

She says, "I'm bribing you with ice cream, okay?"

"Can I go for a swim afterwards?"

"Sure. But take that watch off before you go in."

"It's waterproof to thirty feet."

Vivi gives her a look.

The cash vanishes. "Whatever. I'll get the ice cream."

Vivi watches Melissa picking her way across the pebbled beach, towel wrapped around her waist, up to the kiosk, where she gets in line behind a couple of lobsters in Bermuda shorts and Birkenstocks.

She's not the only watcher on this beach. Some of the boys are also getting an eyeful of Melissa Pappas. They're like birds, chests puffed out, whistling as girls walks by. Melissa's all cool, ignoring them, keeping her eyes on the ground.

Look up and straight ahead, Vivi wants to say. Don't let anyone in this world make you look down.

When Melissa gets back, Vivi says, "You have admirers."

Hair flip. "Whatever."

But she's smiling on high beam, isn't she?

The ice cream disappears fast. Late spring, but the weather is hot. A benevolent breeze carries the sweat away as fast as they can make it.

The question comes out of nowhere.

"Mom? Are we ever going home?"

Home – where's that? There hasn't been time to figure out if Greece is a waiting room or the end of the line.

"I was hoping maybe this would be our new home. Do you hate it here already?"

"No." She says it in a small voice Vivi hasn't heard since the boogeyman days. "I just don't want you to decide without telling me."

"Honey, I wouldn't do that."

"You kind of decided to come here without asking me."

"Remember that day I told you?" Melissa nods. "I only thought of it that morning. As soon as I knew for sure, I told you. I gave you the chance to speak up."

"I said I wanted to stay with Uncle Chris."

"That wasn't an option."

"Maybe I wish it was."

"Mel, I'm not a dictator. But I'm the person who gets to make the hard decisions. Someone has to, for the good of the family. In time, if you're seriously miserable here, we'll go."

"Whatever."

"We can't just turn around now, Honey. We just got here."

"I didn't say I want to leave."

"I don't get it," Vivi says. "You're as clear as mud. You hardly speak, and most of the time you're sulking. We need to work together. I'm not psychic. If you've got things to say, say them."

"Forget it."

"Is this about your father?"

"I . . . said . . . forget it."

Vivi jumps up, starts gathering their stuff as though a tsunami alarm is screaming, telling everybody to get high. "Grab your things, we're going."

"McDonalds?"

She's got to be kidding. "Back to *Thea* Dora's house."

"But her toilet sucks."

Yeah, it sucks. But it's better than an outhouse – right? Maybe she'll offer to replace the thing. She's done it before. She can do it again.

"Well, you're just going to have to get used to it for now."

"But, Mom – "

"Don't like it? Go outside."

✣ 24 ✣

VIVI

EXTRA CRISPY. THANK YOU, Sun.
Underneath her Oregonian pallor, Vivi's got olive skin. Thing is, her melanin has been taking a lifelong nap. It's sluggish, slow to react. It wants to turn brown, but . . . It's a good thing Vivi looks great in neon pink.

Better enjoy the pink now, because red is coming and it's going to kill.

On their way back from the beach, Melissa is dawdling. But that's okay. Vivi loves her girl more than anything, but sometimes teenage Melissa is hard to like, with her claws and fangs and that razor tongue.

But then Vivi has her own sharp edges, too, doesn't she?

She wants to fast-forward to the Julia Roberts part, to the Diane Lane part, to the ending where her character is rebuilt, her soul restitched.

It's fairytale bullshit, but a woman can dream like a girl – right?

Real world, there's nothing to be done except live through it and see what shape she's in when life spits her out the other end.

Nearly noon. Mass exodus, everyone migrating back to their houses for lunch; main meal of the day. In Greece they eat, sleep, then it's back to work-ish.

SEVEN DAYS OF FRIDAY

Vivi and Melissa swap greetings with every passing body.

There's no ignoring your neighbors here. Huge breach of etiquette; Emily Postopoulos would have a conniption. Skip one wave, one hello, and you may as well pack up and leave town, because you'll be on the town's permanent shit list. A million "Hellos" won't make up for that one you skipped that day when that other thing was clouding your mind.

You'll be the talk and talk and talk and talk of the village.

If donkeys are Greek cars, gossip is Greek air. And if today's gossip is on the dry side, they'll add juice. Which is why Vivi hasn't told her aunt about John and his penchant for penis – and never will.

That story has way too much flair, already.

It smells like a *taverna* out here, frying garlic and onions making perfume out of sea air. Vivi is drooling.

"I'm hungry," Melissa says. She picks up the pace, tripping on the pavement to catch up.

"Me too, Kiddo. I could eat a whole what-ever-it-is."

Up at the house, *Thea* Dora is cooking a feast.

"Look at you two!" she says. "You are the color of my flower pots. Why not fix *frappe*? Then we get ready."

"For what?" Melissa asks.

"For the party! Tomorrow you meet your whole family. We will get up early and make lamb on the spit."

Vivi makes the *frappe*. Coffee, sugar, water into the shaker, with ice and a little milk. Could be John's neck, the way she shakes it.

Melissa props her elbows on the table. "But aren't you our family?"

"I am just one aunt. You have many aunts and uncles and cousins."

"Are any my age?"

Thea Dora wrings her hands on a hand towel. Exactly like Eleni. Vivi shakes harder.

"Some are older, some are younger, but I believe one or two are close to you in age. How old are you?"

"Fifteen."

"When is your birthday?"

"August. I'll be sixteen," Melissa says.

"In Greece we would say you are sixteen already. We count ahead."

Melissa's face shines. "Did you hear that? I'm sixteen. Only one more year until I can start dating."

Vivi breaks the seal, pours the coffee. Takes a long, long drink before she says, "Two years."

"But you said seventeen. That's one more year in Greek years."

Tricky position to be in. Melissa is emboldened by her aunt's presence.

"We'll talk about it later, Honey."

Melissa's not dropping this bone. "Mom, it's one more year. You said I could date when I'm seventeen."

"I was counting American years, not Greek. Two more years and that's the end of it or I'll make it three – four if you want to work in Greek years."

"Why do you have to be such a cow?"

Melissa runs out of the room. A door slams.

Vivi winces.

She looks at her aunt, hoping for sage advice. What she gets is: "That girl has her grandmother's temper."

All three of them go to get bread – including Melissa. She wants Vivi to witness her sulk in progress.

No way would this place pass a health inspection. There's a cat in the filthy window, next to an upright basket of whatever baguettes are called when they're Greek instead of French. The baker is dangling a cigarette on his lip.

But who cares when it smells amazing?

Like an addict in an opium den, Vivi inhales.

There's no counter, just a huge butcher's –

When in Greece, don't say *butcher*. Don't ever say *butcher* during any conversation you want to remain polite. If you're a tourist, don't ask for a *butcher's* shop. Swap the b for a p, and you've got yourself a mouthful of slang for male genitalia. It's meat, but (unless you're vacationing in Mykonos) probably not the meat you're looking for.

———

– block that fills half the tight space. The wood is rough and covered with a fine dusting of flour. A tall stack of brown paper sheets sits in one corner of the table, waiting to wrap each plump loaf before it's carried away.

All over Greece there are tiny neighborhood bakeries like this one, Vivi's aunt tells her.

The baker, in his faded blue coveralls and mutton chop sideburns, nods, but he doesn't set aside the cigarette – he grunts around it. He pokes at the wood fire, at the baking loaves, using a wooden pole with a hook attached to one end. Silver scars coil around his arms, before vanishing up both sleeves.

Melissa pats the cat. It's happy for her to pay homage. While she's doing that, a couple of elderly widows enter and wait while the baker shoves a long paddle into the fire and pulls out a bubbling dish.

They do this, *Thea* Dora explains, because who wants to bake at home in this weather when the baker will do it for cheap?

"What kind of bakery doesn't sell cakes?" Melissa asks.

"We will have to go to a *zaharoplastio* for that. There you will find all the cakes, ice cream and sweets you can eat."

Melissa looks at her mother, imploring. "Can we go there next?"

In goes the paddle again, and the baker says, "How many?" Four tins come out; four perfectly formed loaves tumble onto the table.

"Two," *Thea* Dora tells him.

He wraps two loaves in brown paper and drops them into her outstretched arms, all without putting the long neck of ash in jeopardy.

"Yes," she tells Melissa, "we will get some sweets for you to try. But first I need to get some needlepoint silks."

They leave with their bread and take a short walk to a store with a window display that looks like the world's worst swap meet. Souvenirs, silks, statues, yarn, fabric, and jigsaw puzzles. Vivi can't figure that one out. Anyway, it's all covered in a light dust blanket. Also for sale, if what you want is in the window, she guesses.

A small bell tinkles. The bald proprietor shuffles out from behind the counter.

"*Kyria* Dora, how are you on this fine morning? And are these beautiful ladies your visitors from America?"

(*Kyria* = Mrs.)

The man doesn't talk, he oozes.

Thea Dora makes the introductions while the proprietor runs a long fingernail along the side of his chin. The nails on both little fingers are shaped into long points – but only those two fingers.

"Yes," he says after a moment. "There is a definite family resemblance."

Vivi asks if he knew her parents.

"Everybody knows everybody," he says cryptically.

Fingernails (she didn't catch his real name) eyes her while her aunt is busy showing him the list of colored silks she needs. He uses those cultivated talons to lift the correct skeins off their hooks on the wall.

Yeah, he's not at all creepy.

Melissa is all wide-eyed over a squat figurine on a corner shelf. The thing is ugly, unremarkable apart from the huge phallus poking his chin.

"Mel," Vivi whispers. Melissa jumps away.

Fingernails clears his throat. "If she wants the statue, we can work out a deal."

That's a no.

"They're weird looking," Melissa says.

"Probably some kind of fertility thing," Vivi tells her.

Thea Dora says, "Like all Greek men, he is exaggerating."

Fingernails is watching the exchange. "You are not married?"

"Technically, yes, I'm married," Vivi says.

His fingers close around the notes and coins *Thea* Dora dumps in his palm. "Interesting."

"Keep your hands away from her." *Thea* Dora goes *tsk*. "That is Greek men for you – they all believe they are God's precious gift to women, and sometimes men."

The bell above the door tolls, high and childish, and a woman slips through the crack. Plain. Conservative in her skirt and sweater. Odd wardrobe choice for late spring.

"Ah, now this is very interesting," Fingernails says to nobody.

This place is dense with secrets.

"Dora," the new arrival says.

Thea Dora looks through her. "Sofia."

"Have you met our visitors from America yet?" Fingernails is about to piss himself with glee. "This is *Kyria* Dora's niece, and the girl is her daughter. Eleni's daughter and granddaughter."

Thea Dora looks like she wants to wring his neck, but he finds this much too entertaining to stop.

Chilly blue eyes meet Vivi's. "You are Elias and Eleni's daughter?"

"Uh, yes?"

"Are they well?"

"They're great."

She strikes Vivi as a woman left behind, forgotten. A memory; a carbon copy of a more vivid original.

"Do they have other children?"

"I have a brother – Christos. Were you friends?"

The woman's gaze slides back to a scowling *Thea* Dora. Vivi's aunt snatches up her silks, stomps to the door.

"Come, Melissa!" she says. "Let us go and get those sweets I promised you."

The bell tinkles and they're gone.

Vivi stands there for a moment, wondering what the hell is going on. Then the door opens again, and *Thea* Dora barks, "Vivi!"

———

The sun isn't even trying, yet they're all sweating.

Melissa wants cakes and desserts, cakes and desserts she gets. Clear wall-to-wall cabinets filled with sugar, in about a hundred different outfits. Pastry horns filled with cream and custard; *baklava,* and its wooly cousin *kataifi,* drowning in syrup; powder-covered shortbreads; *koulouraki* cookies; stacks of *loukoumades,* a close cousin to the donut hole, soaking up a honey and cinnamon bath. Then there are the cakes. Vivi doesn't know what they're called, but she knows she needs to shove a handful of the tiny confections into her mouth.

Her aunt buys coffee to go and Vivi buys desserts for everyone.

Shameless (and at home), they dive into the box. Who needs lunch when you have cake?

Vivi stuffs down her chocolate cake, then pounces on her aunt.

"Who is she?"

"Who is who, Vivi, my love?"

Like she doesn't know.

Vivi licks the goop off her fingers. No shame when it comes to chocolate.

"The woman from the shop," she says. "Sofia, I think you called her."

Her aunt sighs. "She is nobody."

"Is she a prostitute?" Melissa asks. "Because she didn't really look like one, but you never know."

Vivi stifles a laugh. "Mel!"

Thea Dora's face shutters. "There are prostitutes with far better reputations than that woman. I will say nothing more. Forget her."

Not going to happen.

———

The next morning, John calls in a frenzy because Vivi hasn't called him. But Vivi knows she left a message, and she tells him so.

He covers the phone.

When he comes back he says, "Apparently I missed it. But you should have called back."

"It's not my fault if your boyfriend deletes your messages."

"You don't have to be a bitch, Vivi."

"Neither do you, John. Do you want to talk to your daughter?"

"Put her on," he says bluntly.

Melissa snatches up the phone.

Her aunt follows her into the kitchen. "What is wrong?"

"Nothing," Vivi says.

"It is not nothing. It is something or you would not be upset."

Vivi asks, "Who's that woman?"

"What woman?"

"The one from this morning."

Her aunt gets busy doing nothing in particular, mostly shifting things from here to there. "She is nobody. A nuisance. Nothing more."

An itch starts on Vivi's shoulder. She reaches back to scratch and her nerves combust. "Ow, ow, ow!"

Her aunt's there with a plastic spray bottle of clear liquid. "This will help."

"What is it?" Vivi squints at the bottle. "It's not oil, is it?"

"Vinegar."

The bottle squirts. Her aunt attacks her with it – Vivi's a dirty shower stall that needs cleaning. And lo and behold, the pain fades.

"See?" she says. "Vinegar fixes everything. For anything it will not fix, use rubbing alcohol."

"But you said vinegar fixes everything."

Thea Dora taps her on the back of the head. "You are too clever for your own good. See what happens when you stay in the sun too long? The sun is a snake. He bites if you stare too long."

———

Melissa slams the phone down, then she's gone.

Vivi goes to find her. She's on the bed, hiding behind The Fellowship of the Ring. The book is upside down.

Vivi wonders what the hell John did this time. She puts arm around Melissa, but her daughter jerks away.

"Why did you have to do that?"

Vivi blinks. "Do what?"

"Make me talk to him."

Vivi makes a hand signal: *keep your voice low*. Because she can almost hear her aunt shoving a glass up to the door.

"He's your father and he loves you. If you have a problem with that you need to tell him."

"I'm not going to talk to him if he's there. I'm not."

"He who?" *Thea* Dora asks from the other side of the door. She's not even trying to hide her snooping.

"Did Dad make you talk to Ian?"

"No, but he was making comments in the background."

"Like what?"

"Nothing." Melissa turns the book right side up, flips a page.

"Mel?"

"God, why are you such a nag? Leave me alone, okay?"

There's a big, bold laugh on the other side of the door. "No doubt she is Eleni's blood, even with that pretty blonde hair."

Oh, God. No privacy whatsoever.

Vivi leaves Melissa to her book and her bad mood.

"What am I going to do with her?" she asks her aunt. But her aunt doesn't have answers – she's too busy being distracted by a noise from outside.

There are people out there: a leather-skinned woman and her waif-like moppet. They're dressed as Christmas trees – sort of.

"My Christ, *tsiganes*," *Thea* Dora mutters. "Get out, you dirty gypsies!"

The hunched woman scoots her child forward. Round brown eyes looked up at them, imploring. Working the con. "Please, can we have food or money?"

Thea Dora runs back inside, snatches up the broom she keeps in the kitchen. She waves it like this is Sparta. "You want food or money, get a job! Go, go!"

The gypsy woman grins, showing old, broken piano keys. On closer inspection it strikes Vivi that this woman, with her dehydrated skin and weary gait, probably isn't much older than her.

"A curse on your family," the Romani woman says, her gaze fixed on *Thea* Dora.

Three dry spits in the air. "The Virgin Mary will take your curse and shove it – "

"*Thea*, wait." Vivi pulls out ten euro, holds it out to the kid. It vanishes into a dirty pocket.

A lot of Eleni-like skyward hand waving happens. "No good can come of giving a gypsy money. They will tell all the other gypsies to come here for money. And if you do not give them money, next time they will hit you on the head and rob you."

"My people are not thieves," the woman says. "Thank you for your generosity." She steers her child out the gate.

"Wait," Vivi calls out. "Are we still cursed?"

"Not you." The woman points at Vivi's aunt. "Just her."

Thea Dora is still waving her hands in the air. "You might be Greek, but you do not understand the way things work here. Never encourage gypsies. If you make them angry they will curse you. Curses can be very difficult to break. One day you will wake up dead!"

"How can you wake up if you're dead?"

With a snort of disgust, her aunt shoves the broom into her hands.

"Sweep towards the street. We do not want the bad luck coming into the house."

🦋 25 🦋

MELISSA

MELISSA WANTS IAN TO die in a huge fire.

If Dad had to go all Elton John, why couldn't he have picked a decent boyfriend? She hates Ian, with his shiny suits and brightly colored socks. He always makes these dumb baby voices when he talks to Dad.

And Dad always makes her say hi to Ian when they talk on the phone. It's like he's got this messed up fantasy where she and Ian are friends.

Not happening.

She can practically hear him grinning and gloating. He's glad he stole Dad. He never says it out loud, but she can almost see it on his dumb face.

Mom just doesn't get it. She just goes on and on about how much Dad loves her, and how he's sad he doesn't get to see Melissa every day.

If he's so sad, why did he leave them?

It's dark in the spare room. Cool. Well, cooler. She hugs her pillow, drags the sharp tip of the safety pin across her wrist. Right wrist. The left is raw. Turns out it stings like crazy if you get salty sea water in a cut. She's spent ten minutes digging out specks of sand, but there's more inside. They're squirming deeper inside her. Like bugs. Scabies, or something totally gross like that.

There's a soft knock on the door. "Mel? I'm coming in."

Mel, not Melissa, which means Mom isn't mad. Probably she wants to do the whole "Boohoo, I'm such a bad mother. Forgive me," speech. What-ev-er.

One last poke before sliding the woven bracelets into place. "Yeah?"

Mom's forehead is all crumpled like a tissue and she looks sad. Suddenly, Melissa feels like crap. What's wrong with her? She doesn't feel like she belongs in her own skin anymore. She's a body snatcher, wriggling around in a Melissa Tyler suit. She drove Dad away and now she's making Mom sadder.

You suck, Tyler.

"Hey, Honey." Mom's trying to sound cheerful but her voice is crackling. "If you're going to get dressed up you'd better get a move on. Everyone will be here soon."

More family – what a pain in the ass.

"I don't have anything to wear. I'll just stay here."

Mom picks up a hairbrush from the vanity. "How about that pretty dress we picked up at Macy's?"

It's a cute dress with blue flowers that Trudy would totally dismiss as babyish. Whatever, Trudy isn't here. Just Melissa all alone with all her friends. "I guess."

"I'll let you have a spritz of my good perfume. Your choice."

"Really? What about some powder? I'm glowing in the dark."

It's kind of nice the way Mom sits down and starts pulling the brush through Melissa's hair. It reminds her of when she was little, when Mom did her hair a new way every day. Mom can do any kind of braid, any kind of up-do. All Melissa had to do was point at a glossy magazine picture and Mom made it happen on her head.

"Okay, Kiddo, just this once. But go easy on it." Her smile shines. Melissa realizes she hasn't seen Mom smile – really smile – in a long time. "I'm doing a pretty good imitation of a stop light myself."

Something smells weird. "Mom, you smell like salad."

Mom laughs. For the tiniest moment Melissa feels good. It's almost like the old days.

✣ 26 ✣

VIVI

WHEN RELATIVES ATTACK.
See it now on the *Discovery Channel*.

Apostolia, Apistoli, Giorgios, Yannis, Vasiliki, Vaso, Eleutheria, and a dozen variations – and generations – swarm the evening air. Predatory moths, every last one of them.

Vivi mouths, "*Help me*" across the room at Melissa. Melissa tries a smile, but it's not convincing. Poor kid looks overwhelmed. If she runs out screaming, Vivi will be right behind her.

It's a swirl of names and faces and hugging and kissing and dry spitting to ward away the evil eye. The horde is around thirty strong – not including the demolition team made up of children.

"Out!" *Thea* Dora shrieks when the turmoil turns tornado. The children scamper outside to play in the street. Resigned to being one of the kids, Melissa follows, leaving Vivi with the wolves.

This is Eleni's family. Vivi's father was an only child, and his parents died when Vivi was a kid. They were an anomaly at a time when Greeks popped out a soccer team – if they could. Eleni and Dora's mother made nine of the little suckers, and eight of them are in this room.

———

Now is a good time for a commercial.

Specifically: Hair removal.

This family needs it.

Three aunts, eight daughters, all with chins like the wrong end of a boar. Vivi can't help running a hand over her own chin. Feels smooth enough. But in time? Who knows?

Right now the only body hair problem she's got are her legs, and that's an easy (but not cheap; the price of blades is crazy) fix.

———

"When is Eleni coming to visit?" asks Three of Nine.

Someone passes Vivi a bottle of *retsina*. She takes a long swallow and gasps as the alcoholic Pine-Sol taste punches her in the throat.

"I'm not sure – "

"*Ay yi yi*! She not even come home when her mother died. The shame!" another aunt shrieks.

"And you, where is your husband?"

Can opener tongue. Ass like a shelf. Black hair, black eyeliner, lipstick a life-threatening shade of cyanosis. Ladies and gentlemen, Cousin Effie. Vivi's been listening to her all night, spouting stupidity like she's a devout follower of the arcane science of nonsensical dumb shit. They should put her picture up in schools: see what happens if you don't graduate?

But Vivi's cool – everyone gets a chance.

Thea Dora sidles up to Vivi's interrogator. Never would have picked them for a mother-daughter pair. Anyway, her aunt whispers something in her daughter's ear, and all Vivi can think is: snake; small snake, but a snake is a snake is a snake.

Effie's smile widens – her day just got better.

"So, he won't be coming, eh?"

"Not a chance." Now this is irony. John is the Tyler who belongs in Greece, with its historical fondness for Homo erectus.

"Why not?"

"I know you know we're getting divorced."

"But his daughter is here! What kind of man allows a woman to take his children away?"

"John's a busy man. He can't ditch work to follow Melissa around the world."

"What, in America you can't take a vacation? And they call themselves civilized." She looks to the crowd for confirmation.

"He took his vacation last year. We went to Hawaii."

To be fair, it's only a half lie – the half with Vivi in it. There was Hawaii, and John was there in January for a convention. He'd gone (allegedly) alone. Though now she wonders if Ian went, too, if they walked hand in hand, like there was no Vivi, no Melissa, at home.

"Oh." Her surprise is the only genuine thing about her. "You speak Hawaiian?"

What Vivi tells herself is that this is a joke. A piece of her is waiting for Effie to yell, "Psych!" Then Effie will be like, "Ha-ha, you should see your face. Did you really think anyone could be this stupid and live?"

But it doesn't go that way. So, Vivi's stuck standing there, defending her education and common sense, as though they're the bad guys.

"Hawaii is part of the United States."

"Hawaii is not in America. It is an island!"

"Eight major islands. And they've been part of the USA for nearly fifty years."

The way Effie's blinking, there's no way she's buying it. "No!"

"Yes."

"Vivi!" *Thea* Dora pushes a newcomer between them, sending each bitch back to her corner. "This is your uncle's sister-in-law's cousin's daughter, Maria."

Effie fades away. It's a temporary situation.

Vivi knows two things always come around again: Everything under the sun, and sharks.

27

MELISSA

Y OU DON'T LOOK GREEK," says one of the slightly older cousins. "Do you speak any Greek?"

"Some."

"What?"

Melissa reels off *kalimera, kalispera,* and *kalinykta.* (Good morning, good evening, good night.)

The cousins are unimpressed.

"I know some swear words," she offers.

"Do you know American swear words?"

"Sure."

"What is means 'Son of the bitch'?"

Melissa hesitates, because how do you explain that one?

One of her smaller cousins tugs on her dress. "Melissa, come play with us."

The older cousins laugh. "Go on, play with the babies."

"Go fuck yourself, you sons of bitches," she says.

Cue the "Ooooooooooh, you so bad!" chorus.

———

"Mom?"

Mom looks startled. "You okay, Honey?"

"Can I go and lie down?"

"What's wrong?"

"This isn't really fun."

"It's not, is it? Tell you what, Kiddo. We both have to tough this one out. If you can survive through tonight, tomorrow I'll personally hunt down a McDonald's for you. How does that sound?"

"Sounds great, Mom."

Sounds anything but great.

———

The paper is piling up in the bathroom's wicker trashcan. Skid marks veer off the top piece, plummeting into the can's shitty depths.

Nice.

Whatever. Melissa's not here to pee.

She's not really here to do anything.

She's not really here.

That feeling has come over her again, of being a Melissa puppet, controlled by bored hands. Everything she does, she does because someone else is manipulating her moving parts. Lock the door, Melissa. Don't worry that it's one (sort of) toilet and fifty people, Melissa. Look at your wrist, Melissa. Do you see it? You're filled with sand. That's a problem you need to solve, here and now. Turn your head left. Let me look through the medicine cupboard. I don't see anything that can stop you from turning to sand – do you? No nail clippers, no scissors, no file. I wonder, Melissa, what does your great-aunt do when her toenails get too long? Does she gnaw them in her sleep or –

Never mind, Melissa. Look in the bag – your mother's makeup bag. The one with the white yellow white yellow daisies. Hmm . . . Enough supplies to make the Red Cross envious, but not a one of them appropriate for scraping sand from flesh.

Ah, now here is something. You won't like it, Melissa. But let me promise you that, while this is a tough love intervention, you will be –

in the end – saved. So pick up the palette of sensible neutrals. Drop it. Pick up the glitter, the shards that reveal only slivers of you – an eye here, a nostril there.

You know what to do, don't you, Melissa?

Scraaaaaaaape the sand out and away. Let it ride the red wine river out of your wrist and onto that childish dress you're wearing.

There's a word in her mouth, but it won't come out.

H

E

L

P

It's stuck there, blocking the ME.

Those bored hands drop her strings, and move on and away. They're done with her, done with this booooooring game. The towel is close, but either it's too slippery or the ground is too slick, because she can't stay upright. Her concrete body falls . . .

Stephen King was wrong. The floating doesn't happen down in the sewer, in the yawning pipes below ground. It happens up here, if you're lucky, lucky, lucky.

Melissa . . .

Floats.

❦ 28 ❦

VIVI

T HE *RETSINA* IS STRONG, but hey, it's something to do.
When she spots Effie, Vivi slips out of the room and into another, where she continues her imitation as the sparkling (glowing) guest of honor.

Different room, same questions. And so it goes. She would have printed a FAQ, but she's not sure they can all read.

Now Effie's coming at her from a new angle, dragging one of her kids by the elbow. The poor kid's legs are crossed and he's doing the got-to-pee jiggle.

"Tell her," Effie barks.

Vivi crouches beside the little guy. "Are you okay, George?"

"*Thea* Vivi, Melissa won't come out of the bathroom."

"Wait until she's finished, Honey. Then you can go in."

"But I need to go now, and she's taking forever."

"How long has she been in there?"

He thinks about it for a moment. "Forever. I yelled at her to come out but she won't answer."

"She didn't say anything?"

Shaggy brown hair whips his face. "No."

"Who knows what she is doing in there," Effie says.

Vivi sets the bottle on the nearest flat surface. Then she goes to the bathroom to see what's up. She jiggles the handle.

Locked.

"Mel? It's just me. Are you okay?"

Nothing.

Now her nerves are shot-gunning Ping-Pong balls inside her head. She bashes the door with both fists. "Melissa?"

Thea Dora appears at her side, along with her posse of flapping tongues.

"What is wrong?"

"Melissa's in there."

"Is she sick?"

No time for stupid questions. She needs action, not questions.

"How the hell should I know? She's locked herself in there!"

A big guy pushes through the crowd. One of her uncles – *Theo* Apostoli. He has hair like a lion and a screwdriver in one hand.

He looks at the door. "Good thing somebody put this door on wrong, eh?"

"It is not wrong," *Thea* Dora says.

"It is wrong. Trust me."

It takes forever, the process of digging out the hinges. They've seen a lot of paint.

Then the boulder rolls (slumps) aside and she's in.

Time slows to a drunken crawl. Vivi turns to stone. A Melissa doll is on the floor, broken and drowning in red, red wine.

It's fragmented after that. Some moments are too difficult to swallow whole. Try choking them down and you may as well shove a grenade into your mouth.

Pulse: Yes. Fast, shallow.

Breathing: Yes.

Someone gives her a towel, tape.

She says, "Hospital, now."

"Come," her uncle says. "We go in my car."

Hands reach for Melissa, but Vivi's not giving her up.

Thea's mouth is moving.

"You want me to come?"

"No."

They move through a field of whispers, to the gate. The car is there and it's ready to leave.

Effie is a temporary newel post. Up down, up down, with her stupid clown face. "My Virgin Mary, what kind of mother is she that her daughter would do such a thing?"

A whisper intended to be heard by all.

It's not her way, but Vivi prays.

❦ 29 ❦

MAX

MAX IS AT THE hospital, as (if his mother and girlfriend are to be believed) always.

This isn't his usual stomping ground. Max is in the ER as a favor. It's been quiet, as far as nights go. Not so bad.

Until the woman staggers in.

There's no missing her, the pink woman cradling a blonde girl. Tourists. Probably British or German. Her scaffolding is about to collapse.

Then he sees the dull red flower unfurling on her dress. Her hands are blood and bone.

Max runs.

"Oh my God, please tell me someone here speaks English. Help! Please help my daughter!"

"Why is she still standing there?" he barks at the nurse. "Come," he says in English. "I've got her. He snatches the girl from her, rushes to the nearest empty treatment room

"What's her name?"

"Melissa Tyler," the woman says.

"Stay with me, Melissa," he tells the girl. "We're going to put you back together." He looks at the woman. "Your daughter?"

She nods. Both mother and daughter are bloodless and grey beneath their Hers and Hers sunburns.

"Start an IV," he barks at the nurse, but she's already doing her job.

He takes it easy, in case it's a gusher. But what's underneath the towel has already begun to clot. The girl is lucky her mother is smart.

"The bleeding has stopped. That's promising, Mrs. . . .?"

"Tyler," she says. "Vivi – Paraskevi Tyler."

He looks at the naked wrist. Not a knife or razorblade, but definitely something that enjoys cutting.

The nurse directs him to the girl's head. There's a cut, shallow and short. *Retsina*, she mouths, flicks her eyes at the mother. That will go in the chart. Hospital regulation.

"Mrs. Tyler, did your daughter hit her head, or did something hit her?"

"I . . . don't know. I found her like this on the bathroom floor. We were having a family party."

She never stops stroking her daughter's hand.

"I'm sending her down for a CT scan. Just in case."

"Oh God." Her knees buckle. For a moment he thinks he might have two patients on his hands, but the moment passes and Mrs. Tyler comes back, stronger than ever. "Do whatever you have to do."

"Are you visiting from America?" he asks.

She shakes her head. "I don't know. Visiting, staying, I don't know. My family is Greek. We just got here this week." She honks into a tissue. "Sorry."

He turns away to give her privacy and to prepare sutures.

"So you're Greek. Do you speak Greek?"

Nod. "It's decent, but in this situation . . ."

"You need the familiarity of your own language? I understand." He turns now to the problem that is Melissa Tyler. "Usually a wound like this wouldn't be so bad. Veins don't like to bleed, and they tend to contract to minimize blood loss. But it's a hot spring, and you're both sunburned and new to this country, so Melissa's blood vessels were already dilated. In winter, she would have lost very little blood. Still, the head injury is the more immediate problem. We'll be taking her down for that scan as soon as someone can locate the technician." His fingers weave a crooked bridge of tiny knots. "Do you need us to contact someone – your husband?"

"No," she says. "It's just us. God, what the hell is going on?"

Max is good at stitches, bad at non-medical answers.

"Mrs. Tyler, do you think your daughter meant to do this?"

She hunches forward, sliding her hands through dark, tangled hair. "I don't know. So much has happened lately, and Melissa and I have been fighting every step of the way." A red-rimmed gaze meets his. Under the sunburn she's attractive, beautiful even. "What do you think?"

What does he think? That Melissa Tyler has problems. Her wrists are a spider web of thin white scars and new scabs. He's seen it before, on other girls around her age. Sometimes on boys, but mostly it's the girls. Cutting. Self-harm. A physical release to anesthetize mental pain.

In a fucked up way, this is a blessing. Now she can get help.

"Accident or not, your daughter needs help. We'll make sure she gets it."

Relief blossoms in her eyes. They're the warm, deep amber of cognac.

"I think you could use some, too," he says.

"What I could use is a miracle."

The nurse comes back. "They're waiting for her."

"When you're ready," he tells Mrs. Tyler, "I know a place where you can talk to God."

🌺 30 🌺

VIVI

HEAVEN AND HELL OCCUPY the same disinfected space inside a hospital. Doesn't matter which hospital – they are all heaven, they are all hell.

Vivi has seen both, tonight. Even now she can't help feeling like she has a foot in each.

Melissa is spread out in a hospital bed in a quiet room in the children's ward. It's real, Vivi knows it, but still this can't be happening – not to her baby.

A limp hand rests in hers. Vivi won't let go.

The machines say Melissa is fine, no lasting damage, but what do machines know about minds? What do they know about families and their secrets?

What do they know about love?

31

MAX

I T'S NEARLY TEN WHEN he gets a chance to check on Melissa Tyler. Thanks to a rush in the ER, he's running nearly two hours late for a family dinner at Mama's. Family includes Anastasia, her mother, and her aunt. But not Kostas.

Not exactly a family dinner then, is it?

One of his women will kill him for being so late. Maybe both.

No problem. They can wait five more minutes for dinner, and he can wait five more minutes to die – easy.

Shoulder against the door jamb, he watches the Tylers sleep.

The mother has pulled her chair close to the bed to hold her daughter's hand. It can't be comfortable, the way she's using her free arm as a pillow, but she's doing it anyway. Her slim shoulders rise and fall.

This is love, he thinks. Honest, real love.

He hopes she's dreaming of a place where her daughter isn't lying in a hospital bed.

His boots take him to the nurse's office. He flashes his most charming smile, asks for a blanket.

"Taking this one personally, Max?" one of the nurses jokes.

"They're all personal," he says.

She leads him to the supply closet where the blanket and pillows wait to be useful. "Take care you do not become too attached, eh?"

He drapes the blanket over Mrs. Tyler's shoulders, then walks away.

———

He's a human sacrifice and Anastasia is the volcano.

Mama wants grandchildren, so in he must go.

But he wants this, too – doesn't he? Once he marries Anastasia and their children are born, he'll be a happy man.

———

Anastasia and her family are waiting at Mama's place. They're waving from the third-floor balcony.

Up, up, up the stairs that will take him to his volcano. No point rushing, no point taking the elevator.

The door flies open before he can press the bell.

"*Ay-yi-yi*! Here you are. You are late," Mama says.

He drops a kiss on her forehead. "I had an emergency."

"Always an emergency. Come, we have guests. Perhaps you and Anastasia have an announcement to make?"

"Not tonight, Mama."

"Why you take so long? We are waiting for you. I might die before – "

"Yes, that's what you always say."

"You are not too old for me to smack you!" She wags a finger in his face. "Where is my stick?"

Anastasia is pacing inside, a golden goddess in her gilt mini dress. She grabs his arm as soon as she sees him, drags him out into the empty stairwell.

"We need to talk."

"I'm tired, Anastasia. What's wrong?"

She holds him tight, won't let go. "Nothing is wrong. I missed you because you are late."

His dick – his fucking dick – gets hard. And what happens? He wants to run. He shakes her loose, steps away so he can swallow some air.

"I'm a doctor, Anastasia. Sometimes people get sick and need my help. Maybe I should give them my schedule first. Or, even better, yours."

Her scarlet lips quiver. "Was it an emergency?"

"Yes, and that's why I'm late."

This conversation is in its hundredth rerun. Yeah, his dick is hard, but the only thing she makes him feel is . . . exhausted.

"What happened?"

"Lots of things to lots of people."

Poison Ivy curls herself around him. "I hate them."

His mind blanks. "Who?

"Those people. Because of them you weren't here sooner."

He steps back, because . . . wow. How can this woman be the mother of his children? She's a shark.

"Jesus Christ, Anastasia. They're human beings. How can you be jealous of sick people?"

It's a child's shrug. "I just am. I don't have to explain it."

He moves backwards. She follows. "What do you want from me?" Her hands are all over him. His fucking dick gets harder.

"I want you," she says, playing her seductive best. "I want to see you more."

"We spent almost every night together this week."

"I know. But you always work so late."

"You knew I was a doctor before we met."

Yes, he puts in almost as many hours as he did during his internship, but that's the job. And he loves his work more than any woman.

More than *this* woman.

The door opens again and Mama's silhouette is there. "What are you two doing?" She sounds bright, hopeful.

"Nothing," Max says. "We're just talking."

"Mr. Information. Which is it: nothing or talking?"

"Talking," he says, irritation metastasizing.

"About what? Do you have something to say that you can't discuss in front of family?"

"As a matter of fact, no." He leaves Anastasia there, slack against the wall. "It's just work talk."

"Max has been too busy to see me," Anastasia says in her infantile voice.

He goes numb. Deadened to the two of them.

Mama slaps his arm; she barely registers. "Surely you can make a sacrifice at the hospital for such a lovely girl."

The platinum ring, with its transparent stones, is a lead weight in his pocket, a boat anchor keeping him from moving forward.

"Of course, Mama," he tells his jailer.

———

He drives Anastasia home.

Tonight's the night. He's going to do it.

Over dinner with their families he planned how he's going to shake her off. Nothing elaborate, plain truth: It's not working out. He's done it before, many times. He can do it again. Anastasia, Anastasia's family, Mama, they will all have to get over it.

He parks around the corner from her place. Plans to do it quick. Merciful.

But Anastasia being Anastasia, she has her own plans. Before he kills the Jeep, she's inside his zipper, inside his boxer briefs. "I want you," she says, doing that thing to his ear with her tongue.

The woman works fast but s-l-o-w.

She stops just as he's about to –

"Jesus, Anastasia!"

"Shut up."

Then she's all over him on him around him dress up around her waist and she tastes like honey and cinnamon and all the good things women are made of.

She says, "Just think . . ."

He can't think.

". . . we could do this, be this, every single night."

He can feel the "No" bobbing in his throat. He's trying not to lose it – the "No" or the orgasm. He wants both.

Tonight something's different. Anastasia is different. Hotter, wetter.

A siren goes off in his head, but he's seeing stars as he comes, not blue and red lights.

No condom. His fault, her fault – does it matter?

You know better, Max. Amateur.

The cell door slams. The bolt slides home. The future stretches way, way out. Nowhere to go, nothing to do but live out his life sentence.

It's now or never.

"Anastasia," he says when his breath comes back. "Let's get married."

32

VIVI

HER BRAIN DOESN'T WAIT – it begins its assault in her first moment of consciousness.

Melissa bleeding. Melissa unconscious. The long-short ride to the hospital. The broken doll, spread on the bathroom's marble slab.

That's never going away.

Vivi lifts her head and checks her girl. Still sleeping, face pale with pencil-colored smudges under her eyes. Vivi's hand snakes around her wrist and finds an enthusiastic pulse. Eyes closed, she mouths: *Thank you.*

Her gratitude goes out to all who eavesdropped on her silent prayers.

Now she can step away from her vigil.

The chair squeaks as she unglues her backside from its fake leather. A blue blanket slides off her shoulders, drifts to the floor. One of the nurses must have taken pity on her during the night.

Last night she was too scared to notice much of anything except Melissa, Melissa, Melissa. The room has six beds and three – not including Melissa's – are full. Those children also have their mothers close by, although she's the only one who slept in the chair. The other mothers are curled around their much younger children, punctuating their declarations of love.

Her body complains when she stretches. Empty protest – feels good to move. Then she peers out the door, looking for life signs. It's early and the sun is taking its sweet time showing up. The ward is silent. There's no hustle and brightly lit bustle. No nurses padding in and out of rooms, dispensing medicine and taking temperatures, according to the hospital's biological clock.

She goes back to Melissa and waits for anything to happen.

Melissa wakes. No trumpets and angels, but there should be.

Thankyouthankyouthankyou. Vivi can't stop thinking it. She brushes back Melissa's hair, tries not to cry. She's successful, more or less.

"You're here," Melissa whispers.

"Where else would I be? Nothing matters to me more than you."

The tears are flowing and Vivi's eyesight is drowning in them. She wipes them away with the back of her hand, but more replace those that were lost.

"I don't know." Melissa's eyes close. "I dreamed that you were mad and you went away."

"Oh, Baby. I'm not mad at you. I'm mad at me for not knowing how hard you were hurting."

"You were busy."

"Mel, I'm never too busy for you."

"Yeah, right."

Vivi fishes for a tissue to wipe away her tears. "What happened, Honey?"

Eyes open again. Focusing on some riveting spot on the ceiling. "Nothing."

"Something happened or you wouldn't be here."

"It was the sand. It wouldn't come out."

"You should have told me you'd cut yourself, I could have put some antiseptic cream on it." Vivi lowers her voice, tries squeezing the darkness out of the conversation. "I bet *Thea* Dora has some weird Greek potion for cuts. Probably something like goat saliva. Or freshly-squeezed donkey's feet."

"That's silly." She's not laughing.

"Mel . . ." Vivi starts. She has too many questions. Sorting through the pile isn't easy. Push some aside and others fall into their place. She reaches, grabs any old question. "Mel, is that the only cut?"

Still looking at the ceiling. "Mind your own business."

"You are my business. I love you."

"I don't care."

Vivi's heart cracks. A new fault line is born.

"That's okay. I care enough for both of us."

The morning passes in stifling silence.

———

Dr Andreou shows up after breakfast. He looks important in the daylight, with a string of doctors behind him. Some of them are new, devotees of his every word. The others are every bit as seasoned as the guy up front, but slightly more dismissive. Like most doctors with a few years under their belt, they've seen it all; they have lost and they have found. Melissa is more of the same.

Which isn't bad. It means they know how to fix her broken parts.

They go through the doctor routine, do their song, their dance, then they take their show to the next child in the room.

When they're gone, Melissa's bitter mouth says, "I guess they're not letting me going home today."

What did she expect? They don't let suicidal teens walk out the front door with their incompetent mothers – at least not until they're sure said teenager isn't going to bungee jump cordless off the nearest bridge. But she doesn't say it, because right now Melissa is a delicate crystal bowl, and Vivi feels like small silver hammer.

And anyway, Dr Andreou is striding back into the room, something clearly on his mind.

"Go home," he tells Vivi.

He's nuts. First she thinks it, then she says it. Because this isn't a day where her mouth has a direct line to her brain. The back and forth signals are taking some dark back roads, striking a lot of dead ends.

"Sorry," she says. "It's been that kind of year."

"Tell me about it."

She thinks he's joking, but . . . maybe not? Man looks like he wouldn't say no to poking through her baggage.

None of this is following any script she knows, so she shuts up.

"Backing up," his perfect white teeth and their accompanying smile say. "Melissa is stable and you need a shower. Go home, put on some clean clothes, eat something. You want to take care of Melissa? Take care of yourself first."

"Wow," she says. "Are you always this bossy?"

Nods from the three other mothers in the room.

The doctor laughs, but it's a good laugh. "Guilty," he says. "But seriously, go home."

Vivi looks at Melissa. "Will you be okay?"

Translation: You're not going to jump out that window while I'm gone, are you?

Melissa shrugs. "Sure."

"Okay," Vivi says, "I'm going."

"Can you bring me some books?"

"You bet." Vivi kisses her forehead. Melissa feels warm, alive. Thank every deity ever. "Anything else?"

"I don't care. Whatever."

33

VIVI

O N THE BUS, NOBODY sits near the bloodied woman.
Why would they? She looks like bad, bad luck.

Vivi's cool with that, doesn't mind being in a bubble. Melissa is crystal, but it wouldn't take much for Vivi to shatter. A touch could do it. A word.

She gets off the bus in Agria. Her seat stays empty until all her witnesses are gone.

34

VIVI

HOT WATER IS MAGIC. Pink curls circle the drain and – presto! – goodbye, Melissa's blood.

Speaking of magic tricks: The floor is cleaner than clean.

A person could eat off something that clean.

Someone scrubbed while she was watching the doctor stitch Melissa's frayed edges, made it like Melissa never wuz here.

Vivi needs a closer look.

Her knees say: Lady, you only think you're walking out of here. You want out?

Craaaaaawl.

Too many years on her hands and knees ("C'mon, Vivi, you know I love it this way.") to be happy about it. But this isn't sex; it's a fact-finding mission. Vivi wants evidence. Towel bandaging her core, hands roaming the marble tiles, she gets down to the dirty business of proving Something Bad Happened Here.

She tells herself a nice story. No blood means the whole shebang was a nightmare. Melissa is out in the kitchen, nose stuck in a book, devouring watermelon by the chilly pound. And after Vivi's dressed, she'll go out there, hug Melissa, and say zip about her shitty dream.

Too bad her story is a lie. Because there it is, a thin red-black line between two tiles.

She attacks it with a towel point dipped in shower water. Goes at it the way a dog goes at a bone. Until her shoulder screams, "Stop!"

Clean. Shiny.

No blood. The whole shebang was a nightmare.

Now Vivi is happy, happy, happy.

Everything is fiiiiine.

Pay no attention to the crying woman in the mirror.

———

"You look like a gorgon."

Thea Dora is so helpful. She all but shoves Vivi into a kitchen chair. "How is our girl?"

If Melissa is their girl, why isn't *Thea* Dora at the hospital?

"She'll be okay."

"*Frappe?*"

She's already rattling the shaker, so *frappe* is inevitable. Vivi's getting it whether she wants it or not.

Good thing she wants it. She takes a long drink and waits for the neurological magic to happen.

"*Thea*, can I ask you something?"

"Anything, my doll."

"Your bathroom. How would you feel if I remodeled it for you? As a 'thank you' gift for letting us stay here."

She looks confused. "What is the problem?"

Oh, she has no toilet. That's all.

"It might be nice to have new colors, and maybe even a new toilet. I'll pay for it – and do the work myself."

Thea Dora spends the next two minutes bustling around the kitchen, cleaning clean things.

"No," she says, finally. "This is the man's work. A women does not need to do such things."

Vivi's done it before, gutted the downstairs bathroom in their old house. Dismantled and reconstructed over a long weekend, when John was too busy (sucking dicks) to be home.

"It's not that hard."

"Vivi, it is a nice thought, but I do not need such things. I am a simple woman and I do not need a fancy bathroom. What would I do with it?"

Same clenched jaw as Eleni. No way is Vivi digging out *Thea* Dora's heels without a backhoe. Today, Vivi doesn't have that kind of determination.

"It's just an idea." She rinses the glass, loads a few paperbacks into her bag. "I'm going back to the hospital."

"Give Melissa a kiss from me."

No mention of visiting. Melissa is the family pariah. Last night she tossed a blanket of shame over the lot of them with her faux suicide.

Vivi thinks: Fuck you.

She stomps to the bus stop.

So this is Greece – what a two-faced bitch. One mouth sings a metric ton of love songs, about heaven, and perfect beaches, and all the culture you can stomach, and new, shiny beginnings rooted in timeless tradition.

It's a trap, a covering of leaves over the snake pit.

People are friendly, but they will never trust you. Fingers point, but never at themselves. Didn't see that old woman over there? Doesn't matter, should have waved anyway. Now you're screwed for life. The sun is warm, but it burns, leaves you too lethargic to give a damn that the things depicted in the travelogue are all shine and no substance.

No more blindfold over Vivi's eyes. Something has to change, and history makes it clear that Greece never yields.

Ask Xerxes. Yeah he won a few battles, but Greece turned out to be a huge pain in his Persian ass.

Stay or go?

The bus comes and she gets on it. An old rock takes the seat next to her. Vivi's sunburn screams.

The gulf tries to dazzle her with its sparkling best. Beauty as a diversionary tactic. Look over here! Eyes here! Don't mind the man picking your pocket, sticking the Kick Me sign to your back.

Stay or go?

Go or stay?

She debates herself all the way into Melissa's hospital room, and still she can't pick a side.

Melissa's hunched over a coloring book. She waves with her good hand and makes something like a smile. She's got company. Dr Andreou is sitting on the end of her bed, a coloring pen in his hand. He looks sheepish.

Melissa gets kisses and books. The doctor gets a smile.

"Do I have two children now?" Vivi nods at the half-finished picture between them.

Dr Andreou slides off the bed, hands the pen back to Melissa. "I came by to check on Melissa and got carried away. Reliving my childhood."

"How is she?"

Melissa sticks out her tongue. "I'm awesome. Of course."

"You heard the girl: she's awesome." He leans against the wall. "How you doing?"

"Besides having a complete mental breakdown, I'm peachy."

"Peachy?"

"American expression. It means I'm fine."

He smiles all the way to his eyes. "I'll add that to my collection of Americanisms."

Vivi comes alive.

Good old stress, it crushed her libido into a dormant lump. And before that, all of John's not-wanting made her not-want, too. After a point, that is. She wasted years wishing he'd throw her on the ground and fuck her – face up.

But now? Her libido is stomping the ground, snorting like a bull. It wants, it wants, it WANTS.

Dr. Andreou is off limits, but do you think her body cares? That's a giant, italicized, neon NO.

He's delicious. Face, body, and that mouth.

She looks away. Looks back.

(These two are doing a lot of looking.)

Vivi considers changing the subject, but the subject is already benign.

"Where did you learn English? It's perfect."

He grins. "Directly from the source: England."

"Medical school?"

"All of my education after high school."

"I'll probably send Melissa back to the states for college." If they stay. "So, you're practically British?"

"Sometimes. Mostly I'm Greek."

That smile.

Butterflies in her stomach are rehearsing for Cirque du Soleil. How long has it been since she last had sex?

Um . . . Over a year, definitely.

How depressing. No wonder she's drooling.

Clanking metal throws an invisible bucket of water in her face. Lunch is coming. Meat and green beans and chunks of rindless watermelon. Melissa picks up a book and dives into the watermelon, but she's suspicious of the rest.

Hey, Melissa is alive. She can eat or not eat anything she wants.

"Doctor Andreou," Vivi says, suddenly. "Last night you said you knew of a place where I can talk to God."

"I do."

Things could be so much worse. Vivi owes big.

"Can you give me directions?"

🐾 35 🐾

VIVI

WHEREVER THEY'RE GOING, IT'S by car.
Well, Jeep.

She figured him for a BMW or Mercedes kind of guy. Boy, is she astute.

"Mrs. Tyler, I've arranged for the hospital psychologist to visit with Melissa today. Doctor Triantafillou is very good."

"It's just Vivi. I was wondering when you'd bring up therapy. It's a good idea."

"Great. Greeks aren't big on therapy. Here if you have a problem you go to your family or the church. Not an outsider." He pulls out of the garage and onto the busy street. "I'd like to keep Melissa for a few days, to rest. I think you need it as much as she does."

"I'm fine."

"I don't think so."

She looks surprised. "Does it show?"

"Not really, which is how I know. And call me Max."

Greece is on her best behavior as Max (is that entirely professional?) steers his car up Mt Pelion. Turns out the doctor doubles as an excellent tour guide, pointing out this, pointing out that.

"It was up here on Pelion that Thetis and Peleus, parents to Achilles, wed."

She smiles on the outside, worries on the inside.

Max carries on. "Pelion was also home to the hero Jason, and his Argonauts."

"Now that I already knew," Vivi says.

He takes his eyes off the road for just a moment. "Did you know Pelion was also home to the Centaurs? They came here because the mountain was so rich with healing and magical plant life. Some people believe they still roam, just out of sight."

"I'll keep my eyes open."

Is Melissa okay? What if she needs something and Vivi isn't there?

"If I see one I will point him out," Max says, smiling.

The winding road scales the mountain. Destination: sky. "Where are we going?"

"A small village. There is a church there I want you to see."

"And you go there to pray?"

He holds her gaze a fraction too long. "When I forget myself it helps me remember who I am."

"It's hard to imagine you losing your way. You move like you've got it all figured out."

He doesn't reply.

What did she say? That's the thing about people: they're all walking minefields. Step on a crack, and Mama's back won't break, but her head might explode. Who knows what part of Max just silently exploded.

Finally, he says, "You love your daughter very much."

The Jeep stops. Sheep flock across the street, shepherd coaxing them with his crook. A lanolin and shit cloud wafts behind them.

It's a movie moment, and Vivi falls a little bit in love with the otherness of Greece.

"She's my daughter, I'm her mother. I loved her long before she was born."

"Mothers don't automatically love their children."

"They should."

"I think some love more easily and quickly than others. I see parents with their children every day. Love is not always equal. Sometimes there's no love, only tolerance."

"Maybe," she says. "Or maybe they hide it well. You see parents in hospitals when they're pushed to extremes. Maybe they detach to cope."

"Now who's got it all figured out?" Last few sheep scuttle across the road. The Jeep gets a move on. "My mother, her love is based on conditions. Be good, follow her plan, and she will love you. If not . . ."

"Chop, chop?"

"Yes."

Vivi laughs. "Wait, are we related?"

"You're much too beautiful to be part of my very ugly family."

Clearly the man has never looked in a mirror. Her cheeks go pink on pink.

"Today I feel like I'm the world's worst mother," she says. "Melissa is a fantastic kid. She's my favorite person. It's been . . . difficult lately."

Max slows the car. "She'll be fine. You both will."

Straddling the road up ahead is a calendar-worthy village. It's straight out of a movie, with its rough stone streets and goat herder coaxing his tribe through the thoroughfare. The jingle jangle of their bells reminds her of Christmas.

The Jeep stops outside an iron gate. Nothing behind it except a pair of doors stuck to the mountain's face, and a couple of pink geraniums in those ubiquitous red pots.

The doctor's face gives nothing away. "Come, Vivi. We're here."

He helps her out of the car. Nice touch. Thoughtful. Sweet. His hand is warm and big and strong. Then he drops it and the warmth fades, until the sun picks up where he left off.

Interesting door. She's never seen anything like it.

Max must have a direct line to her thoughts, because he says, "The Church of the Holy Mother is built inside a natural cavern."

She opens the door, steps into night.

Slowly, the stars become candles.

Max takes her elbow, navigates her through the dark maze. He performs the Greek Orthodox ritual, crossing himself, kissing the holy icons.

She copies him, because that's what one does when they're grateful.

The Church of the Holy Mother is anything but typical. The Orthodox Church loves to separate its constituents: men on one side, women on the other, with very few seats for either. Be cohesive, one people, yet segregated. But here are pews in even rows, with no dividing lines.

"Have you brought me a gift this time?"

Vivi jumps. The priest has materialized beside them.

He nods to Max. "I saw the Jeep."

"Vivi, Father Kostas. Father Kostas, Vivi Tyler."

The man in black kisses her hand. He's young and vaguely familiar.

"Shouldn't I be kissing your hand?"

He laughs. "The church makes exceptions for beautiful women. The church also says beautiful women can call me Kostas."

Yeah, that laugh gives away his secret identity.

"You're brothers," she says, almost breathlessly.

Kostas groans. "I hope I'm not as ugly as Max. It is a wonder anyone can stand to look at him."

Max holds his hand up, palm flat facing his brother. "I know this is a house of God, but . . ."

The priest looks at Vivi. "He's an animal. You should have him neutered."

Vivi can't help laughing. A flat palm is the Greek hand gesture for . . . uh . . . Rhymes with mastication.

Kostas's eyes go back to Max. "Is this – ?"

"Vivi's daughter is a patient of mine. I brought her here to see you."

"I hope your daughter is not too ill," Kostas says.

"She's doing better today, thank you. It's been a difficult time for our family – Melissa especially."

"And for you too, I think."

Not easy being around these two. The way they look at her, they see her secrets.

"That's what Max said."

Kostas laughs. "And they say he is the stupid one!"

36

MAX

MAX LEAVES THEM TO it.

This is Vivi's time, not his, so it's back to the Jeep.

Good old Kostas. He should have known his brother would assume Vivi was Anastasia. Who else would he bring here?

Answer: Not Anastasia.

Thing is, up here she doesn't exist, which is why he stopped Kostas from speaking her name. A world without Anastasia is relaxing.

Who is he kidding? Yeah, it's partly Anastasia thing, but also the Vivi thing. Her company feels good and she's nice to look at. Anastasia is all flash and glitter, but Vivi has a quiet, comfortable beauty.

She's easy on the eyes and soul.

And she understood when he mentioned Mama and her mother lode of expectations. He almost told her, then, about Anastasia. But having a woman understand him felt too good. It's been a long time. Now he's wondering if Vivi's mother has her tied up with the same Greek string.

Yeah, there's something about the American woman he finds relaxing and exciting. And, God, she's lovely.

The bastard inside him doesn't want Vivi to know he's engaged.

Not because he's going seduce her, but because he likes the spark, the connection, the zing of potential.

He laughs at himself, because even if there was no Anastasia, Vivi's door is locked. She's got unresolved issues, that much is obvious. And Max likes his love life easy and uncomplicated.

And there is an Anastasia. The Anastasia. His Anastasia. Anastasia who might be pregnant with his child.

In a few days the hospital will discharge Melissa Tyler, and then no more Vivi. She'll go back to her life and he'll go back to his. And Mama will be happy – at last.

They need to announce their engagement, and soon. Otherwise he's going to change his mind.

He calls her – Anastasia, that is. Hearing her voice will keep him focused. If she answers. If she's not already knee deep in bridal magazines and cake samples.

She picks up. He ends the call.

A moment later, his phone buzzes.

"Did you just call?"

He winces. Anastasia is shrill. How did he ever find that sexy? It's high. No soft tones. He can see her ten years from now, still shrieking and nagging about how much time he spends at the hospital.

"Yeah. I just called to see what you were doing."

"I'm working. What else would I be doing?"

Eyes closed, Max leans back in the seat. "I don't know. That's why I asked. I'm up visiting my brother."

"Really? The one your mother hates?" She sounds surprised. How many brothers does he have?

"She doesn't hate him. She's just bitter because she can't manipulate him." Unlike Max.

"I'm a woman, I know these things. Trust me, she hates him."

Her certainty pisses him off. She's never met Kostas and barely knows their mother. She barely knows him.

"I have to go," he says.

"Wait, are we going out tonight?"

"Can't. I have to be at the hospital."

"But you have time to see your brother? Why can't you work now and see me later instead?"

"It doesn't work that way."

"Fine. I'll make plans with my friends." Her voice is an off-key violin.

He doesn't say goodbye, doesn't wait to hear it. Doesn't want her to use those three words he doesn't feel. Doesn't want to lie.

Plain and simple: End Call.

———

He's staring at nothing when a brown blur catches his attention. Some kind of animal.

Max whistles.

The Jeep shakes when a massive dog leaps into the car.

"Get out of here," he says, but his hands are busy contradicting his words. He can't help patting the big brown beast.

He jumps out of the Jeep, calls the dog to him. If Max knows his brother, the man's got room at his table for a hungry dog.

❧ 37 ❧

VIVI

THE PRIEST MAKES *FRAPPE*.

"Did Max tell you anything about our family?"

"No – why would he?"

The view is amazing. Every time she tilts her head, the water morphs to a new blue-green.

"Max is the best of men. He has a good heart. And our mother is taking advantage of that."

That conversation on the drive here. He talked about strings, and she laughed because his mother sounds like Eleni's twin. Now Vivi is doing the math.

"How so?"

"She has nobody, since our father died, except Max. And she pulls his strings and makes him dance and dance. And he does it because he knows she needs one good son."

"She's a Greek mother," Vivi says. "I think they're all crazy."

"Our mother is special. She's a crazy, manipulative witch."

"I told Max we might be related."

Kostas laughs. "If your mother is like ours, you have my condolences. She is the reason my brother looks like a haunted man. I rarely see him, and our mother never writes, never calls.

Not that I'm complaining." There goes the Andreou twinkle again. "Now tell me about you. What brings you to our country, American?"

His tone is kind, easy.

"My marriage broke down after fifteen years. My home dissolved along with it. At the time I felt we had nowhere else to go."

"How do you feel now?"

"It's only been a few days." The damp glass squeaks between her fingers. She hasn't answered his question, so she gives it another shot. "It changes. Sometimes I hate it here. Other times I feel that this place is so much a part of me that it flows through me like blood. To go would be to destroy myself; to stay would be the end of me. And that's just week one."

Kostas nods like he knows. "That's how I felt when I left the army and had to choose between the priesthood and law school. Hard choices, but better to have hard choices than none."

"Did you make the right decision?"

Nothing moves except his hand and the *frappe*'s foam.

"I made the only choice that could give me inner peace. It was not without sacrifices, but it was the correct path. Tell me, your marriage, why did it fail?"

"The real reason or the reason I give people?"

"God will know that you're lying, and I will too." He smiles. "Truth. Let us always be honest with each other, Vivi Tyler."

So she tells him. About John, about Ian, about all of it.

Kostas listens with his impartial ear and serene composure. "And he concealed this from you for all those years?"

"Maybe I suspected. I'm not really sure. Psychologists say we rewrite history in the light of new experiences and information."

"I believe it," he says. "We're all deluded, in our own way. It makes life more bearable."

"Melissa – our daughter – discovered his secret. In her mind, I think, John cheated on her, too. Now . . . now she's in the hospital with a self-inflicted injury and I don't know what to do. Should I stay here and make a home, or take her back where all our demons are at least familiar?"

She looks down at an empty glass. Kostas smiles and makes it full again – with the shaker, not divine intervention.

Wouldn't that be something?

"In time, she will be happy where you are. It is up to you to decide where it will be best for you both to live. But don't make any major decisions until you give Greece a chance. She might just surprise you. Are you staying with friends or family?"

"Family. My aunt."

"Look for your own place. The world is different when you have space to call your own."

"I'm both ridiculous and pathetic. Look at me."

"Vivi, you are neither pathetic nor ridiculous. You've been through many things, and now you've faced a parent's worst nightmare. Do what makes you happy now, and the rest will follow." He pauses. "I hear my brother coming. It's time to speak of happier things."

Good idea. They've shared too much. Now Vivi's thinking about houses and money and wondering if it's smarter to rent or buy.

"Do you know a good real estate agent? Preferably one who can find me a house with a proper toilet."

Max's laugh shows up first, followed by the rest of him.

"Old fashioned Greek plumbing. The newer houses have proper toilets, but the pipes are still last century. It's your lucky day, we do have the name of a very good real estate agent." He clicks his fingers at the top of the stairs. "Come on."

Max has a new friend. No purebred, but the mutt is cute. He slinks across the room, all bones and ragged fur, zeroes in on Vivi.

Love at first sight.

"It's true, the Lord does work in mysterious ways. You have a new friend," Max says

"He's homeless?"

"Just like you," Kostas says.

Vivi looks into those big, brown eyes. "I can't keep the dog."

❧ 38 ❧

MAX

OH YEAH, SHE'S KEEPING the dog.

Animals know. They know how a soul is stitched together. They know what it's made of before anyone else gets a clue. Dog doesn't take a shine to someone, it's a good idea to show that person the wrong side of your front door.

"Looks like he has other plans," Max says.

On the way up, he thought about keeping the dog himself. But Vivi and Melissa need the dog as much as he needs them.

"What am I going to do with a dog? I've never had one."

"Not even when you were a kid?"

She gives him a look. "With my mother? Eleni would never have a dog in her house. Children were bad enough, and we didn't shed."

"Did you jump on the furniture?"

She laughs. "Only when she wasn't home. The armchair had a sweet spot. Extra lift when you're wearing sneakers."

Kostas cuts a chunk of bread, offers it to the bag of bones. It's obvious the poor thing is starving, but he takes it like he's at afternoon tea.

Vivi carries her glass into the kitchen. Her shadow follows, chewing while she washes and dries the glass.

Max tells her she doesn't have to do dishes.

"I'm sorry," she says after a moment. "I can't help myself."

"You're welcome to do my dishes any time you like," Kostas calls out. "I hate housework."

Watching her be normal turns Max on. She moves about the kitchen like she cares.

Max checks out the view – he checks it out hard.

"If you don't mind, I think I'll go downstairs and . . ." Her hands make a steeple.

The dog goes with her.

Max sits in her vacant seat. He doesn't look at his brother. "The dog will be okay with her. Her daughter will love him."

"She's a good woman, but not undamaged," Kostas says cryptically.

"I'm not going to ask."

"And I won't tell." The chair creaks. "So tell me, Brother, how are our mother's plans for your marriage coming along? Did she set a date?"

"Did you say anything to Vivi?"

"I know you and women, Brother," Kostas says. "Don't toy with this one."

"Did you say anything?"

"No. I only told her Mama is insane. You don't sound happy, Max. And you look like shit."

Good old Kostas, reading between the sordid lines. "Anastasia is beautiful on the outside, not so beautiful on the inside. She can be selfish and manipulative. She has no empathy and she's demanding."

There is silence, for a time.

"She sounds like someone else we know."

"Mama?"

Kostas shrugs.

Ouch. Right where it hurts.

"Anastasia is nothing like Mama."

Except, that's not true – is it?

"Shit," Max swears. "You're right. She's jealous of my patients. She flares up every time I mention patients, or when the hospital calls."

His laugh is painful. No humor in the sound. "The other night she said hated my patients for needing me."

"Hate's a strong emotion."

"She's just so ungenerous. I don't know. Maybe I need to spend more time with her. Problem is, there is no more time."

"Are these obstacles you can overcome as husband and wife? Do you believe she can and will change and grow?"

"Anything is possible."

"Wrong. Anything is possible in the *right* union."

Max leans on the table. "What are you saying?"

"Walk carefully, Max. There are some things that cannot be undone, and some things that even you cannot fix."

❧ 39 ❧

MELISSA

SHRINK. THE WOMAN DOESN'T say it, but that's what she is. Melissa knows it.

Dr Triantafillou (that's what she called herself) doesn't seem a whole lot older than Melissa. She looks like she fell out of Seventeen, with her trendy jeans, ponytail riding high on her head. Plus she has an awesome tan – the kind you only get if you spend, like, a zillion years in the sun.

Melissa knows why she's here. Mom and Dr Andreou think she tried to kill herself.

Which is bullshit.

It's not true. She would know if it was. It's her brain.

"You're a shrink, aren't you?"

The shrink is sitting in the same chair Mom sat in while she did her hovering vulture impersonation. It's fake brown leather and it farts if you move the wrong way.

"I'm a therapist." Look at that smile. Perfect teeth. Years of braces – or just super lucky.

"Do you give out pills?"

"No, but I can refer you to someone who does if I think it's necessary. Do you want pills, Melissa?"

Melissa flops back into her nest of pillows.

"No, I was just checking to see if you're a psychiatrist or a psychologist. There's no point talking to someone who wants to dope me up or zap me in the head. You know, like in *One Flew Over the Cuckoo's Nest*.

"That's an interesting choice for a young girl. Did you read it in school?"

"No. Have you read it?" The shrink nods. "I found it at a swap meet. Most of the books were about weird crap like lawnmower repair or Jell-O salad. *Cuckoos Nest* was between *Men are From Mars, Women are From Venus* and a *Weight Watchers* recipe book."

"Did you enjoy the story?"

Melissa shrugs. "It was okay. Do you think if you're crazy you actually know it? Or do you walk around thinking you're normal and the reason people look at you funny is because they don't understand you?"

Dr Triantafillou's smile is broken, stuck in the ON position. "I think we're all crazy in our own way. Is that what you think, that you're crazy?"

Melissa likes her answer, but she won't show it. "I don't know. Maybe."

"What else do you like to read?"

"Most things, really."

"Except old recipe books and relationship advice?"

"I like stories."

The shrink doesn't pull out a file and scribble like Melissa thought she would. She crosses her legs, says, "What would you like to talk about today?" Really casual, like she's asking if Melissa wants Coke or Pepsi.

(The answer is: Either. They taste the same to her.)

Nothing. Everything. "I don't know."

"How are you enjoying our country?"

"It's okay. I've been in hospital for a year now."

Her brows shoot up. "But you were only admitted last night."

"Yeah, but it feels like a year." Melissa picks at the blue blanket draped over her legs. "The beach is nice. Do you go much?" Dumb question, Mel, Where do you think she got that tan?

But the shrink doesn't seem to think it's so dumb. "Whenever I can. My parents have a house on the beach in Platanidia. It's not far from here."

"Lucky."

She thinks about their old house with its jellybean-shaped pool and the tire swing Grampy made for her third birthday. "We used to have a nice house."

"Did your parents sell it to come here?"

"I think Dad wanted to keep it, but his . . . friend said no. They're getting a divorce. Mom hasn't told me yet, but I know it's going to happen."

"And how do you feel about that?"

"I don't know."

"Pick one word to describe how you feel about your parents separation. Any word you like."

She thinks about it for a moment. "Annoyed, I guess."

"Annoyed?"

"Yeah. I mean no one asked me what I thought, if it was okay with me. No one ever cares what I think. I'm just the kid."

"And if they'd asked?"

Melissa shrugs.

"Do you understand that your parents' relationship has nothing to do with you?"

Another shrug. "I guess."

"Anything else you want to talk about?"

Everything. She wants to tell her about Josh Cartwright and how he saw Dad in the park, and how Josh was right and that sucked, sucked, sucked. How Dad left them to be with a man. How much she hates being here, hates being at home, hates . . . *being*. But what comes out is: "Not really."

"Does your mother drink often?"

"Duh, everyone needs to drink to stay alive. Otherwise we'd dehydrate."

She's still smiling. "No, I mean alcohol. Does she drink to excess regularly?"

Melissa thinks about it, shakes her head. "I've never seen her drunk. Sometimes she has a glass of wine, but that's all. And that's, like, only twice a year."

"You don't have to protect her. You can tell me the truth. It's confidential."

What's her problem? "I'm not lying. I've never seen Mom or Dad drunk."

"So she wasn't drunk last night?"

Was she? Melissa can't remember. Everything about last night is hazy. Why is the shrink spoiling things? They were getting along just fine.

"It's very common for children to protect their parents," the shrink continues.

"I'm not protecting my parents." There's a panicky feeling growing inside her, like the time they went to Six Flags and she ate too much popcorn before going on the roller coaster. She puked at the top of the lift hill. *Splat!* All over the guy behind her.

"Melissa –"

"Don't call me a liar. I'm not a liar!"

"No one is saying you're lying. But maybe you're misremembering. Everybody has a tendency to remember things as they choose, not as they really are. Even me. It's possible that your mother was drinking and maybe she'd had enough that she didn't realize you were in trouble."

"That's not how it happened."

"Would you like to tell me how it happened?"

"It was an accident. I only wanted to get the sand out."

No more smile. Her eyes are all sad like she doesn't believe Melissa. "Melissa, this is confidential. You can tell me anything. Lots of young people hurt themselves when they're facing challenges. Sometimes they want to die and sometimes they simply want to choose the type of pain they're experiencing. Physical pain can overshadow the emotional."

"I wasn't trying to hurt myself."

The shrink picks up Melissa's hand, the one that isn't bandaged, and turns it over so that the sunlight hits the other scars. Melissa snatches her hand away. She doesn't want to be touched, doesn't want to be investigated. She wants the shrink to GTFO.

Get The Fuck Out.

"You're wrong," Melissa says. "You're wrong about everything."

The shrink pushes back the chair and stands. It farts, but Melissa doesn't laugh.

"I have another patient to see now, but I'll be back later and we'll set up a schedule for you. In the meantime I want you to think about the things we discussed."

"But I don't want to see a shrink all the time."

The shrink is smiling again. Doesn't look friendly now. "Melissa, we don't always know what's best for ourselves."

"How would you know? You don't even know me."

Under the blanket, Melissa flips her off.

Real brave, Tyler.

❧ 40 ❧
VIVI

COURTESY OF MAX, VIVI has a dog and the name of a real estate agent. Thing is, she's not really sure what to do with either of them.

She leaves the dog in the Jeep and goes to check on Melissa, who is busy playing board games with a couple of other kids. She seems fine enough – busy but bright.

"Yeah okay," she says when Vivi tells her she'll be back later.

Vivi stops at the hospital cafeteria, buys two *tiropitas*. One for her, one for the dog. She eats the feta pie slowly. The dog doesn't. He gulps his then gives her a hopeful glance. So Vivi takes another bite, gives him the rest.

"What are we going to call you?"

He looks up from the pastry crumbs. Got a call-me-anything-just-keep-feeding-me star in his eye.

"You look like a Biff."

He doesn't complain, so Biff it is.

"I don't really know what to do with a dog, Biff. So you're going to have to give me some pointers."

Biff wags his tail. Seems like a good omen.

Vivi has a minor epiphany. If she and Melissa are staying, they need a car. Nothing fancy, just wheels to get them around.

She does the math. They can afford a car if they go simple on the house. An apartment is another option, but that's not fair on Biff.

God, look at her, already worrying about the dog.

John has been generous. Last thing he wants is his client base to find out the truth (come on, John, it's 2014), so he went way overboard. Vivi would never say anything anyway – he should have known that. Strangers, she thinks. That's all they were. Two dumb kids who built a house on a bedrock of lies – well, lie.

Heat shimmers off the pavement in waves; looks like a rainstorm backing up. Siesta time. The Greeks are in their beds, sleeping off the hottest part of the day, but not Vivi and Biff. With Biff's makeshift leash in one hand (a length of slender rope Max found in the Jeep), and a map of Volos in the other, they go walking.

For a dog that has never seen a leash, Biff is cooperative. He only stops to pee on everything. Every time he lifts his leg he looks to her for approval.

What else can she say but "Good boy"?

Six sweaty blocks later, they hit the automobile jackpot. A small used car lot blots the horizon. Beside it, a small kiosk ripples.

Mirage or the real deal?

The heat is taking its toll. Her bra is doubling as a paddling pool.

The ripple steady and solidify.

Hallelujah, not a mirage. She and Biff aren't going to die on the streets of Volos. Silly dog wasted all his liquids spraying Biff Wuz Here over half the city.

"You should have siesta," says the kiosk's toothless proprietor. He takes her money, gives her two bottles of ice-cold water.

"I'm a crazy foreigner," she says.

Biff refuels. Vivi takes a long, long drink, and boy does it taste great. Nothing is sweeter than water when you need it.

Temporarily hydrated, they trot over to the car lot.

Dozens of cars – some she's never heard of. A metallic blue Volkswagen convertible is hanging out in the shade, chilling out until the right buyer swings its way.

An older man approaches, barrel-chested and sweaty, olive oil stain marking his white shirt.

"You want to buy the car?"

"Maybe. How much?"

"For you I give good price." He reels off a number that makes her want to slap him.

Vivi laughs, saunters away with Biff. "I don't think so."

There's a lot of huffing and puffing as the salesman catches up. "Wait, wait. What was I thinking? I got the price wrong. This never happened before, can you believe it? For you it is much less. Very affordable, I think."

He gives her a price slightly lower than the first.

"Is that the man's price or the woman's price?"

He wags a finger. "You are very clever. I will give you the smart people's price. Is special – today only!"

She stares him down. Makes him sweat a bit more. Makes his left eye twitch.

"So, do we make a deal?" he asks.

"Okay."

"Okay! Good! Okay!"

"And I'll want to test drive it, of course."

"Of course!" he cries. "You will not regret this, I think."

She's regretting it twenty minutes later when she pulls the Volkswagen back into the lot. There are road rules but they're serving suggestions. Driving with Greeks equals swimming with sharks when you're covered in paper cuts.

But she buys the car and drives away with Biff riding shotgun. The sleek little VW isn't brand new, but it's got guts.

Her first major John-free purchase.

———

The real estate office isn't far. She parks in the shade and leaves Biff to keep watch.

She's barely through the door when a friendly voice says, "You must be Vivi."

The woman is mid-twenties, polished to a brilliant shine. She's one of those women who can wear linen during the oppressive summer regime and command it not to wrinkle.

Meanwhile, Vivi tries not to drip on the marble floor.

"Come sit, have a drink. Max told me to expect you."

What a guy he is, helping out a pair of strangers.

"You know him well?"

"Of course, we are family. He is my cousin."

That whole family smiles in megawatts.

Still . . . cousin is a nebulous term in Greece. Could be they're first cousins or twenty-fifth cousins, completely removed.

"So you are Vivi and I am Soula. Together we will find you a house. The perfect house. You are looking to rent or buy?" Her perfect nails begin a fast dance across a sleek keyboard.

"I'd prefer to buy something. Nothing too fancy or too expensive. In Agria or very close by."

"How many bedrooms?"

"Two."

"You have a child?"

"A daughter. You?"

"I have a boyfriend. That is a little like having a child, yes?"

Vivi smiles. "I used to have a husband. He was more trouble than a kindergarten full of children."

"What happened to him?" Her voice drops, becomes more intimate. She leans closer. "Did you shoot him?"

"Worse. He left me for a man."

"Better a man than a woman. At least you know what he's got that you don't." She wiggles her pinkie.

Which makes Vivi feel better.

No really, it does. With a few simple words, Soula has given her a fresh perspective. No more sitting around wondering what she could have done differently. Growing a penis is impossible.

(Although, scientists being scientists, you know there's one growing on a mouse's back in a lab right now.)

"At least," Soula continues, "he is someone else's pain in the ass, yes?"

Takes a minute for the joke to sink in. Then a whole ton of pennies rains on her head. She laughs until she's crying, laughs so hard the chair needs a seatbelt to keep her in the upright position. People are looking, but Vivi doesn't care.

Meanwhile, Soula is tapping on the keyboard. She waits for Vivi to stop laughing, then she nods at the screen.

"You point and we will go."

41

VIVI

SOULA SAYS, "YOU DRIVE like an old woman."

"I drive like an American. Plus I just bought this car, I don't want to screw it up yet."

The road is rough. Made of dirt and stones and wishful thinking.

So far they've seen four houses, all of them wrong. The first was too small, the second too big. Three was the little pig's house of sticks.

Vivi says, "How much further?"

"Not too far, I think."

"You think?"

Soula holds up both hands. "Yes, I think."

Greek distance is like Greek time: negotiable.

Nothing much out here except a tiny church, endless olive groves, sooty-faced goats. Cute things with lop ears.

"There," Soula yelps, pointing to the road ahead.

Vivi squints at the cottage. Doesn't look too bad from the road, but it's a postage stamp at this distance.

Zoom zoom.

Up close it looks good, too. Smooth stucco recently whitewashed, by the looks of the crisp white. The cottage is wearing a porch as a wide belt. Irregular flagstones form a walkway that vanishes out back.

Clay flowerpots contain creamy white gardenias and geraniums in shades of cotton candy and sunset. Shutters slick with new brown paint.

Soula is tense with anticipation. "What do you think?"

Vivi shrugs, disappears around back.

Smells like a Fig Newton factory back here. There's a giant fig tree in the yard, branches plunging most of the patio into shade. Its fruit is at that awkward adolescent stage, stuck between green and brown. Biff sniffs about, raises his back leg on the tree trunk. He doesn't make eye contact.

"What do I think?" She looks at Soula, who has wandered back there. "I have to wonder why someone would give up this place."

"Eh." She shrugs. "The owners moved back to England to be closer to their grandchildren. They have no need of this house now. And they didn't have time to tend to the olive trees."

A twist of a key later, she's opening the house for Vivi to step inside.

"The olive trees come with the house?"

"Sixty-thousand square meters. Fifteen acres. About a thousand trees – maybe more."

What the hell would she do with olive trees?

The open floor plan reveals a cozy living space, with four doors leading to, she assumes, the bedrooms and a bathroom. Rustic furniture invites a body to sit, stay, relax. Vanilla paint, textured walls; none of the blinding pinks and blues in older Greek homes. The appliances aren't the trendiest (a wood oven with an aluminum vent pipe running overhead to heat the whole house, gas hot plates, and a refrigerator with the freezer on top), but they're good enough.

Vivi says, "I love it."

She looks behind the doors. Three bedrooms – decent but not huge.

The fourth door is hiding the house's dirty little secret.

"Shit," she says. "Aaaaand . . . now I don't love it."

"What is it?" Soula peers over Vivi's shoulder. "Oh."

Shower, hand basin, medicine cabinet, and a gaping (toilet) hole in the floor.

Vivi spits out a bunch of words she'd never say in front of Melissa.

Soula asks, "Is that physically possible?"

"I've seen it on the Internet. How much do they want?"

"You are still interested?"

"I'm interested. Doesn't mean I'm going to say 'Yes.'"

Soula tosses her a figure.

Vivi throws a smaller one back. "The bathroom needs remodeling," she says. "It's going to cost."

"They won't like it. This is an excellent price."

"An excellent price for a house with a toilet I can sit on."

"You can sit on this one," Soula says, deadpan.

"If I amputate my legs."

"What, you are too good for a Greek toilet? Is your bottom made of gold? Americans," she says, laughing. "You want everything to be sanitary. A little dirt and hardship builds character."

"My mother used to spank me for having too much character. Can you at least try and get me that price?"

"I will try. This is Greece – everything is negotiable except the weather."

"If the owners accept the price, then we have a deal."

Soula goes away with her cell phone, hands doing as much talking as her mouth.

Vivi looks outside at the land she wants. Yeah, she's already imagining Melissa hanging in the yard with her friends, Biff peeing on the trees.

No, that second thing isn't imaginary; Biff really is peeing on all the trees.

Anyway, point is she's fantasizing about this place. Feels good.

Soula's hands and tongue are gaining momentum. Her expression says nothing. Then she drops the phone back into her leather purse.

"You want this house?"

"Yes."

"It's yours."

"Just like that?"

"Well, you have to pay for it, of course. But it's yours as soon as you want to move in." She tucks her arm through Vivi's, steers her back to the VW. "Come, now we celebrate! Wait – first we talk money, then we celebrate!"

———

Surprisingly easy acquiring a home loan in a semi-corrupt country, when the bank manager is your second cousin.

Nepotism is nice when it's in your favor.

"I don't suppose you know where I can buy a toilet?" she asks Soula.

"I know someone who knows a place."

She bought a house. What is she going to do with a house? And all those olive trees?

"Oh shit," she says. "I just bought a house."

❧ 42 ☙

VIVI

THEA DORA SLAPS A triangle of *baklava* onto a plate. The nuts jump.

"Where will you go? What will you do? How will you live? Your child is ill. You cannot live on your own!"

"You live on your own."

"That is different!"

"Different how?"

"It just is."

"We'll be fine," Vivi says. "Melissa will go to school in the fall and I'll get a job."

"What job?"

Biff jumps the fence. The dog's sick of sitting in the car. But once he's over the fence, he gets a load of *Thea* Dora and slams his canine brakes.

"*Ay yi yi!*" she shrieks. "What is that thing?"

"That's my dog."

Thump! goes her palm against the *baklava* container. She mutters something about fleas and plague and Turks.

"He's clean and healthy."

That might be true, or not. But Vivi comes to the dog's defense anyway.

"Vivi, my love, why don't you stay here? I'll be lonely without you and Melissa."

"Can I put in a new toilet and let Biff sleep in the house?"

"The dog cannot stay. Let him loose and he will find somewhere else to go."

Vivi says, "No way."

———

Stale fries and desperation – the hospital cafeteria reeks of both.

Vivi isn't all that hungry, but that doesn't stop her biting into the rubbery *kasseri*. The cheese is paired perfectly with the bread in her other hand.

"You look pleased with yourself," someone says.

What do you know, it's Dr Andreou – Max. He's holding a bucket of hot coffee. Takes his caffeine seriously, that man.

"I bought a house," she tells him.

"Soula told me."

Vivi waves a hand at the empty chair. "If you don't sit, I'll wind up with a sore neck."

"It's my job to make people better, not worse."

"So, sit."

"I am, I am."

Even now, when it's obvious he's coasting on no sleep, he's a good-looking man.

"It takes some getting used to," she says.

"The coffee?"

"Yeah, the coffee."

Max says, "Did you know Greeks drink more coffee per capita than any other country?"

"Ah, so that's why you're all so feisty."

"The caffeine makes us passionate."

"Or neurotic," she says, thinking about the twists in her family tree.

"Are you making fun of our people?"

"No, just the coffee."

Her teeth sink into the bread. She hopes for a dainty bite, but it's more like shoveling coal. With a bit of luck, Max will attribute her pink cheeks to sunburn, never suspecting that she's having a fun time mentally twisting him into erotic poses.

Hey, it's been a long time.

"Did Melissa say anything to you about the therapist?"

Vivi swallows. "No. Why?"

"I'm a curious man. Tell me, how do you like your new house? You'll have to give me your address so I can bring a gift."

"You don't have to."

"I want to." His dark brown gaze collides with hers.

Now she's on fire from the neck down. She tries clearing her throat, but nothing comes out.

"It's not necessary. Honestly."

"Melissa is my favorite patient," he says between gulps. "And I can't help feeling responsible for finding you a house."

Ooookay. She fumbles for paper and a pen, scribbles their new address, her email, and the phone number that will be active when the phone company can be bothered.

Sometime between now and never.

❧ 43 ❧

MELISSA

HOW DO YOU FEEL today, Melissa?"

"How do you feel today, Dr Triantafillou?"

"I'm well. Thank you for asking. But we're here to talk about you."

"I'm well. Thank you for asking."

Now she's getting it. But Melissa figured the shrink would be angry, not smiling. Her teeth are whiter today, or maybe her tan is darker. Whatever. Melissa wants her outfit. She likes the denim pencil skirt and the too-tall wedges.

"It's a common tactic," the shrink says. "But ultimately a time waster. Time we could both be using to help you. Is that what you want, Melissa, to waste your time?"

"How old are you?"

"Does it matter?"

"No."

"I'm twenty-eight."

"How come you told me?"

"Because you asked."

"Oh."

"I'll give you honest answers, Melissa. But you have to give me honest answers, too."

"What happens if I don't?"

"One of two things. They assign you a new psychologist, or they may decide you need . . . a different kind of help."

"Pills?"

"Possibly. Probably a combination of medication and observation, until they're sure you won't harm yourself again."

"I wasn't trying to kill myself. Nobody believes me."

"Would you like to tell me how it started, the cutting?"

"Not really."

"Okay. We don't have to talk about it today."

"Are you going to have me locked up if I don't?"

"No. Only if I think you intend to hurt yourself again. Do you want to hurt yourself again?"

"No," Melissa says. "I wasn't trying the first time. It's just . . . Being fifteen sucks."

"How does it suck?"

"Don't you remember what it's like?"

Dr Triantafillou says, "I think American teenagers have many of the same pressures as Greek teenagers, but also some that are vastly different. Tell me what it's like for you."

Melissa doesn't need to think too hard. "Nobody lets me do anything. Nobody cares what I want. And if they lose their minds and – " she fakes a gasp " – ask what I want, then they ignore what I say and do what they want, anyway. So why even ask me to begin with?"

"It's not easy being fifteen. But you don't have far to go until you're eighteen."

"Almost three years. Basically forever."

"So tell me this: What do you want?"

Melissa shrugs. "I don't know."

"Between now and our next appointment, I want you to think about that. Can you do that?"

"I don't know."

❧ 44 ❧

MAX

THEY TALK TOO MUCH, Max and Vivi. She's becoming a habit.
So, they talk and talk and talk – about funny things, about difficult things – but has he told her yet about Anastasia?

Negative.

"Does Melissa's father know she's in the hospital?"

Vivi shakes her head.

"Why not?"

"Have you ever been through a divorce?"

"Never married," he says.

"That's okay," Vivi says, "this is only my first." She laughs but she's obviously embarrassed. "Bad joke, I know."

"Not that bad," he says.

"Oh yeah, it's that bad. But sometimes you have joke about things to release the pressure, or you crack. I don't know what divorce is like when you don't have kids, but when you do have kids, and they are your world, you do whatever it takes to keep them. If I tell John about Melissa . . . You're right, I should tell him. But what if he changes his mind about our custody arrangement? What do I do if he tries to take my daughter away?"

"Is he a good father?"

"He was always a busy father." Nails tapping on the table. "Yes, John's a very good father."

"So tell him. Be honest. It will save you trouble later."

Isn't that right, Max?

———

He fucks Anastasia, but it's Vivi's name in his throat.

"When's your period due?" he says after.

"Soon," she says.

"Do you think you're pregnant?"

"I don't know, Max. As soon as I know I will tell you, okay?"

She hits the shower without him. While she's doing that, Max Googles "John Tyler" on his phone. Good-looking man. A lot of him in Melissa.

Anastasia wanders back into the room. "What are you doing?"

The phone goes dark. "Nothing."

"Max?"

"What, baby?"

"Nothing," she says.

❧ 45 ❧

VIVI

VIVI CALLS JOHN.

He asks lots of questions, but not one of them is "Does Melissa need me there?" or, "Do you need me to come?"

Does he say: "I'll be on the next flight"?

Nope.

Just: "Keep me up to date."

Vivi doesn't tell Melissa, doesn't put his ugly colors on display.

———

Max takes her all the way to the cafeteria for coffee. Sits her down with a cup of American Joe and a piece of brown cake.

"John really is a good father."

Vivi says it like she's sort of stunned – which she is.

"Maybe he didn't know what to say."

She knocks back a forkful of brown crumbs. Is the cake meant to be chocolate or just chocolate-colored?

"Still," she says.

"I understand," he says. "I do. But he's going through your divorce, too. And maybe he didn't know the appropriate thing to say in that moment. Yes, Melissa is his daughter, but what does he do about you?"

"The part where Melissa is his daughter automatically overrides our differences. I would drop everything and go to her."

"Maybe he thinks you would feel hope if he comes, and that would prolong the pain."

"That's not it," she says, because she's trading with inside knowledge.

"Whatever your husband did or didn't say, you did the right thing. The good thing."

"What if he uses it against me?" Vivi looks down at the cake. Definitely no chocolate in that thing. "He met someone else and dumped me – what do I do if he takes our daughter, too?"

Max goes quiet. Then: "Was he cheating?"

"Unequivocally, yes. For years, I think."

She won't look at him. That's how it goes when the other partner cheats. They fucked up, but you're the one buried under a pile of shame. It's like they put up a billboard telling the world you're not good enough, you're not special, you're not worth fidelity.

Logically, Vivi knows John is the fuck up. Emotionally?

Welcome to Loserville, population: Vivi Tyler.

"Vivi," Max says. "I need to tell you something." The man looks haunted. His brother nailed that observation. There's no time to fret about whatever he's about to spill, because he's saying it, slapping it on the table between them. "I'm with someone. A woman. And it's expected that we'll marry soon."

The "Oh" in her head is flat, disappointed. But by the time she says, "Oh, you're engaged? Congratulations!" she's managed a quick repair job and the words bounce out.

Vivi, Vivi, what did you expect?

Yeah, not this curl of disappointment.

❦ 46 ❧

MAX

Life is good.
He has money to live and money to grow.
Work is satisfying.
And soon he will have a beautiful wife.
Keep on telling yourself that, Max.

❦ 47 ❧

MELISSA

MELISSA SAYS, "YOU LOOK like my grandparents' bathroom."
The days are smearing together. She's using the shrink's outfits as a kind of calendar. Today Dr Triantafillou is neck-to-toe pink. Pink jeans, pink ruffled top, pink Converse sneakers.

She's the Sugar Plum Fairy.

Okay, so it looks pretty great. Melissa can't wait to seize complete control over her own wardrobe. Mom always wants her to dial it all the way down to boring.

"Thank you, Melissa," the shrink says.

Melissa tilts her head. "Why do you always do that?"

"Do what?"

"You're always polite. Maybe their bathroom is the most hideous thing ever."

"Is it?"

"It depends what kind of mood I'm in."

"What kind of mood are you in today?"

Shrug. "Today I like their bathroom. And I miss it."

"Why do you miss their bathroom?"

"There's a proper toilet, for one thing. And there's this window that gives you a great view of the neighbor's backyard. They have this cool dog." Another shrug – she's full of them. "I just really like their dog."

"Pets are great company. And they're good for your body and mind. Have you ever had a dog?"

"No. Dad is allergic. Or so he says."

"You don't believe him?"

"Why would I? He pretended to love my mom for years, when he's secretly gay."

No reaction.

"Your mother found you in the bathroom, that night, didn't she?"

Melissa nods. "I guess so. I wasn't exactly there."

"Mentally or . . .?"

"I hit my head and passed out."

"Has that ever happened before?"

"You mean the other times?"

The shrink nods. "If you're comfortable talking about them."

"No." That's a "No" to both.

"I'm polite," the shrink says, "because it costs nothing and it feels good. I could take your comment as an insult or a cruel observation, but why? The things you say are a reflection of you, not of me or how I dress."

The thing about Dr Triantafillou is that she takes a lot of back roads getting to the point. Melissa wonders if this is a shrink thing or a Dr Triantafillou thing.

"You always wear nice things," Melissa says.

"Thank you."

"I cut myself because it felt good and it cost nothing."

Dr Triantafillou leans forward in the farting chair. "But it did cost you, Melissa."

———

Next time she's white and gold. Very sophisticated. Very European.

Melissa says, "Do you have those big sunglasses that eat up half your face?"

The shrink smiles. "They're in my office."

Melissa closes her eyes. "I figured."

"Are you interested in fashion?"

Shrug. "I guess. I like how different clothes make people different."

"I like that, too. Every morning I look in the closet and ask myself who I want to be today. It's an illusion, of course. No matter what we wear, we are still who we are."

"You're, like, the joy police," Melissa says.

"Do you want to be someone else?"

Stupid question. Who doesn't want to shove their feet into someone else's shoes? Yeah, Melissa wants to be someone else. But she'd settle for being herself with the sadness stripped away.

"Maybe that's why Mom was drinking that night," she says. "To be someone different for a while. Someone shiny."

❧ 48 ❧

VIVI

THREE PEOPLE IN THE room: Vivi, Max (as Dr Andreou), and Dr Triantafillou. The two doctors present Vivi with her options.

It's a no-brainer.

Vivi says, "Let's go with Plan A."

Both doctors nod. They're glad Vivi Tyler chose the first option. Neither of them believe Melissa Tyler is a danger to herself; what happened rattled her cage – and hard. But they don't play the lottery with children's minds and lives, so . . .

"Let's compare schedules," Dr Triantafillou says, "and we'll find a time that works for you and Melissa."

———

Four days later the hospital sends Melissa home. Vivi makes her first outpatient appointment with the psychologist before going up to the ward. Melissa hasn't mentioned the psychologist yet, but she'll chirp when she's ready.

It's frustrating, all this tiptoeing on eggshells, but she'll do anything to help Melissa. She's banking on the new house helping.

Turns out Melissa's happy-cool about leaving. She wants to go home, but she doesn't want to make it look like she gives a damn.

She's shining bright when Vivi takes her down to the parking garage, instead of out front to get a cab.

"You got a car?"

"We got a car."

Vivi hits the remote. The VW's lights flash.

"Sweet!" Melissa says, flopping back in the seat.

Wait until she sees the house.

Melissa looks chill, rested, relaxed with the breeze running wild through her blonde hair. Not all tense and pinched, the way she's been for months now. She's too thin, though, like she's over being a girl. Galloping towards womanhood.

Vivi is all frayed nerves, teeth chewing that bottom lip into a meat doily. The tension is killing her.

They cruise. Melissa fiddles constantly with the radio, checking on the dozens of independent stations. Happens all the time, people jumping on the airwaves to blast an album or two, before fading away until next time the inclination strikes.

Then Vivi eases the car past the turnoff to her aunt's place, and Melissa says, "Hey, you're going the wrong way."

"Am not."

"How come we're not going to *Thea* Dora's house?"

"Because we're going somewhere else."

"Not another doctor!"

Vivi laughs. "It's so much better than that."

"How much better? Better than ice cream?"

"Nothing's better than ice cream."

"So, it's not better than ice cream . . . Is it frozen yogurt good?"

"It's close to ice cream, but it's not chocolate or cake. Or chocolate cake."

The wheels skid on the dirt road. Vivi kicks it down a notch so they don't dislodge any organs or wind up in a ditch. The excitement is making her twitchy behind the wheel. Making her Greek, she thinks.

No more cool from Melissa. The girl is jumpy, practically bouncing on the seat. She's five and it's Christmas Eve; seven and it's the day before Disneyland.

Slower, slower.

Vivi cuts the engine outside the cottage. "This is it," she says. "Not as good as ice cream, but pretty great."

Melissa stares at the cottage, with its white stucco and big, big yard. Her eyes are donut round.

"This is ours?"

"You bet."

"So, we're staying here?"

"Considering I've already paid for it, the answer is yes."

"Good," she says. "I want to stay."

"Are you sure?"

"Yes. But you should have asked me first."

"You're right." Vivi measures her words, tries not to spill the wrong ones. "I should have."

"Whatever."

Melissa doesn't waste time. She's out of the car, racing across the yard. Then she stops.

"Is that a dog?"

Inside, Biff is singing the song of his people.

"Probably just the neighbor's dog," Vivi says.

"What neighbors? This is, like, nowhere."

Smart kid.

Vivi says, "Catch," and tosses her the keys. Melissa opens the door and Biff comes barreling out. Round and round, chasing his own tail, then he's all over Vivi, until he realizes she's not alone.

Spotting the stranger, he sits, head tilted, waiting on an introduction.

Melissa wiggles her fingers. "S'okay, I love dogs."

Biff looks to Vivi for confirmation; he doesn't just believe. "Go ahead," she says. "Mel's the one who's going to spoil you rotten."

The gypsy dog pads over to Melissa, leans on her like she's furniture.

"Can we keep him, Mom?"

"I don't know," Vivi says.

"Please?"

"Maybe."

"Pretty please with two cherries on top?"

"Three cherries," she says.

"Deal!"

Laughing, Vivi kneels beside her daughter and their new best friend. This moment is so much better than ice cream.

———

Melissa's got something on her mind.

"Mom, if I tell you something will you promise you won't be mad?"

"Sure," she says carefully. She came this close to losing her daughter; no way is she going to screw it up now.

"They made me talk to a shrink."

"I know. Did you find it helpful?"

Biff rolls over. Legs stuck up in the air, he could be road kill. Melissa takes the hint, gets busy scratching.

"She wanted to know if you get drunk a lot."

"Try never," Vivi says. "Why did she ask that?"

"I don't know. Something about you being drunk when you took me to the hospital."

She looks at Biff. He's chilling in his happy place. "I wasn't drunk that night. I'd had maybe half a dozen sips out of one of those small bottles of *retsina*."

"Okay."

"Mel, when have you ever seen me drunk?"

"I said okay," she says, with a boatload of attitude.

But Vivi's pissed – not at Melissa, but this quack who already has Vivi strapped to a cross.

"I'm going to call her and give her a few pieces of my mind, then I'm going to demand they find you someone else. Her focus is supposed to be you, and not whether or not I had half a glass of wine at a family get-together."

Melissa's face crumples. "You made another appointment for me to see Doctor Triantafillou?"

Vivi doesn't tell her the part where they gave her exactly two choices, and she picked the one she and Melissa could stomach. It was lock her up or let her go on psychological probation.

"Dr Andreou said he wants you to see her as an outpatient. I was following his advice. I thought it was a good idea, to give you someone objective to talk to."

"Why did you do that? I don't like her. Why do you have to turn everything in my life to shit?" Off she goes, running. A door slams; apparently she figured out which room is hers.

The door opens.

"Biff?"

The dog looks at Vivi, then he's gone, too.

❦ 49 ❧

VIVI

I T'S LIKE CHRISTMAS UP in here.

Vivi unwraps the sticky wax ring. Everything she needs is in this room, right down to the gleaming white toilet.

Melissa and Biff watch from the doorway.

"Gross," she says.

Vivi laughs. "What's grosser: ripping this thing out or squatting to poop?"

"Eww, that's so . . ."

"Gross?" she offers.

"Yeah."

It's been a week since they moved in, and the Tyler women have been maintaining a quiet, fragile truce. Melissa speaks in monosyllabic words and Vivi grovels.

She's been busy this week, repainting the walls, replacing the old shower fixture, painting the ceiling a fresh, clean white. It's a whole new room – one she can live with. No more squatting.

Now it's time to right an oh-so wrong. Vivi gets to work with the pry bar and hammer. She taps and the ceramic yields an inch.

Biff woofs

"You don't get the last word," Vivi tells the mutt.

Probably he wants another meal. Making up for lost time is Biff. His coat has shine now. He's borderline respectable.

Corner to corner, she pries the thing loose. Dried, yellowing caulk dangles. Silly (gross) String. She dumps a bottle of bleach in the open pipe. Sayonara, bacteria.

Melissa still looks unimpressed. "Will we have to put the TP in the trash?"

Vivi considers the pipe. "Let's try it our way and see if the pipes can handle it. Small pieces. If there are any problems we'll have to do it the other way."

Mel shrugs. "I'm going outside."

It's show time for the new toilet. "Sure," Vivi says, absentmindedly. "Just stay away from snakes, and don't eat the fruit until we know what's edible."

Truth is, she doesn't want Melissa out of her sight – just in case. But holding on too tight is only going to make things worse. So, she lets her baby go, while she shows this bathroom how they do things in the New World.

Scrape, scrape, and the old wax is history. She drills holes in the floor, fastens the anchoring brackets; rocking is for chairs, not the bathroom throne. Then comes the part where she staggers across the room, arms struggling with the new toilet.

Nothing easy about it. A toilet is shaped like, well, a toilet. Curves in all the wrong places. But she wins. That toilet goes on exactly like it's supposed to, hugs the wax ring tight, empties and refills right on target.

Hooray.

She takes a step back, then another to admire her handiwork, because from here it looks a-m-a-z-i-n-g.

Next thing she knows, her whole life is zooming by, tangled in that Friday underwear. And she's falling, falling, and the pipe wrench is sailing across the short distance between her foot and the new toilet.

The tile floor catches her. Lucky. She's probably only paraplegic, now. But the wrench falls hard, and that new toilet is no trampoline.

(FYI: In a rock/paper/scissors competition, metal cracks porcelain.)

She sprays the walls with curse words. All the "fuck" and "shit" in the world isn't going to help her situation, but it feels good to let loose.

She hobbles out to find Melissa, jeans wet from the cistern. Looks like she peed her pants. Her daughter's playing fetch with Biff. Sometimes Biff fetches the ball, sometimes he lets Melissa get it herself.

"Change of plans, Kiddo," Vivi says. "If you want to pee you're going to have to find a bush. I highly recommend the back yard. Ask Biff. He knows all the good spots."

"*Yia sou*, Vivi, Melissa!"

(That's Greek for hello, but −)

Fuck. Seriously, fuuuuck.

Max is closing in on the gate, fresh off the cover of That Guy You Want to Bang magazine.

"Hi," she calls out. "What are you doing here?"

He's in denim and crisp cotton, and she's in sewage. And now he knows they need to pee in the garden.

Where's a sinkhole when you need one?

"Mom! He came to see me, didn't you, Dr Andreou?"

He gives Melissa a hundred watts. "Of course. I came to look at those stitches."

"Since when do doctor's make house calls?" Vivi asks.

"Since I brought a gift for your new home. How about I take you both out for *souvlaki*? If you're not busy."

"We're not busy," Melissa yelps. "Don't go without me." She bolts into the house, Biff at her heels.

Vivi says, "Sorry, I don't mean to be rude. Today hasn't gone as smoothly as I planned."

"She seems much better."

God, what is it about these Greek guys? Why do they have to swagger that way? It's . . .

Distracting.

Max is waiting for her to speak. It's weird seeing him on her turf, looking like a man, not a doctor − and her with a blob of wax on her nose. If she crosses her eyes, she can see the damn thing.

"So far. But I'm keeping a close eye on her. Having Biff around seems to be helping."

"Biff?"

"It's a perfectly respectable name."

"You called the dog Biff?"

"My dog, my choice. Hey, you had your chance to keep him."

"Whatever. I don't like dogs anyway," he says.

She laughs at the lie. "Come in, please.

"Looks like you're all moved in."

"Mostly," she says. "The biggest battle is redecorating. I smashed the toilet this afternoon. Come by tomorrow and I'll break some windows."

"Why don't you hire a contractor?"

"Ha-ha. No!"

Greek contractors run on Greek time, which means they'll show up when they can be bothered, and leave on that same schedule. Thanks, but no thanks.

"Let's just say I have more faith in my own abilities."

He looks at her and she looks at him and then she looks at the ground, while he keeps on doing what he's doing, the way he's doing it.

"So, *souvlaki*, what do you say?"

"Is your fiancée okay with this?"

"She's out with friends, and I have to eat."

He looks good – so good. Suddenly, she's starving.

"Wait right there."

50

MAX

MAX DOESN'T WAIT.

He goes back to the Jeep, grabs the two cacti he brought as a gift, sets one at the front door, one at the back. It's a good luck thing.

Superstitions are like salt in Greece: everyone sprinkles it on everything. Two people speak at the same time, they both race to touch something red. Death follows the call of the crow. A cactus wards away evil.

Max figures Vivi and Melissa need all the help they can get, so he brought one for each door.

To be honest, this place isn't what he expected.

But then he doesn't really know Vivi, does he? He just wants to. And after seeing this place, he really, really wants to.

He figured she'd be all about an apartment or a house closer to Volos, or closer to her family at least − not that it's far; everything (and everyone) is still in walking distance.

But this house is a lot like paradise.

And there's a big click in his head, because, man, the Tylers really fit in this house with its fruit trees and its overwhelming sense of home.

Why is he here?

House calls aren't part of the job, though he's been known to follow up if he's concerned.

Yet here he is on a house call, with a gift. Being the good doctor.

Bullshit, Max. Bull. Shit.

He sits on the couch. The house smells of fresh paint and lemons. Is this what it's like, having a home? He can't imagine Anastasia painting or squeezing lemons.

Don't compare them, you asshole.

It's too comfortable, so he gets up. Winds up staring out the back doors to stop himself browsing the family photos set out on the bookshelves.

A moment later, Melissa bounds out of her room with her shadow. The dog is filling out. Won't be long before everyone forgets he used to be unloved.

Now that she's in her own clothes and not in a hospital bed, it's clear Melissa is destined to be a beauty. Vivi eyes, Vivi's cheekbones, but then her father is a looker, too.

Max says, "Is it okay if I check your wrist?"

She hesitates before offering her arm. All that's left of that night is a thin pink line and a row of black knots.

"If your mother has some nail scissors, I can take them out right now." He watches her scratch around the scar. "It itches, huh?"

"Like fire."

"Sure you don't have Biff's fleas?"

She giggles. "Biff doesn't have fleas."

"That's because you've got them now!"

"Mom bathed him with some stinky shampoo. Biff was totally horrified."

Max laughs at the dog. "If I take the stitches out, it won't be so itchy."

"Really?"

"Really. It won't hurt."

It's over in a minute. Melissa looks impressed.

"Is it weird doing stitches?"

"At first. I had to practice a lot on cadavers."

"You stitched real dead people?"

He nods. "First time I saw a dead body I vomited."

"Really?"

"Honest. I prefer the living. You're lucky you're still with us."

She looks past him, temporary cloud darkening those blue eyes. Then it's gone as quickly as it came. "Hey, Mom," she hollers. "Dr Andreou took my stitches out."

And then Vivi's there in a sundress, hair tucked behind her ears, smear of color on her full lips. She looks uncomplicated.

"How does it look?"

"Perfect," he says. "You won't have to take her out back and shoot her."

Vivi smiles. "Good to know. Are we walking?"

"Does it make a difference?"

"Shoes," she says. "It makes a difference."

"Let's walk."

"Mom, why can't we go in the car?"

"Because if we walk five minutes that way . . ." – she points out the door – ". . . we'll hit the beach. And gas is about eighty percent tax."

"But I like the car."

"So do I, but I like fresh air and money more."

"Can Biff come too? He looks hungry."

The dog in question is sitting in front of the refrigerator, tail drumming the floor. Yeah, he looks hungry, but dogs always do.

"Not a chance," she says.

"But, Mom . . ."

Vivi wins this round.

Perfect night. There's a round Camembert moon and a million stars putting on their regular show.

In a different life, he'd reach for Vivi's hand.

But it's this life, so it's just two fledgling friends walking to the promenade, with Melissa charging ahead because it's not cool to be seen with adults.

Greeks are sociable people. Evening comes, and if they're not going out, they're sitting in their front yards, watching their piece of the world stroll by.

They say a lot of "Good evenings," and word moves up the food chain that Vivi Tyler is polite – for a foreigner.

The promenade is blooming, clusters of family and friends everywhere. It's smaller than Volos's promenade, but brighter. More colored lights per square meter. The *tavernas* buttress one another, and along the water's edge it's difficult to discern which tables belong to which establishment.

Melissa is humming with excitement.

"Mom, a pizza place! Can we have pizza?"

"A million miles from the United States and my kid wants pizza."

Vivi laughs, and Max thinks: I want to make her laugh like that.

"Come on," he says. "I know the best *souvlaki* place. You'll never want pizza again."

Melissa looks dubious. "I'll always want pizza."

Max turns up one of the side streets. "If I'm wrong, I'll buy you a pizza."

"Promise?"

"Promise."

"Is this one of those real promises, or a fake one like Mom and Dad's wedding vows?"

"Melissa!"

A quick glance at Vivi then away again. Long enough to see she's dying for the sidewalk to swallow her whole.

"I really promise," he says.

It's not the fanciest eatery in town. The paint is stained from decades of smoke and spitting oil, and it's standing room only. Most nights the bodies are five, six deep. Tonight it's only three, but it's still early. The grill is working hard, sizzling impaled chunks of lamb. One by one, the owner slides the meat into pita bread, and then dumps onions, tomatoes, and *tzatziki* on top. He wraps the whole thing in paper, and that's your cue to get out.

Max pays for three. Two minutes later, they're standing outside, shoveling hot *souvlaki* into their mouths.

Melissa, the hard sell, is groaning. "This is so good," she says. "But I still love pizza."

Vivi taps her on the shoulder. "Don't talk with your mouth full."

She looks at Max. "But she's right, it's one of the best things I've ever put in my mouth."

He doesn't want to do it (yes, he does), but he looks at her mouth. She's not trying to be provocative, but it happens anyway when her tongue flicks out to catch a drop of the yogurt sauce.

Brakes screech in his head. He looks away.

"You okay?" Vivi asks.

"Long day. I haven't eaten since last night."

"You'd think a doctor would know better."

He laughs. "We don't have time to be healthy. My mother is always pushing me to eat more, but time . . ."

"Not nearly enough of that in a day. I haven't stopped since we got here, and now we have the house. I need to find a job."

"What did you do before this?"

"Housewife, mother, slave. I have an MBA, but Melissa's father wanted me at home."

"Mom, don't say that. Say you're a domestic engineer."

Max hides his smile behind the *souvlaki*. The kid is something else. Fire in her belly.

"If you could choose anything, what would you do?"

"Maybe I'll grow fruit and pick olives. I have more trees than I know what to do with."

Melissa scrunches the empty paper, tosses it into the trash. "Could you two be any more boring? Don't answer that – you might bore me to death. Mom, can I go check out the playground? The one next to the church?"

"Aren't you too old for swings?"

"You're never too old for swings," Max says.

Vivi looks at him. "Is it safe, do you think?"

"You won't find many places safer."

"Okay," she says. "Go, but be back in thirty minutes."

Melissa grins. "Why don't you guys come and find me when you're finished discussing career choices?"

Awkward age. Child one minute, woman the next.

"We can walk down and meet her," he says.

He watches her weigh the situation. She's beautiful when she laughs, beautiful when she's concentrating.

"Thirty minutes. We'll be there. No monkey business, and stay away from boys."

Melissa sighs like it's killing her.

"God help me," Vivi says, when Melissa is out of earshot.

"She's all Greek. How is she?"

"Truthfully? I don't know. It's a lame answer but it's the truth. Once minute she's sweet and the next she's a spitting cobra. Who knows what's going on inside her head?"

"That's teenagers for you: stable as the Ring of Fire."

Vivi takes his paper, drops it in the trash with hers.

"At this rate I'm going to wind up modeling straitjackets in the psych ward."

"Has Dr Triantafillou been helpful?"

Vivi takes off. He falls into step beside her.

"Melissa doesn't want to see her."

"What's the problem?"

"She kept interrogating Mel, asking if I had a drinking problem. Mel said the doctor insinuated she's in denial."

Not always a smart man, Max. Pushes when the warning light flashes orange, orange, orange.

"In my experience, children try and protect their parents when they're in an abusive situation. They might have shitty parents, but they're their shitty parents."

"Are you saying she's right?"

Red alert.

Doesn't stop him.

"No, I'm saying we see it all the time, so we have to consider the possibility that the parents are a problem. When you brought Melissa into the hospital, the nurse smelled alcohol on your breath. So I made a note of it. Just in case – for Melissa's own good."

It goes bad – it goes bad fast.

"You're the reason this shrunk is harassing my kid about the drinking problem I don't have?"

"I don't know what you want me to tell you. We do the same for everyone who comes in smelling like a *taverna*."

"Thank you for dinner, Doctor. Goodnight."

Now she's walking away, dress swirling above her knees. He likes the way she moves when she's angry, a summer storm in progress.

He laughs, throws his head back and roars.

"What's so funny?"

"You," he says. "You should see yourself."

"I don't want to be rude, but go fuck yourself."

"Vivi, wait. I didn't know then that we'd be . . ."

She turns around. "That we'd be what?"

"Friends. As your friend, I'm sorry. But I won't apologize for following hospital protocol. Let me help you find someone else for Melissa. Someone outside the hospital."

"I can find someone myself."

"Vivi, come on. My intentions were honorable."

She thaws, but not much. "I don't know."

"Please, consider it," he says softly, reaching for her fingers.

Potential crackles in the night air.

"Max! What are you doing here?"

Shit. It's Mama's oldest, dearest friend, Maria. She's wearing a smile but it's much too bright to be real. He can almost hear her twisting the situation into something the grapevine will love.

"*Kalispera, Thea* Maria." He kisses both cheeks. She doesn't stop gawking at Vivi.

"Who is this?"

"This is Vivi Tyler. Her daughter is my patient."

The wily old woman weighs, measures each word, calculates the value of each. "From the way you two were arguing, a person would think you were having a lovers' quarrel. Is your mother well, Max?"

Like she doesn't know; they see each other every day.

He expects a phone call in ten . . . nine . . . eight . . .

"Last time I spoke to her, both faces were fine," he says. "Goodnight, *Thea* Maria. Vivi, let's go find your daughter."

He doesn't touch her – doesn't dare. The fallout is going to be nuclear. Greece's eyes are as big as its mouth.

51

MELISSA

Y EAH, YEAH, SHE'S TOO old for the swings, but swinging feels
good. She's loose and happy and far, far away from here. Somewhere better, like Disney World. Or a desert island.

"What's your name?"

Her feet hit concrete. The swing jerks to a stop. There's a girl
about her age straddling the other swing. She's snapping gum and her
hair is plum. And – of course – she's wearing shitloads more makeup
than Melissa.

It's not fair.

Mom would flip if she wore that much makeup.

"Who wants to know?" Melissa asks.

The girl pops a sticky bubble. "Olivia."

"Melissa Tyler. You don't sound Greek."

"Canadian."

"Cool. American."

"Cool." Olivia nods at her wrist. "What happened? Your wrist looks
all weird, like the time I fell off the roof and broke my ulna. It hurt like
a fucking bitch."

Mom is going to hate her.

"It's nothing. Just a cut."

They both start swinging. "Are you in school?"

"Not yet," Melissa says. "Are you?"

"Negative. Do you have a boyfriend? Mine is pretty hot, but he only calls when he wants a blowjob. It sucks. I'm dumping him tomorrow."

Melissa can feel herself going all red. "We only just got here but I guess I'll be going to school in the fall."

"So that's a "No" on the boyfriend then?"

"Nope."

"Shit. We need to find us a couple so we can double date. What do you like? Blond? Tall? Older men? You don't want to go younger, trust me."

"Why not?"

"Because you want someone experienced, not a little boy."

Melissa's suddenly full up with hot and cold butterflies. She's a virgin, and it's been forever since she kissed anyone. Not since Matt Riley took her behind the garden shed at his fourteenth birthday party.

"But not too old," Olivia continues. "Anything past twenty is way geriatric. I'd be surprised if a guy could even get it up without porn and a fistful of Viagra after twenty-one. Although, I suppose we had to come from somewhere, right? I mean it's not like our parents were teenagers when they did it with each other."

Melissa can't help thinking about her folks. They weren't much older when she was born. "My parents are separated. What about yours?"

Olivia shrugs, the tops of her shoes grazing the concrete as she slows the swing.

"Sure, I mean they live together. But you should hear them fight. We've been here for three months and they argue every single night. Dad yells, Mom screams. Dad walks out, and Mom goes to sleep crying. By the time I go down for breakfast they're pretending it never happened. I wish they'd just be honest and admit they're screwing other people."

"My dad was screwing someone else."

"Did you ever see her?"

"Him. Yeah."

Olivia whistles. "Wow, your dad was screwing another man?"

"Yeah." It's weird the way she's almost proud of having something scandalous to share.

"Is he gay?"

"Duh, he had sex with a man. That totally means he's gay."

"Maybe he's bi. Lots of people are."

Going both ways seems to be trendy, these days. Girls kissing girls to get a guy's interest. Yeah, there are the kids who genuinely want both, but in high school they're overshadowed by the girls who like putting on a show.

"I think my dad's totally gay. I mean he left us to go and live with his boyfriend."

"That's kind of cool."

Not cool at all, but Melissa shrugs like it's no big deal. "It's okay. I mean it's not like we go shopping and try on shoes together. And his boyfriend's not a designer or anything awesome. He's just an accountant." She leaves out the part where she hates Ian's guts and wants to see him hit by a semi-trailer.

"So your old man's queer, no big deal. No one's going to care." Smile like a predator. Two rows of too-white teeth and pointy canines. All the better to eat you with. "So, Tyler – that's what I'm going to call you – did you cut that wrist yourself or was it an accident?"

Melissa tries to look mysterious. "I'll never tell."

"You're a whack job," Olivia announces. 'We're going to have the best summer."

Yeah, best summer ever.

52

MAX

O N THE WALK HOME, things get better. The conversation flows easy again, and by the time they get back to the house, Vivi is laughing.

Then she says, "Did I leave the inside lights on?"

"No. Just the porch light."

"Someone's inside my house."

"Family, maybe?"

Vivi shakes her head. "No one else has a key."

Melissa has been dawdling all this time, but now she runs to catch up. She's slightly out of breath when she asks, "What's going on?"

"Stay there," he tells them.

Biff's motor mouth starts up, but it's coming from behind the house. The dog was inside when they left.

Vivi rattles the keys. Max shakes his head when the door swings open under the weight of his palm. He knows she locked the door. Saw it himself.

A helmet-haired bird in a navy pantsuit leaps through the opening, almost bowls him off the porch.

"Vivi," the bird squawks, "how many times do I have to tell you not to leave a key in the flowerpot?"

He doesn't see it, but he feels it: Vivi pulling herself tall and taut, ready to shoot an arrow.

"The power of Christ compels you," she says.

The bird reaches past him, slaps Vivi's head.

53

VIVI

ELISSA FIRES HERSELF AT Eleni. "Hey Grams, I didn't know you were coming!"

"There's no key in the flower pot," Vivi says.

"You did not lock the door."

"I locked the door." She looks at Max. "I locked the door."

"You locked the door," he confirms.

Eleni peers down her nose at him. "Why should I believe you?"

Max says to Vivi: "You're right, we're related."

Eleni and Melissa are a tangle of hugs and kisses, but Eleni's eyes are stuck to Max's face. He's a tongue and she's ice. She's Greenland in winter cold. "Who are you?"

Max holds out his hand. "Max Andreou. Melissa's pediatrician."

Eleni beams at Melissa. "Are you okay, my beautiful girl? You look fine to me. What does she need a doctor for?"

"It's nothing, Mom," Vivi says.

"It is something or she would not need a doctor. Darling," she says, clutching at the pearls she isn't wearing. She grabs Melissa's arm with the hand that isn't busy acting in a melodrama. "What happened to you?"

Melissa manages to unravel herself. "It's nothing. I'm fine. Mom, can I go to my room?"

"Sure, Honey. And take Biff with you."

Biff? Where is Biff?

Good question.

"Where's my dog?"

"What dog?"

"My dog. The one that was in here when we left."

"Oh," Eleni says. "I tied him up outside. Tomorrow I will call the dog catcher."

"Mel," Vivi says. "Bring Biff in, please. And ignore your grandmother." She swings back around to the woman who brought her into this world. ("Three days of labor, and still you did not want to come out. The house was a mess when I got home.") "My house, my rules."

"Dogs spread disease."

"Not true," Max starts. "There's a great deal of research that suggests pets boost immunity. They also help lower blood – "

"Silence," Eleni barks. "Are you putting your penis in my daughter?"

Vivi wants a quick death, an instant death; is that too much to ask? And poor Max, he's standing there –

Laughing?

"What's so funny?" Eleni wants to know.

"Nothing." The laughing doesn't stop.

"It is not nothing or you would not be laughing – unless you are crazy," Eleni says. "Vivi, why do you keep company with crazy people? Have I taught you nothing?"

Vivi is stiff and sore from the toilet debacle, but there's some strength to spare. She hoists her mother's two suitcases, dumps them out on the porch. "You can't come into my home, insult my friends, and change my rules. The dog stays, you go. That's how it is."

Max winds down. "I should go."

"Good idea," Eleni says. "Best idea you ever had."

"You stay," Vivi tells Max. "And you," she tells Eleni, "I'll drive you over to stay with *Thea* Dora. Max, would you mind staying with Melissa for a few minutes?"

He nods and Vivi turns back to her mother.

"Mom . . ."

Eleni starfishes the door. "Don't you want to know why I am here?"

"Not tonight, Mom. I'm too pissed off to care right now."

"Please."

This from a woman who hurls words like a teppanyaki chef hurls food?

"Mom . . ." She can't do it, can't toss her mother out into the warm spring night. "One night. Tomorrow you go to *Thea*'s."

"Good. This place smells strange. It smells like . . ."

"Mom. Enough."

"I left your father."

The bottom falls out of the world. It's been doing that a lot lately. But this is like finding out Santa's a big, fat, red and white lie.

"Shit," she says, and Eleni says, "Don't swear," and Vivi says, "Do you want to talk?"

"I'm tired. Tomorrow we talk."

Vivi gets her settled in.

Max stays.

———

Not a featherweight, that one. He could have blown away, but here he is.

He stays after she tucks Melissa into bed, Biff playing second blanket on her feet. He stays after she calms her mother and settles her into the spare bedroom. They go outside and he stays while she curses God, men, and her mother.

He doesn't interrupt, except to pass her more coffee.

"Our mothers bring us into this world, then they think up ways to torture us," he says, during the third cup.

The coffee is hot, sweet, spicy.

Like Max.

"Cynical. I like to think I'm making Mel's life better. Not doing a good job, am I?" His mouth opens. "Wait, don't answer that."

"Don't judge yourself so harshly. Children will grow up and become who they want to be and do what they want to do."

"Like us?"

He laughs. "I was thinking of Kostas. For me, there is no hope. For you . . . maybe. It depends."

"On what?"

He leaned closer, across the chair's slender arm. "On whether you kill your mother and bury her where no one will find the body."

She laughs till it hurts.

They sit there together, two people worn down by family, each with their own set of secrets. The air is thick with all the things that have gone unspoken, and will remain unspoken.

"I could grow old right here in this place." He sighs as though he's trying to lift the world with that one breath. "Vivi, I told you my mother has expectations – for me, for our family."

The bottom is about to drop out of the world again, isn't it?

"You did."

"It's very important to her that I marry – and soon. I was taking too long, so she chose my fiancée for me."

"Ah, the good old Greek arranged marriage. That's before our time, isn't it?"

"It still happens – between some families."

"Do you love her?" Vivi asks, mouth packed with cotton. "Your fiancée, I mean."

"Does it matter?"

"Don't ask me, ask yourself. I'm not the one marrying her."

"I've never stayed with a woman for long. I've never loved any woman enough to get married. So, my mother chose a good friend's daughter. She says grandchildren are long overdue and that my father's name will die if I don't have sons. No, I don't love her – yet. But you must understand, promises were made before I met you."

"Why are you telling me this?" But she knows why – she *knows*.

His hand curls around hers. Heat seeps through her skin, into her bones; his thumb slowly rubs her palm. It is hypnotizing, erotic.

Vivi clears her throat, crosses her legs, trying to deflect the sudden fire.

He doesn't pull away.

"Because if the world was a different place, I could – would – fall in love with you."

Her cheeks burn in the dark.

"But," he says slowly, "the world is how it is."

"Lucky for us we're just friends."

She lets her hand fall away. Something has been lost – there's no picking it up.

They sit that way until the stars tire of watching and move to another part of the world, to observe other people who are lucky not to be in love with one another.

✴ 54 ✴

VIVI

THE VOICE IN HER head screams for blood.

Except it's not in her head, is it?

Vivi bolts out of bed.

She's still in the dress she wore last night. Everything comes back. Her mother is here (shit). Max is not. After he left, Vivi passed out without bothering to change.

No time to change now, either. She throws open the spare room's door. Her mother is in bed, sheets hoisted around her neck.

"Get it away from me," she howls. "It is going to bite my face off."

Vivi looks. She laughs. She can't help it.

"It is not funny," Eleni screeches.

Not funny – hilarious.

Eleni has company. Last night Vivi opened the windows and shutters to let the cool air in, never thinking to close them again before bedtime. Sometime between then and now, a plump turkey found himself a room for the night.

Gobble gobble.

The flabby red wattle below his chin quivers. He pecks at the sheet.

Her mother screams. Eleni Pappas downsized by a turkey – who'd have thought it?

The turkey doesn't give a damn – he's attracted to the screaming. He hops up on the bed, settles on her chest.

Gobble gobble.

"Aww, he wants a kiss," Vivi says, almost choking on the laughter.

Gobble gobble. The turkey's head bobs.

"It is going to peck my eyes out!"

"If you're that worried, close them. I'll get Biff."

Biff isn't in any hurry to leave Melissa's room. Probably thinks Eleni deserves it for tying him up outside. Vivi doesn't say it, but he's right. He pads into Eleni's room, drops his butt on the floor. Does nothing except watch the turkey get comfortable.

Vivi points at the turkey. "Go get him, Tiger."

Biff doesn't get him. Biff sat, and now Biff stays.

So it's up to Vivi to play the hero.

"Fine," she says. "I'll wrestle the turkey. You both suck, by the way."

She pulls an old T-shirt out of the cupboard – one of John's that somehow got mixed up with hers. It makes a decent matador's cape.

"Come on, turkey. Let's do this."

She throws the shirt, but that turkey is faster. He has wings and she has thumbs and a full bladder. But it's all good, the turkey has himself a new perch now: Eleni's head.

Vivi doesn't die laughing, but close. This is one of those MasterCard moments. "Melissa," she calls out. "Get the camera."

"You do that," Eleni bellows, "and I will kill you!"

Melissa appears with the camera. The flash stuns them all for a moment. It's a 10.0 megapixel moment.

In the end, Melissa saves the day. The girl works magic with a whiskbroom, gently shooing the turkey out the front door.

Biff looks baffled by the whole ordeal, head cocked, blinking, wondering what kind of craziness he's been adopted into.

Vivi sits next to the big dog. "You'd have been all over it if he was sliced up on bread." They watch the turkey amble down the road. Periodically it stops to look back and gobble indignantly.

When Eleni reappears, she's wearing a fresh polyester ensemble.

Now Vivi's on inspection. "You are wearing the same clothes you had on last night," Eleni says.

"Maybe because all my clothes are in here and I didn't want to disturb you." Not a great answer, but it's the truth. "I'll move my stuff out today."

"No, it is okay." She puts on her best sad face, the one she wears when her husband forgets their anniversary or Valentine's Day. "You don't want me here. I will go and stay with Dora."

"Mom . . ."

"I know where I'm not wanted. My own daughter . . ." She mumbles something else, but the crunch of bicycle tires mutes her volume.

The bicycle stops right outside their gate. Its rider has burgundy hair, a sweet face, and a bikini straight out of a rap video.

"Mel!" the girl calls out, ignoring the fact that Vivi's sitting right there.

Biff barks, but he doesn't get up.

Out of the house runs Melissa, dressed for the beach. "That's Olivia, the girl from Canada," she says, in the slow, careful tone she uses for her parents and other idiots. "Can I go hang with her?"

Vivi thinks about saying "No." She wants Melissa close, safe. But here is safer — safer than where they used to be. And Melissa, her face is shining and smiling and hopeful. Vivi can't crush that with one sylla-ble; it makes her happy to see Melissa's sunny weather. So she says, "Yes" to the beach and saves the "No" for a more fitting occasion.

Melissa kisses Biff on the nose, and then she's gone. Vivi waves, but it's too late — the girls are lost in their own conversation, making secrets, forming conspiracies, the way girls do.

Behind her, Eleni is dragging both suitcases. They have wheels, but where's the drama in that?

"Why you let her go off that way?"

Vivi says, "Remember the conversation we had last night? My house. My kid. My rules."

"I will call a taxi."

And there goes Vivi's blood pressure, aiming for the sky.

"Mom, I said you could stay here."

"I changed my mind. I want to go."

"Pretty please with *baklava* on top?"

"No, no. I can tell when nobody wants me."

Okay, so Eleni knows how to push her buttons, but Vivi knows how to push Eleni's buttons, too. She punches the big red one labeled CO-DEPENDENCE.

"I could use your help."

It's magic, the way Eleni stops. "What kind of help?"

"I have to get a job, and I'll need help around the house. Maybe you can watch out for Melissa."

"Do I have to wash the dog?"

"No."

"Can I cook?"

"Sometimes."

"Okay," she says. "I will stay, but only because you are begging. Take these bags back inside for me. They are heavy."

———

"So what happened, Mom?"

Eleni's too busy frowning into the refrigerator to answer. So, Vivi attacks the subject from a different angle.

"Greek coffee or American? How about a *frappe?*"

"Greek," Eleni says. "Strong."

Greek coffee is always strong. It doesn't know how to be weak.

The recipe is easy.

One demitasse cup of water per person. Pour the water into a *briki* – that's a small pot with a long handle. Sit the *briki* over the gas flame and dump in one heaping teaspoon of Greek coffee per person, and two spoons of sugar to help this particular medicine go down. If you don't like your coffee sweet, leave out the sugar and . . .

Good luck.

It won't take long for the coffee to boil, the foam to rise. Nothing left to do at that point except pour and wait for the grounds to sink to the cup's bottom. Then sip – sip until you hit sludge.

Which is exactly what these two women do at Vivi's rough kitchen table, with its straw-seat chairs.

"I am glad to see you – "

"Bah! You have a strange way of showing it. But you never could express your emotions properly, so I do not take it personally."

" – but if you left Dad, why come here?"

"I wanted to visit my favorite daughter and granddaughter. To make their lives miserable, of course."

Fact: Eleni has one daughter, one granddaughter. But Vivi lets it slide.

"When did you leave?"

"Yesterday. But your father, he left me first." Eleni pokes holes in the air with her index finger.

Whoa! "Dad left, too? Where did he go?"

"Nowhere. He is still at the house. But he wants to leave. I can feel it in my marrow. He spends all his time out in the garage making things."

All Vivi's life, when Dad wasn't at work, he was in the garage building stuff. Sometimes he made chairs, sometimes clocks, sometimes dollhouses. Sometimes he would sit out there and look at the wood and build nothing.

So in a nutshell, this is nothing new.

But saying that isn't going to win any wars, and anyway, Biff's muttering at the front door.

"Somebody's here."

She wants it to be Max, but she knows it's not. He won't be back, she thinks. A repeat of last night is only going to lead to problems that can't be unraveled.

Staggering up to the house is *Thea* Dora, a sack of angry ground-hogs wobbling inside her dress. That much sweat, she could use an open fire hydrant.

"Vivi!" She waves. "Vivi!"

"*Thea*! What's wrong?"

"Nothing!" Her aunt crosses herself, heaves her bulk onto the porch. "I just saw Melissa. She tells me your mother is here! Where is

Eleni? Eleni, are you here?" She recoils at the sight of Biff, drinking out of her sweat pool. "Mother of Christ, is that creature still here?"

"Why didn't you drive?"

"I wanted to get here fast."

The door opens and out comes Eleni in her polyester separates.

"Hello, Sister. I am here."

Thea Dora leaps to her feet. "My God, Eleni! I thought I would never see you again! You have come home! When did you come? Why do you not come to see me, eh?"

"It was late. Too late to go visiting."

"Bah! You live in America too long! Here we are civilized. We have siesta, remember? No one goes to bed before ten. Come, let me kiss you."

The women hug. *Thea* Dora zeroes in on Vivi's feet.

"Vivi, my love, put some shoes on. Bare feet are for the poor."

"Bare feet are for the poor," Vivi mutters out of earshot.

Let the sisters have their reunion.

VIVI

NICE DAY FOR A walk.
So Vivi walks – shoes on.

Biff comes, too. He knows when (and where) he's not wanted.

She doesn't take the road. Today she wants the thrill of exploration, the unbeaten (to her) path. So she cuts through the fruit trees and segues into the olive jungle.

There's nothing friendly about an olive tree. They're all arthritic fingers and tough bark. And those not quite green, not quite silver leaves make her uneasy. Trees designed for Halloween.

Soon she can't see the house. She panics a bit, grabs onto a trunk while the odd feeling of vertigo or disassociation or whatever it is she's feeling passes. The bark is warm under her palm. Alive. Its cool aura is a trick.

Time stops, but the tree's pulse beats on.

The branches are heavy with green-skinned fruit. How long before they reach maturity and their skins blacken?

Vivi owns this land, but she knows nothing about it.

And it knows nothing about her.

56

MAX

MAX CAN COUNT THE number of times he's wallowed on one hand.

But today?

He's wallowing.

———

Mama calls . . .

And calls . . .

And calls.

Times ten.

When he answers, she goes Vesuvius. Max waits until she's done spewing, then he says, "You chose my wife, but I choose my friends."

"Friend? A man is a friend to another man. A woman is not a man's friend unless she is his wife. If she is not his wife, she is trouble."

"It's not 1950, Mama."

"Maximos – "

Goodbye.

❧ 57 ❧

VIVI

GREAT PLACE FOR AN ax murderer to hide. Or a chainsaw killer.
She's God knows how far from the house now. The ground
is so foreign, with its sticks and stones and pockmarked dirt. She's
creeping. Watching each step before she takes it.

Biff doesn't care. He's a dog. Here, there, all over the place.
Running, peeing, bounding back to Vivi's side as though they're
attached with elastic. He's soaking up everything with his nose. Can
hardly lift his head from the ground, he's so busy.

To her heathen nose it's all wood and dirt after a heavy downpour.
Which isn't bad.

Now there's a dull tinkling, the sound of imminent goats.

The trees break, revealing a chain link fence. It's playing nanny to a
several dozen goats.

The goats storm the fence. New faces, got to scope them out.

Beyond the goats, there's a cottage. It's hanging around, doing
nothing much, letting time have its own way. Grime on the windows,
dandruff flaking off the shutters, a roof that saw better days some
twenty, thirty years ago. Nearby is a shed. Nothing to it but corrugated
iron and a concrete slab.

There's a car, rusted old thing, doubling as a jungle gym for the goats. Two of them are standing on the roof, playing king of the world.

Vivi walks the length of the fence, looking for life signs. The house is a dump, but the goats are in excellent health, all of them clear-eyed and plump.

Someone cares.

She's being watched, and not just by the goats. Under a sprawling fig, a donkey is knocking blowflies out of the air with its tail. Two fingers to her lips, Vivi whistles.

Donkey doesn't care – she's not hay.

Metal creaks and groans. A leather face and one of those giant handlebar mustaches rounds the corner of the shed.

"Take your gypsy curses somewhere else." The old man sounds like a handful of gravel tossed on broken glass.

Hey now, her outfit is colorful, but it's far from the latest in Romani fashions.

"I'm Vivi Tyler, your neighbor." She points in what she hopes is the direction of her house.

His head vanishes. Bye-bye.

Not for long. The shed door bangs open and the old guy steps out.

He stands around watching for a moment, while his thick, calloused fingers roll a cigarette. He takes a long, medicinal puff, then ambles over to where she's standing.

"So you're the *xena*."

She's getting used to the foreigner label.

"Yes, but my family is from here."

He takes his sweet time nodding. "I know who your family is." Then it's back to the shed, coughing up a lung as he goes. "I am Takis. Come, I'll show you something. Gate's over there."

She really hopes show-and-tell doesn't involve his privates.

"Can my dog come too? He won't hurt your goats."

Biff is licking a goat through the fence.

Takis nods. "Goats can take care of themselves," he says. "They might eat the collar off his neck if he sits long enough."

"I can always buy another one."

His face splits in two. Lungs rattle like the reaper's shaking him down for loose change. "You say that now. Come, we don't want the milk to burn."

Milk?

Greece is weird, but she's intrigued.

She lets herself through the gate – Biff, too. The dog karate chops the air with his tail, then gets busy doing dog stuff. You know, the usual: peeing on inanimate objects.

Inside the metal shed, Takis is busy stirring a vat of milk. The whole thing is sitting atop a gas burner.

"Goat's milk?" she asks.

Takis shoves a chair at her. "Half goat, half sheep. I know a man with sheep, and he knows a man with goats. Sit." He reaches down, throttles the gas flow to candle-sized flames. Then he hands her the long end of a long, long spoon. "My goats make the best feta in all of Greece. Stir. Slow."

She stirs. One tiny scorch will ruin the whole batch if she doesn't stir from the bottom.

Takis leaves. Probably to get the chainsaw to cut off her head.

Vivi keeps on stirring. Feels good to do and not think.

And he's back, carrying a thick slab of white cheese on a bread chunk.

Maybe the chainsaw is hidden in the cheese.

One hand snatches the spoon, the other thrusts bread and cheese under her nose.

"Eat. Tell me what you think."

So she eats. Like all good feta, this one has teeth. Sharp, deliciously salty, but with a definite – and unexpected – creaminess.

She meets his expectant gaze and tells the truth. "You're right, it's the best."

"Of course it's the best! You think I lie to you?" He flicks the gas off, sits back in his own chair, legs crossed, foot swinging.

"What happens to the milk now?"

"We wait."

The bread and cheese vanish. Vivi is almost ashamed of her magic trick, but she was starving.

"Good, eh? Some people they buy only the expensive foods. Bah!

This is the best meal in the world. Maybe throw in some olives, and a piece of fruit, and you can eat like a king."

Speaking of olives, some of these trees have to be his. She has no real idea where her property ends and Takis' starts.

"Do you make your own olives, too?"

Rattle, rattle, cough. "Trees make the olives. Don't they teach you anything in your American schools?"

"Do you brine your own olives?"

"Bah! I am old now. Too much work."

An idea happens. Maybe not a great idea, but it's an idea. She has land; she has olives she can't leave to rot on the trees. And she can't spend her days dodging relatives, hoping Max will call.

"Will you teach me?"

All he does is grunt and reach for a plaid thermos. Once again he shoves the spoon at her. He pours slowly and she stirs slowly.

"This makes the milk curdle. I make it myself from nettles."

"Stinging nettles?"

"They don't sting if you don't touch with your bare hands, eh? If you boil the juice out of them they make good rennet. Cheap too." He winks at her. "Tell me, *Xena*, why did you come to Greece? What is here that you could not find in your old home?"

"Peace. Myself. Family. A new beginning. Third-degree sunburn."

"You could not find yourself in America? Maybe not. All those people, it's a wonder any of them can find themselves."

"Maybe," she says. "I needed a change of scenery."

"Bah, what you see can change, but how you feel doesn't change unless you change it. You can't run away from yourself. You know, *Xena*, what it takes to grow olives?"

"Good fertilizer and lots of water?"

He waves a dismissive hand. "Fertilizer makes the olives weak." Now he shows her a fist. "You need rocks and soil to make them strong. They pull their strength from the hard ground. You can't be weak if you want to grow olives. You must commit to them, the way you do a marriage."

He stops for a moment to pour a heart attack's worth of salt into the vat.

"Are you saying I'm not strong enough to grow olives?"

"How do I know what you are? All I see is a very pretty woman who maybe ran away from something difficult. What do I know?"

Anger crashes around inside her head, stomping the furniture, punching walls. She's not some wayward child, pissed at her parents.

And it must show, because:

"You don't agree with me," he says, smiling beneath the bushy mustache.

"I think you're over-simplifying the situation."

Silence while he unfolds a large cloth square, covers the milk. Says, "We must wait again."

"How long?"

"Half a day, maybe longer."

"So slow?"

"If I put more nettle in it will go faster, but I like to do it slow."

He opens the door, pushes her out.

"Come back tomorrow and I will let you drain the curd for me."

———

Twenty minutes later, Vivi and Biff pop out of the grove almost exactly where they entered.

Are her survivals skills good or what?

The two sisters are still talking, only now there's a mountain of food in the kitchen, all of it sugar-based.

Vivi knows good *baklava* when she sees it. She grabs a plate and –

"Where have you been?" Eleni asks.

Her aunt says, "Who did you see?"

Okay, so she's a teenager all over again. Does Melissa find her this annoying?

She gives them the Cliff's notes, and her aunt says, "You cannot grow olives. This is a man's work."

"That is the bull's shit," Eleni says, punctuating the air with a wooden spoon. "My daughter can do anything she chooses!"

❧ 58 ☙

MELISSA

OLIVIA SMACKS THE WATER. "Come on, Tyler. You know you want to."

She's right, Melissa wants to. But the water is a murky green. Anything could be in there, waiting to bite off her legs. Or her arms.

"Chicken," Olivia says.

"Am not."

"So jump already."

Melissa holds her breath, leans forward. Gravity does the rest. It drags her, stomach first, into the sea.

And now her belly is on fire and she can't. seem. to. breathe. Her oxygen is gone and there's no refill handy.

But it doesn't kill her – not even close.

Feet peddling the water, she slowly spins around in time to see Olivia hoisting herself onto the dock.

"That was a crappy dive, but at least you had balls enough to jump in."

And she's flying again, more graceful in her tiny red bikini than Melissa will ever be.

The boys are impressed, too.

Melissa's pretending not to notice, but four of them are lined up further along the pier, watching. Every so often they jostle each other and laugh, but they never take their eyes off the girls.

"It's fun – right?" Olivia asks breathlessly.

"It's a rush!"

They do it over and over, diving, swimming for a bit, diving again. It's not so bad after the first time, after Melissa perfects her descent.

The boys keep watching. They move to the edge of the pier, where the girls' clothes are folded in neat piles. They're all super tan with messy hair and white teeth. Melissa feels full up with bubbles instead of blood.

"Which one do you like the best?" Olivia doesn't whisper. "And don't pretend you haven't noticed them. They're practically drooling on us. I bet they've all got hard-ons under those baggy shorts."

"Shh! Don't say that, they might hear us."

"So what if they do? We've got what they want. We're the ones with the power." She swims over to the side of the pier. "Aren't you guys going to swim today? You should. It's hot, and my friend and me could use the company. I mean what if a shark bites us? We could drown."

"Then you should learn to swim faster," the brown-haired boy says. They all laugh.

"Are you American?" another boy asks. He has dark, nearly black hair. He's cute, but not nearly as hot as the blond boy in the blue shorts.

"Canadian." Olivia hooks a thumb at Melissa. "Melissa is American."

"*Me-lee-ssa*. Do you taste like honey, Melissa?" he calls out.

She's not exactly sure what he means, but her skin does. It spontaneously combusts and she goes neon.

"Melissa's shy," Olivia tells them. Melissa wants to tell her to shut up, but she doesn't want to lose the only friend she's made so far.

Black hair jumps up. He points to himself first, then the others. "Kristos, Apistole, Vassili, and the loser on the end is Thanasi."

Thanasi. The blond one.

He locks eyes with Melissa and smiles, and she glances away quickly because she's a humungous wimp. She swims in the opposite direction, treading water near an orange buoy. Looking at him makes her feel too much of everything.

The boys dive bomb the water, legs pulled tight against their chests.

"Catch me if you can," Olivia shouts, her arms cutting a smooth freestyle in the water. Not only is she bossy, she's hogging all the guys for herself.

Melissa doesn't love it. Olivia is a flirt and she's a shy, nerdy loser. No one is going to like her – ever. She's a dropout from an 80's teen flick. And she can't seem to let go of the buoy.

Some primal instinct kicks in and she goes still. Thanasi has broken off from the group and he's swimming her way. If she doesn't move he won't see her.

She wants/doesn't want the attention.

Thanasi moves like he's boss. Long, easy strokes, commanding the water to get lost.

Melissa Tyler will go down in history as the biggest failure with guys ever. People are going to point and laugh in the streets.

Don't be so lame, Tyler. What Would Olivia Do? Be flirty, of course.

"Hi," Thanasi says, in thick English. His hand brushes against hers as he reaches for the buoy.

She says, "It's easier to float here."

Is her dialogue killer, or what?

Thanasi doesn't look fazed. Total opposite of that. He's checking her out – up down, up down – painting her with his gaze. "You look sad over here."

"I'm not sad."

He looks back over his shoulder at the others. They're splashing around a shrieking, giggling Olivia. And she's not envious – nope, not at all.

"I can go if you like."

"No," she says quickly, in her crappy Greek. "Stay."

Thanasi smiles.

She smiles.

He's a honey with his messy boy-band hair. The guys at her old school never looked this good. The few hot ones were real dicks that preferred cheerleaders to girls like Melissa. Like . . . oh, Josh Cartwright.

"Your Greek is very good."

"My grandparents, they made my parents send me to Greek school. I haven't been since I was twelve. It was embarrassing."

"Why?"

She doesn't want to explain, but he seems interested and she really wants to keep talking to him. "It made me different."

"And this is bad?"

"In America? Yeah, if you're a teenager."

It's not the real reason she's unpopular, but it's not exactly a brilliant idea to tell the hottest guy ever that she was considered a total dork that would rather read than go to parties and make out.

Okay, so maybe she does want to make out – sometimes.

"No boyfriends then?" His smile never quits.

"Some." Liar, liar.

His smile goes supernova. "I like you. You have a very beautiful face." His leg touches hers in the water, now she's burning up. But she doesn't pull away, does she?

"You're beautiful too," she blurts. Recovery is a hasty: "I mean, what grade are you in?"

"Eleventh grade this year. What grade will you be in?"

"How do you know that I'm not already in school here?"

"Because if I'd seen you before, I would have remembered you."

"Ten," she says quickly. Gaze slides to her watch. It's nearly noon and she promised Mom she'd be home for lunch, didn't she? "I have to go."

"But we just met. Stay."

God, the boys are so smooth here. So much smoother than at home. Satin. Silk. Marble cool. She's way out of her league, but Thanasi is talking to her and smiling at her and she really wants him to never stop.

"We can meet again," she says. "Me and Olivia come here practically every day."

Not true, but so what?

(Tyler, Tyler, how very Olivia of you.)

"You want to come and watch us play football?"

"When?"

"Tomorrow afternoon up at the fields. Your friend will know where."

Olivia gives her a thumbs up.

"Sure," Melissa says, with some other girl's voice. "We'll be there."

———

"Friends are good for the soul," Dr Triantafillou says. "It's great you're making some. Healthy."

Melissa says, "I guess. Do you have lots of friends?"

"Not as many as when I was younger. But enough, yes."

"What happened to them?"

The shrink taps a pen on her knee. Jeans again, and those wedges Melissa likes. They're sitting in a sunbeam on the hospital's third floor. Big sunbeam, spilling all over the shrink's office. Melissa didn't picture it this way. She imagined the room stuffed with generic furniture and a fake leather couch. Surprise, surprise: no couch. And the chairs are super-comfortable. Definitely not hospital issue.

"Life. As you get older, you change, you grow, you get busy, they get busy. Tell me about Olivia."

"What's to tell? She's a girl, that's all."

"Do you like her?"

"She's my friend."

Smile, smile. "That's not always the same thing."

"I guess I do. She's kind of . . . Is it okay if I stand up?"

"Of course. You're not a prisoner."

Melissa goes to the window. It's big – floor to ceiling. Hence all the sunlight. Not high enough to transform people into ants, but they're definitely doll-like. People coming, people going, people grinding the hot end of cigarettes into the concrete. Gypsies –

– Romani. Mom will kick her ass if she hears her call them gypsies

–

– scattered all over the place, like the hospital is their watering hole.

"Olivia is okay. She's not a bad person – she's just kind of an asshole sometimes. Is it okay if I say 'asshole'?"

"If that's the word you mean to use, sure."

Melissa nods. "She's kind of an asshole. But not all the time. Just sometimes. I haven't decided if she's a nice person with a shitty – can I say shit?"

"You can say anything here, Melissa."

How cool is that?

Mom wanted her to switch shrinks after the drinking thing. But Melissa told her if she had to see a shrink, she wanted Dr Triantafillou. Mom shrugged and said, "If you're cool with that, I guess I am, too."

And now here she is.

Olivia doesn't know. Melissa isn't sure she can be trusted. Could be she's one of those people who bottles up secrets, saving them until she can spray them over a crowd and look cooler, bigger.

"I don't know if she's a nice person with a shitty shell, or a shitty person with a candy shell. Does that make sense?"

"Yes. I know people like that."

"I'm waiting to see what she's really like, I guess."

"That's very mature. What about this boy?"

"He's just a boy."

Casual shrug to a casual observer.

Dr Triantafillou is anything but casual.

𝕩 59 𝕩

MAX

MAMA IS LIKE GOD: her eyes are everywhere.

Back in the old days (cold days?) in England, he would jerk off in the dark under the bed covers so the fly on his wall wouldn't see and report back to its Greek commander. So he's not surprised when she calls again. Took her a while; gossip train must be malfunctioning, unloading the details one car at a time.

"This woman is a *xena?*" Like the word is shit-dipped.

He counts to five. "She's a friend. Her daughter was my patient. And she's not a foreigner, her parents are from here – which makes her as Greek as you."

"She's an American! A whore! A married woman who leaves her husband to cavort with my son! Anastasia will not marry you when she hears of this, the poor girl.

"Mama, you're overreacting." That's new, isn't it? "She's alone in this country with a sick child. You raised me to help people and now you complain when I do?"

"I raised you to heal people, not take them out for dinner and walk arm-in-arm on the promenade! What is wrong with you, Max? What would your father say? This must stop. You and Anastasia must

234

announce your engagement formally and set a wedding date. And you must never see that woman again."

He makes a fist.

Why the hell can't he stand up to one sixty-year-old woman?

She wants him to be a boy, not a man. But this man makes his decisions. He conquered university. He survived the brutal residency.

He put in the hours.

"No. This is my life, Mama."

"Yes, Max. This is the way it will be. You will bring dishonor on this family – on me – if you keep seeing this whore. And if you don't marry Anastasia . . . Oh, the shame, after I made a promise to her mother! It will be the end of me. No beautiful grandchildren to show people. Who will carry on your father's name? Kostas? He is not a man. He is little more than a eunuch! That thing lies useless between his legs."

"Mama, enough! Kostas is still your son and my brother. You will not insult him again or you will lose another son! Then you will be a woman with no sons and no grandchildren."

End Call.

He stalks toward the cafeteria, veins throbbing.

A small boy is walking the halls with his mother. She's wheeling the IV stand while he shuffles. The little guy waves, smiles.

Max stops to say hello. He pockets his anger with the phone. This isn't the time, isn't the place.

❧ 60 ❧

VIVI

ANOTHER DAY, ANOTHER WHIRLWIND.

Vivi wants to sleep, but Dora is dragging them all over town, visiting family, showing off Eleni. She won't shut up about how good Eleni looks with her dyed hair and Jane Fonda waistline.

Her mother looks like she'd rather be hanged. But she's enthusiastic enough – eager to catch up on years of gossip, maybe knife a few backs while she's at it.

The family wants to know everything about life in America. (How much is this? How much is that? How much does a house cost? Can you buy Greek food there?)

Beautiful afternoon under the trellis at cousin Effie's house. Ice cold *frappe*, sweet and sour preserved cherries for dessert. Can't complain. Every Greek home seems to have one room set aside for company. It's always done up with fancy linens and too many shiny things. But not Effie's house. If she has a room like that, they're not allowed in.

Keeping the riffraff out.

"How was your flight, *Thea* Eleni? I hope you weren't too frightened on the plane," Effie asks. As usual, she slapped on her makeup with a bucket and trowel. Looks like she's auditioning for The Cure with that lipstick.

"It was good. Comfortable. The food is another matter. All that money I pay and what do they give me to eat? Cardboard. Whoever is responsible for the food . . . their mother should spank them."

"Did you take off your clothes?"

Eleni blinks. "For who?"

"The security," Effie says. "That is what they say on the news: that people in America are strip searched before they get on the plane, that everyone is guilty of some crime until they prove otherwise."

"That is not true," Eleni says.

"And they look in your ass for drugs and bombs." (Vivi doesn't dare make eye contact with her mother; she'll lose it if she does.) "I saw this on the TV so it must be true." She looks around and everyone else makes agreeable noises. "They do not lie on the news."

Vivi can't help herself. "They only strip search people who ask stupid questions."

But it's lost on Effie, who continues her interrogation in some weird game of one-upmanship only she understands.

"Why would they say it on the news if it is not true?"

"Television always lies," Eleni says. "Anything to get higher ratings."

Vivi nods. "Reality TV."

"I couldn't fly." Effie is on a roll. Good thing she's the perfect shape for it. "Planes are so small. How can people survive for so many hours in such a small space with no fresh air? I do not understand."

"They're not at that small," Vivi tells her. "In fact, a lot of them are huge. Imagine about fifty people lying end to end in the street here. That's about how long a 747 is."

"I do not believe it. Something that large cannot fly! How does it get off the ground?"

"A 747 is seventy-six meters long, so believe it. Google it, for crying out loud!"

"Now here is some good news!" *Thea* Dora comes to the rescue. "Vivi is going to start her own business!"

Yeah, not a rescue. More like tossing a honey-coated Vivi into a bear pit.

Effie goggles. "Why would you want to do that?"

"There's this really neat invention called money," Vivi says casually. "You can buy stuff with it. Been around for centuries."

"So get a job or get married like other women," Effie says.

Because that worked out well for Vivi, didn't it? "Thanks but no thanks. I like the idea of being my own boss. Flexible hours, and I can choose who I want to work with."

"You can't do this. What will people say?"

"Why would they say anything? Lots of women all over the world run their own businesses every bit as well as men," Vivi says.

"Maybe in the rest of the world, maybe even outside Agria, but here it is different. Here women get married and raise families. That is a woman's work," Effie insists.

Vivi feels sorry for her, because Effie's got this desperate look in her eye, as though once upon a time, she had dreams but they turned to shit, and now here she is: a mother, a wife. Been nowhere, going nowhere.

"Look!" *Thea* Dora yelps, pointing at Vivi's cup. "You spilled the coffee in the saucer!"

"I'll clean it up," Vivi says. Eleni glares across the table at her. "Don't worry, I won't lick it."

"No, no, leave it," her aunt says. "It is a sign of good luck. It means that money will soon come to you." She waves her hands in a hurry up motion. "Finish it. I will read the grounds for you."

"Do not start with that hocus pocus, Dora," Eleni says, but she knocks back the last drop of her own coffee, swirls the grounds, upends the cup on its delicate saucer.

Thea Dora wags a finger at her. "Hocus pocus, eh? I remember one time many years ago when I read your grounds and warned you –"

"Enough, enough. Always with the talking," Eleni says. "Go on, read her grounds and make up something good, eh?"

"Bah! I make up nothing. The grounds tell the truth. Vivi, my love, swirl the cup, turn it three times counter-clockwise, and place it upside down on the saucer."

She swirls, she dumps. "What now?"

"We wait for a few minutes for the grounds to harden. Eleni, give me your cup."

Eleni slides the demitasse her way, taking care not to break the seal between cup and saucer.

Thea Dora peers in the cup.

"The bottom of the cup represents the past," she says for Vivi's benefit. "The curved part where the bottom meets the side represents the present. And you will find the future near the top." She looks up at Eleni. "What I once saw in your future is now in the present as well as your past. Strange."

"That is impossible."

Vivi asks, "What do you mean? Is it time travel? Because it sounds like time travel."

They ignore her.

"How can it be impossible if I see it? You are here, are you not?" *Thea* Dora says. "Now, in the future – I think the near future because it is a little low – I see a doorway. You will have an important meeting with someone from the past."

"So basically everyone here?" Vivi asks.

"Mock the grounds if you must, but believe in them, Vivi, for they hold the key to our destinies. Now give me your cup."

Vivi doesn't believe in fortunetellers or horoscopes, and she doesn't want her destiny spelled out. What if it spells f-a-i-l-u-r-e?

Not cool.

What the hell, it's just a bit of fun, isn't it? The future isn't really hiding in a dirty cup, waiting to be read by a superstitious aunt.

Is it?

"I see two men in the bottom – "

Vivi thinks: John and Ian.

" – and a line. A journey. Of course you are here, so there is your journey. I see a snake in your present."

"Sounds ominous."

"No, this is good. It means something you desire deeply will come to pass very soon."

"What about her future?" This comes from a scowling Effie, who doesn't look like she wants anything good to swing Vivi's way.

Thea Dora says, "I see a bridge. You must make an important decision soon. Only you can decide if you want to cross it or not. But there's a line through it. Something, or someone, will try to stop you."

"Will I win?"

"Eh." She shrugs. "Maybe. The cup does not say. We try it again another time."

Effie thrusts her cup at her mother. "Do me."

"Bah! I don't need to look in your cup to see your future, Effie. You have a husband and children, what more do you want to see? Old age?"

"Maybe you'll be surprised," Effie says.

"Some people do not have surprises in them."

————

There's a small bouquet on Vivi's front doorstep. Wildflowers tied with yellow ribbon.

Eleni hovers at her elbow. "Who are they from?"

"No note."

"Why no note?"

"Here, let me pull out my psychic whodunit guide and I'll tell you."

"I bet they are from that doctor."

"No, Mom. They're not from that doctor. He's unavailable. Maybe they're for you."

"Okay, I will take them."

61

VIVI

THE NEW, NEW TOILET doesn't break.

After it's in place, Vivi trudges through the olive grove, back to Takis's mansion. Biff comes along for the goats.

She wasted a lot of time last night, beating her thoughts into submission. Now she knows two things: Takis will teach her everything he knows about harvesting and processing olives, or she'll pester him until he drops dead or files a restraining order.

The other thing is Max. She can't see him again. *Ev-er.*

No way is she going back there, to that place where she can't have what she wants. One sham relationship is enough.

There was love – there was. In a distant sort of way. She and John were shopping lists and renovation and a wan sort of friendship. But she wants shopping lists and renovation and friendship and fire.

Max is fire, but he's not destined for her fireplace.

And Vivi isn't an asshole.

She's not like him – John's boyfriend.

It's a problem. No painless fix, either.

Yeah, they could be friends, she and Max. But what happens when he's married and she's in love?

She's doing her best not to care. Melissa and olives are her future, not Max. And in the immediate future there is Takis and his cheese and his goats.

Vivi likes goats and cheese, and in time she might like Takis.

———

The goats are less curious today, too busy eating stuff that shouldn't be edible. Biff takes a long drink out of their trough, then goes to chill with his bleating peeps.

Takis is sitting outside the shed, hand-rolled cigarette bobbing on his lip, peeling an apple with a pocketknife. He's wearing a shirt that was clean maybe ten years ago. Vivi is an optimist.

"You want?" Apple pinched between his fingers and knife, he offers the slice.

She wants. It makes her a child again, grasping a giant apple in her hands, teeth grazing the shiny skin. The apple slice is all juice and sugar.

Before she can bite again, Takis stands.

"Now we have work to do. I hope you're strong." Sounds ominous. "First, go wash your hands and arms, over there. Use soap." He points to the outdoor pump near the trough. A fat bar of soap sits in a plastic tub on top of the pump, up high where the goats can't eat it. It's covered in leaves.

The soap has an odd green tint.

Olive oil, maybe?

Olive empire expanding in her head (Vivi Tyler, a modern day Onassis), she goes back to Takis. He's in the shed, slicing the curd into strips. When he's done cutting one way, he gives Vivi the knife.

"Now you cut."

She cuts.

"Smaller pieces!"

Smaller pieces.

"Now you mix – use your hands," he says when she's done cutting.

"What, all of it?"

A dull ache sets into her shoulder. Her neck muscles are starting to whine. Her body doesn't like the burn, but her head does.

"Put your arms all the way in and break up the curd. It won't kill you. The wetness you feel in there is the whey. Soon we will drain it."

That explains the cheesecloth and bucket nearby.

Takis presses the loosely woven fabric down into the large bucket, clips the overflowing edges to the side with clothespins. When he's satisfied, he nods.

"I just scoop them in?"

"What else would you do? Sing them a song? Dance?" He slaps his thigh, cackling, coughing.

"Wise guy."

Doesn't take long. When only the whey is left, she looks up for directions.

"Pour it in. We will use it later for the brine. Feta becomes too dry if you do not keep it covered in liquid. Now, tie a big knot in the end of the cloth. Then take sieve, place it on the bucket, sit the cloth on top of it."

It goes okay.

Exhausted, she drops into the chair. "Now will you tell me about the olives?"

Takis makes a sucking sound through his teeth. "You have a child?"

"A daughter. Melissa is fifteen."

"Where is she now?"

"With a friend."

"Girl friend or boy friend?"

"Girl friend."

"Yes? Are you sure?"

"Melissa wouldn't lie to me."

Would she?

"Bah! Children always lie. But at least children only lie to others. Men, women, they lie to others and themselves."

Now she notices the black band he wears high on his shirtsleeve. Takis is a man in mourning.

"Do you have children?"

"Eh, three. And many grandchildren. They have their own lives. They do not come around so much since their mama passed."

"I'm sorry. When did she pass?"

"Twenty years, but it still feels as fresh as that cheese."

Drip, drip. The curds slowly expel their whey.

"Pain doesn't get much fresher than that," she says slowly.

He shoves her out the door. "Come back tomorrow."

"Then will you teach me about the olives?"

"Eh . . . Probably not."

❧ 62 ☙

MELISSA

THE HILL WON'T QUIT, and neither will Melissa.

Olivia is panting beside her. The football fields are somewhere up ahead – allegedly. Behind them is an unraveling mile of
Greek road.

Olivia says, "Look at you, Little Miss Eager Beaver."

"What do you mean?"

"The other day you were practically shitting yourself at the idea of
meeting boys, and now you're totally wetting your pants to watch them
play soccer."

"Am not. This hill sucks, that's all."

"You're practically desperate. Be careful," Olivia says. "Boys can
smell desperation a mile away. You don't want to be too eager. Flirt
with some other boys, too. It'll drive him crazy."

It's dating advice straight out of Cosmo, circa some other decade.

When they get to the top of the hill, the game is on. Melissa spots
Thanasi at the far end playing goalkeeper.

It's a fan club up here. More girls than boys watching on the
sidelines.

Olivia reads her mind. Melissa hates it when she does that. It's like
an invasion of privacy.

"Don't look so pissy, Tyler. Competition is good. We just have to prove we're way hotter. And we are. Let's go."

They go to where they can see Thanasi without a zoom. Close enough that Melissa can see the outline of his −

"Don't stare so hard. Remember what I said, look at other guys too. Practice looking at them like they're a delicious candy bar. Like this."

Olivia makes a weird duck face. Very MySpace (which is dead), very Facebook (which is death spiraling). No way is Melissa going to copy her and sit here looking like Nemo.

She doesn't know anything about soccer, but it looks like Thanasi is good at what he does. All her smiling and cheering pays off.

"Chill, Tyler," Olivia warns her.

"I am chilling."

"Stop smiling so hard."

She tries, but her face has other plans.

After the game, Thanasi jogs over to them, and Melissa says, "See? My way worked fine."

Not a word from Olivia; Vassili is running their way and she's duck facing even harder.

Yeah, not laughing at her is HARD.

"You came," Thanasi says, out of breath. "How did I look?"

"Great! I don't think I've watched soccer before."

"Here we call it football. Do you know how to play?"

Melissa shakes her head.

"Here, let me show you."

He walks her to the net. His fingers curl around her hand. Heat shoots up her arm, makes her face all bright and shiny.

He moves her into position. "Stay."

A group of girls hovering nearby glare at her, but she doesn't care. He picked her, didn't he?

"What are you doing?" she asks.

He moves behind her, brushes her ponytail aside. "That's all there is to football. You stand there until the ball comes close, then you kick it." His hands rest on her hips, chin drops onto her shoulder. "I want to kiss you."

Something sucks her guts out, fills the space with hot water. "Here?"

"We can go over there." He indicates the dense woods surrounding the field.

"Is that a good idea?"

"If we don't go there, I'll kiss you here."

No Olivia anywhere. She must have gone off into the woods with Vassili. So Melissa goes, too.

Mom would K-I-L-L her. Good thing she'll never know.

When they reach the tree line she says, "Okay. But not too far."

Does she mean don't go too far making out, or into the trees? Same thing really, she figures.

As soon as the field is out of sight, Thanasi stops.

"You've done this with other boys, yes?"

Can't speak. Only nod.

Once, but who's counting?

(Answer: Melissa.)

She presses her lips to his, expecting a gentle touch. But Thanasi's all open mouth and tongue, and he's daring her to do the same. So she does it, opens her mouth and moves her tongue against his. They're like eels, she thinks, wet and slippery, fighting over bread someone tossed into the pond.

She's excited, turned on. Disgusted.

Now he's getting all handsy, working the button on her shorts, tugging the zipper down, down.

Melissa freezes. She's wearing old underwear, ones with bees buzzing all over her butt. Kids' underwear.

No way does she want Thanasi thinking she's a little kid.

She wriggles away.

"You don't like me?"

She likes him.

But his tongue is a square peg in her round mouth. And Melissa has a feeling both pieces should be squares, or round, or whatever. She's also fifteen (and Thanasi is super cute), which means she's worried her piece is the wrong shape – not his.

"I like you. And I really want to hang with you again. But I have to go."

She bolts, stupid kid.

Vassili is on the field, talking to a group of girls. He waves and she flips a lame wave back. Wherever Olivia is, it's not with him.

"Are you going so soon?" he calls out.

"Parents," she says.

He laughs like he knows. "Parents!"

———

Home again.

Mom is in the kitchen poring over a picture book.

Biff's a life support system for a wagging tail.

"How's my ickle bickle puppy doggie?"

Mom looks up, smiles. "Hey, Honey. Olivia not coming in today?"

"Nope. She had to go."

"What did you girls do today? Anything fun?"

She shrugs. "Nothing much. What about you?"

"Nothing much."

63

VIVI

MAY BLEEDS INTO JUNE. The heat is sharpening Vivi's edges. She's tense, jittery. Needs something to do with these hands.

Pretty much every morning, St George's bells chime. Bright, cheerful peels in honor of saints' days; slow, mournful monotone when they're putting someone in the ground.

Flowers come almost every day, sans note. And Biff is no Dr Watson. Does he bark when the mysterious florist sneaks onto her property?

Nope.

Eleni always hogs the flowers. They die in jars all over her room. Every day she calls her husband and leaves a message on the machine, but she refuses to speak with him directly. She wants the poor man on his knees, crawling.

Vivi spends a couple of days painting her aunt's bathroom a pale, inoffensive pink. Not an Eleni Pappas eye bleeder. *Thea* Dora gets a new toilet, too. No more hole-in-the-ground. No more squatting. She took one look at Vivi's new bathroom and she coveted – hard.

What was Vivi to do?

Renovate, of course. She's grateful for the time filler.

When it's all done, her aunt waddles in, carrying a bulky bag.

"My Virgin Mary, it is a paradise! I am almost afraid to use it."

"You won't feel that way after a glass or two of *frappe*," Eleni says.

A painted wooden box tumbles out of the bag. Two compartments: one wide, one narrow.

"There," *Thea* Dora says, with a satisfied smile. "Now I have somewhere to put my crochet and my TV Guide."

Whatever works.

"Now we need to get ready for the party," *Thea* Dora continues.

Uh . . ."Party?"

"Yes, you have a new house, I have a new bathroom, so we will make a party at your house this weekend. Apostoli will be there early to make the *kokoretsi* and put the lamb on the spit."

Vivi can't help herself: she invites Max.

Because she and Max have a thing. Not a romantic thing – a friend thing.

And because she's an idiot.

———

The afternoons d-r-a-a-a-a-g.

Vivi can't sleep. Too hot, too dry, too used to not sleeping during the day. She's a woman, not a cat.

After the first week, she doesn't bother trying. Instead, she uses the time. Takes lots of notes. Business ideas, research, hours and hours with her good friend Google.

Takis hasn't ponied up the (olive) goods, yet. That man is all about the cheese and the cryptic messages.

If the hot afternoons take, the nights give.

Greece is a different woman after dark. Her flower-scented breeze refills Vivi's reservoir. Without the nights she'd be a parched husk with nothing to give her family.

Another reason to love the night: Max almost always comes, because (sigh) Vivi never sent him the "We can't be friends" memo.

And now she's pretty fucked, in the figurative sense.

Everyone goes to bed, and Vivi carries a cool glass of spring water to the back porch. She sits, sips, listens to the trees conspire.

On the good nights, she hears the Jeep's tires kicking stones, throwing dirt. The engine clicks off, leaving a heavy, fraught silence in its place. Doesn't take long for Max to slide into the second chair.

Sometimes they don't speak, other times they can't stop.

But their hands, their bodies, are constantly caged.

One night, he says, "I lost a patient today."

Grief bends him into a new, sad shape. He sits, head in hands, heart on sleeve.

It could have been Melissa. "I'm so sorry."

"I am, too. It's not right. Death is natural, but not when it's a child."

She goes quiet, lets him use the silence his own way.

"The boy had asthma. The first we've had. It's not common in Greece. Instead of weaning him off steroids as I instructed, one of the other doctors cut him off completely. The relapse happened quickly and his heart and lungs gave out."

"My God, the poor baby. What will the family do? Do you think they'll sue?"

It's dark, his head a shaking outline. "You are thinking like an American, Vivi. The boy has no family. He came to us from the orphanage. He leaves no one behind who will miss him. I should have been there."

"It's not your fault, Max."

A fox appears out of nowhere. Time stretches as the fox satisfies its curiosity, watching them watching. Then, as quickly as it appeared, it melts back into the shadows.

"Do you miss your husband?"

Good question. Does she miss John or does she miss the intermittent companionship he provided?

"I miss who he could have been, who he never was – with me, at least. It's nice sharing a life with someone, until they throw you away and you discover they've been sharing that life with someone else."

"Were you ever unfaithful?"

"There was only ever John."

The night grabs its stars, its moon, and moves slightly west.

"Did you want to be unfaithful?"

"I wanted someone to think I was the most beautiful woman in the world. I wanted to love and be loved exclusively, even if I wasn't being loved by John. I craved passion and romance, but wouldn't have taken it from the first hand that offered it to me. I would have wanted to, though. Is that infidelity? I'm not sure, maybe."

This is a first, admitting to another person what a soul sucking void her marriage had been. Vivi doesn't like to cry and tell.

"What about you? Do you plan to be faithful to this woman your mother wants you to marry?"

"Vivi . . ."

"Go on. I gave you an honest answer."

Tick, tick, tick.

"Yes. She will be my wife and I will be faithful."

"Good."

"Is it? Anastasia is very beautiful, but . . . It's a difficult relationship. Anastasia loves my work, but is jealous of it at the same time."

"She loves that you're a doctor?"

"Yes."

"With all the financial rewards that field can bring?"

"Yes. You make it sound as if she just wants me for my money."

Vivi laughs. "Come on, you have plenty of other charms to offer a woman. Besides, money isn't always that big an incentive. Not all of us want someone rich."

"I'm not so sure about that."

"You're cynical for someone who's never been married. Some women who want money actually go out and make it for themselves."

"Like you?"

"I have to support myself and Melissa somehow. And look at Soula. She works hard to make her living in real estate, and she's very good at it."

"Only until she finds a husband."

Vivi laughs until it clicks he's not joking.

"You've got to be kidding if you think Soula will give up her independence entirely when – if – she gets married."

"She will when she has children."

"Lots of women who have children work. Being a mother isn't a disability. You're an educated man, you know I'm right."

"Perhaps. But the mother of my children won't need to work."

"Need and want are two different things, Max. You may find your fiancé won't want to give up her work." They say nothing for a minute. "You're serious, aren't you?"

"Of course. It's the traditional Greek way."

"So is arranged marriage, but you don't seem to care for that too much." Vivi shuts up because she's gone too far, and Max is a friend. "Sorry, that was rude."

Two chests rise and fall in the dark.

"Sorry," she says, quieter this time.

He stands and stomps to the porch's edge. He's going to leave and it's her fault for being pushy. But he doesn't. He turns back and their solitary spheres collide.

Max grabs her, steadies her, doesn't let go.

Vivi doesn't mind. If he wants to hold on forever, that's okay with her.

Except: she's not an asshole.

Is she?

"I want you," Max says. "I'm trying to stop, but I can't quit coming here. Because of you." His fingers do delicious things to her hair and then he pulls her close and his mouth is all over hers – oh God. She should stop – she will stop – but for now she's leaning into the kiss, giving more, taking more.

"We can't," she tells his warm lips.

But they do and she lets the hot ripples wash over her. Every ounce of passion missing from her old life explodes in this one kiss. He wants, she wants, they want – in the exact same way. His arm curls around her waist and pulls her closer, tighter, hard against his hips. She wants it to stop, never wants it to stop.

But it does stop, and it's Max who does the stopping. Lips fall away first, then his arms. There's another kiss, but it's stamped on her forehead in burning ink.

"Goodnight, Vivi."

She closes her eyes. "Goodnight."

❧ 64 ❧

MELISSA

SAME TIME, SAME PLACE, same sun-filled room.
Dr Triantafillou says, "Do you think maybe you like the idea of him more than you like him?"

Melissa shakes her head. "That's not it."

"Are you sure?"

"Yeah. Thanasi is so cute. Like, the hottest guy I've ever seen."

"So why did kissing him feel like it didn't fit?"

"I don't know. What's wrong with me?"

"Nothing," Dr Triantafillou says. "Cute doesn't mean compatible. Chemistry is more than a face you like. Are you going to see him again?"

"Olivia is dating his best friend, so yeah."

"How do you feel about that?"

Melissa shrugs. "Good for them, I guess. Vassili is a pretty cool guy."

———

That "pretty cool guy" is outside the hospital waiting for a ride when Melissa spots him.

He waves first.

She swallows the lump in her throat and manages to say, "Hi." It's not an attraction thing. It's an "Oh shit, what if he tells Olivia and Thanasi" thing.

"You need a ride?" he asks.

He's tall.

Built lean. Good for soccer (football, Mel. Duh!), she's found out.

Very David Beckham, except not old.

He's looking at Melissa like he's happy to see her; like it's not weird she's there.

"Aren't you going to ask why I'm here?"

"Do you want me to?"

"Not really," she says.

"Don't worry, I won't ask. I won't tell, either."

"Why not?"

Vassili shrugs. "You looked afraid when you saw me. And Olivia is not always a kind person."

Half of her is offended on Olivia's behalf, but the rest of her gets it.

"So why are you with her?"

He says, "You never said if you need a ride or not."

A horn beeps. Mom.

"Got to go," she says. "See you."

———

The VW does a slow crawl along the beachfront road. A mile of cars behind them. Mom's a cautious driver, but this is nuts.

"Mom?"

"Yeah?"

"You okay?"

"Yeah, why?"

"You're totally holding up traffic."

Mom glances in the rearview mirror. "Huh."

"Are you going to speed up?"

"Nope."

"Why not?"

"I don't feel like it."

"Can we stop for ice cream?"

"Sure."

Wherever Mom is, she's not behind the steering wheel.

"Pizza?"

"Okay."

"We should get matching tattoos."

"Sounds great, Honey."

And she's the one seeing a shrink?

65

MAX

WHAT A BASTARD.

Max has been thinking that a lot, lately.

Two women in his pocket and he can't have both. But let's be real, both isn't what he wants.

Vivi's mouth stays with him all day. Every time his mind drifts – and it drifts a lot – she's there with that sweet mouth.

Goddamn, she's delicious.

And she's a good woman, too. Kind, funny, smart as hell. The type of woman a man wants to keep for a lifetime, not just a night or two.

But, Anastasia's going to be his wife.

Yeah, he's a bastard.

———

At noon he rides the elevator all the way up. The meeting is in about ten minutes, with the Chief of Pediatrics.

He's the first one there and what does he do?

Close his eyes and replay that kiss.

"Holy Mother, Andreou, you look like shit." Philipous, also a pediatrician, drops down next to him, a cup of what smells like coffee in one hand. "You keep forgetting you're not an intern anymore. You've earned the privilege of sleep. Try it. You might like it. Here." He shoves the cup at Max. "Looks like you need this more than I do."

Max pushes it back. "Any more coffee and my teeth are going to shake loose. Five cups, so far."

Philipous whistles. "Impressive. So is she hot?"

"Who?"

"The woman you were with last night. A man doesn't look that tired unless . . ." He makes an O with one hand, pokes a finger through it.

"There was no woman. Just one of those nights."

"I hear you're getting married." Dr Maria Ioanni takes the third seat. She's the reason for this meeting, for the dead child. His face stays neutral. The poor woman looks miserable – he's not going to add to the shit storm rolling her way. "The nurses were talking about it. They're all weeping now that you're off the market," she continues.

"Nurses, they talk too much." Philipous winks at Max. "You can tell me later."

Tell him what?

That he keeps popping a boner over another woman? That he wants to fuck her and cuddle her for the rest of his life? Or that he's breaking a date with his fiancée to attend a party at the other woman's house?

Maybe he should. Enough people tell him he's an asshole, maybe it'll sink into his thick skull.

This morning Anastasia threw a tantrum. He doesn't blame her. They're supposed to go to her cousin's wedding this weekend, but he made up some excuse about work. If he goes it will be hell. Endless questions about when they're getting married. Inevitable, bold inquiries about how many children they're planning, when they'll start. Sly glances at Anastasia's belly, while they try to guess if she's already knocked up or not.

She's not. Thank God.

But now he's trapped for no good reason. Children, at least, would have soothed the rope burn around his neck.

Condoms only from now on. Anastasia won't catch him off guard again.

But anyway, Anastasia had her tantrum and he weathered her storm. The next one will be along before long; Anastasia is hurricane season, all year long.

At Vivi's party there will be family, but they don't have expectations. He is a friend to her, nothing more. He won't have to smile, perform, pretend to be the successful doctor with huge monetary ambitions. There will be time to sit with Vivi and talk. And when he smiles it will be real.

They won't kiss again. He's sure of that.

The Chief of Pediatrics walks in, takes her rightful seat at the head of the table as god-in-residence.

Judgment is nigh.

Doesn't raise the dead, does it?

Untitled

———

A head rolls, but it isn't his. He's in the clear.

❧ 66 ❧

VIVI

TODAY IS THE DAY. Max will be here and they're going to talk. Vivi's going to make sure of that.

They can't be friends – there is no way. Vivi wants too much, covets too hard. Not thy neighbor's house, but close enough. Stay on this path and her heart will be in pieces.

Again.

Theo Apostoli arrives at dawn with a dozen male relatives, a large barrel sliced in two (each half with legs welded to the curved underbelly), and something massive and dead, wrapped in butcher's paper. They sweat a lot, but they don't stop until each half-barrel is stuffed with a nest of glowing coals.

Some of the cousins bounce up the road in a pickup truck, dozens of chairs stacked in the bed. Another isn't far behind, hauling long tables nested four deep.

Bottles of lemonade, *retsina*, and beer wait inside crates of ice, ready to be popped open when the heat makes death threats.

Vivi's kitchen is the women's new home. They've brought Tupperware.

Taramasalata (a pink dip made from roe), tiny spicy meatballs, feta pie, *spanakopita* (spinach and cheese pie), potato salad tossed

260

with lemon juice, salt, and onions (not a hint of mayo in sight), *dolmades* (grapevine leaves stuffed with rice). And every Greek dessert ever.

Vivi wonders how big this party is going to get.

She doesn't ask. Better she doesn't know.

Popping the lids off a dozen beers, she prepares to hydrate the masses.

"*Thea* Dora tells me you renovated your bathroom all by yourself," her cousin Nikki says, tearing aluminum foil off the *baklava*.

"It is true! And she fixed mine too – it is a paradise now! I go there just to knit sometimes." *Thea* Dora has come up behind them, toting a bucket of so-red-they're-purple cherries. "Come, we will go see. Come, come see what Vivi did!" Twenty women surge toward the small bathroom.

Vivi leaves them to their fun, takes the beer out. The dead animal is up on the spit, performing a slow pirouette over the hot coals. Lamb, the whole lamb, and nothing but the lamb.

It still has eyes, and it's watching her.

No eye contact – no way.

The second spit is mystery meat. All she knows is that it's dead and tightly wrapped around the metal rod, the whole lot secured with string.

The men take the beer, wade back into the amateur political arena. They're performing the Greek custom of drowning out the other guy. Who's right, who's wrong, doesn't matter. Be big, be loud, be deaf to other arguments.

Too much noise for her. She goes out front hoping for some peace and quiet, and finds Biff making eyes at Max, while Melissa talks the doctor's hind leg off.

The world drops away and it's like they're in the movies. Nothing but him and her and (oh, God!) the tension.

Get a grip, Vivi. That's for other people – not you.

The countdown starts to their friendship's demise.

"Hello," she says lightly. "You came."

"I can't stay long, but I wanted to see you both. And Biff, of course. That's still a stupid name."

"My dog, remember?" Vivi looks at Melissa. "Did you invite Olivia to the party?"

"No, should I?"

"She's your friend. She might be hurt if you leave her out of a good time. Go on over and ask. Don't be too long though."

"Okay. Bye, Dr Andreou." She peddles off down the road, the woman-child.

Vivi watches her go, and then it's back to Max.

"You look like you need a stiff drink and a month on a desert island. Is everything okay at the hospital?"

"The hospital is fine. It keeps me busy – too busy sometimes for my friends."

"You're a doctor," she tells him. "Just be grateful you have time to breathe."

"How do you do that?"

"Do what?"

"Always say the right words." His eyes say there's a storm headed her way.

So, it's going to be like that. He's here to dump her, dump their friendship, dump the everything (and the nothing) between them.

Good for him. It's the right thing to do. The best thing.

For both of them.

Now there's no plug for her to pull. That's something – right?

"It's a first," she says. "Do you at least want to eat something?"

"I can't. I can't keep coming to see you at night. It's . . ." He looks at the ground, looks at that tree over there, looks at Biff. "I have to marry Anastasia. It's expected. If I keep seeing you, eventually I'll be unfaithful, and I'm not that man. When I kissed you last night . . ." He kicks the ground like it's the problem. "Shit . . ."

(Conversations like this are always cobbled together with ellipses.)

He's not an asshole. It's not like he's hurting her to be cruel. But it sure as hell feels like he's knifing her in the gut.

Worst rerun ever.

"Jesus, Max, I would never be your mistress. Do I look like a whore?"

The words have steel capped kick. Her regret is instantaneous –
John is the oath breaker, not Max.

Grim eyes, grim mouth. "Vivi, there are more ways to be unfaithful
than sex."

Her bottom lip is getting that wobble. It's unresponsive to her bite.

"We're just friends. I'm not even divorced yet. I don't want a relationship."

Liar, liar. Pants on –

"But I do." He reaches down to scratch a languid Biff. "My heart is
here with you – as your friend, but I have a duty to my family to marry
and have children."

"Enjoy your mother's cage."

"That's cruel."

"It's true."

They're silent for a moment. He uses the conversation's gap wisely
– leans forward, kisses her cheeks. To an onlooker it's a simple farewell.
To Vivi it's goodbye.

Funny how neither of them says it.

He leaves her there in a dust cloud, cement boots on her feet. She
stays because she can't move; this is the place she didn't say goodbye
to Max.

❧ 67 ❧

MELISSA

O LIVIA NEVER SAYS "NO" to a party, is how Olivia puts it.
Anyway, no food in the house. Her parents are AWOL and
she's s-t-a-r-v-i-n-g. A party sounds like the best thing ever.

Melissa asks where they are and wins a shrug.

"Don't know, don't care."

Must be nice.

Must be awful.

❧ 68 ❧

VIVI

THE FOOD DOESN'T QUIT coming. Vivi stuffs a bit of everything in her mouth, hoping it will tamp down the pain.

Doesn't work like that. Now she's miserable *and* bloated.

Melissa returns with Olivia just in time to eat. They get busy building a mini Mt Olympus on each plate.

"You'll need ropes and a pick to dig into that," Vivi tells Olivia. "Have you got some *kokoretsi*? It's amazing.

Olivia makes a horrified face. "I don't eat guts and gross stuff."

Vivi looks at her plate, loaded with round two. "Guts?"

"Yeah. I've seen them cutting up the hearts, lungs, livers, tying it to the spit with stringy intestines. Do you know how long those guts – ?"

Vivi holds up one hand. "I don't want to know. What about the lamb, it's just lamb, right?"

"Yeah, I guess," Olivia says. "Baa baa, dead sheep."

Vivi doesn't do offal, but she makes an exception for heaven in her mouth. She plonks herself on the couch, stares at the food. Wonders if these guts can divine the future.

The screen door goes wild. Someone's trying to bash its mesh face in.

Vivi wants it to be Max, but it's a woman. Older, with a lived-in face. No cosmetics, total stranger to tweezers. A "walking dead" way about her – soul long gone, body animated through the will of Hades. A shade.

A metaphorical bell rings.

"I'm looking for Elias, is he here?" Husky voice, seen too many years of tobacco and *retsina*. Her teeth confirm Vivi's suspicion.

"No . . ."

"Your mother is here, yes? I thought they would be together."

What does she want with Vivi's father?

"She's here, but he's not," Vivi says. "Can I help you?"

The bell quits ringing, because now Vivi remembers. The woman from Fingernails' shop. The one *Thea* Dora said was nobody.

And look, nobody is here on Vivi's doorstep.

Vivi's curiosity explodes. "Who are you?"

"May I see her . . . please? You are her daughter, you can make her speak to me."

"Ha-ha," Vivi says. "Obviously you're not an old friend or you would know: nobody makes my mother do anything. Can I help?"

Nothing.

Vivi doesn't budge.

"Go and get her. I'll wait by the tree." She says the words slowly, precisely, issuing a challenge.

"You do that," Vivi mutters.

"Vivi, my love, are you talking to yourself?" *Thea* Dora asks.

Her mother and aunt are back inside – with knives. They get straight to work, chopping a pile of tomatoes, onions and cucumbers.

"She does that," Eleni tells her sister. "This is what happens when you go crazy."

"You talk to yourself," *Thea* Dora says.

"Vivi and Christos make me crazy. The spirits tell me my children should listen to their mama more often."

She wishes.

"I'm not that crazy yet." Vivi gets another paper plate. Time to feed the sadness again, see if she can squash that bastard. "There's a woman looking for you, Mom."

"A gypsy," her aunt says with conviction.

Vivi looks out the window. The woman's still out there, resting against the tree. "She's not Romani."

"A Jehovah's Witness! Is she carrying those booklets? They make good fire."

Vivi peers again. "No. She knows the family."

"Well, why didn't you say so? Probably she is a cousin."

"No, it's that woman. The one you said was nobody."

Thea Dora nudges Vivi aside with one overabundant hip. "My Holy Mother of Jesus, what is that woman doing here?"

Some bull she is – doesn't even bother snorting, stamping. Goes right into CHARGE.

"Who is it?" Eleni asks. Without dropping the knife, or wiping her hands, she trots out the door after her sister.

Well, Vivi's not going to let them go alone, is she? Her curiosity is spiking into the red zone – proof that she's Greek enough.

Her aunt is just one person, but she's surrounding the woman.

"What are you doing here? You have no place here!" *Thea* Dora is saying.

The woman looks unafraid, unperturbed. No expression but the one she'll wear when she meets God. "I want to see Elias," she says, repeating her earlier request.

"Sofia, your business with this family is long over. You cannot be here!" *Thea* Dora says.

"But I have to see him. She is the one who should not be here!" A finger stab at Eleni, who is stiff cardboard, knife in hand.

"Would someone please tell me what is going on here seeing as this is my house and my tree?" Vivi says, to no one in particular.

They ignore her.

There's nothing for her to do except stand on the porch and watch the play unfold. If a minor skirmish breaks out, at least she's got this handy paper plate.

Eleni is mobile again. "I could kill you where you stand, feed you to wild dogs, and no one would care that you are gone."

"Do it!" Sofia roars. "All you would do is prove that my Elias is too good for your black heart."

"*Skasmos!*"

(Translation: Shut up.)

Thea Dora grabs the woman's arm, pulls her to the gate. Pitting a sumo wrestler against a rag doll.

Sofia breaks away.

Pointless, really.

Except she performs a mean windmill, arms spinning, wheeling toward Eleni. It's a toddler's pro move.

But Vivi's mother is smart – the woman survived two toddlers. She feints, lets the woman kiss dirt.

The victory doesn't last. Sofia snakes around, grabbing Eleni's ankles, and Eleni teeters. *Thea* Dora bustles past her, into the house.

Vivi can't help herself. She's angry as hell at Max and needs something to smash. She's all over the woman, slapping with the paper plate, dumping leftovers in her face.

Paper cuts. Lots of little paper cuts.

Vivi straddles her chest, lets her have it.

Eleni rallies. "You are my daughter, no question!" She sounds proud. So they're – what? – bonding over a bitch fight?

Stranger things have happened.

It gets stranger when Eleni rips off Sofia's shoes, tickles the woman's feet until she's squealing like a pig.

Vivi stops. "Why are we doing this?"

"Because she is a mad woman!"

Good enough. Sofia's a decent surrogate for Max, John, John's boyfriend, and . . .

Everyone, really.

It lasts until the hand of God (*Thea* Dora, it seems, is omnipresent), drags her away. With her free hand, her aunt dumps a pitcher of water over Sofia's head.

Vivi falls back, panting.

Fighting is better than:

Zumba, yoga, Pilates, calisthenics, running, jogging, and spending an hour on the elliptical, loping to nowhere.

It's not over.

The uncles are suddenly there, dividing the women into four spitting piles.

Sofia's not going quietly. This is her time. Her reckoning.

"I curse you," she screams. "I curse you and the children you brought into this world. May the devil take your souls and wash them in blood and fire for all eternity!"

Very dramatic. Very Greek.

The uncles load Sofia into the pickup truck and drive away.

The three women stand there panting for a bit.

"Well," Eleni says. "Whatever she is selling, we certainly don't want any."

Vivi laughs, because the whole thing is a fucked up kind of hilarious. She looks at her mother. "So who is she? You kind of owe me – "

"As your mother I don't owe you anything except life. And I've already given you that." Pretty much beheading Vivi's snappy retort.

Her mother stomps off. *Thea* Dora follows, pitcher swinging in her hand, and Vivi stands there wondering if the gods have painted a huge target on her ass.

Apparently, yes. Because the next person out the front door is one of her cousins.

"Vivi?" she says. "I think your toilet is broken."

🎏 69 🎏

VIVI

It's a lake. A shit lake.

"Lake Peepeekaka," Vivi says.

Her family has vanished. Very clever of them.

"Mom?" Melissa appears at her elbow, eyes donut-wide. "What happened?"

"It's nothing. Just a family curse."

Biff comes rolling in. The dog can't believe his good fortune. He lunges at the bathroom buffet. Vivi's fast but not that fast, and Biff gets his lick in.

"Shit," Melissa says, matter-of-factly.

"And piss."

70

VIVI

CLEANUP TAKES HALF AN hour.
Vivi rejoins the party wearing eau de lemon bleach, falls into a chair.

A couple of cousins brought their bouzoukis (they're like guitars, except not), one uncle brought an ancient accordion, and together they spin off one unfamiliar tune after another.

She doesn't know the dances, either. But she knows happy people when she sees them doing a Greek jig.

Melissa kneels beside her, so Vivi knows there's going to be a question.

"Mom? We're going to the beach – is that okay?"

How can she say no? Melissa's cheerful and sweet, these days. Agria is good for her, and what's good for Melissa is good for Vivi.

It's safe here. Eyes and ears everywhere. One foot out of line and she'll know before Melissa steps through the door.

The grapevine is a mother's best friend.

(And a woman's worst enemy.)

"You let her go this late?" Eleni asks.

"It's only three. The beach is a whole five minutes away. She'll be fine."

"Humph."

"What do you want me to do, Mom? Put her in a plastic bubble?"

"Eh, that is not such a bad idea."

Vivi flops facedown on the couch. She wants this party over, these people out. Find herself a nice hole and hide. Conduct a postmortem on Max's permanent departure.

Instead she's playing starfish on the couch, while her mother keeps secrets and her cousin rifles through her belongings. Nosy cow.

Speaking of . . .

Effie asks, "Are you sure that is where Melissa is going?" She's flipping through a thick book from Vivi's shelves, looking at the pages like they're pornographic. Probably never seen a book before, which would explain a lot.

"Are you calling my daughter a liar?" Vivi asks.

"I hear stories . . ."

"What stories have you heard, Effie?"

She shrugs. "Eh, she is your problem, not mine. Have you ever been here?" Effie waves the cover under her nose. British castles.

Vivi lets it go; one catfight a day is sufficient.

"Britain? No."

"Why you have the book, then?"

"I like castles."

"Maybe you think you are royalty, eh?"

"Yes, Effie, that's it."

"You will not think you are so special when you go there and you can't find your castles."

Vivi's mind boggles. "What do you mean?"

Effie shrugs. "I don't understand why people go where they don't speak the language."

"And I can't go to Britain because . . .?"

"You speak Greek and American, not British."

Vivi's head explodes. First Hawaii, now Britain. Effie is a one-woman chorus of stupidity.

"Jesus Christ, Effie. Americans speak English. The British speak English. The accent is a bit different, but it's the same language."

The expression on Effie's face says there's no way she's buying what Vivi's peddling.

"How stupid do you think I am? It is a different country with thousands of kilometers of water in between."

Pretty stupid. "And yet, we all speak the same language. It must be magic."

Effie is turning red. No – purple.

"That's not true. I heard it – "

"Let me guess, on the television? Or maybe you read it in the coffee grounds. Because you sure as hell never heard it from any intelligent source!"

"*Thea* Eleni?"

Because Vivi's word isn't good enough.

Eleni is trying hard to stay out of it. "Vivi is right."

There's a minor commotion as Effie shoves the book back into place.

"You know everything, don't you, Vivi?"

Then she and her butt wobble out the back door.

"Was she dropped on her head at birth?"

Eleni makes a face. "She is not a bad girl. She has not had your opportunities."

"Yes," Vivi says. "Everyone needs a gay husband to turn them into a decent human being."

"That is not what I mean and you know it, Vivi. Effie has lived here all her life. She left school at fifteen. She was married at seventeen. She knows only what she reads in magazines and hears from the television."

"And whose fault is that?"

"Do not judge her, Vivi. She is ignorant but she is still your cousin. Blood is important."

Vivi's had enough. She looks for her purse, for her keys.

"Where are you going?"

She whistles and Biff comes running. He's licking his lips, so she knows someone's been feeding him.

"Want to go for a drive, boy?" The dog pants. "Yeah, I'm going to check up on my daughter."

"You cannot go after her now," Eleni says.

"I can't let her go, I can't go after her. Will someone around here give me the rule book that isn't scratched in shifting sand?"

Eleni's mouth keeps moving, but Vivi doesn't listen. All that blood swooshing in her ears is drowning out the world.

Biff doesn't mind. He takes shotgun with a grin.

Any chance she can trade her family for five bucks and watermelon? Maybe sell her life on eBay?

She feels like shit. Partly because her mother's right about Effie, partly because she's driving and driving, following the path the girls should have taken to the beach, and . . .

Nothing.

No sign of them on the beach. Or on the way to the beach. Or anywhere near the beach.

Back and forth, back and forth. A few red bicycles, but none of them Melissa's.

Where the hell is she?

Panic streaks naked through her veins. Her heart's ramping up for bad, bad news.

The VW hooks left. Next block. And the next.

Nothing.

In a minute she's going to park, start pounding on doors.

She's thinking every way but straight.

Melissa lied. Is it the first time? Vivi's trying to be a good mom, trying to balance freedom and trust and age-appropriate caution.

And what happens?

She fails all over the place.

Oh God, please just be in one piece.

Blocks of nothing much. Flashes of bicycles that aren't Melissa's. Glimpses of girls who aren't her.

She's going hot, going cold. Going crazy.

Lucky break when she passes the old railway tracks. Vivi slams the brakes, burns rubber in reverse. Smoke everywhere.

Melissa's there. Olivia, too. With a couple of boys.

Boys? Ha! Try almost men. These Greek kids have a way of looking older than they are. Vivi knows trouble when she sees it. Not when she marries it – but definitely when she sees it on someone else's arm.

Melissa's gazing up at the blond kid like he's Santa Claus.

Santa Claus, her ass. The kid's a predator. Look at the way he's leaning into her, pants riding low, no shirt, following her with his eyes. Melissa giggles and he brushes the hair away from her eyes.

Vivi's going to rip off his dick. Maybe hit him with it when she's done. Maybe throw it to Biff, let him use it as a chew toy.

Olivia spots Vivi first. A sly look flits across her face and she nudges Melissa.

I'm on to you, you little bitch, Vivi thinks.

Biff at her side, she stalks across the tracks.

Melissa looks like she wants to d-i-e. That can be arranged. "Mom, what are you doing here?"

She's panicking.

Tough shit.

"Wow." Vivi glances around. "Funny, this doesn't look like the beach. You did say you were going to the beach, right?"

The wheels turn. "We were just on our way."

"Did I miss the detour signs?"

"Somebody's got menopause," Olivia mutters. Because she's the kind of girl who likes to act tough to make up for her own parents not giving too much of a shit what she does.

"You're not in this conversation," Vivi tells her. "So stuff a sock in it."

Melissa tries a new angle. "What are you doing here, Mom? Is Grams okay?"

"Nice try. Who are your friends?"

"You already know Olivia."

Vivi gives her the you-are-so-grounded look.

"Fine," Melissa says, with every ounce of teenage exasperation she can muster. "This is Vassili and Thanasi."

Mr. Asshole with the blonde hair and twenty-something body is Thanasi.

"Okay," Vivi says. "Say goodbye. We're going home."

"But you said I could go to the beach," she whines.

"You did, I heard you," Olivia says. The little snot.

"I said Melissa could go to the beach. Does this look like the beach to you? Last time I looked the beach wasn't two blocks away from the ocean and covered in grass and rail tracks."

"Mom – "

"Melissa, get in the car."

"But my bike – "

"How do you think I got it to the house in the first place?"

The other kid – what was his name? Vassili – helps her out. Nice kid. Blondie is standing there looking equal parts pissed and amused.

Basically, fuck that guy.

But as they drive away, Vivi feels better. Melissa is safe and some of the pressure's gone.

"He's cute," she says.

"He's okay."

"Do you like him?"

Melissa shrugs, but she's turning pink.

"You can invite him to dinner at the house if you like."

"I don't want to."

"Fine."

Melissa swivels in the seat, gives Vivi a look that's way too old for her face. "Are you pissy because Dr Andreou didn't stay for the party?"

Ouch. The kid nails it.

"No. This is about my fifteen-year-old daughter lying to me about where she's going."

"I hate you," she says, sagging against the leather.

"There's a line. Take a number."

✿ 71 ✿

MAX

MAX GRIMACES AT THE piece of shit staring back at him in the rearview mirror. He'll never forget the way Vivi looked as he drove away. Her in that white sundress with the blue flowers.

He slams his fist on the steering wheel and nothing happens. It doesn't hit back.

Maybe they'll meet again someday. In another life – it would have to be. They can't be friends in this one.

Not after today. She's lost to him, now.

It's for the best. Vivi's. Anastasia's. Mama's. He can't love his friend the way he'll never love his wife.

He puts on that face where he looks pissed at the world.

He could go to Anastasia, lose himself in her body for a few minutes, but she's at that wedding. Right now he doesn't want to touch her, anyway.

He never wants to touch her again.

Where does he go?

———

Kostas isn't home.

Max wanders the village alone, traipsing up rough steps cut into the rock, dodging goat herders and their flocks, trying not to make eye contact with the locals.

Head down. Eyes down.

See nothing and be seen by nobody.

Until he spots Kostas drinking Coke in the town square. It's a flat piece of rock, jutting out from the mountain's face. Tree-canopied, perfect in summer. Tables around the rim, amazing view from every last one. In the center, peddlers hawk their wares. Business is good, busy. Lots of tourists looking to buy something – anything. Everything Made in China, or someplace equally plastic.

As soon as Kostas sees his brother, he nods to the waiter.

"I'm so fucked," Max says, sliding across from him.

"And a good day to you, too."

"I'm serious."

"What's wrong?"

The waiter comes back with two Cokes. Max dumps some bills onto the tray, tells him to keep the change.

"I'm in love with someone who isn't my fiancée."

Kostas says, "Vivi."

"Is it that obvious?"

"You forget, Brother, I've seen you with a lot of women. Some you like for a while, but mostly you're indifferent and you bore easily."

"Am I that shallow?"

"Shallow? No. Sometimes it takes the right woman to open a man's eyes. Before that he is blind and a fool."

"Says the priest." But he's laughing because he remembers how Kostas used to be. The man didn't come to the priesthood a virgin. "Shit. I should have met her sooner."

They drink, watch the view, say nothing for a while.

Kostas says, "Under different circumstances you wouldn't have appreciated her."

The Coke is so cold and sweet it makes his teeth ache, and still it tastes bitter. It's not the drink – it's him.

"I don't know what to do."

"Break your engagement. You and Vivi can be together."

"I can't. I already told Vivi we can't be friends anymore."

Kostas slams his palm on the table. The wood shudders.

"What the hell is wrong with you? You can't allow Mama to control you! This is your life. She had her chances. She made her choices. Now it is your turn. She tugs on the strings she tied to you, and you jump around like her marionette! Be a man, not her little boy!"

"If you were anyone else I'd punch you."

"If you were anyone else I'd give the exact same advice – minus the 'hell.'"

Max smiles. It's a grim thing.

"Brother," Kostas continues, "it's time to let go of your guilt about our father. Let. It. Go. Don't be bound to our mother forever. She is poison."

Max knows his brother is right, but things are complicated.

They don't talk much after that. Just horsing around.

"Any chance you want to come down to Volos and see a movie?"

"Anything suitable for a priest playing?"

"I was thinking of something with guns, violence, and aliens. Maybe some breasts."

"And you think this is the antidote to your problem?"

"No, but it can't hurt."

Kostas drains his glass. "Yeah, I'm in."

72

VIVI

J ULY IS A REAL bitch. Every day a new disaster.

Her whole calendar is framed with the misery of missing Max.

Day one, it rains. Not normally a problem, but there's a hole in the roof. Good thing she bought a bucket. Now instead of the *plinks* and *plops* of water on marble, she's hearing the same sounds on plastic.

If marriage is about sleeping in the wet spot, being single is about walking through it.

"Do you have a phonebook?" Eleni asks.

"What for?"

"What, you think that roof will fix itself?"

No. Just . . . No. Last thing she wants is some contractor showing up a week after he promised to be here.

"Forget it," Vivi says. "I'll do it myself. Now."

Eleni looks horrified. "Are you crazy? It is raining. Of course you are – what am I thinking?"

"Which is why I'm going up there now. Too much longer and I'll have to replace that chunk of the ceiling too."

Ladder, toolbox, raincoat.

"Be careful," Eleni calls out. "If you fall, do you want them to keep you on life support?"

Vivi scales the ladder. Throws the toolbox up ahead of her. The hole is tiny, but a hole is a hole. Looks like animals have been throwing a party up here. She patches it as best she can. When the rain stops she can do it right.

The rain stops. The gray skies shrivel away. Patches of blue spread like a welcome virus.

Figures.

In the distance, a megaphone is crackling. The Romani hawking their melons. It's not long before the rickety pickup stops outside her gate.

She climbs down to buy a watermelon. They all look good, but what does she know?

The guy looks as clean as his melons. He shoves the knife into Vivi's first choice and pulls out a wedge. Bright red. Perfect.

"I'll take it."

She counts the coins into his dirty hand. It takes a while. Learning new currency is one of those pains in the asses no one warns you about.

Melon tucked under one arm, she hoofs it back up the pathway, mouth watering in anticipation.

Her ankle twists and she falls. Goodbye, watermelon.

That thing can fly – fly until gravity snatches it out of the air.

Watermelon everywhere. A red-green halo.

Bad day for Vivi, happy day for Biff. He goes at the mess like it's Thanksgiving and he's been fasting since Halloween.

The pickup truck is shaking with all the laughter.

"You want another melon?" the Romani guy calls out.

Vivi says, "Not today."

Biff goes on licking.

She limps inside with what's left of her dignity.

———

Caterpillars. A plague of them.

They eat their way through all the plants on the patio, except the cacti from Max. It takes a noxious mixture of soap and water to kill the bastards before they migrate to the trees.

Her aunt is a walking encyclopedia of natural cures.

"You must spray them each week to prevent further infection," she says, rinsing each leaf with the soapy mixture. "Yanni, George, get out of that tree!"

Effie's boys have freshly shaved heads – to prevent head lice, *Thea* Dora said. Now they're having a spitting contest up in the plum trees. It's hard to say who's winning.

They ignore their grandmother – of course.

Vivi and her aunt wander to the front yard, *Thea* Dora's mouth doing its best to conquer any stray silence.

"Alternate this with a spray of garlic water. You put a whole head of garlic in the pot with water and boil. Hot peppers are also good, but careful, do not put them on your fruit. It will spoil the taste – "

She breaks off suddenly. In the same moment, something cracks, someone screams.

They run.

Vivi gets there first.

Yanni is on his back, broken tree limb wedged under the curve of his spine. George is standing over him, poking his brother with a stick.

The boy looks up. "*Yiayia*," he says to his grandmother, "I think he's dead. Wake him up. I was about to win the game."

But Yanni is moaning – a definite sign of not being dead.

Eleni rushes out of the kitchen, sees the boy there. "Jesus. I will call 911."

"Mom, you can't do that," Vivi says.

"But the boy – "

"We're not in America, remember? Dial 100. And hurry."

"Wait! We do not need the ambulance," *Thea* Dora calls out. "Eleni, get the rubbing alcohol. Quick!"

"He doesn't have a fever," Vivi starts.

A moment later her mother reappears, a clear bottle of blue rubbing alcohol in one hand, vinegar in the other.

"I brought this, too. Just in case."

Vivi gawks at her. "Did you call 100?"

Eleni shrugs. "Dora knows what she is doing."

"But he could have a spinal injury!"

It's horrifying, the way her aunt rolls the boy over and yanks up his shirt. The bottle squirts his back. She rubs in widening circles.

The boy shudders, moans, sits up.

Vivi goes weak with relief. "You could have killed him! If his spine was broken, rolling him over would have snapped it in two. We'd be carrying him out of here in a box."

"Nonsense!" her aunt proclaims. "The rubbing alcohol cured him. Without it he might be sick, yes, but now he is fine. Look!"

Yanni is already halfway up the tree again, swinging like an ape.

Vivi can't believe it. Rubbing alcohol for a fall . . . She bet Superman's specialists never tried that after his incident with the horse.

Footsteps crunch up the path and . . . here's trouble.

"Mama, what is going on?" The words rocket out of Effie's mouth.

"It is nothing. Yanni fell out of the tree. Look," Dora points up at the tree where the boys are reloading their ammunition, "he is fine."

Effie saves her dirty looks for Vivi.

"He could have been killed," Vivi exclaims, still horrified at what passes for medical attention in her family.

"Probably you should take him to see that nice doctor," her mother says. Vivi's eyes narrow, daring her to keep talking.

"What doctor?" Effie demands. She clomps over to the tree, shrieks, "You boys get down here now!"

Balanced on a branch, George drops his shorts. His Batman underwear is the next to go. Listen to them: pair of cackling hyenas, those kids. George dumps the offending garments on his mother's head.

Effie's screws loosen another half turn. In a flash, she's halfway up the tree, yanking George's leg. He's the church bell in this scenario, and she's Quasimodo (who else?)

It's obvious she's done this, or something like it, before.

The boy falls. She catches him. Then she picks her way across the yard, holding him out from her body by his arm, a game piece from a Barrel of Monkeys.

His brother (the almost paralyzed-for-life boy) stays in the tree, eyes as round as the fruit in his hand. He knows things are about to get bad for George.

And they do.

Effie slaps that boy on every inch of bare skin her hand can find.

"You will not show your backside to me like that again, you little bastard! I'm going to spank you so hard you can't climb a tree again for a year. If I so much as see you near a tree I will beat you," she squeals. "When your father hears about this you are going to be sorry."

Snot bubbles down George's face. Poor kid. "Don't tell *Baba*!"

"I think I am going to call him now and he can take you home!"

"No, Mama! No!"

The two older women do nothing. But Vivi can't sit here and watch the boy take a beating. A slap is one thing, but Effie is a hitting machine. She leaps up, stops Effie's arm mid-strike.

"Enough already. All he did was drop his pants."

Her face goes as red as her son's ass. The symmetry isn't lost on Vivi.

Effie drops the boy. He bolts. "This is none of your business. Why are you interfering?"

Vivi points at the tree. "My tree, my house."

"He's my child. It is not your place."

"You want to beat your children at home – fine. But you won't do it in my house. You'll regret it later, you know."

Effie and her halitosis get up in Vivi's face. "Are you threatening me?"

"No. Jesus. I mean you'll feel bad about it later. You'll hate yourself for hitting him that way."

"Mama says you're a bitch who can't keep a man," Yanni says from his perch in the tree.

Thea Dora's head jerks up. "Effie! What kind of talk is this?" She gathers her skirt, waddles over.

"I never said that!" Effie says.

"Yes, you did," Yanni says. "You said she was a bad mother and Melissa tried to kill herself to get away from her."

"I guess things could be worse," Vivi says calmly, though her anger is quietly going Chernobyl. "I could be an ignorant peasant who beats her children over nothing."

"Vivi," her mother says. "Don't be rude."

"She started it."

"What, are you a child?"

"You're the one who's treating me like one," she tells Eleni.

"You think you're so perfect." Effie says, stabbing the air with a finger. "If you knew what I know, you wouldn't be so high and mighty."

Thea Dora is all over that. Her hand snatches up a handful of Effie's hair, twists it at the roots. "Keep your mouth still. Tend to your children."

Red-faced and getting redder, Effie reloads her hate rays, shoots them at Vivi. She's daring Vivi to open her mouth just one more time.

"Now!" Effie's mother barks.

Effie snatches up George's clothes, glare bolted to her face. "I wish you had never come here."

"We don't always get what we wish for," Vivi says. "Watching you beat your children isn't a dream come true for me either."

Eleni slaps the back of Vivi's head. Skirmish over.

Can't outgrow some things.

❧ 73 ❧

VIVI

THE VETERINARIAN IS THE doctor; the doctor is the veterinarian. Very chicken and egg.

Biff doesn't care – he's got balls to lick.

The clinic's waiting room is full of people (and pets) putting a lot of effort into ignoring the dog – Vivi included. She's here because Biff's full of worms.

The clinic is a sort of optical illusion: outside it's a snub rectangle, but inside it goes forever. One single hallway with at least twenty doors, no air conditioning, two ceiling fans, and a dozen plastic chairs in reception. White-on-black plaques on all the doors.

After a half hour wait, Doctor Papadopoulos's door swings open. A whiskey and cigarette voice hollers, "Next."

Vivi is next, so off she goes.

Doctor Papadopoulos isn't much more than a kid, but he's adding decades with that mustache. Big handlebar of a thing, no sign of his mouth. Pale for a local boy. Probably no time to make friends with the sun when you're both doctor and veterinarian.

"Why are you here?"

Friendly guy. Really putting himself out there.

Meanwhile, Biff carries on licking. Her dog's upwardly mobile, going from balls to butt.

"Worms," Vivi says.

"Eh?"

"Worms. My dog's got worms."

"Worms?

"Worms! Little white squiggly things."

"Oh . . .WORMS! You've got worms!" Top of his voice. Loud, excited, thinks he's Archimedes in the bathtub.

Today's news, fresh off the grapevine: Vivi Tyler has worms.

No such thing as doctor/vet/patient confidentiality around here.

She points at Biff. "No. The dog has worms."

Yeah, he doesn't believe her. Not with that look on his face. His hand shoots out, zips his pen across a prescription pad.

"Two medicines. One for you, one for the dog."

What else can she do – she takes it. "Thanks, but I don't have worms."

He looks past her. "Next!"

———

The envelope arrives on a motorcycle. Thick, yellow, business-sized. American stamps in the top right corner. John's handwriting. Addressed to her, not her and Melissa.

Which means . . .

Divorce papers. She's officially single, according to some judge named Wayne Porter III.

There's no note. Nothing from John to say he's sorry about how things didn't work out. Just the papers and a check for child support.

Piece of shit.

She's angry all over again. It's tidal, lately. Ebb, flow. Ebb, flow. Right now she wants to punch John in the throat.

It's –

———

" – The curse," her aunt says.

Eleni says, "There is no curse."

"There might be a curse," Vivi says, being all open-minded about the possibility. This much bad luck, why couldn't the curse be to blame?

"There is no curse," her mother repeats.

"Trust me, it is the curse," *Thea* Dora says.

"She did curse us," Vivi reminds her glaring mother. "Who is she again and why did she curse us?"

Her aunt gets busy fiddling with the tablecloth. "Why not tell her, Eleni?"

"No!"

"Fine," Vivi says. "I'll ask strangers. Everybody here knows everything, and they love to talk."

"You will not ask anything, do you hear me?" Eleni barks.

"Yes . . ." *Thea* Dora is rubbing her chin, playing the bearded villain in an old silent movie. ". . . that crazy *putana* put a curse on this place, I am certain."

———

The good news is there's an ancient ritual for that.

It's super-secret, passed down from one generation to the next. Some say it goes from mother to daughter. Others believe it hops man to woman, woman to man. And it may or may not be taught only on Good Friday. In some retellings, it skips a generation.

Like any good ritual, it's a lot like a recipe:

1 bowl of water.

1 bottle of olive oil.

1 (or more) potentially cursed person(s).

1 woo-woo person.

———

Method:

"For a woman to pass it to her daughter, she cannot speak it directly," *Thea* Dora emphasizes. "She must write the necessary words on paper, and place it in a bible for her daughter to read on Good Friday."

"Do you know it?" Vivi asks her mother.

"No. Our mother passed it to Dora, not me."

"Why?"

"You ask too many questions, Vivi. Why did I raise such a curious child?"

Her aunt recites a prayer, keeps it down low where Vivi can't pick words out of the lineup. Sign of the cross over the bowl with her hand. A few drops of oil in the bowl. They immediately separate.

Vivi's not tired, but she yawns.

"There!" *Thea* Dora says. "You have the evil eye from that woman."

"Yawning means I have the evil eye?"

"Don't mock the evil eye, Vivi," her mother says.

"I'm not. I just didn't realize all those times I thought was sleepy I was really just evil eyed."

Eleni gives her the do-not-mess-with-me look.

Thea Dora points to the bowl. "Swish your finger in the water and rub it on your lips. Three times."

And now Vivi really wants a salad.

"Good," Eleni says after her sister traces an oily cross on Vivi's forehead, then repeats the ritual on Eleni herself. "Now that Vivi is no longer cursed, we can trust her to take us somewhere. I need to get outside before I go crazy."

Vivi raises an eyebrow. "Before?"

✺ 74 ✺

VIVI

S O WHERE ARE THEY going? That's today's flammable discussion. Eleni wants out of town. *Thea* Dora wants *frappe*. Melissa, when she shows up, casts a ballot for shopping. Vivi wants them to hurry up and make up their minds.

Bicker, bicker, bicker. Dogs chasing their tails.

Not Biff—he's under the table enjoying his worm-free existence.

Vivi slams the metaphorical hammer. "I want to see some history," she says. "And guess who has the car keys?"

———

They zip out of town in Vivi's VW, headed NW to Dimini.

Dimini: Population three thousand – give or take a goat or two.

No good reason to go there except the ruins. Way, way back, a Neolithic civilization settled on the hill. They moved on, died out, evolved (take your pick), and then *Mycenaeans* decided they liked the view and built a palace on top of the bones.

The people and their buildings are long gone, but the foundations are stubborn.

Very Greek of them.

Vivi helps her aunt out of the car. There's not much room in the back, and her aunt is a woman who needs a lot of room.

"Remind me why we care about this old crap," Melissa mutters.

"Because it is history," her grandmother says. "One day someone might be looking at the ruins of your house, wondering how you used to live and what sort of person you were."

Melissa is pulling her sheet of hair into a tight ponytail. "It's creepy if you ask me."

"Then you should leave them something good to talk about, eh?" Eleni says.

Vivi pays for the tickets. Melissa's technically a child so she gets in free. The cashier passes out electronic guides with numbers corresponding to each pile of rocks.

Thea Dora is moving slow. Vivi hangs back to keep an eye on her aunt.

"*Thea*, are you okay?"

Sweat rolls down her face, a river looking for the sea.

"It is hot, and that hill . . ." She waves at the landscape.

Not much of a hill – more like a pimple. But in her aunt's condition it may as well be Kilimanjaro.

"It's steep for me, too," Vivi says. "Let's take it slow. Leave the rushing to the fools."

Short stone teeth jut from the ground – ancient pickets. Other stones sit stacked in gray and brown layers. To the west is the Mycenaean settlement with its big tourist draw: a *tholos* tomb cut into the hill. Curvy walls, base wider than the top. The beehive roof collapsed centuries ago, and the tomb's thirty-five-hundred-year-old occupant is long gone.

Chances he walked out alone are slim.

The Neolithic ruins are fading from the hill's memory. Scraps of five circular walls and several single-roomed dwellings. Nothing left of them but foundations.

Vivi squints and tries to invoke the past. No television, no fast food, no cell phones. Peaceful in a way the world today isn't.

"Vivi." *Thea* Dora drags her back to the present, with its iPods and McDonald's and constant static. "Who is this girl Melissa sees?"

They pause for a moment on the hillside. Further up, Eleni is snapping a photograph for a couple of tourists.

"Olivia? Her family is Canadian, that's all I know."

Listen first; speak later – after her aunt shows her hand.

"Is it a good family?"

"I don't know. Why?"

"The girls have been seen in the company of some boys."

"Isn't that normal? Teenage boys and girls go together like teenage boys and girls. Is there some problem I haven't heard about?"

No way is she about to mention the incident at the train tracks. That stays between the two of them. Anyway, no one gets a say in how she raises Melissa – except John, and he's not here, is he?

"Girls that age should have a chaperone."

Vivi says, "A chaperone? How last century."

"I do not think she should keep company with the boys. One of them, Thanasi is his name, comes from a very bad family."

"What, are they Turkish drug lords or something?"

———

Turkey and Greece are longtime frenemies. They go way, way back to the 15th century, when the Ottoman Empire snatched up bits of Greece and stuffed them in its bulging pocket. In 1821, Greece waved bye-bye to its overlords, had a bit of a war, gave themselves a public holiday to celebrate. After that, Turkey and Greece spent forever bickering over custody of Cyprus and swaths of the Aegean Sea and its airspace. Raised their fists a couple of times – in the eighties, in the nineties – but never came to blows.

Now they're in time-out, each country back in its corner, glaring across the ring.

———

"His great-grandfather and your grandfather were friends. Best friends. They were inseparable, those boys. Every year they would dive together for the cross on Epiphany. Do you know how cold the water is here in January?" No waiting for an answer. "Then one day his great-grandfather stole from your grandfather. After that everyone knows they are a bad family."

Small-town Greek logic.

"So let me see if I've got this straight. Because Thanasi's ancestor took something from Melissa's ancestor, it means this boy is no good?"

"Yes. Very bad blood."

Oooookay.

"What did he steal?"

"A chicken," *Thea* Dora says.

"A chicken? Like, one chicken? Not all the chickens?"

"One, yes. She was a very good egg producer. It was a great loss to the family during the war."

Vivi can die now, because she's officially heard everything.

"All this is about a chicken? I'm supposed to chaperone my daughter, out in plain sight, because of a chicken?"

"Who knows what this boy is capable of with the blood of a thief in his veins?"

Vivi thinks about it. "Melissa doesn't have a chicken."

But from the set of her aunt's lips, Vivi knows she's thinking cherry trumps chicken.

The older woman continues. "Do you want Melissa to have a bad reputation?"

"Why would she have a bad reputation? None of our relatives were donkey thieves, were they? Did they sell black market firewood?" She's trying not to sound indignant, but it's happening anyway.

"Vivi, my love, do not be naïve. Reputation matters in a town this small. People talk. You do not want your daughter to be the focus of their gossip. You and I know what a good girl she is, but not everybody knows her like we do, eh?"

Vivi looks to the rubble for wisdom, but rocks don't say much.

"Do you suppose these people gossiped about each other for no good reason?"

Thea Dora puts an arm around her shoulder. "Of course. It is the way of all people. We enjoy a story where someone else is suffering for a change, instead of us."

"Hurry up," Eleni calls out. "We are going to the tomb." She and Melissa wave frantically. Vivi waves back with a lead hand.

Chaperone? Melissa will hate her.

Correction: Melissa will hate her more.

But what choice is there? Keeping Melissa safe – from harm and gossip – isn't optional.

Chaperone. Even the word pisses her off. She wants more freedom for Melissa, not less.

Vivi doesn't want Melissa to grow up to be her.

75

VIVI

TAKIS IS UNDER THE tree with his ass.

"*Xena*, you are just in time."

Vivi won't make eye contact with the donkey. "Let me guess: You're making more feta and you want me to help?"

"No, I need someone to brush my donkey. My knees hurt. It will rain tonight, I think."

"He looks fine to me."

"Do you want to learn about olives or not?"

"Does he bite?"

"Only if he's in a bad mood."

Vivi asks, "Is he in a bad mood?"

"He is a donkey."

Takis gives her the brush, rolls a new cigarette with his two free hands.

"Does he have a name?"

"Eh, I call him *Gaidaros*."

Creative, that Takis, naming his donkey Donkey. He crouches on the ground, smoking, watching Vivi brush. So far the donkey is cool, happy enough to let her brush him with long strokes. His tail is tangled up in twigs and leaves, but he seems okay with Vivi's attention there, too.

What the hell is she doing here?

Not dragging Zeus-knows-what out of a donkey's tail, but here, meaning in Greece. Peeling away the layers, there's nothing underneath except a thin, selfish hope that they could be happy here.

She goes all tough love, tells herself what she did was the expensive, grownup version of running away from home. Yeah, she ran – far away from her problems. And her problems were cool with that. They knew a fresh batch of their foreign cousins would be waiting here for Vivi.

Problems: they're the Interpol of the psyche.

If she had any stones she'd pack them up, move back home, deal with her problems like an adult. Set up visitation with John so Melissa can have her dad around. Find a job, go back to school. Night classes. Do something she's always wanted to do. But what? That MBA is flopping around in her résumé like a dying fish.

Donkey is sick of her. His rear hoof shoots out, nails her in the thigh. Vivi's whole world explodes in a mixture of fire and glitter. She cries because *goddamn*.

"That was just a tap." Takis rolls another cigarette. "What have you learned?"

"Never stand behind a donkey?"

"Greece is a donkey. She will kick you if you try and catch her from behind. You must always come from the front!"

Vivi is hopping around on one leg, eyes throwing wet streamers down her face. "Really?"

"No, I just make that up."

Great joke, from the way he slaps his thigh, rocking back and forth, cackling. Not so funny from the splash zone.

It takes a while, but the pain loses its bright edge and her woes start slamming into each other, jockeying for attention. And suddenly she gets it: every time Melissa cut herself she was purposely standing behind a metaphorical donkey, because physical pain is a hog. It's not big on sharing. A cut, a kick, a slam (choose your own flavor of self-harm) elbows its way to the front of the line and demands immediate attention. Mental anguish has no choice but to skulk to the back and wait its turn.

She goes back to the donkey. This time she stands off-center.

Brush on, brush off.

✿ 76 ✿

MAX

WORK IS GOOD, BUSY.
Life is okay.

He doesn't have Vivi but he has his health.

July comes along and every day is the same. Hot, hot. Lots of sun. The tourists are happy: this is the Greece they paid for.

July's new moon means it's festival time in Agria. Fisherman's Night, they call it, but it's two nights not one. Locals, visitors, tourists, all of them welcome to dance, sing, eat fish soup and anything else the fishermen catch that day.

Good times.

Max doesn't want good times, he wants busy times. Can't keep his head on straight unless he's too busy to think.

But Anastasia says they're going. So . . .

They're going.

❧ 77 ❧

VIVI

THE COTTAGE SHIVERS. IT'S earthquake proof (Greek regulations call for concrete and rebar), but building inspectors don't care if a house can withstand teenagers.

"That went okay," Eleni says. She's by the phone waiting for Vivi's father to leave for work. How can she leave a message if he's home?

"Understatement of the year," Vivi says. "I'd call it spectacular."

"Is the door broken?"

Vivi shakes her head. "Not this time."

"Well, there is always next time."

❧ 78 ❧

MELISSA

W E'RE GOING TO THE festival, Mom said.

It'll be fun, Mom said.

You have to stay with your grandmother or me. No wandering off on your own, Mom said.

Melissa slams the door with her foot.

Mom's new rule S-U-C-K-S. She looks for the loophole, but there isn't one big enough to shove her whole body through. Mom says she has to be chaperoned – and that's that.

Olivia is going to laugh herself sick. Melissa can hear her now, gloating about how her parents let her do whatever.

An hour later she's telling Dr Triantafillou all about it. Painting Mom black, a halo circling her own head.

The shrink (red dress, red espadrilles with red ribbons) takes it all in. When Melissa's done ranting, she says, "If you want freedom, you have to prove you can handle it. What have you done to show your mother you're an adult?"

"Why are you taking her side?"

Arms folded, legs crossed. Melissa knows she's closed for all reasonable business. But so what? Whatever side she's on, she's always standing there alone.

"I'm not here to take sides. Amongst other things, it's my job to help you reason your way through challenges, in a healthy way."

Yeah, yeah, yeah. So she says.

But what has she done to show Melissa she's a rock steady shrink?

Except be there.

❧ 79 ❧

MAX

VIVI IS HERE – SHE has to be. Everybody is here.
He wants to see her, but he doesn't want her to see him with Anastasia.

(Asshole, Max. Asshole.)

Two shots. Maybe she's coming tomorrow, not tonight.

Is that lucky or unlucky? He can't say.

Anastasia's clutching his hand like he's a lifejacket, and all he can think about is shaking her loose. He's tired of saving her from being single. Tired of the nagging, the tears. He wasn't going to come tonight, but this morning it was stay and fight or get to the hospital on time. The hospital couldn't wait, and he didn't want it to, anyway. It's where he gets to be him.

So he didn't want to come, but here he is.

The waterfront street is alive. Lights everywhere, fresh seafood on display. Tourists are going crazy for a giant (dead) octopus. Great for photo ops, bad for eating. Much too tough without lengthy preparation. But they don't care. They're posing next to the dead cephalopod, "cheese-ing" into their cell phones.

The promenade is bulging with celebrants. Walking, talking, eating, drinking. The ouzo flows. Waiters dance across the street, trays of *mezedes* balanced high. Marinated peppers, grilled zucchini, *dolmades*, spicy bites of *kalamari*, keeping appetites satisfied, but not sated, until entrees hit the table.

The no-traffic zone stretches way, way past its usual end. A carousel marks the new stop. Workers have been busy all week, erecting the stage for dancing.

(Not that Greeks need a stage to dance. They dance anywhere, anytime. Even on a bus if the mood strikes. You could say life is their stage.)

Bumper cars, Ferris wheel, food carts. Something for everyone.

Speakers crackle. Time for dancing.

First up: traditional dances and traditional dancers.

Anastasia drags him that way, following the *Rembetika* folk music that (to him) is nails on a chalkboard. The diamond he bought her is cutting into his palm. It's large and flashy on her finger. Fitting that the physical symbol of their union causes him physical pain.

He pulls her in a different direction, toward a cart where corncobs are grilling over hot coals. Anastasia makes a face when he asks for two.

"Max, I can't eat that, it will get stuck between my teeth. What if someone sees me that way?"

"Come on, corn is healthy. Lots of vitamins."

"There you go being a doctor again. Can't you leave the hospital behind for one night?"

Max shrugs. He eats without mercy; the salty-sweet corn is out of this world.

"Your loss," he says.

Anastasia being Anastasia, she's suddenly penitent. "Sorry, my baby, I don't mean to be angry. When we are married I am sure we'll have other things to talk about. You won't want to stay so late at the hospital then."

"Wanting to stay late and having to stay late are two different things. I can't control it."

True – to a point.

Yeah, he's been working later and later. Finding excuses to break their dates. His desk is clean, his charts organized. When there's nothing left to do, he zips to the ER. He's useful there. Busy.

"Forget the hospital, start your own practice."

Round and round. Same old argument.

"I don't want my own practice. I love the hospital."

"But that's where the money is."

"Not everything is about money, Anastasia. I'd be bored working on my own. The urgency and rhythm of the hospital excites me. I'm not going to sit behind a desk and prescribe anti-fungal creams until I die."

She steps back, away from him. "How will you support us when we have a family? All you think about is yourself."

"I make good money now. It's not a fortune, but it's more than most people have. A lot of people have raised families on much less – including our own parents."

"I want more. We will have even less when I quit my job."

Vivi is on his mind – again. (Did she ever leave?) That conversation they had about women and work.

Vivi, Vivi, Vivi. He hurt her – and himself – and for what? To appease Mama and Anastasia.

But they're not worth it.

Too late now. He said what he said, did what he did, and now here they are. A man accepts consequences of his own making; otherwise he's still a boy.

Someone taps his shoulder.

Is it – ?

No. His cousin Soula.

He throws one arm around her shoulder, kisses her shiny hair. "And now you've got corn in your hair," he says.

She laughs. "It will be a snack for later. How are you, stranger?"

"Good. Where is your boyfriend?"

"He was boring, so I gave him back to his mama."

Kiss, kiss. Both cheeks. She repeats the ritual with Anastasia.

Soula says, "Sounds like you're giving my cousin a hard time."

"Men, you know." Anastasia turns away, but Max knows she's rolling her eyes.

Soula raises an eyebrow.

Max says, "It's nothing. Soula, you want corn?"

She pats her flat stomach to the tune of heavy bracelets jangling. "I've had two already and I'm getting ready for *souvlaki*. Have you seen Vivi? I wonder if she's here . . ."

His face says nothing. "I haven't seen her or Melissa."

"Too bad. I think I might go up and drag her here. She would love this."

Anastasia is suddenly attentive. "Who is Vivi?"

"A friend," Soula says. "I sold her a house."

Next: "And how do you know her?"

One wrong word and – say "Bye-bye" to your balls, Max.

"Her daughter was a patient. I introduced her to Soula because she needed a house."

Eye rolling, eye rolling. "Enough with the patients already." Moving on. "I'm going to touch up my lipstick. Soula, are you coming?"

Soula threads her arm through her cousin's. "No, I need to ask Max for some medical advice. Take your time."

Anastasia stalks away, all legs and miniskirt. Heads turn, ogle her body. Max doesn't care. Watching her move used to turn him on. Now he wants her to keep on walking.

"I'd rather eat crunchy glass flakes than play best friends with her. Sorry." Soula doesn't look sorry.

"Don't be."

"Do you really have to marry her?"

"Soula . . ."

"Fine, fine. Forget I said anything. You want to leave her here and come up to Vivi's with me?"

Does she know? He can't tell.

"I can't."

The folk music dies out. Something that was hot in the 80s takes over. Teenagers swoop the stage and Max laughs. He danced to this song when it was new.

"Maybe I can find her a good man. I found her a house; I can definitely find her a man. Blond or dark? What do you think?"

"She's been through a lot. Let her make her own choice."

"Sounds like you know." Eyebrow raised. No, not suspicious at all. "Pity you have to marry Anastasia, otherwise Vivi would be perfect for you. I wonder if Kostas would consider leaving the church?"

Was a time he couldn't imagine his brother in black. Now he can't imagine him the other way.

"Yeah, I don't think so."

"Let's ask him. Kostas!"

Speak of the –

Well, not the devil.

Anyway, Kostas appears, robes swirling around his feet.

"Look who came down from his mountain," Max says.

They hug. Lots of back slapping.

Kostas winks at Soula. "The food is good and I like to look at the pretty women."

Now Soula's got a cousin on each arm. They walk all the way to the Ferris wheel.

"I was just telling your brother it's a shame he's marrying Anastasia. If either of you were free, you'd be perfect for Vivi."

"Ah yes, Vivi." Kostas doesn't make eye contact. "She's a good woman. Just ask Max."

"Kostas – " Max starts.

Soula looks interested – very interested. "Do tell."

But Max doesn't kiss and dump and tell. (And look, Anastasia's headed their way.) Says, "You should come to the hospital, Kostas. The children would love to hear some Bible stories."

No time for Kostas to say anything – Anastasia's back and she's pissed.

"You left me," she announces.

"And you found us," Soula says.

Anastasia ignores her. "I thought you had gone home without me."

"Max wouldn't do that." Soula's smile is brittle. "It's my fault. I wanted to take my handsome cousins for a walk."

Anastasia notices the priest. "You are him."

"Holy Mother of our Lord, I am him. At least I think I am." He looks at Soula. "Am I?"

Soula smiles. "You look like him."

"Since the lady is never wrong, I must be him." Kostas takes Anastasia's hand. "And you must be my worthless brother's beautiful fiancée."

Embarrassing how fast she jerks her hand back.

"Max, your mother would be angry if she knew we were socializing with him."

Max has never hit a woman, but he wants to slap Anastasia.

"Kostas has a name, Anastasia."

That woman has no self-control. She turns on the other brother. "Why didn't you honor your parents wishes the way Max did? Your mother deserves better."

Max grabs her arm, jerks her away from the group. She winces but he doesn't let up. He pulls her close, gets up in her face. He doesn't want to be misunderstood.

"He is my brother." Teeth gritted, face dark. "Show some respect for him and for the church. And for me!"

"What do you care? Your mother – "

"To the devil with my mother! He is the most important person in the world to me."

Her lip shakes. "I thought I was the most important person in your life."

She does this: softens him up with her baby routine. Now it makes him sick. He wants a woman, not a girl.

"You won't be part of my life if you can't accept my brother."

"Look, Kostas. The lovers are fighting," Soula calls out. "You're meant to save that until after the wedding."

Max gives her the *not-now* look.

"Come on, I'm going to buy *souvlaki*," Soula tells the priest. "If my stomach gets much louder they'll have to turn the music up." She kisses Max on both cheeks, and Anastasia, too. "If I don't see you both later, I will definitely see you next weekend," she says.

Max says, "Next weekend?"

"*Thea* is throwing an engagement party for you and Anastasia – an official one. So you'd better be there."

"Party?"

"She didn't tell you?" To Anastasia: "You knew – right?"

Anastasia knew; it's on her face. He's going to strangle Mama. Slowly. Until her bones snap.

"Nobody did," Max says.

Soula shrugs. "If Kostas won't be my date, I'll ask Vivi. She might enjoy a Greek engagement celebration." But the twinkle in Soula's eyes says she's playing. She reaches up to hug him, keeps her voice low, for his ears only. "Cousin, if you want to get out you better hurry. Do it quick, like pulling off a sticky plaster."

Then they're gone. The crowd eats them whole.

"What did she say?" Anastasia demands.

"Nothing."

"Don't lie to me. She said something."

"If you want to know Soula's business, ask her."

"Okay. I'll go and ask her. I'm going to be your wife, you should be telling me everything. If I don't like what she tells me, I'm leaving."

"You do that."

"You better be here if I come back," she says.

"And if I'm not?"

"Then it's over."

"Okay," he says. "It's over. We're done. Goodbye."

"It's over when I say it's over!"

He holds up both hands. "Goodbye, Anastasia. Have a good life."

She walks away – that's what she does. Hips swaying, demanding attention from anywhere she can get it. But Max won't give her another minute.

He's free but he doesn't feel it yet.

That's because he knows:

There's going to be war before it's really over.

❦ 80 ❦

MAX

FOR A WHILE HE'S lost.
     That's okay, he wants to be lost.

Lights flash. From the bumper cars, from the carousel, from everywhere. Children shriek.

Happiness bleeding all over the place.

This is how it's supposed to be.

He makes a light pole home. Crosses his arms, watches life. Teenagers flirting, vanishing into the long, dark stretch of the promenade. Full of hope and fun. Certain that life and love will always go their way.

Been about a thousand years since he was that young. Tonight, maybe longer.

An engagement party. Fuck. That means wedding plans are underway. Imagine if he'd prolonged this. He'd wake up one morning to a text demanding he be at the church that afternoon.

His phone rings.

Ignore, Ignore, Ignore.

He doesn't pray much, but he prays now – for salvation, for freedom without bloodshed. He saved himself, now he needs saving from what comes next.

And when he opens his eyes, she's there.

His salvation.

❦ 81 ❦

MAX

S HE'S IN YELLOW AND he's in trouble.

Aphrodite in her sundress, hair spilling over her shoulders; his heart aches just looking at her.

He misses her face, misses her conversation. A life with Vivi would be one of fire and friendship. A good life.

"I wasn't going to come over," she says. "Then I was, then I wasn't."

"Then you did."

"Apparently."

"Soula and Kostas wondered if you were here."

Vivi glances around. "Are they still here?"

"Somewhere. They got hungry."

Small talk mimicking mortar, filling in the cracks, holding the conversation together long enough for it to step onto solid ground.

"Is Melissa enjoying the festival?"

Vivi shrugs. "I don't know. She's here somewhere. My mother has a leash on her. The family suggested it might not be a hot idea to let her be so free. She exploded when I told her. Said I was ruining her life. The exact same thing I told my mother when I was her age."

"What do you think?"

Vivi looks up at the stars. "I think they're full of shit. I want to protect my daughter but not to the point where she can't have any fun with her friends. Apparently she has to pick her friends based on the family's approval, too. No whores, chicken thieves, or people whose families vote for opposing political parties. At this rate all that's left are imaginary friends." Her gaze drops, finds his. He tries not to look at her mouth. "What do you think?"

He abandons the pole for a nearby bench. A couple of kids were on it – now they're not. He sits, she sits.

"When I moved to England for what you call college, I was just a kid. At the time I thought I was badass. I loved that nobody knew me there. Nobody cared what I did or who my friends were. I could party as I pleased – no judgment."

"Okay . . ."

"Greece is different – especially here where the town is small. They thrive on knowing what everyone else is going, and they talk and talk and talk. The bigger the scandal, the more excitement it produces. If there are no big things, they magnify the small things. That sustains them between major dramas. The trick is to not let their talk stop you from living your life. If you want to do something, do it. Just be aware that they will talk about you, and all of them will have advice or tell you how you could have done it better."

She moves her eyes to the constantly shifting crowd. "So I should just let Melissa do her thing?"

"Within reason, of course. She's still so young. It would be nice if family feuds weren't passed down to the next generation. In the grand scheme of things a chicken thief is not so bad."

"It's not exactly murder," she says. "What were you like in college?"

"Horny."

They laugh together. He holds out his hand. Vivi makes a fist against the yellow.

"Dance with me," he says.

"Okay, but I have to warn you . . ."

❧ 82 ❧

VIVI

"... I DON'T REALLY DANCE."

Max leads her to the stage. She takes in the other dancers, the worn, scuffed planks, the instability of it all.

"Is this thing safe?"

Max laughs. "Yeah, it's safe. They've been using the same wood for fifty years."

He's joking. He's joking?

"While I have confidence in your confidence, a lot of things have been going wrong lately. Dragging me up here might end in disaster – just so you know."

"It's not much of a drop. Chances are we'll make it."

He curls his hand around her hip. Nice, she thinks. Too nice. But she steps closer, embraces the nice. His body runs hotter than hers, but hers runs wetter.

Bodies do their own thing. They don't wait for permission. So Vivi's body is getting ready for the possibility of getting what it wants. Doesn't matter what her head has to say.

"Is your fiancée okay with this? I don't want her coming after me with a meat cleaver."

His hand goes north, cups the back of her neck.

"It's just a dance," he says.

"Just one dance. This can't go any further. I won't be the other woman."

Yeah right, her body says.

"Anastasia and I are done. It's over. There's no engagement. No relationship."

She stops. Doesn't know what to think, doesn't know what to say. What's appropriate when someone loses something you didn't want them to have? Aaaand, what's appropriate when your last thought was purely selfish?

"I'm sorry," she says. Silence. "Wow, when did that happen?"

"Not long ago."

To an outsider, it looks like she's relaxing into him.

That's a no. She's tighter, tenser than she's ever been. They could use her nerves to restring an orchestra. Max's hands are on the move again. Down, down, to the small of her back. The S curve. The yes, yes, yes curve.

"Wait," she whispers. "I don't want to be the headline news in tomorrow's gossip fest."

The dancing horde doesn't give them much room. Max moves back maybe an inch.

"Better?"

"Better," Vivi says. And worse.

Max closes the distance with his head. His breath is hot against her ear. "I'm going to fuck you so hard and good you'll never stop craving me."

Vivi scans the crowd, scans, scans.

The music is loud, yeah, but what if there's spy equipment about? People this nosy, can't have them missing any of the juicy stuff.

"I don't have an addictive personality," she says.

"I can change that."

"When did you plan on starting?"

"As soon as we get back to the Jeep."

"Where is it?"

"Not far."

She thinks about her mother and Melissa and how she should tell them she's leaving. But Melissa is safe with her grandmother, and if Eleni sees her with Max there will be questions. Too many questions.

So: "Everyone needs one addiction – right?"

Right.

———

World's oldest teenagers, these two. Back to the Jeep and he's up her dress and down her dress and into her with his fingers.

He stops long enough to drive, but he keeps one hand on her and in her.

Max makes her crazy for two whole minutes with his small talk. Don't talk, she thinks. Do. As in, do me.

He talks and talks and she can't because his fingers aren't letting her.

The Jeep jerks to a stop outside her cottage and Max changes the subject – to them, to her, to what he's going to do with her.

To her.

"Just shut up and do it," she says.

"Trust me, it's hotter if I tell you first."

He's down and out of the Jeep and opening her door. And then he lifts her out and bends her over the hot, damp seat.

"I'm going to keep talking and you're going to keep listening. Okay?"

Can't speak. She's too busy raining all over his fingers.

He stops before she explodes, pulls away. Her world is instantly ten degrees cooler.

"Inside," he says.

"Inside."

She can hear the promenade's music from here. *Thump, thump.* Her pulse is racing to keep up. She unlocks the front door and Biff bolts out.

The look on his face says he's real sorry he's interrupting. He pees. Then it's back inside to the cool kitchen floor, as though he's been there all evening and the dog hair scattered on the couch is an illusion.

Max knows which room is hers, so he takes her there.

She feels wild and awake and simultaneously hazy. Too hot to care that there's never been anyone but John. She should tell him, but not right now. No way does she want to dislodge his fingers from the underwear he's pulling down, down, down with her dress.

Now she's naked and he's not and her shyness kicks in. He grabs hers wrists, stops them from doing a shitty job of covering herself up.

"I want to look at you," he says.

"I want to see you, too."

She gets one wrist back so he can unbuckle his belt and shuck his clothes. Talented man, that Max.

"Can you see how much I want you?"

Like she can miss it.

She kneels in front of him, looks all the way up.

"Show me."

❧ 83 ❧

MELISSA

S LIPPING HER GRANDMOTHER IS easy. Melissa waits until she's too busy socializing to notice her fading away. She knows she shouldn't be doing this, but whatever. It's too late now.

Come at eleven, the note said. She found it this morning, wedged in the gap between her shutters and the window.

Didn't tell Dr Triantafillou, did she?

An hour ago she was fretting, trying to figure a way to meet Thanasi without Mom finding out, but then Mom let her go one way with Grams, while she went another.

An opportunity presented itself so she took it.

She's wearing her favorite outfit and Mom's least favorite. *One or the other, Mel*, she always says about the pink pleated miniskirt and the white top with the spaghetti straps. But Melissa's clever. She hid the top under a T-shirt, and now she's stowing that T-shirt on the far side of the tiny church near their house. That way she can find it easily later, before she sneaks back to the promenade with a mouthful of excuses she's already thought up.

Thanasi is going to go wild when he sees her outfit. At least she hopes so.

Doesn't she?

But by the time she reaches the meeting place, the buzz is mostly gone. Suddenly, meeting a boy in the dark doesn't seem like a great idea. She can't back out now, though, because Olivia's voice is whistling through the night. "Woo . . . Tyler, is that you?"

She can hear Olivia, but she can't see her.

"No, I'm a psycho with a chainsaw, and I'm here to eviscerate you," Melissa calls out.

"Eww, gross," Olivia says, but she's laughing. "Don't be such a loser. Come on. Wait. Put this on."

Makeup changes hands. Melissa sets her font to bold. Then she steps into the olive grove. The town lights give one last flicker before vanishing.

Olivia is there. Vassili, too. And next to them Thanasi is smiling, his teeth almost glowing in the dark, like they're painted with the same spooky stuff they put on those sticky stars and planets.

She smiles back, but it's cool plastic. She remembers the kiss and how it didn't fit.

"We're going over there." Olivia points to a spot in the distance. Doesn't matter, Melissa can't see it anyway. "You guys go over there."

"Shouldn't we stay together?"

"Why? Are you into four-ways, Tyler? I had no idea you were so kinky. Let's see if you can at least hit a home run, first."

The guys have no clue what she's saying, but Melissa gets her message loud and clear. This isn't just a make-out session. Olivia is daring her to hook up, to go all the way. Be like me, she's saying.

"If she doesn't want to go – " Vassili starts, but Olivia shuts him up by dragging him deeper into the black.

And now Melissa's alone with Thanasi, whose hands are getting too friendly.

She wiggles away, tries to put some distance between them.

"Come on, Melissa, don't you like me?"

His touch is doing weird things to her, making her hot and cold at the same time. She's frozen, but she wants to run.

"Can't we just, you know, talk?"

"Of course," he says lightly.

Olivia's giggles fade.

Thanasi sits on the ground, his back supported by the rough twisty trunk of an olive tree. Melissa kneels beside him, fighting to stay cool and not freak out.

"Do you like sex, Melissa?"

"I – "

———

One bite at a time.

———

Thanasi pulls her hand until –

   – swiveling her legs –

   – straddling his lap –

"– are you my girl? Show me – "

She doesn't say yes, doesn't say no.

"– something for me. All the girls do it – "

   – metal scratching metal –

"– your hand . . . please."

Please, he says. As though she's directing this teenage train wreck.

Except he's pushing her down on the ground into the ground pushing up her skirt pushing into her. And she can't scream doesn't scream won't scream because you're supposed to say "No" before screaming.

And she never said "No."

She never said, "Yes" either, but everyone knows "No" is the power word.

And she never said it. She's sure of that.

Isn't she?

Then it doesn't matter because he's done and she's as cold outside as inside. And she's sore and stretched the way she felt when she was six and she shoved Barbie's leg up her nose.

She makes two Melissas. Cuts herself down the middle. Melissa girl. Melissa woman. Melissa woman feels all grown up. Melissa girl is crying, crying, wishing she could go back in time and scream, "No."

"That was fun," Thanasi says. "Maybe your friend can teach you how to give head. She's a pro."

Melissa girl, Melissa woman – doesn't matter which one speaks. "It's not nice of Vassili to tell you about him and Olivia."

Thanasi laughs. "He didn't tell me."

"You and Olivia . . .?"

"You had me all hot and hard the other day. She was something to do. Men get sick if they don't . . ." He jerks his fist in the air.

Both Melissas go icy cold. "But she's my friend."

"So?"

"Why didn't you tell me before we had sex?"

"Would you be here if I did?"

"No."

"So, it was good that I didn't. Come on, Melissa, you liked it. It's good."

It's not Melissa woman or girl who makes the next move. It's Melissa, daughter of Vivi, granddaughter of Eleni. She takes one small step toward evening the score. Knees his balls right out of the court.

"You're a fucking asshole!" she shouts to the tune of his gagging.

Stupid little girl, she's crying and crying as she waits for Olivia at the edge of the grove.

She doesn't have to wait long.

"Oops," Olivia says. "Looks like someone popped a cherry."

"What do you mean?"

"Let's just say I'd wash that skirt in some cold water before your mom sees it, or she's going to totally freak out."

Olivia is right: the sun is setting on her skirt. A long copper smear. Mom buys her pads, so there's no way she'll believe Melissa has her period.

Their friendship shatters. She looks at Olivia, former friend and backstabber.

"Screw you, Olivia. And by the way, thanks for sucking Thanasi's dick."

"At least I'm not a tease. You lead him on, pretending you liked him while your legs stayed shut. He needed a real woman, so I gave him one."

"You can't even imagine how much I hate you right now."

"Not nearly as much as I hate your boring, pathetic ass. No wonder you tried to kill yourself. Figures that you'd manage to fuck that up too!"

It gets physical.

Melissa slaps Olivia.

Olivia slaps Melissa.

Melissa shoves the other girl as hard as she can. Olivia's feet shoot out from under her. Her arms windmill, trying to stop the fall, but it's way too late. Melissa doesn't mean for Olivia's head to crack against the sharp rock, but it does.

Terrified, she runs. Leaves Olivia there, running nowhere, staining the sticks and stones with her broken bones.

84

VIVI

VIVI IS GLOWING IN the dark.
 That's how happy the woman is.
In this moment her world is perfect.
Makes a nice change.
COME ON, YOU ALREADY know that won't last.

❧ 85 ❧

VIVI

VIVI SAYS, "DID YOU hear that?"

Fun and games over (and over and over), Max is flat on his back in the sexual recovery position, Vivi draped over his bare chest. His fingers are doing this delicious thing where they dance up and down her back.

Capital B-L-I-S-S.

The shutters are wide open, the windows, too. And now every little noise is a huge deal. Cicadas and their monotonous friction sound multilayered, complex.

"No. I'm dead."

"That came on fast," she says.

"You should know. You killed me."

Yeah, not that dead. He rolls toward her, hands up, up, up her arms until they're pinned above her head.

"It's a miracle," he says.

"Zombie. I should cut off your head."

Then she hears it again, an undercurrent below the cicada symphony. A small, sharp noise. The sound of dying.

Vivi is out of the bed and into her dress.

"It sounds like something's hurt."

Max pulls on his jeans. "If it was trouble Biff would be all over it."

Louder now.

"I hear it," Max says. "Let me go first." He points to the side of the house.

Outside, the dark is too stubborn to let the porch light creep far, so all they see is night. But there's something inside the darkness, on the house's right side.

Vivi squints, and soon her eyes get the message.

"Jesus," she whispers. "Turn Melissa's bedroom light on, and open the shutters!"

He does it – and fast.

That doesn't stop an eternity passing while she waits.

The shape in the dark is Melissa, crouching and sobbing and scrub, scrub, scrubbing something under the outside faucet. Biff is at her side, lapping water.

The girl jerks at the sudden light spilling from the room, staining her with its aura. Vivi can see her daughter's eyes are wide and red-rimmed. She looks surprised – no, horrified – to see Vivi.

"Mom, what are you doing here?"

"I live here?"

Mama bear runs to her daughter. She's all over the girl with her eyes, making sure, making doubly sure she's physically okay.

She's okay. Her shell's not cracked.

But her face tells a horror story. Black makeup flows downhill from her eyes, and Vivi knows Melissa wasn't wearing a river's worth of makeup when they all the left the house together. In her hands is something wet and twisted.

"What's this? Melissa, what's wrong?"

Then the picture soaks in another inch, and Vivi realizes her daughter is crouching there in her underwear.

"Is that your skirt?"

"Yeah."

Melissa's bottom lip is shaking the way it did when she was little. It never happened unless she was hurt – and hurt big – which is why Vivi's insides are freaking the hell out.

"Mel!" She grabs the girl's shoulders. "What's wrong? Why are you washing your skirt?"

"It's nothing."

"It's not nothing. Show me."

She's gentle about it – easing, not prying Melissa's fingers away from the sodden fabric. When she holds it up to the light she sees the monochromatic rainbow.

"Did you hurt yourself?"

Vivi can't help glancing at her daughter's wrists, but they're unbroken. There's nothing but scars, and they're not much more than the memory of bad times.

Another light comes on. Then another. Max is giving her all the light the house can give. Then he's back at Melissa's window, looking out.

"Is she hurt?"

No. Yes. Maybe? She can't tell and it's driving her crazy.

"I don't know. I don't know anything right now. Mel, is someone else hurt?"

"No."

Vivi tries doing the math, but the numbers keep changing.

❧ 86 ❧

MAX

Not Max, though. He's adding things up just right.
   "Were you out with a boy?"

❧ 87 ❧

VIVI

M AX – " VIVI STARTS, BUT her mouth snaps shut when Melissa nods.

"What were you doing?" he asks.

Vivi groans. "Was it Thanasi?"

Melissa pauses. The pause turns into a nod.

Shit. Shit, shit, shit.

"Did he hurt you?" Max asks.

"Yes. No." Melissa's crying, making big snot bubbles. "I didn't say 'No.' I wanted to, but I never said it. Olivia told me – "

"I'm going to kill her," Vivi says. "I knew she was trouble. I could see it in that little bitch's eyes. She won't be smirking when I tell the police she facilitated a rape."

She's boiling over, pacing back and forth like a madwoman.

Same way Eleni does.

But Melissa eyes are wide and haunted. Something else is wrong or Vivi doesn't know her daughter.

"Vivi," Max says softly. He's behind her now, touching her shoulder. "She said this was consensual. Maybe we should believe her, eh?"

"What, am I supposed to believe my baby has been flat on her back with some boy? She's fifteen. *Fifteen*. She barely has boobs yet."

"Mom!"

"Vivi," Max says, "don't overreact."

"I'm not overreacting! I'm freaking out because my baby is having sex. You don't have children – you don't know. It's bad enough that people are talking about her and that boy, but now her reputation is ruined."

Shutting up sounds great, but the secondhand words keep strutting out, every last one of them puffed up with indignation and anger. On the upside, she's digging herself a nice, deep pit. Good place to bury herself later.

"Ever since I got here everybody has been telling me how to raise my daughter. I just want her to be a child for a while longer. I don't want her putting out for some asshole – "

"Like you, you mean?" Melissa says, the question all ugly and malformed.

Whoosh! Say goodbye to Vivi's steam. She doesn't look at Max. She knows when she's on her own.

"Your father didn't touch me for months at a time. Just how long am I supposed to stay celibate? Until my vagina has cobwebs?"

"You and dad could have – "

"Honey, your dad is gay. He's just not interested in what I've got to offer. He never really was."

"So?"

"So, he likes penis. Something we all apparently have in common," Vivi mutters.

"Mom . . ."

"Are you hurt at all? Do you need to go to the hospital?"

"No."

"Okay. That's something." Vivi rubs the new crease on her forehead, but it's sticking around. "This isn't over. For starters, you're grounded until I decide what to do."

"But, Mom . . ."

"But nothing. I have to put that skirt in the washing machine before the stain sets."

Max follows her inside. "You want me to take her to the hospital for a physical?"

"Why? So they can tell me what I already know?"

"Melissa is a good girl, Vivi. She just made a bad choice she's not ready for emotionally."

"She could have said 'No.' She could have chosen not to sneak away. Clearly I can't trust her, and I hate that most of all."

"If I was her father – "

"Well, you're not."

Insta-regret. But there's no backspace on the spoken word.

"I have to go," he says stiffly. "Work in the morning. Unless you guys need me."

Vivi shakes her head. "Max . . ."

"Is it true what Melissa said about your ex?"

"That's he's gay? Yeah."

"Idiot."

"Him or me?"

But it's too late. Max is gone.

❧ 88 ❧

VIVI

VIVI MAKES COFFEE, THEN she makes more coffee. Somewhere along the way she realizes she's made three cups and finished exactly zero.

Lights switch on and off in her head.

She gets up, goes to Melissa's room. Her daughter's not even pretending to sleep.

"Melissa," she says. "Where is your grandmother?"

———

Melissa doesn't know.

Vivi doesn't know.

"You want to talk about what happened?" Vivi asks.

No, Melissa doesn't.

✤ 89 ✤

ELENI

I T'S BY DESIGN THAT the two women meet, but not Eleni's.

"Eleni?"

Eleni looks around. "Who is there?"

The woman steps out from behind the tree at the bottom of Dora's street.

"Sofia? Is what you? What do you want?"

"I want to talk."

"I have nothing to say to you."

"I said *I* want to talk. All you need to do is listen."

Eleni does not want to listen. She has never had time for Sofia's foolishness. Not all those years ago, not now.

"I am dying. It is cancer."

"So?"

"I thought you would be glad."

"Sofia," Eleni says. "All this time you think I care? I have never cared if you live, if you die. You were nothing to me. You are still nothing—a mosquito buzzing around my head."

"You took everything from me. But I took something from you, too."

"What did you take from me?" Eleni sounds bored, tired, too old for cryptic conversations. "Say what you mean to say, then go away."

Sofia tells her.

❦ 90 ❦

VIVI

IVI KNOWS A LOST cause when she sees one. She gathers up her
fury, her anxiety, her worry, and dumps the lot on the couch. No
point going to bed. May as well sit there and pretend to read.

Once again, her life is taking the fast train to Bedlam.

Melissa is out of (her) control.

Eleni is currently AWOL.

Max is gone – and by the way, thanks for the sex.

Biff . . . Well, Biff's cool. So there's that.

Stew, stew, stew. Marinating in misery.

Melissa is alive, but almost lost to her. Vivi knew Olivia was a
problem (sometimes you just know) but she wanted to give the girl a
chance. The way . . . Well, the way Greece is giving her a chance.

Now Olivia is all out of chances. So is that kid, Thanasi. But she
can't ruin him without ruining Melissa, too.

She thinks about killing him, about hiding the body deep down. It's
a nice idea, a fun fantasy, but he's someone else's kid. Someone else's
beloved problem child.

What's wrong with this family?

Better question: Is there anything wrong with this family?

Maybe this is how families are, how life is. Every day is a minefield, and the goal is to get to the other side without blowing up the people who matter most.

God, the smell of Max won't go away. It's sticking around when he's long gone. Spicy citrus all over her, around her, in her. Her bedroom reeks of him.

She can't be with him. They argue too easily, too passionately, and about things that matter. He's entangled in every disaster she's stepped in since they got here. And his engagement is barely broken.

An engagement of his mother's design. Where's the spine in that? But. . .

She's in love with him. She wants him back here, now – not just for the sex, but also to have a wall to flail against and hold.

And she wants him to stay the hell away.

———

Night does its thing – slowly.

Sometime after three, the front door opens and Eleni skulks in.

Vivi slaps the book shut.

"Go to bed, Vivi. It is only me."

"I was worried about you."

"Do not be so needy. I was at Dora's house, celebrating the festival."

Oh really? "Did you forget something?"

Eleni pulls the silk scarf from her neck, drops it on the kitchen table. "No. I forget nothing."

"Like, maybe your granddaughter."

Silence. Eleni does a lot of things before she speaks. Dumps two teaspoons of Greek coffee in the *briki*. Sugar, water, lights the gas. Doesn't say a word until the coffee is in her cup.

"The world does not revolve around you, Vivi. It is time you realize that."

Say what?

"Excuse me? One time I ask you to look out for your grandchild and you screw it up. Do you know what happened tonight?"

"Is she alive?"

"Yes."

"In one piece?"

"Yes."

"Then what is the problem?"

"I left her in your care."

"Vivi, Melissa is your daughter. It is your job to look after her. You let her run wild, and now you complain about it? I raised you to be smarter than that."

Vivi laughs, cruelly. "I raised myself. You were too busy looking out for your own interests."

"You see what you want to see, my doll. Look at John. I have my own problems right now. My past is bleeding into my present, just like Dora saw in the coffee grounds."

"Is it that woman?"

Eleni finishes her coffee. "You take care of your business and I will take care of mine. What did I tell you, Vivi? Coming to Greece was a bad idea. Now we are all suffering because of your foolishness."

"In that case," Vivi says, "suffer on your own."

❧ 91 ❧

VIVI

S TRANGE MORNING.
Could be a movie set – nothing is as it seems. Everyone's lines are rehearsed.

"I am going to see Dora," Eleni says, sometime after the watermelon truck swings by. "Do not fuss if I come in late."

Vivi does a Melissa. "Fine. Whatever."

Dusting, sweeping, dishes, laundry. A place for everything, and everything in its place.

Melissa is sleeping off her rough night.

Good, Vivi thinks. The girl is going to need it. She's got a lot of things planned for her daughter. Time-consuming things. Fruit picking, olive picking, school. If she likes the olive grove so much, Vivi can make it her second home.

After the harvest, she'll reevaluate.

One toe out of line and Melissa will be picking olives until her twenty-first birthday.

Biff is restless. Back and forth, back and forth.

Constantly alert.

What does he know that she doesn't?

92

MAX

D OC," VASSILI SAYS, "YOU were right about the scars."
"Huh?"

The kid is looking at him like he's lost it. "The scars from the needles. Girls like them."

Max comes back to earth. This isn't the time or place to get lost.

"You move fast. Who's the lucky girl?"

"Just a girl. Not the one I really like. She's into my friend."

"So steal her."

Vassili grins. "I don't think my girlfriend would be happy."

Max returns the grin. "You're all clear. I'll see you in a month."

"I've got a football game coming up. Can I play?"

"If you feel good enough to play, play."

Then it's back to kicking himself. It's keeping his erection away.

Vivi's the problem. He can't stop thinking about fucking her. And then fucking her over.

What's he going to do?

His phone has been a brick all morning. No good news, no bad news. No Vivi, but no Mama or Anastasia.

One of those mixed blessings people are always talking about.

———

Anastasia doesn't call.

Anastasia shows up.

Marches down the hall on her long legs, cutting a clean path to confrontation. She's wearing an inch of war paint.

Looking at her now, she seems so obvious. Even if he never makes things right with Vivi, Anastasia's no longer a contender. Better to be alone than married to misery.

His head nearly comes clean off his shoulders when she strikes, but he doesn't hit back. Doesn't say anything, either. Let her play out her melodrama. Have her five minutes of attention and years of (hospital) infamy.

"You . . . you . . . gypsy! You dog!"

She hits him again, and he gives her the same nothing.

"I can't stand to look at you," she says.

"So don't look at me. The door is that way." He points back the way she just came. "I'm trying to work here, and I don't want you scaring the children."

"Always with the children! Aren't I important too?"

"We broke up, Anastasia. Last night. If you've got amnesia, I know a guy."

But Anastasia, she talks right over him. "Every time you tell me you have to go to the hospital, I pray the children will go away so that you can come back to bed. You give everything to this place, there's nothing left for me."

Now she's attracting attention from people with bigger problems. Nurses, parents, patients – all curious.

He tries steering her into the waiting room. She slaps him away.

"Stop pushing me, Max. This is the problem, this hospital. We would be fine if you would just open your own clinic – "

"That's not what I – "

"We could be happy, and your mother could have her grandchildren."

" – want. I don't want children with you. I don't want you."

Third strike and he's out of patience. He's ready for her incoming hand. He pushes it down to her side.

"We're done," he says. "I told you that last night. Believe it."

"It's because of her, isn't it? That American *putana*."

"Vivi's not a whore."

Still holding her wrist, he steers her into the waiting room. Only one woman waiting, nose in a magazine. He gives her a look and she's gone. "Vivi or no Vivi, you and I are finished. Done. No more. No wedding. I'm sorry, but that's how it is."

That's her cue to cry. "But I love you."

"No, you love that I have earning potential."

He shakes her off, but she's not done with him yet.

"I forgive you," she says, dangerous glint in her eyes. "But I told you, if I find you cheating, I will kill the other woman. You'll never have her again. I followed you last night, I know where she lives."

Max shoves his finger in her face. "Touch her and I'll kill you. I can make it look like it was God's will."

93

VIVI

Sirens mean it's howl o'clock – just ask Biff. The dog is determined to drown them out with his voice.

Not happening. Those sirens are getting closer, louder.

Vivi shuts him inside, runs out to investigate. There's a bitter taste in her mouth, a bell in her head.

Police car. Ambulance. Police car.

In precisely that configuration. Which means there's trouble and somebody is hurt.

All three vehicles stop outside the gate.

Melissa appears at her side. She's paler than the chunk of feta in their refrigerator. "Mom, what's going on?"

She puts an arm around Melissa's shoulder, fakes confidence she doesn't feel. "I'm sure it's nothing."

But it is something, isn't it? Otherwise she wouldn't be looking at three key pieces of evidence. The whole thing makes her want to run for the phone, call her aunt to make sure her mother made it over there okay.

Car doors open and cops step out into the sun. They're all wearing shades, so Vivi's the only one squinting. The stout one comes over. He's bulging over the holster strapped to his waist.

"Paraskevi Tyler?"

"I'm Vivi Tyler."

He looks past her, not at her. Up, up, toward the trees.

"We need access to your land."

Her pulse is going wild. It's pushing all the blood away from her head to her feet.

"Of course, whatever you need to do. Is someone hurt?"

"Dead." He nods to the paramedics, gives them the go-ahead. "There a road up there?"

"No road."

"We're on foot then," he calls out. They're pulling a stretcher out of the ambulance.

"Can you tell me anything else?"

"Can't tell you what I don't know," he says.

———

It's wildfire, the way the news spreads. Soon half the town (it seems like) is outside her house. This is primo gossip and they want to drink straight from the source.

She locks Biff in the bathroom so he doesn't go *Cujo* on them.

An hour and counting since the cops and paramedics vanished. Every so often she spots another one traipsing up to join them. A news van shows up, but the crowd swallows them. If the townspeople can't get information, no one can.

Melissa's one of the walking dead. She's been in a chair on the porch this whole time, staring at nothing, saying nothing.

Vivi picks up a box of plums. If she doesn't do something with them soon, they're going to rot.

"Want to help me, Kiddo?"

Melissa shakes her head slowly, fate of the whole world balanced on top.

"Suit yourself. I'm going to feed the masses. It's not fishes and loaves, but then I'm not Jesus."

Big crowd.

"I can't offer much," she calls out. "But I have plenty of home grown fruit right here. Help yourselves."

"What's going on?" a woman shouts.

"I know as much as you do," Vivi tells her. "Which is nothing."

She passes the box over the fence and goes back inside.

The phone rings.

"Vivi? It's Max. Are you okay?"

She's disappointed and excited. What a combination.

"Yes . . . No. I'm not sure. Max, the police are here – "

"Good," he says. "Make sure they stay there."

"You heard about the dead woman all the way over there?"

There's a pause, then: "Dead woman?"

She fills in the blanks. It's sketchy, at best, but it's what she's got.

"I'll be right there, Vivi. If Anastasia shows up, don't let her in."

"What does she have to do with this?"

"Nothing, I hope. God, I want you."

Click.

He wants her. John never wanted her.

She drops into the chair beside Melissa.

"Mom," Melissa says. "I need to tell you something."

94

VIVI

VIVI IS LOOKING INTO a black hole.

"Don't be mad, Mom," Melissa says. "I was scared. We were yelling at each other, and when she hit that rock – "

"I get the picture." Vivi rubs her face. "So let me get this straight. The body up there is Olivia, and she's dead because you two had a fight and you pushed her?"

"She had sex with Thanasi."

"Okay, I think we've already established that he's a douche." Think, Vivi, think. "Was she still alive when you came back to the house?"

"I don't know!"

The poor kid is shaking. She's white-knuckled and pale-faced. Vivi wants to hug the stuffing out of her, make everything okay, but first . . .

First . . .

"Sit. Stay."

Right now she needs to do normal. What's more normal than Coke?

Nothing, except maybe pizza.

She pours two Cokes into tall glasses, dumps a couple of ice cubes in each. Then it's back to Melissa. Coke in hand, it's easy to believe the police aren't combing the property for the girl Melissa killed. An accident, of course.

"The moment this Coke is finished, I'm going to call a lawyer. If the police ask you anything, don't say a word. Let the lawyer be your mouth, okay?"

"Okay. But – "

"Drink up," Vivi says. "Let's be normal for five minutes."

Suddenly, there's motion on the edge of the grove. Three policemen stomp over the rise. The paramedics follow, two of them stringing a gurney between them. As they get closer, she gets a look at the black bag.

"What's the black thing?" Melissa wants to know.

"Body bag. They put the . . . the body inside to protect it." And us.

"Oh."

No telling from here who is inside. A body bag is manufactured to be ambiguous. Even the size and shape of the deceased is a mystery.

What if it's not Olivia? Vivi thinks. What if it's Mom? How can she call her father and tell him that?

What's she going to do without her mother to spar with?

Olivia, Mom, whoever – there's no happy outcome here. Even if it's a stranger, it's still someone who is lost to someone who cares.

———

She doesn't hear the Jeep – how could she with this ruckus?

The tension is high. So when Max sticks his head in the door she jumps.

He looks good, but now isn't their time. Which is why they both leave a wide stretch of warm air between them.

"Hey," she says.

Yeah, he looks good, but also tired. His hair's tousled and his five o'clock shadow got an extension to early afternoon.

"I got here as fast as I could."

There's no time to act all cool and nonchalant because he's not alone. Behind him is Eleni, sans body bag. Vivi could be a rocket ship, the way she launches herself at her mother. Feels great to hug her, but she never noticed before how fragile and tiny Eleni is.

Death shoves everything under a lens.

"Mom, you're okay!"

"Of course I am okay. Why would I not be okay? I told you not to worry – no? What is going on? It is worse than the zoo out there. What did you do, Vivi?"

Things, they never change.

Which is why people freak out when they do.

"I picked her up outside the church," Max says.

Vivi turns on the high-wattage smile. "Thank you."

"You guys okay?" he asks.

"We're okay," Vivi tells him. Or maybe not . . .

"Okay," he says, looking out the window. "I'll be right back."

"Wait – "

Too late.

They go out onto the porch, where Melissa's stretching out that Coke.

Eleni doesn't sit. "Now will you tell me what is going on? Why are the police and the ambulance and half the town outside your house?"

Vivi doesn't look at Melissa.

"Somebody's dead. We don't know who, yet."

"And you thought maybe it was me?"

"Maybe."

The older woman laughs. "Silly Vivi. Look: I am as healthy as an ox. Maybe five oxen. I could pull a plow, no problem."

"I'll remember that if I ever buy a plow." Melissa finally hits the glass's rock bottom. Vivi says, "I'm going to make a quick phone call. This time, stay with Mel, okay? Don't wander off."

Eleni follows her into the house. So does Melissa.

Vivi looks at them both. "What did I say?"

"Eh, who knows?" Eleni says. "I want to see what your doctor is doing out there."

"Not my doctor. He's just a friend."

Yeah right. Last night? Definitely not what "just friends" do.

"He's handsome and not gay," Eleni says. "You could do worse. Look at John."

"Hey, John is still Melissa's father. And Max's mother is crazy."

"All mothers are crazy."

Vivi says, "I'm not crazy."

"Of course you are, Vivi."

Melissa laughs.

"You're grounded," Vivi tells her.

"No, you're not," Eleni says.

Melissa says, "I'm already grounded."

"Why is my granddaughter grounded?"

"I need to make a phone call," Vivi repeats.

Eleni shrugs. "So make your phone call. We are going to watch out the window."

Vivi stands there, because what's she going to do? She doesn't want to call a lawyer with her mother in spitting distance. Doesn't want to tell her Melissa's business, at least not until they know something.

"He looks at you like you are a slice of my *galaktobouriko*," Eleni says from the window.

And Vivi thinks: Yes, and last night he ate me like I was, too.

"Mom, I know it's not your *galaktobouriko*."

"Whose is it then? Your father cannot cook."

As the adage goes: If you can't beat 'em, join 'em. Vivi shoves her face alongside theirs at the window. It's a circus out there. No animals, but a lot of clowns.

Max and the chubby cop are talking. The policeman nods and Max walks over to the paramedics and their black bag. More conversation, then Max opens the bag, takes a good look inside.

Melissa recoils. "Eww, how can he do that?"

"He's a doctor, Honey. They see death all the time, the way your dad sees houses."

Vivi's heart is going wild. The gushing blood is making it hard to hear, to think. She's telling herself to be calm, but she can't be calm until she knows who is or isn't in the bag.

Too far away to read Max's lips. And they're talking at a gallop, anyway. Is it her imagination, or did he just glance their way?

The bees in her ears won't shut up.

Finally, he zips up. They all do a lot of hand waving to punctuate the conversation. Then they're done, and police and paramedics are on their way.

Max jumps the fence, cuts across to the house. Vivi is going to explode if he doesn't get here right now.

"Well? Who is it?" Eleni demands.

Melissa's complexion is going gray.

"It's a woman. Badly bloated, so there is no ID yet. Normally decomposition wouldn't be so far along, but the heat . . ."

"What was she wearing?"

"All black. Some gray hair. She is – was – an older woman."

Vivi's knees wobble. It's not Olivia.

But now there are two new questions on the table: Who is the dead woman? And what happened to Olivia?

"She could be anyone," Max says. "An old man up in the woods found her hanging from a tree."

Takis. It had to be.

"Was it a suicide, do you think?" Eleni wants to know.

He shrugs. "Hard to say." But his expression is shuttering.

Vivi makes coffee. That way she looks busy. "Do you think it was murder?" she asks.

"That's for the police to determine."

Not exactly reassuring.

"Coffee?" she asks.

Max says, "Can we talk?"

Eleni is all over that. "What about?"

"Yes." She gives her mother a dirty look. "Mom, make the coffee."

She leads him outside, out back where the people aren't. Her heart is thumping with a new kind of anxiety.

He looks at her. She looks at the trees.

"I ended my engagement."

"You already told me."

"I know. I ended it last night."

So recently? Not even a page between women.

"Before we had sex? Please tell me it was before we had sex."

"Yes, of course."

She switches her gaze to another equally fascinating tree. Fabulous leaves. Strong trunk. Won't fall down in a storm. What is that fruit called again?

"Okay, so I'm rebound woman. But at least you didn't cheat."

"Vivi, you're not rebound woman. You're not meant to be anyone's consolation prize."

"Logically, I know that," Vivi says. "But I feel like the runner up."

He takes her hand. This – this is what she knows. The sales pitch. John was a salesman and now Max is, too.

Too bad she's not in the market for bullshit.

"Anastasia was never my choice. But I went along with it for all the wrong reasons. Then I met you. There couldn't be an Anastasia after that. You are my first choice – she was my mother's last resort."

"Max, you need time between women. You can't just hop from one bed to the next."

"That's not how it was."

"But it's how it looks. And looks matter here. People will see us together and they'll think I was the other woman."

"So let them think it."

She shakes her head. "Anywhere else, I'd be okay with that. But I brought Melissa here for a new life – a new life for both of us. I want to build that life right, strong from the ground up. You don't know what it's like to have the life you've built crumble because the foundation wasn't solid. And you – you need time, too. Make a life for yourself, one you're steering. You can be a good son and your own man."

Max goes blank like the stucco behind him. "What about us?"

"I could use a good friend," Vivi says. "Maybe in time . . ."

He nods, looking at the same tree Vivi found so interesting seconds ago. "Yeah, thanks. But I have plenty of friends."

His phone jangles. When he glances at the screen, Vivi can tell it's Mama Dearest calling.

"Okay," he says. "I'm out of here. I'll see you around. If Melissa needs help, call."

"Max."

He doesn't turn around, but he lifts his hand; the most dismissive of goodbyes.

There's a knife in her heart, and its blade is bright and cruel. She doesn't complain – she's the one who put it there.

🦂 95 🦂

VIVI

THERE'S NO TIME FOR a pity party.

Vivi wants to throw herself at her bed and cry herself dry, but Eleni is there with coffee and questions. Vivi takes the coffee, ignores the questions. Eleni isn't too persistent – not when she has an audience outside. She goes out with the broom, makes a performance of sending everybody on their way.

And they go happily because the story is unfolding somewhere else now, anyway.

———

Or so they think.

———

The police don't knock on Vivi's door because it's wide open and they can see her on the couch.

Vivi can see them, too.

Shit, she thinks. Shit, shit, shit. She's sitting there looking like she's got a rampant case of pink eye, when in reality she's spent the last hour boohooing over Max.

Eleni, of course, isn't around. She and Melissa are both sleeping off the morning. It's peak siesta time.

Two cops. The guy with the belly and another guy in plainclothes.

Cop Number Two introduces himself as Detective Lemonis, then he gets right down to business.

"Mrs. Tyler, do you have an Eleni Pappas staying with you?"

Deep voice. Good for playing bad cop.

"Do I need to call a lawyer?"

The policemen swap looks.

Lemonis says, "Why would you need to call a lawyer?"

"I was born in America," Vivi says. "We don't do anything without a lawyer."

"Maybe you need a lawyer. We don't know yet."

This all feels very circular, very strange. There's still the matter of Olivia and her whereabouts, yet here they are asking for her mother.

A door opens and Eleni strolls out in fresh makeup. "Vivi," she says. "Have you got pinkeye? Don't touch me until you see the doctor."

"The police are here," Vivi says.

Detective Lemonis says, "Eleni Pappas? We have questions for you."

"I do not know anything about anything or anyone."

There's a first time for everything.

"Are you acquainted with a Sofia Lambeti?"

Now Vivi really doesn't like where this is going. She looks at her mother. "Don't say a word, Mom. I'm calling a lawyer."

"Vivi, be quiet," Eleni says. "I know that whore. She opens her legs for everyone. Maybe you ask her customers if they know her, eh?"

"Mom, be serious."

"I am serious. Everybody knows she is a whore."

Detective Lemonis and the chubby cop exchange glances.

"Mrs. Pappas, Sofia Lambeti is dead. We found her on your daughter's property this morning. Do you have any knowledge of how she got there?"

"No." Wide-eyed. "Do you?"

"We have information that you and she had a confrontation last night."

"Maybe we did. I don't remember. Why are you asking me questions when you already have the answers?"

"Mom, enough," Vivi warns her. "I'm calling a lawyer right now. Don't say another word."

"Bah! I do not need a lawyer, Vivi. As soon as they start asking people, they will see that she was a lunatic, a crazy person."

The cops aren't laughing. Chubby cop steps forward with his handcuffs.

"Eleni Pappas, you are under arrest for the murder of Sofia Lambeti."

"I am not!" Eleni sits on the floor, arms folded.

Hello, headache. "Mom, I kind of think you are."

"Why, God? Why did You give me a traitor for a daughter?"

Policeman on either side, both of them trying to pull her off the ground, but Eleni is doing that dead-weight trick, straight out of a toddler's arsenal. She curls her legs around the nearest chair.

It's a sixties-style protest.

Vivi doesn't know what to think, but she knows what to do.

"Listen to me. Right now you don't have a choice," she tells her mother. "They're taking you whether you fight it or not. You can either go willingly and I'll find you a lawyer, or I'll call Dad and tell him to get his butt here and bail you out himself."

Eleni is aghast. "You wouldn't!"

"Try me."

"Fine, I will go. But if any of those lesbians try to squeeze my cheeks, I will bite their fingers off. And I will never make my *galakto-bouriko* for you again."

"Too bad," Vivi says. "Guess I'll have to buy it from the Greek restaurant, same as you always do."

That one moment of shock gives the cops a foothold. Eleni goes, kicking and screaming. No dignity, that one. No dignity all the way into the police car.

Vivi watches the car kick up stones and dust. She watches until it's like that small storm never happened.

What a day. Mother of a murderer one minute, daughter of one the next.

Some new beginning.

She goes back in and finds the phone.

Two rings, then: "Eleni?"

He can't see her, but Vivi shakes her head anyway.

"It's me, Dad. I really need you to be here. And Mom does, too."

❦ 96 ❦

MAX

MAX DOESN'T FUCK AROUND. He's a man on a mission. Target: Mama.

He's got things to say, things she needs to hear, starting with his broken engagement.

"You look terrible," she says, when she opens her front door. "See, this is what you get for fooling around with foreign whores. Maybe you should go to the doctor and see if you caught a disease." She clutches her chest; same old, tiresome melodrama. "I told you, but you never listen to me."

"Enough, Mama."

He takes a seat at the kitchen table. He's eaten here a million times. Won't make it to a million and one if this doesn't go his way.

"Don't you tell me enough. I say when it is enough!"

"If I hadn't listened to you for all these years I wouldn't be in this mess. All you want to do is make me miserable. You pushed my brother – my best friend – away from this family because he wouldn't bow and scrape at your feet. If you wanted someone in the family to be a lawyer, maybe you should have done it yourself."

Her fists connect with the tabletop and its plastic cover.

"I am a sick old woman and this is how you speak to me? The

shame! The devil will come and cut your tongue from your wicked mouth!"

Max leans back. "You're not old or sick. You just like pretending you are so everybody will play your games. I'm done playing, Mama. Anastasia is not for me. I won't marry her, and nothing you say can change that. I don't care if you're the shame of the whole country because of it. You should be ashamed for forcing your will upon your grown children. Shame on you. Shame on you for not loving your youngest son enough to accept his choices. You cannot love, you can only manipulate."

She says nothing. For a long time, nothing.

Then: "You must hate me."

Yeah, whatever he was expecting, that wasn't it. He reaches across the table, takes her hand.

"Mama, I could never hate you, and neither could Kostas. But your time of controlling our lives is over. If you want to see either of us again you have to accept our choices. We're men, so let us be men, eh?"

Of course it's not that simple, is it?

The doorbell chimes, and, after one last mournful look, Mama scurries off to answer the door.

Anastasia. Listen to the vicious rhythm of stilettos on marble.

"I knew that dog would run to his mother." She shoves her way into the kitchen. "I told the gypsies downstairs they could piss in your car."

Max smiles like he's never known rain. "Don't be so bitter. It's not like I asked for the ring back."

"Of course I would not give the ring back. Your whore will never have my ring." She's all lit up like a maniac. "Guess what I heard, Max? Your whore is a murderer."

"Enough of the lies, Anastasia. Your problem is with me, not with Vivi."

"Is this true, Max?" Mama asks

"No, a woman died on her property this morning, but – "

"See, I told you," Anastasia crows.

Mama looks at him. "Max?"

" – they don't know if it was murder or suicide."

ALEX A. KING

"She was a murdered," Anastasia continues. "What decent person has bodies littering their land?"

"Anastasia," Mama says. "Enough!"

Isn't that a surprise?

But Anastasia doesn't stop. She's nowhere near a stopping point. In fact, she's winding up for the big one.

"The police arrested the whore's mother just now. Maybe she helped her mother, eh? Will you write to her in prison, Max? Apply for conjugal visits?"

Max thinks Anastasia sounds much too happy for it to be a lie. And she works for a law firm, so she'd know. He pulls his keys out of his pocket.

"Mama, I have to go. Vivi needs a friend."

Okay, he said he couldn't be her friend, but that was then. Things have changed.

"I need you," Anastasia says.

Always with the little girl routine.

"I have nothing to give you, Anastasia. I don't want you."

The woman doesn't have wings, but that doesn't stop her from flying at him. Fists, scarlet nails, teeth. Only thing missing is Wile E. Coyote's dust cloud.

Max doesn't fight back – he steps back.

Anastasia falls forward. It's enough to throw a spanner in her assault. Deprived of her primary target, she picks another.

Nice teeth, that girl. And they should be: she spent a couple of years with a silver smile. Seems like a shame to sink them into her former fiancé's shin.

Suddenly, she's sliding backwards, arms waving for him to save her. It's like a scene out of a horror movie. Doesn't matter which one – they've all got a scene just like it, where the about-to-be-deceased gets sucked into the darkness.

Mama is the monster (although to Max she looks like an avenging angel) standing over the spitting woman.

"I didn't bring him into this world so you could bite him like a dog," she says. "Get up!"

356

Anastasia stands, legs shaking with a mixture of anger and fear. "But I want him to marry me."

Mama grabs her by the hair. It's beautiful, really, the way she shoves Anastasia out the front door. "Apparently my son does not want to marry you. Out!"

On the way back into the kitchen, Mama drops the ring in his hand.

"It's a lucky thing you did not marry that one," she says. "I always knew she was crazy."

———

Mama walks him to the Jeep.

"You shamed me, Max. But I think perhaps I deserved it."

"You think?"

"Don't push me, my boy. One thing at a time, eh?"

"Okay."

They hug, she kisses him on both cheeks, and that's that.

"Maybe you can bring your brother for dinner soon, eh? It's time we were a family again."

❦ 97 ❦

VIVI

I T'S USEFUL HAVING A superhero in the family.

Thea Dora comes to the rescue. One of the cousins is a lawyer, and she convinces him that the family name is in jeopardy – and does he want his children to live with that stigma? And his grandchildren? And their grandchildren? No, she does not think so – so it is in his best interests to help.

She doesn't give him a chance (or a second chance) to say no.

Consider it his housewarming gift, she tells Vivi.

So while Cousin Pavlos is at the police station making deals with the blue devils, *Thea* Dora insists on entertaining Vivi and Melissa.

Which is how Vivi winds up sipping coffee under her aunt's grapevines. Melissa is out in the street with the neighborhood kids.

Effie swings by, which . . .

Sucks.

"What's it like to have a criminal in the family?" she whispers as soon as her mother is out of earshot.

"You tell me," Vivi says. "She's your family too. Wow, I hope her criminal genes weren't passed down to our kids."

Effie throws a worried glance at George. The boy is trying to shove his big toe up the garden hose.

It's kind of fun to wind her up and watch her spin. But they're swimming in the same gene pool, aren't they? Effie has her own bag of mean words and tricks to rattle.

"Maybe the police will have lots of question for you, too. Who knows where you were last night?"

"I was at the festival, with everyone else."

"Not for long, eh?"

"If you have something to say, Effie, say it."

Effie looks away first. "When are you leaving?"

Thea Dora picks that moment to bustle out with a tray of cherry sweets. "Nobody is going anywhere. Eat up, Effie. You don't want your backside to get small like Vivi's!"

Best joke ever, you'd think, from the way she's shaking. She's laughing, laughing, and Effie's scowling like she wants to slam a stake through her mother's heart.

"Enough, Mama, I'm on a diet." Still, she doesn't say "No" to the sweets, or the spoon that comes with them.

Behind her daughter's back, *Thea* Dora wiggles her eyebrows in a passable Groucho Marx imitation. Only one thing can save Vivi from laughing: eating.

Her aunt sits between them. The chair sighs as she lets the wood take her weight.

"*Po-po*," she groans. "I hope Pavlos does not keep us waiting. I cannot stand for Eleni to be all alone in a cage with all those lesbians."

Vivi says, "She's not in prison, it's just the local jail. Worst case, she's in there with some drunk who's sleeping off a pint of ouzo. And I don't think any self-respecting lesbian on this planet would want to feel up Mom in her polyester stretchy pants. Her disposition alone is a turn-off."

"I know you are right, but poor Eleni. That Sofia has been nothing but trouble for this family. It is a good thing she is dead." She says it matter-of-factly.

Effie scoffs. "Mama, don't defend what has happened here. A woman is dead and *Thea* Eleni killed her."

"Effie, this is my house. Have some respect. Eleni would not kill anybody, not even that woman. Why would she need to? She won her prize already. Sofia was eaten up inside with jealousy and hate. It ate away at her brain for all these years, until finally her wits were completely gone."

"Prize?"

Aunt and cousin exchange glances. There's a story here, Vivi knows, and it's juicy.

"Tell her, Mama." Effie looks downright happy, a definite sign this story is juicy-bad, not juicy-good.

Her aunt groans. A few minutes melt away while she gets her crotchet ready. The silver hook is making pretty flowers.

"I will live to regret this when Eleni finds out I am the one who tells you. But some things are not content to remain in the past where they belong. Even when the police find that my sister is innocent of this crime, other people may not believe it to be true. You will be of more help to her – and yourself – if you know the truth."

"I need to know," Vivi says. True. She also wants to know.

"Yes." *Thea* Dora looks sideways at her niece. "I think it is time. Many years ago, long before your parents left Greece and you and Christos were born, your mother was one of the prettiest girls in town. So many boys she had begging for her attention, that our mother would throw old bread and scraps not fit for the animals at them when they came calling. Eleni, she was not so interested in any of them, although she thought them amusing. Mostly because she could make them do anything she wanted. Then one day she met your father. He was very handsome, but quiet and much more shy than Eleni."

"He still is," Vivi says.

"He is a good man, your father. Effie's father was a pig, but he could show a woman a good – "

"Mama!"

Now here's a first: Vivi agreeing with Effie. Some things don't need to be said or heard. Where's the brain bleach when you need it?

"When they met, Eleni fell in love with him like that!" Finger snap. "He was all she would talk about, all the time. Our father made her sit outside to eat so he would not hear 'Elias this, Elias that' all through the meal. But your father was already promised to another woman – a woman his family had chosen for him."

Aaaand there's the juice. Bitter, bitter juice.

"Sofia," Vivi murmurs.

"Yes, Sofia. She was very quiet like your father, but sneaky, like the fox. And Eleni, she was not discreet. Always she says what she thinks and feels, so it did not take long for talk to reach Sofia. She was furious when she discovered Eleni was in love with her fiancé. Before long, she was following Eleni all over town, checking to make sure she was not with Elias. Of course, as soon as Eleni realized what Sofia was doing, she would walk for miles out of her way, with Sofia sniffing her footsteps like a hound. At the time, we had many laughs about it. We would take turns constructing new routes and creating fake rendezvous, all to make Sofia crazy.

"Somewhere along the way, Elias decided he had enough of Sofia's accusations and suspicions, so he convinced his parents that if he married Sofia, their children might be crazy, too. By this time they heard all the rumors and decided that their son was right, Sofia was not an appropriate bride for their only child. They wanted good strong grandchildren who would carry on the family name.

"Once the engagement was broken, Sofia became even more crazy. In the middle of the night she would throw rocks on our roof. When Elias and Eleni began courting, Sofia would often follow the couple, screaming obscenities at them. She set our father's motorcycle on fire. She strangled our cat. She told anyone who would listen that your mother made witchcraft with her vagina and used it on your father – can you imagine? Then one day she stopped, just like that. Eleni and Elias became engaged, and they married soon after.

"Eleni was so beautiful on her wedding day. You have seen the photos?"

Vivi nods. "She was beautiful. They looked happy."

Happier than she was on her wedding day.

"Sofia came into the church screaming that she was pregnant with Elias's child. Eleni snapped. She marched through the church, a warrior of Artemis in her long white dress, and grabbed Sofia's ear. Almost pulled it off her head! By the ear, she dragged that woman from the church and threw her out like a bag of garbage. Can you imagine, your tiny mother doing such a thing?"

"Was Sofia really pregnant?"

Her aunt shrugs. "Then? Who knows? Not long after, there were rumors Sofia was sneaking around in the woods with different men, many with poor reputations, some married with their own families. She left town for a while and came back with a daughter, but was it your father's? Nobody knows. Maybe not even Sofia knew.

"Not long after, your parents left for America. Sofia kept her distance from the family until Eleni came back. And now she is dead. It is for the best – a blessing."

Holy shit. Vivi's hands shake when she picks up the coffee cup. She's full and fat from so much information.

Before she had no answers and one question; now she has answers but also a hundred questions.

And another (painful) thing: she and Max are her parents, all over again. Maybe he wasn't happy with Anastasia but he was content, until Vivi shook him up like a Pepsi Cola. He could have had a happy life with another woman, one who was young enough to give him a dozen chubby-cheeked babies. One who wasn't toting Vivi's emotional baggage all over town.

A hundred questions. She starts with one.

"What happened to Sofia's daughter?"

Effie pounces. "What, you think she would want to see you now, after your mother killed hers?"

"No good can come of it, Vivi. It is best you leave it – and her – alone," *Thea* Dora says, without looking up from her crochet.

"If you wanted me to leave it alone you wouldn't have told me." Vivi looks at her aunt, sees the truth of that comment smeared all over her face. *Thea* Dora is itching for her to go out there, settle the town gossip once and for all. Is Sofia's daughter her half-sister? Vivi's blood can answer that question.

Goodbye, last untainted sip of coffee. Hello, sludge.

Thea Dora sets aside her hook, her yarn, her cotton flowers. "My love, let me read your cup."

Why not? She slides the cup on its saucer.

"I can see it now," Effie says. "Suffering, disaster."

Thea Dora tilts the cup this way, that way.

"I see a gate. Much success will come your way. That is good, yes?"

"I'll take it," Vivi says, not buying a word of it. On the other hand, a tiny piece of her wants to believe – but only when the cup is showing nice things.

"Trees, also. This means good things are coming. But there is an eye, the sign of a duplicitous person. Someone is jealous of you and they will betray you. Maybe they already have. I cannot say for sure. It is on the cusp of future and present."

"Cheerful." Vivi peers in the cup. Nothing but brown blobs. You could say it's all Greek coffee to her.

Effie pushes her cup forward. "Now do mine, Mama."

Dora picks up her crochet. "We already know your future, Effie. You will get fatter, your children will grow up to have many sons, and your worthless husband will continue to sleep with that donkey from the supermarket. What do you want to know?"

Effie glances at Vivi, but Vivi's doing the right thing, looking far, far away.

"Stop spreading lies, Mama."

"Bah. Just last night after Eleni left, I went to get water, and what do I see? I see him driving to her house. He was not home at midnight, was he?"

"We were at the festival," Effie says.

"Oh?"

"Mama, stop! Not in front of her!"

Her. Like she's dog shit on a shoe. Still, she cuts Effie a lot of slack this time. Vivi's not the only one with parental woes; lack of empathy runs through the family veins.

She holds out a shaky olive branch. "If you ever need to talk, Effie . . ."

"I don't need your pity!"

Smack. Goodbye branch.

"I only meant – "

"Once again it's all about you," Effie says. "You should never have come here."

"Enough!" *Thea* Dora slams her fist on the table, makes a small earthquake.

Vivi says, "Hey, my husband was a cheating bastard, too. I thought we – "

"Don't compare your troubles to mine! Mama, you need to still your tongue."

"Effie," Vivi's aunt says, "we are all family here. Everybody in town knows. It is no secret."

Vivi (in a rare Eleni moment) says, "I didn't know. So not everybody. Technically, now everybody does . . ."

Yeah, the death toll in town is high enough today.

Anyway, the conversation is destined to get cut short. Somewhere down the street there's a commotion. Melissa shoots into the yard, panting.

"Mom, it's the police. They're coming."

Thea Dora drops the crochet needle, heaves herself out of the chair. It sags with relief.

"Good," she says. "They have let Eleni go free, of course!"

That doesn't sound right. The police don't drive you home the morning after – or the day of. It's the drive of shame, for you. Get a ride from a cab, from a lawyer. Walk if you have to. Just get out of here.

And don't leave town until we say it's cool.

Vivi, Effie, *Thea* Dora, and Melissa all rush out into the choking street. It's all very Three Stooges, the way the car bumps and bounces. Every few feet (meters, if you're living the base 10 life) there's a new thing to dodge. Bicycles, kids, chickens – none of them step aside with gusto. The whole neighborhood is there to watch this hot, new show.

"Maybe they want to arrest you, too," Effie says. "You and your mother could be cellmates."

"Or maybe they just found out you beat your children."

Bicker, bicker.

The police car is getting a workout, today. It's the same one that came for Eleni. Two uniforms. Younger and in much better shape (read: not donut-shaped) than the cops who arrested Eleni.

"Paraskevi Tyler?"

Effie points.

Thanks for nothing, Vivi thinks. She raises her hand the grade school way. "I'm Vivi Tyler. Is my mother okay?"

"Paraskevi Tyler, you're under arrest for your role in the murder of Sofia Lambeti."

Where's the part where they ask questions before jumping to conclusions?

Where are her Miranda rights?

(Same place as Ernesto Arturo Miranda's bones: back in the USA.)

"Mom?" Melissa's shaking and white. Vivi hugs her as hard she can.

"Stay with *Thea* Dora, okay? If I'm not back by this evening, make sure she takes you to feed Biff. I love you, Honey."

No melodrama for Vivi. She offers up her wrists and goes without a fight.

"This is a mistake."

Snap, click.

"That's what they all say," the cop tells her.

Not only is she an alleged criminal but she's common, too.

"Make sure Biff goes potty before you lock him back up again," Vivi calls out.

Her aunt waves like Vivi's going on a cruise. Only thing missing is the *"Bon Voyage!"*

Vivi slumps against the back seat. This day is perfect – puuuurfect.

The police car rolls down the hill – backwards.

The cop who isn't driving turns around to look at her. "You are American, eh? Do you know Robert DeNiro?"

❧ 98 ❧

VIVI

S ECOND TIME VIVI'S BEEN in a jail cell this year (if she's counting twelve-month stretches, not the calendar year). How does this one fare?

She takes inventory.

One granite mattress, two sandpaper sheets, one pillow with an eating disorder. The blanket is woven from Europe's finest steel wool.

Vivi can't sleep in this palace.

It's not the bedding. It's not that night two of the festival is happening a block over and doesn't care that she's trying to sleep. *Boom, boom, boom.* Singing, laughter, and the occasional squeal.

That's not so bad. It's good to hear people celebrating.

The main reason she can't sleep is on the bottom bunk.

Eleni won't shut up. On and on, mouth chewing air. Bringing up this, bringing up that, dredging up crap that happened thirty years ago. Raking muck. Cursing that one plumber for traipsing his filthy boots over her clean kitchen floor.

Vivi thinks about killing her just to get some peace. Finally, she says, "Did you kill Sofia?"

That makes her mother clam up. Temporarily. Vivi pictures her

SEVEN DAYS OF FRIDAY

down there, opening and closing her mouth, a guppy in a metal-barred fishbowl.

"Of course not! What would make you think such a thing?"

"I don't know, Mom. But the police must have something or you wouldn't be here."

Eleni climbs out of her bunk bed, looks Vivi in the eye.

"They arrested you, too. Did you kill that worthless donkey?"

Touché. "No. But then I had no motive. You did."

"Dora!" she curses. "She told you!"

Vivi can't do this lying down. Now they're both pacing the postage stamp-sized floor.

"Why not? Everyone else seems to have scoop on our family history. It's like John all over again, me being the last to know. Why didn't you tell me I might have a half-sister out there?"

Eleni stops mid-pace. "She is nothing to you! That woman opened her legs for so many men the Virgin Mary Herself probably does not know who the father is." Back to pacing. "Do not stir up the past, Vivi. Nothing good comes of it."

"In case you have noticed, the past is beyond stirred. Someone shook it up and let it fizz aaaaall over the place! That woman is dead and they think one of us – maybe both of us – killed her. Your past could stop us from having a future. What about your granddaughter? Do you want her to grow up without a mother and grandmother?"

"Vivi, why do you say such ugly things to your mother? This has nothing to do with Melissa. We are both innocent, the police will see that."

Vivi climbs up on her perch. Back to the wall, she bangs her head lightly on the cinderblock. Repetition – it's great for concentration.

"Lots of innocent people in prisons, Mom. The news is full of them." *Tap, tap.* "Think, Mom, there has to be a reason we're in here. They have something that makes them certain one or both of us are guilty. What could they possibly have besides an ancient grudge?" *Tap, tap.* "I'm the worst mother in the world." Eleni stays silent. "No, no, don't contradict me."

Eleni takes the low bunk – again. Vivi goes back to sifting her 'what ifs' and 'if onlys'.

What's Melissa doing?

Is she okay?

Did she feed Biff?

If only John hadn't bounced out of the closet with CPA Joe. If only he'd been honest with himself years ago. Yeah, it's been hard for her, but how hard was it for him to live a lie? Poor, stupid bastard.

Rewind: If only John hadn't bounced out of the closet . . .

Melissa wouldn't have cut her wrists.

She and her mother wouldn't be in jail.

Melissa wouldn't have lost her virginity to some smooth-talking Romeo with a loaded missile in his boxers.

They wouldn't be in Greece at all.

And she wouldn't have met Max.

Vivi thinks impure thoughts, fucks Max in her head, over and over. Feels the way he made her feel. He's a talented man, but that's not his bottom line by a long shot. He's kind, affectionate, sensible, and –

———

"Mom?"

"What, Vivi?"

"Where were you last night?"

"After the festival I went to Dora's house."

"And after that?"

"I walked back to your house."

"No," Vivi says. "*Thea* said you left, then she went to get water around midnight. That's when she saw Effie's husband. You came home hours after that."

"Maybe I was having drinks with the rest of the family at the festival."

"I don't think you were."

"Well then, Miss Know-all, where was I?"

Vivi scoots forward. Her legs dangle over the edge. "I think you went to Sofia's house to confront her. Or you came across her somewhere and somebody saw you together. That same somebody told the police that maybe you were the last one to see her alive."

"Where is the harm in talking to an old acquaintance?"

"Nemesis. And everybody knows it."

Silence.

Vivi says, "But that doesn't explain why I'm here."

Back to the cinderblock wall, to the tap, tap, tapping.

"Stop that. You are giving me a headache."

"You're giving me a headache," Vivi says.

"Ungrateful brat."

"I'm grateful," Vivi says. "Being in jail is awesome. Everyone should try it sometime."

One block over, the festival is winding down. Happy, tired voices dance along the street.

"Yes, I spoke to Sofia. She came to me. Leaped out from behind a tree as I was leaving Dora's house. She wanted to let me know that she took something from me just as I took something from her. I took nothing! Elias never wanted to marry her."

"What did she take?"

"It is nothing. Old business."

"Mom . . .

"What she told me was a lie. The same lie she has been telling for years. She said that she had your father's first child – not me. She said she took that first from me. No matter what I do, Elias's firstborn child will always be hers. Like I said, a lie. Her daughter is not your father's."

"Do you know for sure?

"Of course I know!"

"Okay, okay."

Another stretch of silence. This time Vivi almost misses the talk.

"Say something," she says.

"Your father and I," Eleni says from her bunk, "before I left, we had a fight, and he said maybe he should have married Sofia instead of me."

"Whoa, what? Why didn't you say something?"

"And what would you have done? Pitied me?" The bunk creaks.

"You were such a happy baby, Vivi. It broke my heart when you married John."

And the revelations keep on rolling.

"Why? I thought you and Dad loved him, even though you objected at first."

"Your father always wanted another son. John filled the position. But I knew different. Something was not right about him, I saw it the day you brought him home."

"I wish you'd told me sooner," Vivi says.

"Would you have listened? Just like your mother, nobody tells you how to live. When you married John, I could see you were not happy, not the way a bride should be. You did not have that glow from lots of good sex."

Vivi's horrified, and rightfully (in her mind) so.

"Mom!"

"We are grownups, no? Then we can talk of sex. But it was more than that. John was not attentive to you the way a man truly in love is. His eyes did not follow you when you left the room. There was no excitement when you came back. You were always the one reaching out to him."

Wow. Her mother is Oprah. Greek Oprah.

Opah?

Whatever. Vivi is all shook up. All these years, she thought Eleni adored John. Her beloved son-in-law. If she had a choice between sides, she always joined Team John.

"I thought you liked him more than you liked me."

"How could I love anyone more than I love my little Vivi? You have all the good pieces of your father and me, and maybe some of the bad too, eh?" Eleni's voice is smiling. "You are better off without John. I am glad he left you. Look at you now – you are strong!"

Vivi's face glows red, her mouth goes Sahara. Feels good, in a weird way.

The John years were filled with probability.

The Vivi years are filled with possibility.

Anything can happen. It doesn't matter that Melissa (sweet, vital

Melissa) is stumbling; Vivi's going to take her hand, show her where the steel lives.

Eleni makes a self-satisfied noise. "You are smiling again. Good."

"I'm not smiling," Vivi says. "There's no smiling in jail. How long until Pavlos comes back?"

"That crook. I should have known Dora would send for him."

"I can find another lawyer."

"No, a crook is good. A crook that is family, even better."

✼ 99 ✼

V I V I

NOT EVEN LUNCHTIME AND the cop has *tzatziki* on his upper lip.

"Visitor," he says. Then he gets out so the visitor can get in.

Eleni gasps.

(Vivi doesn't, because Dad being there isn't a surprise.)

"Elias, what are you doing here?"

What is he doing here? Reaching for his wife, that's what. The man practically crawls between the bars so he can get ahold of her. Then it's hugging and kissing and –

Love. Real love.

Vivi looks out the window. Nice blue sky. Lots of sun. Not too far away, someone's cooking *souvlaki*. Too bad some partygoer urinated beneath their window last night.

Eventually, her dad drops the dime on Vivi.

"Vivi called. She thought you needed me. She was right."

Eleni gives her the look, but Vivi can tell she's secretly pleased. "You silly man," she says.

Vivi's father glances from one woman to the other. "Will someone please tell me why both my girls are in jail?"

"You didn't tell him?" Eleni asks her daughter.

Vivi shrugs. There was no time. The moment she mentioned her mother and trouble, her father was out the door.

"It is nothing," Eleni continues. "They think we killed someone."

"Sofia Lambeti." His face gives nothing away.

"Don't tell me you're upset!" Eleni says.

Elias Pappas turns his attention to his daughter. "Vivi, I brought you a present."

"Do I get a present?" Eleni asks.

"When we get you out of here, then you can have a present, eh?"

Vivi's present walks in the room, rough, tired, no sign of his usual swagger.

"Surprise, I'm a jailbird," Vivi says.

Max laughs. "Suits you."

"You haven't lived until you've been arrested in front of the whole neighborhood. Have you seen Melissa?"

Her father nods at the door. "She's in the waiting room. My poor girl is terrified you're going to the electric chair. I told her that they used to have a firing squad, not the electric chair."

"Not since 1972," Max says. "Greece hasn't executed anyone since 1972."

Vivi says, "Shit."

"Language!" Eleni barks.

Vivi doesn't bite back.

———

She's watching herself earn her place in this cell. Slowly wringing the neck that put her in here.

It's okay that she's here. There are worse things, worse places. Sometimes life turns strange corners. Go to bed one night and the world is one way, wake up in a world gone mad.

It's okay.

Vivi can live in a behind bars if she has to. She can eat their bread and cheese, drink their water, pee in a lidless, stainless (not-stainless) toilet. She can go to court and watch her character go on trial, listen to the other guy tilt the truth until it fits his template.

And that's okay, too. Vivi is (if anything has been proven thus far) a survivor. Three parts woman, one part robot.

What's not okay — seriously NOT okay — is Melissa being frightened.

That's the complete opposite of okay.

Vivi knows she didn't kill Sofia, didn't help Eleni (or anyone else) kill Sofia. While Sofia was busy dying, Vivi was busy doing . . .

Well, doing Max.

Which means someone around here is a major-league liar. And because of that lie, her daughter is afraid Vivi's going to do life or give life.

Vivi's doing the time, so she thinks it's perfectly acceptable to commit a few rounds of mental homicide.

It's amazing what a furious mother can do with an imaginary lead pipe, barbed wire, and zero consequences.

———

"What did the police say?" Eleni asks her husband.

He shrugs. "Nothing. They tell me nothing." A nod in Max's direction. "But to him, they talk."

"They know me," Max says, in his own defense. "A witness saw Mrs. Pappas arguing with the deceased before she died. Then someone called in an anonymous tip, that the two of you killed the woman together. Vivi, you allegedly lifted the deceased into the tree at your mother's request."

"Ha-ha," Vivi says weakly. "It's a lie, of course."

Max nods. "I told them we were together at the time, and after I left Melissa was there. Which she confirmed. The good news is that you're both free to go — for now. They're processing the paperwork."

"They're letting Mom go, too?"

"New evidence, they said."

"I told them you would kill each other if they leave you in here together," Vivi's father says. "The paperwork on two dead women in their custody would be taller than Mount Pelion. And Greek police, they do not like paperwork so much."

"Ha-ha," Vivi says.

Ha-ha.

🦋 100 🦋

VIVI

MELISSA IS FULL OF tears and hugs.
That's okay, Vivi is, too.
"Allergies," she says.
Nobody suggests otherwise.

———

You'd think she'd been gone a year, the way Biff acts.

It's undignified, how she rolls around on the ground with him, but who cares?

"So who do you think called in the tip?" Max asks.

Vivi shrugs. "Could be anyone."

"Who hates you?"

"I'm sure there's a list."

"Be serious, Vivi."

"I am serious. Let's see. Ian – that's my ex husband's boyfriend. Your fiancée – "

"Ex fiancée."

" – my cousin Effie. Melissa's friend Olivia. This Sofia woman's daughter – who may or may not be my sister. I'm sure there are more. Like I said: a list."

"Do you think she's your sister?"

"It's possible." She thinks for a minute. "Who knows if she even knows I exist? If her mother was as secretive as mine . . ."

They look inside at Vivi's parents and Melissa working in the kitchen.

Vivi says, "We never really know our parents, do we?"

"No, but they know us. They used to be us."

———

She might talk a lot of sunshine and light, but Vivi is worried.

Somebody here hates her. Somebody here hates her enough to lie to the police.

That's not exactly small potatoes.

Nobody leaves anonymous tips for funsies. It's a calculated tactical move. That anonymous someone wants:

———

Vivi in jail permanently.

Vivi in jail temporarily.

Jail or no jail, Vivi's reputation shredded.

———

So, she's worried. For now, she's out of jail and home with her family, but what's next?

When someone's gunning for you, they usually bring more than one bullet.

She keeps her cool, though. Doesn't melt in front of her family. Doesn't cry again, until she's tucking Melissa into bed that night.

It's been years since Melissa asked to be tucked in, but tonight is special circumstances.

Biff settles his big bones on the end of Melissa's bed and tries to look small. Melissa's not trying to look small – she is small. Tonight she's maybe five, maybe seven.

"Mom, you're not going back to jail, are you?"

"No, Honey. Max vouched for me, and they know his word is good."

"Then why did they arrest you?"

"Because someone told a lie."

"Why would they do that?"

It's a million-euro question. "I don't know. People do all kinds of awful things for all kinds of reasons. Maybe it was some kind of crappy joke."

"It's not very funny," Melissa says. Her bottom lip is starting to quiver. "Are you mad at me, Mom?"

"Yes, but also no. Does that make sense?"

"Not really."

"I don't like that you lied to me, but that's only one tiny crappy thing. There are a billion other wonderful things about you. If you could stay away from guys until you're thirty, that would be awesome."

"Are all guys assholes?"

Well are they?

Consider the two men in the other room.

The man who boarded a plane, and took on the world, the minute Vivi called, the minute he knew his wife was in need.

The second man who (Vivi knows) would do the same for his own wife, if necessary. The man who saved Melissa, who saves children every day. The man who told the truth so she could walk free.

"No," Vivi says. "Most men are pretty great. Just be patient."

🜲 101 🜲

VIVI

I s my Melissa okay?" Elias asks.

Vivi nods.

"I should go," Max says.

"Or you could stay," she tells him. "For a while."

He glances at her parents.

Eleni says, "If you put your hands on my daughter, I will cut them off and feed them to the dog."

"Leave the man's hands alone, he's a doctor," Elias says.

"Only a surgeon needs hands."

———

Vivi gets down to (personal) business.

"I'm sorry about yesterday. I didn't want to hurt − "

"I'm in love with you."

It's not midnight, but it sure looks it. The moon is too new to matter. All they've got for light is the stars, and even they're limping, worn out from last night's merriment.

Vivi panics. This isn't how the script in her head goes. And when it comes to Max, she's not good at making it up on the fly. She can't be trusted with herself.

That's okay, Max has more words for her.

"I think I loved you from the moment I saw you standing in the emergency room, holding Melissa in your arms. You were terrified, but at the same time you were strong enough to carry her in there on your own. Yes, I want to be your friend, but not just a friend."

He loves her. He loves her.

And yeah, she loves him.

Or at least she thinks she does.

It's hard to say. She lived a make-believe love for so long that now she can't tell the real thing from the impostor. Doesn't want to love a sheep and find out he's a wolf.

"I'm not looking for an answer, tonight," Max says. "I'm giving you your time. Giving myself time. Then I'm coming for you, Vivi. Believe it."

Oh.

102

VIVI

"ELENI! VIVI! HURRY, HURRY!"

Mid morning. They all slept in.

At least until the *Thea* Dora juggernaut started rolling their way.

Now they're leaping out of their beds, running to see what today's drama is all about.

Vivi is in yesterday's clothes. Max left minutes after his revelation, and things got hazy after that. Getting changed seemed like a waste of potential sleeping time, so she let herself fall, let the bed catch her.

She and Eleni collide at the front door. Her mother squints at the figure of her impending sister.

"My God, Dora, what is your problem?"

"Virgin Mary be praised, you are both here!" She glances around furtively. "I hope the lesbians did not touch you."

"No lesbians, *Thea*. Just me. And Mom's not exactly my type," Vivi says. "They tossed us in a cell together."

"And nobody beat you?"

"Not even at cards."

"Oh, thank Jesus and God and the Virgin Mary!"

It's exhausting, watching her heave herself up the steps.

"I heard a rumor, Vivi, that your father broke you out of the jail. If you need a place to hide from the police I know a good one. It is under my house. Your late uncle, he dug a big hole there in case the Turks came."

Eleni has a funny look on her face.

"We didn't break out of prison," Vivi says. "They let us out."

"Really?"

"Yes," Eleni says. "The walls are made of concrete and steel. How would we break out?"

"Maybe Elias tied rope to a car and pulled the window bars." She sounds hopeful.

Vivi doesn't laugh – she doesn't.

"You are ridiculous, Dora," Eleni tells her sister. "Come, have coffee."

"No, no, I cannot stay. You must come to my house immediately! We must remove the evil eye. Sofia is dead so her curse should be gone, but someone else still wishes you ill or you would not have been arrested."

"Dora . . ." Eleni starts.

"Bah! You have lived in America too long!"

"I suppose it cannot hurt," she says. "Vivi?"

It's unconventional. Weird. Hocus-pocus. Crazy. Start believing in the evil eye and you may as well start living your life according to the horoscope scribbled in the back of the newspaper. It's one step away from throwing your life savings at some psychic hotline, where the only accurate prediction is your inevitable bankruptcy.

"I thought you already got rid of the curse. Why do it again?"

"Curses can be like a burr," her aunt says. "This one could be stuck to you."

What would The Amazing Randi say?

"Um, okay?"

———

Vivi thinks her aunt doesn't look so hot, so she offers to drive. She doesn't frame it like that, though, doesn't tell her aunt she looks like one small hillock away from heart failure.

She's diplomatic about it. Blames it on her own frailty and the heat.

Melissa stays behind with her grandfather. Vivi thinks how lucky she is – lucky to have Melissa in her life. She's the world's biggest silver lining.

They're still in first gear when Eleni says, "Look, here comes Melissa's friend."

Vivi glances in the rearview mirror.

Friend, her ass. But she's glad to see Olivia is alive and capable of steering a bicycle. She doesn't like the girl, but she's somebody's baby. And, yeah, this lets Melissa of a huge, bloody hook.

"Hang on," she says.

Reverse, reverse, until she's alongside Olivia.

The girl looks startled, at first. It's obvious she was waiting to catch Melissa alone, but she makes a smooth recovery.

"Mrs. Tyler, is Melissa home?"

"Not to you."

"Why?"

Gee, where does she even start? "Because you're a shitty friend and my daughter deserves better. That's a good enough reason."

The girl leans on the handle bars oh-so casually, puts on her best smirk. Vivi wants to slap it clean off her face.

"Did Melissa tell you everything?"

Figures. Vivi is so not surprised. A snake is a snake is a snake. But Vivi's a good Girl Scout – she came to this confrontation prepared.

"Everything." She stretches that word to its limits. "Including the part where you had sex with Thanasi."

Goodbye, smirk. Hello, fear.

"I could have died," Olivia says.

"But you didn't."

"But – "

"You didn't."

Olivia looks away.

"I highly recommend looking for another friend. Melissa is unavailable."

Vivi hits the gas. The tires spin and as she zooms away, all that's left in the rearview mirror is a sepia-toned girl.

❧ 103 ❧

MELISSA

MELISSA WATCHES IT ALL go down.

Olivia rolls up on her bicycle and Melissa freaks out, because either that's a ghost out there or Olivia has come to kick her ass for kicking her ass.

But she's not a ghost. Melissa figures that part out quickly when Mom throws the car into reverse.

So Olivia's not dead. That's good. That's great. No juvie for Melissa – if they even have juvie out here.

Which leaves the ass kicking. Best-case scenario, Olivia's going to yell a lot of horrible things. She doesn't care what Olivia tells Mom, but she does care what Olivia tells, oh, the rest of town. School is starting in another month, and Melissa doesn't want everyone to hate her before they've had a chance to know her. There's, like, one high school in town. It's not as if she can just go somewhere else nearby. Changing schools would mean catching the bus into Volos every day.

"What's so interesting out that window, Sweetheart?" Grampy asks.

"Nothing," she says vaguely.

He looks outside. "Who is the girl?"

Melissa shrugs. "She used to be a friend."

"Heh, heh. Look at your mother. She is telling that girl something she does not like hearing."

He's right. Olivia is making a face like Mom's flinging poop at her. Then Mom zips away, leaving her in a dust cloud.

Pretty awesome.

Grampy smiles out the window. "Your mother and grandmother, sometimes they remind me of very short amazons."

Yeah, her mom is pretty cool. For a mom.

❧ 104 ❧

VIVI

BOWL, WATER, OLIVE OIL? Check.

Same ritual, different time. When *Thea* Dora drips the olive oil into the water, the droplets immediately separate.

Vivi yawns.

"You have the evil eye again! And it is very strong this time. See how fast and wide the oil spreads? It is like an egg."

Of course.

Thea Dora draws a wet, oily cross on Vivi's forehead, then it's Vivi's turn to swish, swish her finger in the bowl.

"Rub it on your lips," her aunt instructs her. "Now, I do your mother, okay? Then we will do you again, to make sure you are clear."

Exact same ritual, but her mother's drops stay tight and whole.

Thea Dora smiles. "Sofia's curse has gone to the grave with her body." She dry spits into the air three times. "Just in case. Come, Vivi. Let's make sure you are not still cursed."

But Vivi's curse is sticky. It likes her too much to leave.

Thea Dora shakes her head. "Someone is very persistent. We must try something else. It could be that this person went to a professional to place the curse."

"Mama, are you here?" Effie's voice booms from outside.

"Come in, Effie," *Thea* Dora screeches. "We are in the kitchen!"

A moment later, Effie barrels through the door. She's cultivating a nest of long-legged black spiders in her armpits. And she doesn't look happy to see Vivi. How surprising.

"Why are you here? I thought you were in jail."

"Don't be rude, Effie," her aunt says. She's busy poking through the spice rack. "Make some coffee."

Effie hesitates, but not for long. Her face is pinched and pissed as she dumps coffee and sugar in the *briki*.

"Hold out your hand." *Thea* Dora drops something in Vivi's upturned palm.

Vivi looks up. "A bay leaf?"

"Chew it. While you are chewing, concentrate on turning the curse around, away from you and back to the person who made it. Afterward, I will give you three bay leaves to keep in your pocket – or your purse if you do not have pockets. Keep them with you always."

"And this will work?" Potpourri as a shield against evil. Huh.

"If it was good enough for the ancient oracles, it is good enough for you!"

Eleni says, "Do it, Vivi. What harm can it do?"

Vivi shrugs. Why not? It's not like it's poison – right? "Bottoms up." She chews. "This is the second worst thing I've ever put in my mouth."

"Concentrate." *Thea* Dora pats her arm. "Turn the curse around."

The bitter, oily eugenol is making it hard to concentrate on anything. Still, Vivi bundles up every tiny mishap from the time they arrived – Melissa's wrist, Biff's worms, the roof – all the way up to her night as a jailbird, then fires it off towards the unknown target.

Effie screams.

She's covered in scalding coffee. Steam rises in a thin sheet from the coffee pool widening around her feet.

Thea Dora is on it. She snatches up the long handled whiskbroom and starts whipping Effie's legs with sharp, vicious strokes.

"My God, Dora, have you gone mad?" Eleni yells.

Effie's screaming and screaming, like someone stuck a knife in her.

Thea Dora isn't in a listening mood. She hits and hits and hits.

"What kind of woman are you to put a curse on your own cousin? Is this how I raised you? You are not too old or too important to take a beating."

Wait, what? Vivi thinks. Effie cursed her?

She's horrified but not all that surprised, now that she thinks about it. Effie hated her pretty much on sight. But this level of hate is crazy.

"Why couldn't you just go away?" Effie screams. "You should never have come here!"

Eleni tosses Vivi a towel.

"I have as much right to be here as you do." Vivi kneels at Effie's feet, soaks up as much brown as the white towel can take. The broom whistles past her ears.

Effie doesn't want help. Correction: Effie doesn't want *Vivi's* help. Her foot jerks, nails Vivi in the ribs.

Vivi yells and rolls sideways. She kicks and she kicks hard. Right in Effie's groin.

"If you had a problem with me, you should have had the ovaries to say something," Vivi says.

"You think you are so wonderful with all your education and knowledge about every little thing in the whole world. You know nothing!"

"Ha! I know you're an idiot who might actually get a friend or two if you'd crack a smile."

"*Putana.*"

"Cow. Mooooo."

"You turned your husband into a homosexual!"

Vivi says, "Bitch, if you want war, you can have one." Her left hook is mean. It should be – it's never been used. Got about thirty-four years of resentment behind it.

It knocks Effie back. She rebounds off the counter, wrestles Vivi to the ground. Then she grabs Vivi's hair and twists.

Vivi's eyes flood. "I'd kick you in the ass," she says, "but my foot would bounce right off all that Jell-O." She stabs Effie with her elbow.

Eleni and *Thea* Dora are background noise.

"Should we stop them?"

"I say we let them fight. No need to panic until there is blood. Tell me, Eleni, how do you do that neat cross-stitch? All these years, still I cannot master that one stitch."

Vivi sinks her teeth into Effie's ear. She feels the satisfying crunch.

"It is all about where you slide the needle. You want that thread to go next to the neighboring threads, not on top of them."

It's a sideways punch, but it's a good one. Hot blood spurts out of Vivi's nose. She hooks a foot behind Effie's knee, flips her, straddles her chest. Now she's bleeding. All. Over. That. Bitch.

Effie spits, right in Vivi's face.

"No spitting, Effie," *Thea* Dora says passively. "Spitting is for lower-class *putanas*."

"That's why I'm spitting at her, Mama."

"I said no!" she barks. To her sister, in a sweeter voice: "How do you tie such neat knots on the back?"

Vivi pins Effie to the floor with one hand, wipes the spit off her own face, smooshes it into Effie's. "Here, you left this behind, Miss Piggy."

Effie clamps her teeth on Vivi's finger. She bites until she's violating the space between bones. A thin whine in Vivi's head turns out to be her own crying. She hits and hits and hits. Effie's jaw springs open.

Then she's seeing stars. Cartoons, apparently, have correctly nailed the aftermath of a successful head-butt. All these years, she figured it was animated hyperbole. She staggers to her feet.

Is it over?

Hell no.

She snatches up Effie's hand, wedges her cousin's arm between her knees, bends that middle finger back, back, back. The crystal vase on the table considers shattering under the pressure of Effie's squeal.

"Stop!"

"Apologize," Vivi says, panting.

Eleni peers over. "Is that blood?"

"Yes, but it is just her nose," *Thea* Dora says. "No vital organs."

"Thank the Virgin Mary."

"I'll die before I apologize!" Effie screams.

How far back can a finger bend before it snaps off?

Vivi doesn't get a chance to find out. There's a loud crack inside her skull. She drops Effie's hand, staggers backwards.

Her cousin is gasping on the ground, one end of the broom clenched in her hand, the other half at Vivi's feet.

"You should be in jail! I told the police you did it – why did they let you go so quickly?"

Silence. No more talk of needlepoint.

"Wait – you called the police and told them that my mother and I were killers?"

"Not *Thea* Eleni. Just you."

Small miracle. Tiny. Miniscule.

"Why?"

"It was the only way to get rid of you! My life was okay until you came here. Now it's all 'Vivi this, Vivi that.' Even my children are second best now. You are all anyone talks about – not just in the family but also in town. No one asks how I am doing, they just want to know about you and America."

"Effie, you do not know what you have done," her mother says.

"You are the worst of all, Mama. My husband is cheating and did you offer me a place to stay? No! You just gossip and joke about it with your friends. But your precious Vivi comes crawling here because she doesn't have the strength to face life, and you throw the doors open wide for her."

"Effie, Vivi is family! What would you have me do? Turn her away?"

"Fuck the Virgin Mary," Effie yells. "I am your family, too!"

Screw this, Vivi thinks. This isn't about her and Effie – it's a mother-daughter thing. And mothers and daughters need to figure things out their own way.

Her face is on fire, her head's pinging like a sonar, and a big red bird is unfolding its wings on her dress.

"Vivi, where are you going?" Eleni asks.

"Running away again?" Effie snarls.

Vivi shrugs. "The hospital, I guess."

🦋 105 🦋

MAX

VIVI SAYS, "I THINK by dose is broken."
      Then she falls at his feet.

Max picks her up.

He doesn't mind her falling at his feet. What he does mind is that someone did this to her. Right now he's rethinking that whole Hippocratic Oath. Thinking about breaking some bones. Thinking about Anastasia and her threats.

He sits her on his desk. Her nose is a big, black balloon. The rest of her isn't in much better shape.

"What did this? A boulder?"

"Close: Effie."

"Is anything else broken?"

"I want to shake my head, but it hurts."

He gets a wheelchair, rolls her down to radiology.

———

Nothing broken but her nose, and that will take care of itself with time.

"They can shoot you up with something good to dull the pain," Max tells her.

"Is it chocolate?"

That's a no.

"I'll pass. I really want some chocolate."

"I can get you some chocolate on the way home."

"You're taking me home?"

"What else can I do with you?"

She (almost) smiles.

He says, "We could hit Effie on the head and donate her body to science. I know people who could really use her organs."

She (almost) laughs. "Effie's probably taking a vinegar bath."

He punches the elevator button. "Vinegar and rubbing alcohol are sound remedies for some things. I wouldn't be so quick to dismiss them."

"Like what?"

"Alcohol is good for a fever. It evaporates and – *boom* – lower body temperature. But dilute it first – a lot. Otherwise you cool down too fast. Vinegar can soften calluses, and it's good for nausea."

The elevator doors ping and they're down and out. Vivi's riding in her super cool wheelchair.

Max takes the VW. Vivi looks in the mirror and gasps.

"My nose is huge."

"It's okay," he says. "You just look more Greek."

———

Max makes a stop. "You have to do this," he says.

"Effie's my cousin."

"So?"

He parks and walks her into the police station.

Quiet afternoon. Two cops hunched over their desks, and a woman in the corner, waiting.

The cops look up.

"Hey! Did you come back for more bread and cheese?"

"Ha-ha," Vivi says. "I'm here about that anonymous tip."

"What about it?"

"My cousin called it in."

"Proof?"

Max says, "There were two other witnesses present when she confessed."

The cop glances back at Vivi. "Which cousin?"

"Effie. Eleftheria."

"Which one is that?"

Vivi looks up at Max. "I don't even know her last name, to be honest."

The other cop says, "The one whose husband is boning your sister."

"Oh, her. Let's bring her in, scare her a bit," he says. To Vivi: "Why would she do that?"

"She hates me. And the right situation walked into her hands. That poor woman died and – "

"Vivi?" The woman from the corner stands. "Are you Elias and Eleni Pappas's daughter?"

Vivi squints at her. "Only if saying "Yes" won't land me back in jail. Otherwise, no."

That's his woman, Max thinks. Not today, maybe. But she will be.

"Hello, Vivi," she says. "I think perhaps we are supposed to be sisters."

❧ 106 ❧

VIVI

Wow. What do you say to a bombshell like that?

Vivi takes the high, classy road. Says, "Hello, I'm Vivi. I'm sorry about your mother." Offers her hand and an appropriate smile for the somber occasion.

She's looking for similarities, differences, clues that they crawled out of the same gene pool. But there's nothing. All they have in common is dark hair, dark eyes. Not a rare bird around here.

The other woman nods. "Thank you. I'm Nitsa Lambeti."

Vivi analyses, analyses, but the only thing familiar about Nitsa's smile is its sadness. Wasn't long ago when Vivi's face was set to grief.

A door slams in the guts of the building. A moment later, Detective Lemonis appears.

He says, "Your sister – or not – has something she wants to share with us. If you two can delay the family reunion, I think she has something that might affect you both."

Vivi's got nothing but questions, and now they have to wait. Meanwhile her broken nose is beating along with her heart. She's trying to be tough, but . . . *goddamn*.

Nitsa retrieves a piece of paper from her very nice handbag. Vivi knows the brand – it's expensive and hard to get. Now they're standing side by side, she can see they're the same height, a similar build. But Nitsa is more polished, fashionable.

Everyone leans over to look.

"It's a letter," she explains. "From my mother. You may read it aloud."

Detective Lemonis clears his throat and reads the words of a dead woman.

———

My daughter, my love,

I cannot love you with my whole heart in this life because it is full to the brim with hatred for the woman who denied you a father. She took away that which I loved above all (before you came along, of course). Therefore it is fitting that that the one who caused me so much pain will be blamed for my death, at least for a short time. It will be her turn to walk around, accusing stares piercing her weak shell, wondering how deep her sins truly run.

Nitsa, you have a sister and brother. They are only half, but blood is blood. While they carry the bad blood from their mother in their veins, do not forget that their father's also flows through them, and he was the best of men. Perhaps there is still time for you all to create a bond that goes beyond that of blood. Perhaps they will help you to know your father. This is my sincerest hope.

It is time for me to go. I am old, I am sick; my heart has been cracked for too many years. I am dying, yes, but it is I who will choose my time, my place. Do not cry.

You are my heart,
Mama.

PS: When you receive this letter, take it to the police. I would not deprive your sister and brother of a mother the way their mother deprived you of your father.

———

It's a Hallmark moment, the two sisters hugging.

"So we're sisters," Vivi says.

Nitsa says, "Uh, no."

❧ 107 ❧

NITSA

Turns out Nitsa Lambeti is a woman with resources and curiosity in abundance. She has an excellent job at a television network, and she knows how to ask the right people the right questions the right (productive) way.

All her life, she heard Elias this, Elias that. Her mother was like a parrot with a one-word vocabulary. Nitsa was raised by half a mother and the shadow of Elias Pappas.

She spent her teens poring over photographs of her alleged father, searching for proof or rebuttal. Growing up in Agria, there was no way she could sidestep the gossip about her mother and potential fathers. Her mother denied the others, of course, said Elias was the only one. And Nitsa, who grew to recognize an obsession when she saw one, nodded and said she believed her mother.

Because there's nothing else to be done when you love your mother and she loves you.

Nitsa dug in secret.

Digging in secret became easier when she relocated to Athens for work. She found Elias Pappas, his wife, his two grown children. She called and spoke to Elias, and he was as good as her mother said.

Too bad he's not her father.
The DNA test was clear about that.

❦ 108 ❦

VIVI

L AZY AFTERNOON ON THE porch. Summer is taking its pound of sweat and salt. Nobody is sleeping; nobody wants to waste this one perfect day.

"I knew it," Eleni says. "I knew she could not be your sister. Now I have proof that her mother was a madwoman."

Melissa is sprawled out on the patio, flipping through a magazine. The words are for her, the pictures for Biff.

Vivi's scraping her espadrille along porch's edge, her back flat against the support post. She's alternating between balancing a bag of frozen peas on her nose and draping it with a vinegar soaked cloth.

"You have proof of nothing," her husband says.

Vivi looks at her father and remembers the box. Now she knows it was the test Nitsa sent. Mystery solved.

"But – "

"Eleni, leave it alone. The woman is dead."

"Yes, and that is a good – "

"Eleni!"

Vivi says, "Nitsa's lovely. If you speak out against her mother now, you'll only hurt her more."

Eleni scoffs. "Just put that ice on your nose and be quiet. The swelling will go down faster if you do not speak."

"Now that I think about it, Nitsa was always a good girl," *Thea* Dora says, without lifting her head from her crochet.

Melissa looks up from her magazine. "Do I have to call her *Thea*?"

"Of course not," her grandmother says. "She is not your aunt."

Vivi doesn't bother pointing out that everyone here calls everyone Aunt or Uncle or Mr. or Mrs. if they're more than five or so years older. "You'll have to ask her what she wants you to call her," she says.

"What is the world coming to? My daughter is a traitor."

"Nitsa has no one," Vivi says, "and I like her."

"Then she should get married," Eleni says.

"Not everyone wants to get married," Vivi says.

Thea Dora lowers her crochet. "Why not? All women want to get married. It is the natural order of things."

Vivi waves. "I'd just like to point out that, except for Melissa, getting married didn't work out too well for me."

"Yes, but you married a *pousti*," her mother says. "It will be different when you marry Max."

Thea Dora jumps up. "Vivi, you are getting married? We must celebrate!"

"Sit back down, *Thea*. I'm not getting married – to Max or to anyone else."

"If you're sleeping with him you must marry him," she says. "Eleni, are they doing the sex?"

Time for Vivi to crawl under the porch and die. "Mind your own damn business," she says.

Eleni says, "I think so."

"Be quiet, Eleni," Elias says.

"About Sofia I will be quiet, but we are discussing Vivi's sex life now."

Oh really? How about no?

"By the way," Vivi says, "Nitsa's coming over this evening."

🌾 109 🌾

VIVI

SHE FINDS TAKIS SITTING beneath an olive tree, smoking one of his hand-rolled cigarettes.

"Did they put her in the ground yet?"

Using her foot, she kicks away the rocks and sticks, and then she sits beside him, cross-legged. "Tomorrow."

"Good. Even in that tree, she was starting to stink. July is a witch. But August will be a bigger witch." He nods at the purple-green patchwork on her face. "Wrestling donkeys again?"

"More like a gorilla."

He grunts. "I hope the gorilla looks worse than you."

It hurts like hell, but she smiles.

Takis says, "What have you got to smile about?"

"Everything, apparently. Turns out I'm pretty happy here."

She expects questions, but what she gets is laughter. It starts with a chortle, than erupts into a guffaw. Then he's coughing all over the place, spraying the parched air with wet flecks.

"You!" he says, once his spluttering stops. "I never knew a *xena* could be so funny. You should have seen your face when the donkey kicked you. You wanted to cry, but you didn't. And look at you now. Someone kills herself on your land, your mother goes to jail, you go to

400

jail, you take a beating from your cousin, and what do you do? You tell me life is good."

"You forgot the part where my ex-husband is gay and my daughter tried to kill herself."

He laughs again, and Vivi laughs, too. Yeah, it's been the year from hell, but she survived, didn't she? They survived – she and Melissa. That's got to be worth at least a few cosmic brownie points.

Takis stands, squashes his cigarette. "Get up, *Xena*. We have work to do."

"More cheese?"

"You want cheese, we will make cheese. But not today. Turns out you are strong, like these trees of yours. The world gave you rocks and dry dirt, and still you survived. Maybe you even grew a little, eh?"

She holds out her hand for him to pull her up. "Are you saying you're going to help me?"

"No, I'm saying that I'll teach you what I know about olives, then you can help yourself."

❦ 110 ❦

VIVI

I N THE END, VIVI stands behind Nitsa as she commits her mother
to the ground. St George's bells have been weeping all morning.

They're all there: Vivi, her parents, Melissa, and *Thea* Dora.

Most of the town is there, too – partly out of morbid curiosity. But
Vivi is there because she cares.

It's been three days since the police ruled Sofia Lambeti's death a
suicide, but Vivi and her family are still the hot gossip.

Eh, it won't last. Soon enough there will be fresh meat. Someone
will steal a goat, flash a tourist, and the great gossiping mouth will
swing away to chew on the fresher story.

Eleni is on her best behavior. She's managing to ratchet her melodrama from Gabor down to Mercouri. Vivi's father is same as he always
is; with no woodwork to do, he's betting ten euros here, ten euros
there, on the *Pro Po*, always favoring his beloved Niki – the local pro
soccer team.

Melissa is beautiful in her black dress, her long golden hair tied
back in a low ponytail. School's not far away now. Her scars will fade. A
year from now, no one but Vivi will remember how close she came to
losing her favorite person.

Melissa isn't alone, and neither is Vivi. Max is beside her. Tall, strong Max. He's here – his choice.

A somber situation, yes, but every so often he looks down at Vivi and smiles.

It's real, what they have. He is for her, and she for him.

She knows it with as much certainty as she knows they belong in Greece.

His mother is coming for dinner tomorrow night.

❧ III ❧

VIVI

T HE KID IS ALONE in the front yard, busy with a broom. Greek boys know if their mama says, "Sweep," they better sweep.

"Hey, Thanasi."

The sweeping stops. First reaction is fear. Kid doesn't look so tough now, so adult, so cocksure. His inner child knows he fucked up big. He slaps on a smirk, but it's wrapping paper; Vivi already caught a glimpse of what's in the box.

"One day you might have a daughter," she says. "Then you'll know."

❦ 112 ❧

S O MUCH CHANGE IN the family.

Vivi was talk of the town for five whole minutes when Max moved in. Not to be outdone, Effie kicked her husband out, moved her girlfriend in, and lost fifty pounds. Max gave Vivi an engagement ring and Effie shaved her head.

When Vivi's business grew wings, and began exporting olive products to gourmet markets in the United States, Effie was filming the first season of *Greece's Top Hoplite*. Thank you, Nitsa Lambeti.

Effie won.

They invited her back as a judge for Season Two. Greek viewers love to hate her. German viewers love to love her.

❧ 113 ❧

MELISSA

M ELISSA OFFERS HER WRISTS to the sun, lets it see what's left of the pale bracelets she carved there so many months ago.

"It's funny, I can hardly see them, now."

"The scars?"

Melissa nods. "I thought they'd always be there. Like an expensive souvenir from my first summer in Greece. It's only been a year and a bit. Next September they'll be all the way gone, Max told me."

Dr Triantafillou says, "You almost sound sad. Will you miss them?"

"Not enough to make new ones." Her smile comes easy. The girl doesn't have to work at it, now. Things have changed, the way things inevitably do. "Olivia left – did I tell you?"

"No. What happened?"

"Her parents pulled her out of school last week and they went back to Canada. There's a rumor going around that she's pregnant."

"What do you think?"

"I think people here talk a lot. And sometimes that's good, and sometimes it's really not."

Melissa feels sad and glad Olivia is gone. It's very Dr Seuss.

"That's a healthy position to take," the shrink says, smiling, smiling. Dr Triantafillou has changed, too. Same smile, same a-m-a-z-i-n-g style, but it's all maternity clothes, now. She waddles to the door, sees Melissa out, and they hug the way they always do.

The T-shirt, the poster, the bumper sticker, the mug, they've all got it wrong, Melissa thinks. It's not shit that happens, it's change. And sometimes the change is shit and sometimes it's flowers.

Like the flowers Vassili left for her.

Like the flowers Vassili brings her still.

❦ 114 ❦

ELIAS – THE FINAL WORD

A MAN WILL DO ANYTHING for a wife he adores. Remember that and do not judge him. Do not judge him when you see Vivi, see Nitsa, and notice the way both women stand, the way both women walk. Do not judge him when you see a picture of his own grandmother and see Nitsa all over her face.

Peace is expensive, eh? Peace is expensive, but it is good. Remember that.

THE END

THANK YOU FOR READING SEVEN DAYS OF FRIDAY! If you don't want to leave Greece yet, you don't have to! Stay in Agria with One and Only Sunday, where an arranged marriage kicks off the second book in the Women of Greece series. Or snap up the Women of Greece Box Set (Books 2-4) and save a few bucks!

Turn the page for a special preview of *One and Only Sunday*.

If you can't wait to plan your next trip to Greece, subscribe to Alex A. King's newsletter right here (or go to: http://eepurl.com/ZSeuL), or like Alex A.King on Facebook (https://www.facebook.com/alexkingbooks) for news about limited-time deals on new releases.

Thank you!

ONE AND ONLY SUNDAY PREVIEW

There is a special place in hell for people who enforce childhood promises on adults, and Margarita Andreou is on her way there in a pale blue dress with a modest neckline.

It's Kiki's wedding day, but does Kiki want to get married?

That's a big fat Greek NO.

"Today I hate you," Kiki tells her mother's reflection in the tall, oval mirror.

"Of course you do," Margarita says casually. "And I hate my mother, too. Why do you think I am always trying to kill her? When I am old and feeble, you will try to kill me. That is how it is in our family."

Kiki glances over at Soula, who is shimmying into her bridesmaid's dress. Mama's choice—of course. Kiki isn't the kind of woman to inflict that shade of green on anyone she loves. Still, Soula being Soula, she forces the dress to suit her. She's old school glamorous is Soula, with that black-blue hair (salon-bought) and red lipstick. The kind of woman who—when she lights up a rare cigarette—makes a person forget lung cancer isn't cool.

"What about Soula? She's not trying to kill you."

"She took her turn when she was born, that ungrateful girl. There I was, giving her life, and what does she do? She almost kills us both."

"I don't want to do this," Kiki says. "My hair ... I'm Medusa."

Soula jumps in. "Mama, look into Kiki's eyes. Let's see if she can turn you to stone."

"You are almost thirty, what else can you do? Work?" Very convenient, the way her mother sidesteps Soula's offer.

Lipstick skates over Kiki's lips. A daring shade of her-lips-but-dimmer. Not her choice, but on this day, what is? Despite her objections, she's a good little Mama-bot, isn't she? "I work now. And marriage isn't a job."

"Of course marriage is a job—a thankless job. You are a teacher." Usually it's Margarita's hands that punctuate her sentences. Today, it's a hairbrush, in between smoothing invisible stragglers from her own neat French twist. Wave, wave, goes the brush. "That is not work, that is torture. Why you want to raise other people's children?"

Kiki wants to shake the stupidity out of her head. Only on Mama's planet is a teacher not a real job. Kiki teaches junior high and high school English (the two schools are mixed in together, in the same building), and when she's not physically present, work is swallowing her free time. If teaching is not work, then why is it so much, well, work?

Mama doesn't understand. She chose family over a career, and now that her daughters are grown, her marbles are rolling all over the floor. Nothing to do except keep trying to off *Yiayia* and sell her daughters to family friends.

Now it's time for Kiki to stuff herself into that awful dress. Stand her next to the wedding cake, nobody will be able to discern which is cake and which is woman, unless they get a good look at her sad, sad eyes.

Jesus, this stinks. Everything from the dress to the groom. Inside her head she screams for help.

"I really don't want to do this."

"So don't do it," Soula tells her, voice husky from a long night of wine and laughter. Last night—Kiki's last unmarried night—they partied like her world was ending.

Which—in her estimation—it kind of is.

The older Andreou sister wins a slap around the ears from their mother.

"She has to do it," Mama's fuchsia-colored mouth says. "Otherwise the family will be shamed. Do you want the family to be shamed? I do not think so!"

The argument rides to the church with them in a white limousine. Bicker, bicker, all the way up to the front doors.

St George's isn't the church Kiki wanted, but the Holy Mother is too small to hold all the family, the friends, the friends of family, the friends of friends, and the tourists who want to gawk at a Greek wedding. So it's here, or cast the guests out into the late April sun. If she was marrying a man of her choosing, she would have fought for the Holy Mother. It's tiny but it's personal, and not just because the priest is her cousin.

It's where she goes to beg for freedom.

Everyone is packed into the bigger church. It's strange, she knows most of these people, but right now they're one long smear. Only a few faces stand out: cousin Max and his American fiancée, Vivi, her daughter Melissa (also one of her students), Kostas and Max's mother —her aunt—and her about-to-be in-laws. *Yiayia* is there, too in her wheelchair, head slumped on her chest.

She's in a coma—a different one this time.

Kiki glances from mother to sister, shrugs. Something's missing. That would be the groom. "So where's Stavros?"

Stavros should be out here. That's how Greek weddings go. The couple meets at the door, and then they walk in together. A Greek woman doesn't stroll into marriage on her father's arm. Fathers palm their daughters off on the groom as quickly as possible.

"Not here yet." The voice comes from the church's open doorway. Stavros's *koumbaros* (best man) and best friend, Akili. He's holding the *stefana* (flowery halos, tethered together with a single ribbon to symbolize the union), in one hand, punching letters into his phone with the other. The thing about Akili is that he's an ass. And like any ass, he doesn't miss an opportunity to kick her in the teeth. So the lack of kick means he doesn't have clue one where Stavros is.

"He will be here," Mama says. "Or I will cut off his—" she wiggles her little finger.

Is Kiki mad?

Nope. Every second that passes without Stavros showing up is a better one. Obviously he doesn't want to be here any more than she does. He just got smarter, that's all, and skipped church.

Too bad he didn't let her know so she could skip church, too.

Time ticks onward. The spring sun is transforming this wretched dress into a torture device. High afternoon now, and all she wants is a *frappe*. She needs the caffeine punch. This is how lamb feels on the rotisserie, Kiki thinks. Every last hair on her head is scraped into a high, tight ponytail, before exploding into manmade curls. Beads of sweat creep between the captive strands. She wants to shake the whole mess loose, rip off the dress, roll her bare skin over the concrete until she quits itching.

Almost worth doing it to watch Mama explode. She deserves it for this ... this ... *wedding*.

Inside the church, the natives are restless. No air conditioning, all that incense. There's the eager hum of gossip behind hand-covered mouths. Usually the entertainment starts after the wedding, but she's okay with them getting started early. If the town is going to gossip about her, well, it could be worse, couldn't it? Stavros standing her up outside the church is pretty benign.

People start flooding up the steps, dressed in celebratory threads. Another wedding is on its way. Hopefully one with a groom. The bride shows up in a limo identical to Kiki's. She's wearing the dress Kiki wanted, a simple slim column. Kiki remembers her from school, back in the days when she was a fledgling bitch.

"What's the matter, Andreou. Did you get stood up?"

"I think so. Isn't it wonderful?" Kiki says sweetly. No way can she be mean when she's feeling this great.

Best day ever.

Gathering up her skirts, she stomps into the church, as much as anyone can stomp in pencil-thin heels. "Everybody out," she announces. "The groom is a no-show, and there's another wedding about to happen."

Hooray!

——————

Nice day for a wedding. Not Kiki's wedding, but *a* wedding.

Everyone congregates outside the church. Nobody wants to leave—what if something dramatic happens and they miss it?

"Hold up your hand if you've heard from Stavros since last night," Soula hollers.

Nobody has heard from Stavros since last night—not his mother, not his father, not his friends.

"Well," Soula says, bunching up that ugly green dress, "he's not coming." She looks at Kiki. "Beach or dancing?"

"Beach first. Dancing later."

Mama's hand snaps out, grabs Kiki by the curls. "She cannot just leave her own wedding!"

"What wedding?" Soula says, repressing a grin. "There is no wedding. No Stavros means no wedding."

It's the best news ever. Kiki can't help herself—she laughs.

And laughs.

And laughs.

Beside her, Soula starts to cackle. Two women laughing this hard, it sounds like a chicken coop outside the church. It's infectious. The priest is the next to fold. Kostas Andreou is her cousin, which means he knows this whole wedding thing wasn't Kiki's idea. About a thousand times since he joined the priesthood, she has wandered into the Holy Mother, begging God to shut this particular door and shove her out a window.

And look, it worked. Here is her window.

Everything is good. Everything is fine. If the bride is laughing instead of crying, then the guests feel okay about laughing in front of her, as opposed to behind her back.

"This is not funny!" Mama barks. "How do you think it looks, eh? My daughter stood up by that—"

Thea Helena moves into range with a granite face. She's in a silvery silk dress that's wilting like warmed lettuce. "By that what, Margarita?"

It was a rare childhood photo that didn't capture the two women together, but now Mama is standing under the spotlight's hot glare while her best friend tries to snap a new picture that speaks of an alternate ending to their lifelong friendship.

The answer dies in Mama's mouth.

Things are bad when Margarita Andreou's mouth dries up. It's one of the signs of a very small, very Greek apocalypse.

Kiki slides into her mother's orbit, changes the subject to something that won't cause a friendship derailment. "I hope he's okay."

"Why wouldn't he be okay?" Same question, two mouths.

Both mothers dive to touch the nearest red thing—in this case, a clutch held by somebody's aunt's third cousin. Kiki doesn't know her name, but from the way she slaps at the women with her bag, it's obvious that somebody's aunt's third cousin has mistaken them for purse-snatchers.

(It's a Greek thing, the touching red when two people speak the same words simultaneously. If they don't, it's a sign they're going to fight.)

"I'm sure he's fine," Kiki says.

And she *is* sure. This is Agria, a small town on the Pagasetic Gulf, near the foot of Mount Pelion, where death is mostly natural causes, and crime is something that happens to a cousin's uncle's best friend's chicken. It's big news if someone steals an armload of firewood.

Okay, so years ago there was a flasher, and that same summer one of the local cops died when a pair of clowns robbed one of the village's two pharmacies. But those are outliers.

Accidents are few and generally limited to tourists accidentally wandering into the merciless Greek traffic, or someone falling out of a tree they shouldn't have been climbing to begin with. And they're easily fixed with liberal applications of rubbing alcohol or vinegar. Need the big guns? Use both.

So the odds that Stavros Boutos is anything other than okay are extremely low. He's probably holed up somewhere with a bottle of ouzo and a couple of his favorite naked friends, doing her the favor of a lifetime.

Tonight, she'll crack open the champagne and toast her thanks. To life, to Stavros, to freedom.

"Kiki ..." Soula nods toward the road.

Snugging up to the curb is one of the town's police cars. She knows the young constable from school, and she knows Detective Lemonis by sight and reputation, mostly. There's no mistaking him for anything but the law; even in plainclothes he looks like he knows how to sniff out trouble and slap it with cuffs.

They tramp up the stairs, gazes combing the crowd. A hand shoves Kiki forward. Mama. Somebody has to be the mouthpiece, so—tag —she's it.

"Is there a problem, Detective?"

"Helena and Kristos Boutos, are they here?"

Her hot Greek blood turns cold.

ABOUT THE AUTHOR

Alex A. King is an American author (by way of several countries, including Greece), who divides her time between writing, thinking about writing, and reading Seuss's HOP ON POP for the millionth time. She lives in the Pacific Northwest with her family.